THE GOBLIN KING'S MISCHIEF

BOOKS BY D. LIEBER

Minte and Magic

The Exiled Otherkin

The Assassin's Legacy

Intended Fates Trilogy

Intended Bondmates

Intended Strangers

Intended Enemies

Council of Covens

Dancing with Shades

In Search of a Witch's Soul

Also by D. Lieber

Conjuring Zephyr

Once in a Black Moon

A Very Witchy Yuletide

The Treason of Robyn Hood

The Curse of Moonseed Manor

The Goblin King's Mischief

THE GOBLIN KING'S MISCHIEF

D. LIEBER

Ink & Magick, LLC
Kenosha, Wisconsin
contact@inkandmagick.com

Hardcover ISBN: 978-1-951239-31-2
Paperback ISBN: 978-1-951239-32-9
Ebook ISBN: 978-1-951239-33-6

Cover by Artscandare Book Cover Design
Edited by Olivia Kalb at oliviakalbediting@gmail.com
Proofread by Samantha Talarico

SPECIAL THANKS

Thank you to my beta readers: John, Megan, Amy, Trish, Aunt Debbie, and Joyce.

CONTENTS

THE GOBLIN KING'S MISCHIEF

CHAPTER
ONE

I inhaled the scent of evergreens and last year's leaves underfoot. The full moon was bright overhead, illuminating the meadow before us well enough for even my human eyes to see clearly. My ears pricked at every bird call and the soft skittering of the forest animals hidden from view. I held my breath when a thumping reached my ears, hoping to distinguish it from the hammering of my own heart. But as the rhythmic drumming grew louder, I knew it was the sound I'd been waiting for—the sound of horsehoofs on the forest floor.

"I don't think this is a good idea," my brother Graeme whispered, crouching beside me as we looked over a tangle of bushes to the meadow.

I scowled at him. "And whose fault is it? If you'd just sent that letter, I wouldn't need to do all this."

"It wasn't only my fault," he grumbled. But when my gaze flicked to his, he lowered his sea-glass green eyes in guilt. He'd said he was sorry too many times to count, but that didn't change my situation. He pushed one final time. "What if it doesn't work?"

"It'll work." *I know it will.* My heart drummed as the galloping horse drew nearer, and I strained my eyes in the direction of the sound. "Now?" I asked my brother.

"Not yet," Graeme murmured, his sharper, sidhe gaze staring out at the meadow.

I shifted my weight, readying myself for action. My legs tingled from being in the same position too long.

"Now," he urged.

On cue, I let out the loudest scream my lungs could muster and launched myself over the bush, running away from our hiding place like my life depended on it. "Help! Somebody help me!"

I was a quarter-way across the meadow when the elf arrived on his horse. His ruddy blond hair fluttered behind him as he galloped toward me. When his dark eyes met mine across the distance, I nearly tripped.

Steeling my nerves, I looked behind me in a panic—my signal for Graeme to start his pursuit. He jumped out, his face covered with a hood.

I let out another scream as Graeme raced toward me. "Please!" I reached toward the rider. "Please, help me!"

He set his jaw and urged his horse forward.

I stumbled and fell, hissing when my knees hit the ground. My long, chocolate-brown hair flew into my face. I peeked through the waves, lowering my head in a cower.

Graeme was nearly to me now, but the rider was faster. He hopped down from his horse and drew a dagger in a smooth motion. He stepped between my brother and me, raising his weapon.

Graeme pulled up short, hesitating at the threat.

My heart squeezed as they stared each other down. Then

Graeme turned and sprinted away, back into the safety of the surrounding forest.

My defender tensed as if to pursue him.

"Wait!" I cried. "Please! There are too many of them. If you follow him, they'll overpower you."

I watched his back as he stood firm before me, his quiver of arrows slung across his torso. I winced. *Good thing he didn't choose his bow instead.*

He sighed heavily and turned, peering down at me.

My heart swelled and cracked when the elf looked at me without recognition. "Thank you, sir," I whispered, the lump in my throat all too real. I moved as if to stand, then let my knees buckle beneath me.

He knelt to help me up, and as I met his gaze, his eyes held the same warmth I remembered. "What happened? How did you get here? This is no place for a human to be unaccompanied."

I slipped my hands into those he offered, blinking the unbidden tears from my vision. "I was running errands for my mistress," I said, my voice shaking as I spoke my practiced lie. I felt his arm wrap securely around my waist. His gentle warmth sent a jolt through me, and I leaned heavily against him. "I'd been there a million times before..." My voice thickened as if I were reliving an unpleasant memory. "Someone grabbed me from behind and covered my head. We rode for a long way... Where am I? I managed to escape, but I don't know where I am." I widened my eyes, trying to communicate panic as I pleaded for an answer.

"You're in Goblinwood."

I gasped, shrinking from him—slipping the ring from his finger as I did so. My heart pounded. I used my fear of discovery to color my words. "Oh, no! I can't be."

He shushed my hysterics. "You're safe. Do not fret. Where do you live? I'll be sure to get you home safely. Along the way, you can tell me what you know about the people who took you."

I looked up at Aodh, taking in the face I used to know so very well. His features had sharpened in the last ten years. His thick hair—which had been quite messy when it was shorter—now fell in long locks that could no longer hide the pointed tips of his ears. The groove between his straight nose and wide lips had deepened, and he still had a tiny break in the hair of his left eyebrow, a scar too small to see if not for the space where the hair no longer grew.

I took in the sight of him, memorizing the small changes that had taken place since the last time I'd seen him. He'd grown both taller and wider—his shoulders now the broad and strong shoulders of a man. Though, despite the added years, his eyes had changed the most. They were much darker than I remembered, not in color but in substance. He'd helped me as I knew he would, but he no longer had that carefree glint in his eyes. The lack of that little light of mischief hurt more than anything else.

"Miss?" he called. "Where do you live? What's your name?"

I let my mouth widen in a smirk of bravado. "Me? My name is Lady Melody Píobaire, daughter of the Earl of Piskishire." I swallowed my heart. *He's not going to like this.* Raising my left hand, I displayed the ring I'd just sneaked from his finger onto mine. "I'm the goblin queen, and you can come for me at Maplecrest, my family home, whenever is convenient for you, husband."

Aodh's eyes widened but only for a second. Then he snatched my wrist and squeezed. "Give it back," he growled, his expression turning dark and menacing.

My stomach clenched, but I kept the smile plastered on my face and tilted my head. "Why would I do that? I've followed the rules. I outsmarted the goblin king. That makes me the goblin queen and your future wife."

His nails dug into my arm, but I didn't wince. Even the pain of his touch seemed a relief after not feeling him for so long. "No one witnessed this. If you give it back now, I will let you go free with no repercussions."

I raised my chin. "Despite what they say, there *is* honor among thieves. Even the goblin king himself, the leader of all the criminals and outcasts in Tír, has some honor." I raised an eyebrow at him. "Or would you prove otherwise?"

His nostrils flared as he sighed through his nose. "You have no idea what you've gotten yourself into."

I stroked his hand, which still held my wrist. "I look forward to finding out."

As he flinched away from me, a cold hardness entered his gaze. "Suit yourself." With a loud whistle, he called to his horse, which was happily munching on some wildflowers at the edge of the meadow. "A human as clever as you can surely find her own way home." He mounted gracefully and pulled the reins to urge the horse away.

"I'll be expecting you at Maplecrest shortly, Your Majesty!" I called after him.

He didn't look back as he disappeared into the trees, but I knew he would come for me. He had to. Even if he wanted to hide the fact he'd been bested, it wouldn't be long before someone noticed the ring, which bespoke his station, was gone. He'd have a hard time explaining that. That's why, out of all the options I'd considered, I'd chosen that one.

I smiled to myself, a warm glow blooming in my chest, a glow I hadn't felt in too many years. I'd known the trade would be worth it. I had to admit: giving up the lightning bird egg had smarted a little. It was a rare and valuable commodity. But the drake I'd bribed had been accurate in what she'd told me about the Goblin King's—not so secret— secret monthly rides.

A shiver ran through me as the image of Aodh's cold glare resurfaced in my mind. I pushed my apprehension away. *I knew he wouldn't be pleased at first. He never did like losing. But I know I can win him over again.* I hesitated at the edge of the meadow, looking over my shoulder at the full moon above the trees. *I know I can.*

Shooing my fears with a shake of my head, I started into the forest and made my way to where I was supposed to meet Graeme. He wasn't far away, just far enough Aodh wouldn't know he was there.

"So"—Graeme stared down at me from the branches of a wide tree—"did it work?"

I grinned at him and showed him the ring on my finger. "You may call me 'Your Majesty' from now on."

He snorted and slid lightly to the ground. Taking my hand, he analyzed the ring, then frowned. "Mum and Dad won't be happy about this."

My heart sank, and I sighed. "Let's get home before them. I'm going to have a lot of explaining to do, and I'd rather talk it out before Aodh comes for me."

Once we were through Goblinwood, it was only a matter of picking up our buggy at the nearest roadside inn. We made quick work of it. We had to get home before our parents returned, or Graeme would be drawn and quartered for sure.

Luckily for my brother, we were home before our parents. I stared past the glimmering gates of Maplecrest, glinting gold in the entrance torchlight. We hadn't been back for very long from our over two-cycle absence. And while the cozy swath of trees leading up the hill to the elegant country mansion held many happy memories for me, I hadn't gotten used to calling it home again after being gone for ten years.

There was no hiding the fact we'd left without permission, so we didn't bother to try to hide our return. We didn't ask the servants to lie for us. My parents would find out what we'd done soon enough. We only wanted to ease them in, soften the blow, and not send them into a panic if they'd arrived and we weren't there.

No one greeted me at the door when I alighted, leaving Graeme to put the buggy away. But Eithne arrived in my bedroom before I'd even gotten my shoes off.

She stared at me from the doorway, her sharp eyes alight

with apprehension above her turned-up piskie nose. "My lady?" It seemed Eithne had crawled from her bed in a hurry; her feet were bare beneath her nightgown. Her long, red hair—characteristic of all piskies—was plaited over one shoulder, and her pointed ears peeked out from the fiery waves.

I smiled softly and nodded. "Everything is all right now, Eithne."

Eithne stepped forward to assist me in changing my clothes, worry still painted all over her face. "What happens now?"

"Now? We wait."

Eithne frowned. "But you've waited so long already, my lady."

I smiled at her. She was such a loyal and caring fae; she'd even kept my scheme a secret from my parents. But I knew she wanted what was best for me, and she didn't believe that was the Goblin King. I wondered if she'd want to accompany me despite not agreeing with my decision. "Yes, but this time, he has no choice but to come for me."

She pressed her lips together in an expression I recognized as disapproval.

"Do you have something more to say, Eithne?" I thought she'd long since said her piece.

She bit her lip, then sighed. "I just don't think you can force someone's love. Giving him no choice... It doesn't seem like it will work out if you go about it this way."

Dread momentarily clenched my heart. *Will Aodh forgive me when he finds out?* Ordinarily, I would agree with Eithne. People didn't take kindly to being forced into things. I didn't either. But this was an extenuating circumstance, surely. I'd made a promise I intended to keep. But I knew Aodh hadn't been given a fair shot at making the choice on his own, so if

—when all was said and done—I couldn't win his heart again, I would return his ring and set him free.

"I'm sorry, my lady. I spoke out of turn."

I shook my head. "You're fine, Eithne. I appreciate your wisdom. And I've told you many times you can speak openly to me." I gave the piskie a reassuring smile, then slipped my robe on over my nightgown. "I've heard what you said, I promise."

And though Eithne returned my smile, the apprehension in her eyes didn't wane. "Get some rest, my lady."

"Thanks, Eithne. Sweet dreams."

CHAPTER
THREE

After Eithne left my room, I doused the light and went out onto my balcony. Sitting with my back to the wall, I gazed up at the sky.

The full moon hung close to the treetops in the west, and I knew it wouldn't be long before the sun started to lighten the eastern sky.

The night seemed chilly now that I didn't have adrenaline pumping through me. I pulled my robe tighter. *I should try to get a little sleep before Mum and Dad come home.*

But even as my mind urged me to crawl into bed, I didn't move.

A sudden presence, like a tickle on the back of my neck, made me turn toward my open balcony door just as Tadhg slipped out of it. The spunkie's luminescent blue glowed brightly, and I smiled because that meant he was happy to see me.

Tadhg's default orb flowed into that of a cat, the form he always took when he wanted a cuddle.

"Aw, come here," I cooed, lowering my knees from my chest to give him space to crawl into my lap.

Tadhg settled in, purring loudly.

Despite his ethereal body, he felt very much like a real cat. Even as my hand passed through the lines of his shape, my brain told me I was stroking the soft fur of a glowing, blue feline.

I sighed contentedly as my mind drifted. "He's so much the same as before, Tadhg. I would have recognized him anywhere."

Tadhg blinked his big eyes at me, and I smiled as I cast my mind back to the first time Aodh and I had met.

～

"I know where you're going," I said to Graeme, casually leaning against the side of the carriage house in the dark.

My brother jumped, his head snapping toward my voice.

As I stepped into the dim light, he squinted to see me. "What do you want?" he asked uncertainly.

I smiled an easy smile. "You're sneaking off to Goblintown again. I want to go with you."

"You can't be serious," he said and huffed a laugh. "You're fifteen. What could you possibly want in Goblintown?"

I pursed my lips. "I'm not a baby anymore. And you know what I want: ingredients. I've heard you can get stuff they don't sell anywhere else. I want to try some advanced potions. I'm tired of this kid stuff."

My brother shook his head. "They don't sell them anywhere else because they're illegal. What if you get caught with them? You'll be able to do proper magic once you become the Crown Prince's royal mistress, once you become a banshee by coupling with him. Can't you just wait until then?"

I crossed my arms over my chest. "That's five years away. And what are you saying? Would you turn in your own sister?"

Graeme rolled his eyes. I wasn't getting anywhere. Sighing, I tried another approach, puffing my lips into a pout. "Come on, big brother. Please? I won't be a bother. I promise."

His hard expression started to waver. "I can't stay with you the whole time. I'm going to be too busy to watch you."

"You don't have to watch me. Look, I put on my simplest dress, and I'll wear a hood. I'll stay right where you leave me. I won't wander. I'm only going to buy ingredients. Surely, that isn't dangerous. It's like going to the market." I reached out and tugged Graeme's hand. "Hmm?"

His face crumbled. "Fine. But a hood won't be enough. You'll have to glamour your appearance. It's risky enough with you being so young, but no one can find out you're human."

My heart soared, and I flung my arms around my brother. "Really? Thank you!"

But as I pulled away, he met my eyes gravely. "I'm serious. None of your usual mischievous antics. I will take you to a shop I know, and you have to stay there until I pick you up. And don't remove your hood either."

I held up my hand solemnly. "I won't."

Graeme watched me for another moment, then nodded. His apprehension eased from his gaze. "Go get your glamour potion. I'll meet you at the front gate."

He didn't need to tell me twice. I slipped into the house and raced up the back stairs as quietly as I could. Once in my bedroom, I passed through to my workroom and snatched the corked bottle from my neatly organized shelves.

The house was quiet, even Tadhg's glow was muted and dim as he slept on my bed.

I was at the gate when Graeme reached it. I let the buggy out and closed the gate before climbing in beside my brother.

"When should I take it?" I asked him.

"When we get closer to Tally's. It'll last longer that way."

I could hardly quell my excitement as our horse pulled us closer and closer to our destination. I knew my brother had been going to Goblintown for months on some errand for our father, and my list of illicit potion ingredients was burning a hole in my pocket. There were so many things I wanted to try, and I was finally getting the chance.

As we neared a small roadside inn, Graeme slowed the horse and glanced over at me. "What do you want?"

I thought about it. Hair would work, but spit would be even better. I uncorked my potion bottle and handed it to him. "Spit into this."

I wasn't exactly thrilled about drinking my brother's spit, but then again, I'd put far grosser things into my mouth for the sake of my hobby. It was the only way a human like me could do magic after all—since the magic came from the ingredients rather than a proper spell—at least until I coupled with a sidhe to became a banshee. Even so, it wasn't perfect. I couldn't glamour myself to look completely like Graeme—not that I wanted to.

Graeme did as I asked, then handed the bottle back. "It's too bad you couldn't get some of Eithne's hair or something. Glamouring yourself as a piskie would be far better than a sidhe in this case."

I shrugged. "I'll have my hood up anyway, so this is all

just a precaution." Then I downed the bottle in two gulps. It tasted like strawberries, honey, and hay.

I pulled my brown hair forward and saw it had lightened to the same golden brown as my brother's. I could only assume my turquoise eyes now appeared a sidhe sea-glass green, that my human features had smoothed into the beauteous features of a sidhe.

Once we pulled up next to the inn—after insisting that I raise my hood and stay quiet—Graeme negotiated with Tally, the piskie innkeeper. A stable hand was soon leading our horse and buggy into the stables.

"We aren't even going to ride Violet?" I asked my brother, my voice softer and more musical after taking the potion. I understood why we wouldn't want to bring our nice buggy into Goblintown, but did we really have to walk through Goblinwood?

Graeme shook his head though I could hardly notice the gesture from under his green hood. "Violet is better off here, too. Unless you want to stay with her the whole time?"

"No, I'm coming." But even as the confident words left my lips, I trembled a little.

I'd been told stories my entire life about Goblintown and the woods surrounding it. Goblin was the worst label someone could be given in Tír. It could be earned by anything from murder to petty theft. But it always meant one was a criminal—an outcast—abandoned by even their closest friends and family and forced to leave home to live with the other goblins.

I clenched my jaw. I'd asked to come with Graeme, and I wouldn't let my fear get the better of me. It would be too shameful to ask him to take me home now. Still, I moved a little closer to him, taking comfort in my shoulder brushing up against his arm as we started down the winding forest road.

CHAPTER
FOUR

The cool late summer air sent a shiver up my spine, or rather that was what I chose to believe was the cause, as we trekked through Goblinwood.

I couldn't get rid of the feeling we were being watched, and I looked over my shoulder for what seemed like the hundredth time.

"Scared?" Graeme teased.

I threw my shoulders back and tossed my head. "Not at all."

He chuckled, and I chose to ignore it. At least his challenge made me push my fear away.

"Why has Dad been sending you to Goblintown of late?" I inquired.

Graeme was quiet for long enough to make me worry he wouldn't answer. "I suppose there's no reason not to tell you. Do you remember Lord Kelpania?"

I thought back to the many parties and balls I'd attended. "Brochfael's father?"

Graeme's hood dipped in a nod. "He's been hiring goblins to build his ships."

I shrugged. "Is that a problem?"

"It's a problem when he doesn't pay them properly. He doesn't pay them as much as he would if they weren't goblins. And he forces them to buy their tools from him at an elevated rate to get the job, so most of their meager wages go right back to him."

My stomach dropped. "They're slaves?"

"Very nearly."

"But what does that have to do with Dad? Surely, he isn't participating in such horrible acts?"

"Of course not," Graeme scolded. "Dad has been sending me to Goblintown to buy their debt and offer them higher paying jobs based on their skills. We pay off what they owe Lord Kelpania, find them better work, and they pay us back as they can."

I frowned. "But how is that any better than what Lord Kelpania is doing? Now, they just owe us instead of him. Why wouldn't Dad just forgive their debt?"

"It's worlds different. We don't charge them interest, and we don't charge them more than they can afford. We may be wealthy aristocrats, but even *we* would run out of money if we just forgave everyone's debt. If we did that, we wouldn't be able to help more people."

I saw his logic, but it still felt like a slight distinction.

"Besides, just because they're goblins, doesn't mean they don't have pride. People want to feel they've earned what's given to them."

"I guess so. But why is Dad sending you? No offense, but you're only just twenty. He could do it better himself."

Graeme scowled. "It's a good thing Dad has more faith in me than you do, or I might never become earl. Lord

Kelpania has a lot of influence with the King. If Dad did all this himself, it could hurt his standing at court."

My face flushed. *It could hurt my future with Lorccán, he means.* "Does the King know what Lord Kelpania is doing, then?"

My brother shrugged.

Graeme may not have known whether the King was privy to Lord Kelpania's deeds, but I couldn't believe Crown Prince Lorccán knew about the situation. He would've done something.

As I was about to ask another question, I saw a break in the trees ahead and the distant buildings of Goblintown. While we neared the outskirts of the city, I took in my first sight of it.

Unlike Sifra, the city where the sidhe king of Tír dwelt, Goblintown didn't have any walls or guards who watched stone gates. Goblintown could be entered from wherever one left Goblinwood.

As for Graeme and me, we followed the path before us. If Goblinwood had swallowed us, it felt like we'd reached a churning stomach as we stepped into Goblintown.

Houses of wood or stone with thatched or tiled roofs, some missing or broken, lined the dank streets. I didn't know why the whole place was wet and musty because it hadn't rained recently. But when an elf opened her shutters and threw liquid into the street from two stories up, I figured it out.

The streets were cobbled but in serious need of repair. As I watched a cart ramble and rattle farther ahead, I was glad we'd left the buggy at the inn.

Graeme touched my arm, and I swallowed a yelp at suddenly being grabbed.

"Listen," he murmured. "Remember what you promised

me. I won't be long. Don't wander, and don't trust anyone. Got it?"

I nodded deeply so he could see the gesture even with my hood on.

Graeme led me around with a confidence that said he was comfortable there, and I wondered how much of that was a front.

Those we passed didn't meet our eyes or attempt to talk to us, lending an air of unfriendliness to the already oppressive atmosphere.

My brother halted outside a well-lit shop with dirty windows. The sign above the door identified the place as Swonghilder's Potions and Apothecary. After turning to me, Graeme rested his hands on my shoulders.

"This is it. There should be plenty for you to look at while I'm gone. Go inside, and don't come out until I come to get you."

"All right," I said, annoyed now that I'd promised so many times already. "I'll see you in a while." Slipping from his grasp, I opened the door and stepped inside without glancing back at him.

Swonghilder's looked exactly like every shop I'd ever been in to buy ingredients for my potions, if not a little more cluttered and with a little more dust. The shelves were well-organized and clearly labeled.

There were a few customers talking to the clerk at the far end, so I just started wandering around in search of the rare, and illicit, ingredients I was after.

It didn't take me long to realize they didn't have what I was looking for on display. They had herbs and crystals, extracts and ash. But I could get any one of those things at a shop in Piskishire.

Of course, why would they display them? Who puts illegal

items out in the open? Even goblins were smarter than that. I waited patiently for the other patrons to leave before I approached the counter.

"Excuse me," I said politely.

The puck clerk glanced up at me from the ledger he was writing in. I hadn't ever seen a puck in person before though I'd seen depictions of them. He was shorter than I'd expected but still taller than me. He had the curly brown hair and hazel eyes most pucks were said to have, and I could see his pointed ears. I eyed his mouth, wondering if it was true that pucks had pointed teeth. But I didn't dare look beneath the counter to see if his feet were indeed hoofs.

Now that his steady gaze was on me, I couldn't quite put my words together. "D-do you happen to have a...um, the scale of a mermaid?"

That was the least controversial item on my list. Though it fell under the ban that prohibited the selling of fae parts, mermaids shed their scales every so often, so it wasn't necessarily something acquired by nefarious means.

The puck stood from his stool behind the counter—much taller now that he was at his full height—his hoofed feet clopping on the floorboards as he walked around to my side. "Are you asking me if I carry *illegal* mermaid scales in my honest shop?"

I winced as he smiled at me—flashing his sharp teeth.

"Um..."

He pointed a finger toward the door. "Get out of here."

I blinked. "What?"

"You heard me, missy. I don't sell things like that here. You want something like that, you go to Redcap Row."

"But—Hey!"

The puck grabbed me by the arm and dragged me

toward the entrance. Then he unceremoniously shoved me into the street.

I stumbled but caught myself before I fell. As he slammed the door shut, the bell rang with the sort of finality I didn't dare challenge.

I looked around at those who passed me in the street; no one even hesitated at the scene they'd just witnessed.

"Well, shit," I muttered. *Now what am I supposed to do?*

I shoved my hands into the pockets of my apron. *Redcap Row? That doesn't sound good.* Redcap was the distinction for the worst kind of goblins, those who'd actually killed someone. And any street named after them wasn't a place I'd likely want to wander around. It certainly wasn't a place my parents would ever want their precious daughter to be. And, of course, I had promised Graeme.

But I can't just stand here in the street… Maybe it isn't as bad as it sounds. It's not as if I want to hire a killer. I just want to get a few mermaid scales. I won't be long. I'll be back before Graeme even knows I'm gone.

CHAPTER
FIVE

Though I'd made the likely ill-advised decision to go to Redcap Row, I didn't have the first idea of how to get there. I looked around at those who passed me, scanning their faces to determine who appeared friendly enough to ask.

A few yards ahead of me, an older gnome hobbled along, pulling a handcart behind her. One wheel wobbled on its axle, ready to fall off at any time. As a rule, elemental fae usually put me on guard. They seemed more wild, more unpredictable, than other fae. However, as earth elementals, I felt gnomes were the most stable of the elementals. But perhaps my comfortability with them had more to do with the fact that I'd been exposed to them more than the other three. My family always stopped in Gnomeburgh for the night on the way to and from Sifra.

I moved toward her slowly so as not to alarm her, and it didn't take me long to catch up. "Excuse me, can I help?"

The old gnome turned toward me; the fringe of her long grey hair, wet from her exertion, covered the top half of her face. I couldn't read her expression. She faced me for a long while, heaving breaths.

"If you're thinking because I'm a gnome I have anything valuable to steal, you'd be sadly mistaken," she said finally. "The only thing I have worth anything is this"—she pulled a sharp and jagged dagger from her apron—"and I know how to use it."

Despite the gnome's feeble appearance, the steel in her voice mimicked that of the steel in her hand, and a shiver ran up my spine.

I'd never met someone so openly untrusting. But then, I'd never been in a place such as that. I frowned. *How hard is her life that she's suspicious of a little help?*

Then again, what has she done to earn herself a place here, to be labeled as a goblin?

I showed her my palms. "I wasn't trying to rob you. I just saw you struggling and thought I'd offer my help. But you obviously don't want it, so I'll be on my way."

I turned to head in the direction I'd come from. *Perhaps I'll just park myself outside Swonghilder's after all.*

But as I took a step to leave, the old gnome cleared her throat. I looked over my shoulder at her. She'd already tucked her knife back into her apron.

"I'm only heading up the hill." She pointed.

I nodded and slipped between the two handles of the cart. I had no idea what she had under the tarp, but it was the heaviest thing I'd ever encountered. Granted, I was just a regular human compared to her. It seemed even elderly-gnome strength was not to be taken lightly.

She walked beside me as I pulled, her steps much less labored now that I was carrying her load. I could feel her eyes on me even though I couldn't see them beneath her hair.

She didn't say anything while we moved up the hill, not that I was capable of conversation as I huffed and puffed. If she noticed I wasn't as strong as her despite my younger age, she didn't let on. She stopped before a small, wooden house with a thatched roof that bowed in the middle. Its unpainted door was crooked with large gaps between the slats.

My heart pounded as I tried to catch my breath, but I resisted the urge to clutch at the stitch in my side.

"Thank you," the gnome said. "It's rare to find kindness in strangers."

I nodded.

Again, I felt her eyes on me. "You should get out of here while you still can."

My breath hitched. *Does she know I'm not a goblin?*

But she had nothing more to add and turned her attention to whatever was in her cart.

I hesitated, second-guessing my earlier decision. "Um… you can probably tell I'm new to this area." I acknowledged my vulnerability because she'd already seemed to have picked up on it. "I'm looking for something special, and I was told I could find it on Redcap Row… Could you tell me where that is?"

She looked at me again with that same inscrutable expression. "You don't want to go there. You don't belong there."

"It will only be for a moment," I argued.

The old gnome shook her shaggy head. "If you insist." Then she gave me directions to the place before issuing a final warning. "Be careful, young one."

As I headed back down the hill, I wondered one last time if I shouldn't just stay where my brother had left me. But when I peered into the dirty glass window at the puck clerk of Swonghilder's, a feeling of defiance crept into me.

I came all the way here because I want to advance my potion-making. I could have stayed home in my nice, cozy bed if I wanted to play it safe. I'm getting those mermaid scales.

With a set jaw and steeled nerves, I marched in the direction of Redcap Row.

As sad and derelict as Goblintown seemed so far, the farther I went from Swonghilder's, the worse it got. Even the torches seemed dimmer—they were certainly less frequent.

My heart hammered in my chest, and my skin prickled as if every window had eyes that watched me slip through the night toward my unknown fate.

There it is. I stopped at a corner and looked up at the painted image of a clurichaun on a tavern sign overhead. He looked like a leprechaun who'd had way too much wine— short with grey skin and a red nose and a silly drunken grin.

The windows of the tavern were alight from within, and the mingled sound of a crowd filtered through the open door into the night. Laughter, a slurred sea shanty, annoyance, and anger—the tavern's patrons went about their lives in ignorance of my silent steps.

Peeking around the corner of the building, I squinted into the darkness. There didn't seem to be anything there, just the shadows of an ordinary alley. As I strained my eyes, I thought I could make out the outline of a clothesline, linens swaying in the breeze, strung across the space.

Is it really here? The old gnome had assured me I would see it once I entered the alley. I wasn't convinced. But quirking my mouth, I shrugged my shoulders and stepped into the shadows.

CHAPTER
SIX

As I stepped past the mouth of the alley, the shadows I'd seen before lifted from my eyes. The clothesline was still strung overhead, but beneath it was no longer empty. Shops and stalls, dim and dirty, lined the walls. Cloaked patrons browsed the full buckets and tables as sharp-eyed shop owners looked on.

The place wasn't as crowded as market day in Piskishire, but it wasn't close to empty either. Perhaps it was the hushed tones of conversation, barely heard above the shuffling of shoes on pavement, that made it seem less populated than it was.

Pulling my hood closer, I tried to ignore the heaviness pressing in on me, squeezing my lungs as if trying to suffocate me.

I passed a permanent shop on my right, its sign promising exotic human realm animals. A simple table was set up outside. A rough-looking trow—about a foot shorter than me—played a fiddle, his large eyes closed as his light brown skin practically glowed while he lost himself in his music. He wasn't nearly as handsome as the other trows I'd seen. His blond hair looked dirty in the dim light, and his grey cloak was tattered. As he played, a portune—a tiny woman, no bigger than my thumb—danced among a set of objects on the table. I eyed the strange collection: a knife, a rope, a club, and an empty vial. The sign on the table just said, "for hire" and had a price ten times what any of those things were worth—even the knife, which was likely the most valuable object there.

A few feet away, I came upon another table with an enclosed tent set up behind it. I stalled my quick pace when I noticed bowls and vials of potion ingredients lined up in messy rows. I reached for a colorful snail shell in a bowl full of them. It wasn't an illegal item, but it was rare to find snail shells with such vibrant colors. They would hold powerful magic. I examined it, looking to see if it was authentic or had been painted.

"Oh, it's real, all right," the shop owner declared, exiting his tent.

I looked up at the salamander. His yellow eyes glowed in the dim light of the alley although his red skin seemed muted more than enhanced. I stiffened a little at his approach. The salamander may have taken humanoid form, but I knew his fire elemental spirit was always just below the surface.

I pushed my unease aside and put the shell back with the others. "I wonder"—I stepped closer to the salamander and lowered my voice—"do you have any mermaid scales?"

The salamander's dry lips stretched into a smile, and I stiffened again despite myself. His glowing eyes looked me up and down, and I was glad for my glamour, and especially my hood.

"Of course," he replied smoothly. "I've got a whole tank

of 'em in the tent." He lifted the flap door, and I could see there were packed shelves farther in. "If you'll just step inside, I'm sure I can help you with whatever you need."

My stomach fluttered, and I took a step forward.

"Don't do it," someone said from behind me.

I looked over my shoulder at an elf I hadn't seen arrive. He stood in a relaxed posture, his hands in his pockets. He appeared about the same age as me, tall and lean in an always-hungry kind of way. His blond hair was ruddy and messy enough to cover his pointed ears. If it wasn't for the shape of his eyes, I might not have known he was an elf at all.

He smiled lopsidedly at me. "I wouldn't go in there if I were you."

My gaze lingered on the elf, my cheeks heating. "And why is that?" I asked, my voice softer than intended.

He shrugged. "Because once you do, he won't let you leave."

My heart raced as panic seized it. My eyes flicked to the salamander. He sneered at the elf, all traces of his friendly smile gone.

"Mind your business, boy. This doesn't concern you."

I shrank from the shop owner, but he snatched my arm before I could take a step.

His yellow eyes burned with flame, and his dry skin started to heat on mine. I winced, knowing the warmth would soon turn to searing pain as he flared his fire elemental energy.

A loud clatter crashed beside me, and I turned to see the elf knocking over tables and scattering potion ingredients all over the alley.

"Why you—" The salamander released my arm to make for the elf, who deftly avoided him.

The elf held out a hand to me. "Come on!"

I took his offer without hesitation, and we both started to run toward the exit of Redcap Row.

My chest heaved while we raced out of the alley, and I looked over my shoulder to see if we were being pursued. But my arm was yanked as the elf kept on going.

We ran through streets and cut through alleys, past shops and dark houses. The cool air felt good as it blew over my cheeks and through my hair. The elf eventually slowed his pace as we neared the edge of Goblinwood, and we stopped before the ruins of what looked like an old guard tower. It was taller on one side than the other, and there wasn't but one story left as far as I could tell. Boards had been affixed to the slanted hole like a makeshift roof, but there was a door.

With the danger passed, I became very aware of the boy's warm hand gripping mine, his fingers slender but his grasp firm.

"That should be far en—Whoa…" His dark eyes widened as he glanced over at me.

My heart fluttered at the wonder in his gaze. I couldn't seem to look away from his face despite my inexplicable embarrassment.

"I knew you had money, but I didn't think you were a sidhe," he said.

My mind twirled in confusion, then I sucked in a breath. My hands flew to my face; I was much too late in realizing my hood had fallen away while we'd been running.

I decided to go with it. He could tell from my glamoured sea-glass green eyes I was a sidhe. And as all sidhe were aristocrats, he could infer I had money, but how had he known before he saw my face? "What gave away my status?"

He smirked. "Your clothes may lack embellishment, but no one in Goblintown could afford fabric like this." He reached out and rubbed his fingers against the edge of my hood.

When I pursed my lips in a pout, he laughed.

"Did you think you were fooling anyone?"

I clicked my tongue, feeling annoyed at myself for thinking he was handsome for even a second. "There's no need to rub it in."

He raised his hands. "Sorry."

I sighed through my nose. "Well, in any case, thanks for saving me back there. I don't know what would have happened if you hadn't stepped in." I put all of my sincerity into my tone. He'd saved me like some hero in a storybook. He'd been bold and brave and looked good while doing it. He deserved my thanks if nothing else.

His face sobered. "No, you don't. And you shouldn't be wandering around a place like this if you aren't up for it."

"Are you scolding me right now?" I frowned.

"Call it what you want. But I marked you as out of place the moment you got thrown out of Swonghilder's."

A shiver ran through me, and I analyzed him. *I don't want to believe it, but he is a goblin after all.* "You followed me all the way from there? Why? Were you planning to rob me?"

The elf scowled, and my stomach clenched. "Wow, I just saved you from a world of suffering, and you promptly accuse me of being a thief? Your prejudice is showing, princess. And what exactly are *you* doing here in Goblintown, huh? No one wanders into Redcap Row if they aren't planning on doing something illegal. So who's the criminal here? You better get out of here before this place eats you alive." He turned to leave.

My face heated—that time in shame. "Wait." I grabbed

the back of his tunic. "I'm sorry. Really. That wasn't right of me. I don't know anything about you."

With his back still to me, he said, "You might think everyone here deserves to live like this, that everyone is a criminal, but some of us were just born here. And even if someone did commit a crime, they've already served their time. Don't you think they would have returned to their own communities if they could have?"

I'd never really thought about it. I'd always been told goblins were criminals, but now that he pointed it out, he was right. They wouldn't be out in the public at all if they hadn't already received their punishments. And it had never once occurred to me goblins could start families and have children who'd never done anything at all.

"You're right," I answered contritely, dropping my hand from his shirt. "I'm really sorry for my ignorance. Thank you for correcting me. Can you forgive me?"

Turning toward me, he gave me a good-natured grin. "Since you're so pretty, I'll let it slide this once."

I blushed—even my ears radiated heat—as my breath caught. Then I quickly tempered my internal pleasure, quirking my mouth. *He's not complimenting me. This isn't my real face.* "A-anyway, thanks again for helping me out."

"If you really want to thank me, you can give me a kiss as a token of your heartfelt appreciation."

My heart leapt into my throat. My eyes snapped to his, but I didn't see anything menacing in them. "Is that why you brought me way out here? To extort my first kiss out of me?"

He chuckled. "There you go again, jumping right to criminal accusations. No, I brought you out here because this is my safe place, where I go to get away from home. I guess I just came here out of reflex."

I barely heard his words as my mind imagined what it

would feel like to grant his request. I scolded myself, tearing my gaze from his lips. *These are not appropriate thoughts. Not from me. Not about him.* "Is your home life very hard, then?"

He shrugged. "It's not too bad. The orphanage takes care of us as best they can. They don't mistreat us or anything, so it could be much worse."

My heart squeezed. *An orphanage? Was he abandoned by his birth parents as I was? Surely, the elves have orphanages. He must have been born in Goblintown.*

"But it can be sort of overwhelming what with all the other kids, so I come out here when I need some time alone."

I was deep in thought, distracted by his words, so I didn't notice he was staring at me. I dropped my gaze, praying my face wasn't as red as it felt.

"What's your name?" he asked.

"M-my name?"

He smirked at me. "Surely, a high-class fae like you *does* have a name. Even I have one, and I don't have anything else."

Considering I was in disguise, it wouldn't do to give him my real name. I cast my mind and landed on the nickname my brother had always called me. "Mischief. My name is Mischief."

The elf gave a graceful little bow as if he'd long practiced court manners in preparation for that moment. "Delighted to meet you, Lady Mischief. I'm Aodh. It would be my honor to escort you back to Swonghilder's if you will."

I smiled and curtsied as if he were a noble I was meeting for the first time. Even though it was all playacting, it felt like familiar territory to me. "Why thank you, kind sir."

Continuing with the charade, he offered me his arm, and

I took it—embarrassed to the core when a giggle escaped my lips.

As Aodh led me through the streets of Goblintown, I tried to mark the way though my gaze always seemed to return to his face.

"So what brought you here anyway? Potions stuff?"

I raised my eyebrows at his guess.

"You were thrown out of Swonghilder's, and you stopped at an ingredient merchant," he explained his conclusion. "Swonghilder may be a goblin, but he takes great pride in following the law. He'll have no illicit ingredients in his shop."

"Yeah, I gathered that a bit too late. I came here for mermaid scales and some other things. Trust my brother to take me to a shop that doesn't sell what I want."

"You came with your brother? Why didn't he stay with you?"

I shook my head. "He has some things he's—" I pulled up short, halting Aodh in the process.

"What—?"

I shushed him and drew him to a nearby corner, so I might hide our presence.

"What are we looking at?" Aodh whispered, his lips close to my ear as he watched over my shoulder. A pleasant shiver ran through me.

"That's my brother," I said, nodding to Graeme. His green hood obscured his face while he stood on the pavement talking to a male sylph—his conversation seeming to be much more genial with the air elemental than mine had been with the fire elemental.

"But why are you hiding?" Aodh murmured.

"I wasn't supposed to leave Swonghilder's."

Before Aodh could respond, Graeme shook the sylph's hand in what appeared to be a final farewell.

"Let's go," I said. "He looks like he's leaving, and I have to get back before he does."

There was no more pleasant conversation between us as Aodh led me to Swonghilder's. We had to run to get there before Graeme.

Aodh slowed, pulling my attention back to him as we neared the shop. "Well, this is it. I don't expect to see you anymore. But it was…eventful. Be more careful from now on, Mischief."

With a stiff nod, Aodh moved to pull away from me. I grabbed his sleeve to stop him. His dark eyes seemed to glisten with hope as they clung to mine.

"My brother comes here every three days. I'll be waiting at the guard tower two hours after dusk if you'd like to meet me."

He didn't hide his smile as he nodded.

Standing on my toes, I pressed a quick kiss to his cheek.

His face turned red, and a little gasp escaped his lips. Despite his earlier bravado, I knew he hadn't expected it.

"Thank you for everything, Aodh. I'll see you again," I whispered.

I pulled up my hood, hoping a sidhe glamour could hide my matching blush, and ran toward Swonghilder's without looking back.

∾

The warm memory kept the chilly night air out on my bedroom balcony at bay. The hazy image of Aodh's expression of embarrassed delight when I'd pecked him on the cheek floated before my eyes. I ran my fingertips over my lips, which had stretched into a reminiscent smile. *How much has he changed?*

Tadhg's cat ear twitched, and he raised his head, hearing something I didn't.

I squinted in the direction he looked, and thoughts of my first meeting with Aodh faded into the past as I heard the clip-clopping and rattle of my parents' carriage approach.

Guess it's time.

CHAPTER

SEVEN

I stalled at the top of the stairs, leaning against the wall so my parents couldn't see me from the foyer. After closing my eyes, I took a deep breath.

I knew they would hate the idea of me becoming the goblin queen, especially given my commitments. And though I'd prepared myself for their disappointment, I wouldn't be pressured into a life of unhappiness "for my own good."

They loved me, had loved me from the moment they'd found me abandoned on the moors of the human realm. I just had to trust their love for me would outweigh their prejudice against the goblins and their ambitions at the sidhe court.

Sighing heavily, I stepped out of the shadows.

My father was helping my mother take off her cloak. They were as gorgeous and youthful as the first day I could remember them. It was no wonder the sidhe were considered the most beautiful of all fae and why they ruled the various communities of Tír. With hair that always had a golden hue and hypnotic sea-glass green eyes, no one would ever mistake a sidhe for a human despite having no outwardly fae features. And if someone should make that costly mistake, the sidhe's superior magic would correct them most severely.

My father wore green that evening, his jacket elaborately embroidered in gold, which matched the shine of his golden hair. My mother's ball gown was a creamy yellow with intricate lace, and it made her sea-glass green eyes seem that much brighter.

She was the first to notice my arrival, and she smiled in greeting.

"Oh, you're still awake. How are you feeling, dear?"— she didn't wait for me to answer—"You missed a wonderful party, as expected of the Duke and Duchess of Westcount. The King asked after you."

She beamed with pride, and my heart stung.

"May I speak with you both?" I asked.

My mother tilted her head at my serious tone.

"Of course," my father responded. "Come into the drawing room."

As if my brother had known exactly how it would happen, he was already waiting in the drawing room when I came down the stairs—seated comfortably on the window seat.

My parents lowered themselves onto a couch, and I sat facing them, my brother's eyes encouraging me from behind them.

I cleared my throat, which seemed very dry under the expectations of their gazes. "I know this isn't what you wanted for me, but I have to follow my heart. Tonight, I did something that cannot be undone... I became the goblin queen."

My mother's face paled as she gasped; my father turned red.

He swiveled around to glare at my brother. "And how *exactly* did that happen?" he demanded.

To Graeme's credit, he didn't flinch at the anger directed toward him. But then, he'd probably expected it. He was given the task of "watching out for me," after all. And my failure to follow the rules would be considered just as much his fault as it was mine. He was the elder sibling, he was fae, and he was male. It was his duty to act in my best interest. Of course, it was that attitude that put us in the current situation to begin with.

"Graeme had nothing to do with this. Don't blame him. Even if he'd locked me in my room, I would have found a way." I drew my father's ire back toward me.

"I don't understand," my mother whimpered. "What is your *obsession* with goblins? We uprooted and went all the way to Olympus to get you away from there. It hasn't even been a season since we've returned. I thought you'd finally let this nonsense go."

I sighed. "I'm not obsessed with goblins, Mum. You tore me away from the boy I loved. You didn't even let me say goodbye. And now that boy is the goblin king. I made a promise to him all those years ago, and I'm keeping that promise."

My mother scowled. "You speak of promises, Melody? What about your promise to King Lorccán?"

"I never made that promise. You and father promised I would become the royal mistress before I knew what it meant, before I understood what it entailed. I wouldn't even be King Lorccán's proper wife."

"I didn't know you wanted to be queen of Tír." My

mother frowned. Even if it was something I wanted, Lorccán already had a queen, a sidhe queen.

"I don't. That's not the point."

She continued with her lecture. "You know how sought-after human mistresses are. It's so hard for fae to have children, and the Queen is too important to be risked in such a way. As the King's mistress, you'd be taken care of the rest of your life, you'd have the King's ear, and you'd be mother to the future king. You've known King Lorccán for most of your life. I thought you liked him. He has such affection for you."

I thought about Lorccán's hungry gaze—his whispered promises—the last time we'd met. He'd never looked at me like that before my recent return to Tír. I knew how impatient he was to make things official, and that impatience had only fueled my determination to become goblin queen all the sooner.

My father clicked his tongue. "I wouldn't have brought you back from Olympus if I'd thought this would continue. You have obligations to the King. And your little *mistake* will never be repeated. The binding is still in place."

My jaw clenched at my father's mention of the binding spell he'd placed on my whole family—the spell that made it impossible for any of us to tell Aodh that Mischief and Melody were the same person.

I forced my teeth apart. "He wasn't a mistake. And I don't need to tell him outright. He'll fall in love with me again, or he'll figure it out on his own. He's clever. He's the goblin king."

My father raised his lip in distaste. "He can call himself whatever he likes, but he has no power in Tír. His only authority is given to him by King Lorccán, and it extends only to the edge of Goblinwood. Goblintown is part of Tír, and the only reason the King allows this little playact is he has more important places to put his energy. Better to let the goblins govern themselves than to constantly wrangle them."

I frowned. "His power may be given by the grace of King Lorccán, but his impact in Goblintown is all-reaching. You sound as though you don't see the goblins as fae. I know you don't believe that. You've done so much work in helping them. I will be able to do even more as goblin queen. I know you two are upset and surprised right now. But you taught me to be empathetic and kind to everyone, especially those less fortunate. How can you say that in one breath and tell me I can't marry a goblin in the next?"

"Yes," my mother said in her most reasonable and patronizing tone. "They are fae, and they should be treated with empathy. But you can't forget they also chose this path for themselves. Actions have consequences, and their criminal actions have led them to Goblintown."

I snorted. "You sound as if every community doesn't have criminals in it. Not everyone who commits a crime ends up in Goblintown. If you have enough power and influence, not only do you escape punishment, but the community turns a blind eye to it entirely. Did Lord Kelpania ever go to prison when the previous king found out he was using near slave labor to build his ships? He didn't, right?"

My father's face darkened to a shade of purple.

I sighed before he could speak. "Listen: I love you both, truly. I appreciate everything you've ever done for me. I know that if you hadn't found me and brought me home, I would have died long ago. You've raised me with love and care, and I don't want to have our relationship end here. But you cannot ask me to not be who I am."

I glanced at my brother, who gave me a small smile.

"King Aodh will be coming for me very soon. I apologize if this has thrown a wrench into your political plans, but I'm sorrier if I have hurt you. I know this is a lot to take in, so I'm going to give you time to calm down and adjust for now." I rose from my chair, meeting the startled and confused eyes of my parents who had loved and nurtured me my entire life. "Thank you for everything. I love you. Goodnight."

CHAPTER

EIGHT

I didn't sleep well that night though I did try—forcing myself to lie in bed and close my eyes. Tadhg must have sensed I was unsettled because he shifted into a luminescent blue dog to lay beside me, the form he always took when trying to protect or comfort me.

The argument with my parents swirled in my mind. On one hand, I was one step closer to my goal. They couldn't make me become the royal mistress. But I hated fighting with them. It wasn't that I didn't want to make them proud, but I couldn't be true to myself and give them what they wanted.

Still, as I lay in bed, I felt guilty for hurting them. I could only remember all the joyful memories from my childhood: my mother teaching me to brew my very first potion, my father teaching me to dance in preparation for my first party, them laughing and clapping as Graeme and I put on little plays in the drawing room with a sheet strung across the room for a curtain. We'd all been so happy, and I could only hope I would see them smile with joy and pride at me again someday.

But they weren't the only ones I was hurting. Lorccán would be surprised at best and upset at worst to find out his promised mistress had run off to marry a goblin. And even though I had full confidence he could easily find a replacement for me—anyone in Faerie, even those in countries outside of Tír, would be thrilled to be with him—it would be an embarrassment for him. I'd known him for a long time, and I thought of us as friends if nothing else. He'd always been kind to me, well before he'd ever seen me as a woman. I was relying on that kindness now. He would find out at some point what I'd done. I would tell him as soon as I found the right words.

Guilt gnawed at my gut. I curled onto my side, squeezing my eyes shut as a bittersweet memory replayed in my mind.

～

With my head down, I carefully watched the cobblestone street past the ruffled hem of my skirt. It was my first time wearing heels outside. And though I'd practiced in preparation of that day, the uneven, sloped street was making me feel a little wobbly.

I teetered to one side, and a firm hand caught me at the waist to steady me.

The Crown Prince chuckled under his breath as he tucked my hand under his arm. "Why don't we sit on that bench over there? We can watch the ducks. You love the ducks."

I pursed my lips in a little pout. I had met with Lorccán many times before for these planned meetings where we were supposed to get to know each other—at least twice a year since our parents first promised us to each other when I was eight and he was thirteen. I'd wanted today to be different. I was thirteen already. And I hadn't understood before what it would mean to be bound to him.

"I'm not a baby anymore," I muttered while he led me slowly toward a bench facing the river that ran through Sifra.

His sea-glass green eyes were a few shades darker than most sidhe, bordering on emerald. At eighteen, he was already a man in my eyes. He had the lean strength of a warrior despite having never been to war. His golden hair glistened in the sunshine, almost as brightly as the indulgent smile he gave me.

He settled on the bench beside me, and I stifled my sigh of relief at taking the weight off my feet.

"That's true," he agreed. "You're not a baby, but don't be so eager to grow up. You should enjoy your childhood. You'll be longing for these days once you have to bear the burden of adult responsibilities."

I puffed out my cheeks.

With a grin, he pinched my cheek playfully, and I flushed with indignation. That was not at all what I wanted. Didn't he know I was a woman now? I'd had my moontimes for two years already! Why did he still look at me as if I were his little sister rather than the future mother of his children?

"Are you *certain* you don't want to feed the ducks?" Lorccán asked as he produced a cloth bag from his pocket.

My gaze drifted to the summer sunlight glittering off the rippling water of the river. A mama duck swam under a cobbled footbridge in our direction, her ducklings drifting close behind. I bit my lip at beholding their adorableness— still so small and soft looking.

Lorccán sighed heavily. "Oh, well. I guess I'll just have to give them these grapes all by my lonesome…"

With a smirk, he rose from his seat beside me and sauntered toward the riverbank. Slipping my shoes from my feet, I left them under the bench—the grass lush and green on my soles as I ran after him.

He rewarded me with an easy smile when I reached his side. "Hold out your hand."

I offered him my palm to receive some of the grapes. But instead of giving me the fruit, he placed a golden bangle in my hand. My heart warmed at the gift. Its metal swirls twisted together like the tails of shooting stars during a meteor shower.

"Happy birthday, Melody," Lorccán said.

"Thank you, Your Royal Highness."

Lorccán made a show of looking around us. "Do you see anyone else here?"

I shook my head. I knew what he wanted, but my face heated regardless. "Thank you, Lorccán."

He rewarded me with another smile and offered me the bag of grapes.

CHAPTER
NINE

Tadhg nudged my hand with a whine, and I opened my eyes to see dawn had long passed. I'd drifted off, but I wasn't rested.

"All right," I murmured, getting out of bed. I shuffled to the door, a little unsteady on my feet as my head spun, and opened it for Tadhg. He bounded out happily to get his breakfast, his dog's tail wagging. He clearly wanted me to follow him, or he would have just slipped under the door on his own rather than waking me.

But I didn't go with him. Instead, I sat in my bedroom chair, gnawing on my lip—a habit my mother had long scolded me for. *I shouldn't go down to breakfast. I should give them more time to adjust before facing them.*

Whether it was cowardice or prudence, I couldn't say. But I ignored my grumbling stomach in favor of starting the day. I was changing my clothes when Eithne entered with a tray of food.

I turned toward her.

"You missed breakfast, my lady. And when I saw Tadhg come down, I knew you must be awake," she explained.

My savior. "Thank you, Eithne."

Eithne eyed my attire, which was simple and comfortable. "Are you romping today, my lady?"

My mouth twitched into a smirk. Romping was how Eithne always referred to my various shenanigans—the ones Graeme called mischief and Mother called unladylike.

"Not today, no. Today, we're packing in preparation for King Aodh's arrival. I don't know when he'll come, but it will be very soon, and I want to be ready."

After I ate breakfast, Eithne and I began packing all of the things I would take with me to Goblintown. She concentrated mostly on my clothes while I carefully packed my workroom.

Hours later, as I soaked in a hot bath, I ticked off all the things on my list. There wasn't much left to do now but wait.

The candlelight glistened gold off my wet skin, and the slight fragrance of jasmine hung in the air from the oil Eithne had added to my bathwater.

I breathed deep the scent, remembering the first time I'd smelled it.

~

I stuck my nose in the drawstring pouch and breathed deeply, excited about the purchase I'd just made. I'd always wanted to smell jasmine, but it didn't grow in these parts of Faerie.

The magically preserved flowers looked as though they still grew on the vine, and they wouldn't lose that property until heated or crushed, or so the saleswoman had told me.

Aodh chuckled. "You're going to faint if you don't stop doing that. I think your brain could use some fresh air."

I smiled at his teasing. They just smelled so wonderful that regular air didn't seem good enough. But, if I was honest, I did feel a little light-headed. Heeding his advice, I pulled the pouch closed and placed it beside the candle burning steadily on the weather-worn table between us.

Over the last few months, I'd grown to love the crumbling guard tower Aodh had turned into his hideaway. It didn't have much by way of decoration—a table and a few stumps we'd rolled in to use as chairs. But the way the stone walls sparkled slightly in the candlelight, the way they muffled the sounds of the chilly wind and the forest just outside the door, made the small round room feel safe and cozy.

"Have you really never seen jasmine before?" he asked. "It's not like it's illegal. Don't they have things like that in your fancy sidhe shops?"

He wasn't wrong. Even though I'd never seen the flower in the shops of Piskishire, I probably could find it in Sifra. At the very least, I was sure Lorccán would get some for me if I asked. But I didn't like asking him for things. From our scheduled visits and monthly letters, I knew Lorccán very much wanted me to live a normal life. He didn't want me involved in courtly matters until it was absolutely necessary. That was one of the reasons he'd insisted our arrangement not be public knowledge until I became his royal mistress officially in five years—when I turned twenty.

I frowned, a queasy feeling twisting my gut, remembering Lorccán's most recent letter. He'd cancelled our next meeting. He was twenty, and his marriage was only months away. The idea of sharing him with the future queen of Tír had never much bothered me in the past—that was just how things were done. But recently, I'd started to see things differently. Was it so wrong for a human like me to want to be someone's only love? Did Lorccán even love me in that way at all? He'd always been kind and gentle toward me. But, if he loved me, it was platonic.

"Is that not right?" Aodh asked. "Are jasmine flowers so rare?"

My eyes met Aodh's in the warm glow of our single candle. Of late, thinking of Lorccán had made me uncomfortable in a way it never had before. But it wasn't really the thought of sharing him with another. It was the twinge of guilt that pricked my heart. When I thought of Lorccán, I couldn't help but compare him to Aodh. The comparison was the difference between a pencil sketch and an oil painting. Being around Aodh made me feel like the world was full of colors and textures I hadn't known were missing.

"Yes," I answered his question. "They're quite rare in these parts. I've been to ingredients shops everywhere from here to Sifra, and I've never seen them before."

Aodh nodded, his ruddy hair catching the light in such a way that it blazed like fire. He frowned slightly. "What's it like outside of Goblintown? What's it like to be a sidhe? To get to go wherever you want whenever you want?"

I analyzed his tone but found no bitterness, only curiosity. I sighed through my nose. "I wouldn't know what it's like to go wherever I want when I want. My life it quite structured. You have no idea the number of rules I'm breaking to be here. I do have a certain amount of freedom, of course. But most things—what I wear, who I socialize with, even who I m-marry..." I stumbled on the word. The truth was I would never be allowed to marry, not really. But without revealing I was a human and promised to the future king, I had no other way of putting it. "The big things are all decided for me by my parents."

Wincing, he dropped his gaze to the candle's flame. "You're almost making me glad I don't have parents," he murmured.

I watched his expression carefully, trying to distinguish if there was any disappointment at hearing I was effectively spoken for.

"At least I can wander within the confines of Goblintown as I like."

My heart sank at hearing his thoughts. *Why did I think he would be disappointed?* "There's no place else quite like Goblintown. I can tell you that. There's so much diversity here. You rarely find outsiders within the communities of Tír. You're not going to find a trow in Manderfeld for instance."

"Have you ever been to Elfton?" His tone carried a weight it didn't have before.

I shook my head sadly. "You?"

He mimicked my gesture but smirked with a shrug of his shoulders. "Even though I wasn't the one who was cast out, I doubt I would fit in there. Besides, I'm proud to be a goblin." He sat up straighter on his stump. "Hey, you up for a walk? It's cold out, but I want to show you something."

I nodded and rose to my feet—grabbing my pouch of jasmine and tying the drawstrings at the back of my apron.

CHAPTER

TEN

I followed Aodh out into the night. The weather had turned cold since the beginning of the winter half of the year. We hadn't yet had snow, but ice had already formed on the surface of ponds and water troughs.

I shivered, wrapping my arms around myself as a chill blew down the street. Our footsteps shuffled softly on the uneven stones of the road. I had no idea where he was taking me, but I knew I could trust him to keep me safe should we run into trouble.

I glanced over at him walking beside me. Though his mouth was set in that easy smile of his, his eyes still seemed contemplative. I bit my lip. I'd wondered something for a while, but it had never felt like the right time to ask. *Well, he asked me a prodding question…*

"How well did you know your parents before…?" I inquired softly.

Even in the torchlight, I could see his face pale.

"You don't have to answer if—"

He shook his head to cut me off. "No, it's…fine. My

mother died in childbirth." His soft words were hardly above a whisper as if he were trying not to disturb the spirit of the mother he'd never had the chance to know.

I frowned. It was all too common a story in Faerie though most babies didn't survive either.

"And my father, or rather the elf who called himself my father"—he lifted his hand to the tiny scar that broke his eyebrow—"Let's just say, I wasn't overly upset when I found him dead in the alley on my way home from school."

His gaze seemed to stare at something no longer there. He suddenly looked years older. Compulsively, I reached out and touched his hand.

He flinched and halted to a stop. When his eyes found mine, I thought I saw a flicker of hope there. My heart pounded, and I struggled to swallow. My whole body tingled as all my nerves stood on end. I held my breath.

What would it be like to kiss him for real?

My stomach fluttered. *Stop it. Don't think about things like that.*

Lacing his fingers with mine, he started walking again. As warmth spread through me, I wondered if the rosy tinge to his cheeks was from the cold or something more.

I couldn't lie to myself about what I was feeling.

I'd met plenty of boys in my life, everyone from lords' sons to stable lads. I'd danced with them, had tea with them, chatted about their families or nothing at all. But I'd never met a boy quite like Aodh.

Oh, there were plenty who were attractive, kind, and even humorous—Lorccán was chief among them. But Aodh was different. He was brave enough to take on a salamander to save a naive stranger, savvy enough to navigate Goblintown and all its dangers. And he was kind. He may be boastful, and he teased me every chance he got, but he was also just as free with his compliments. I could hear how warm his heart was when he talked about the other children at the orphanage and the goblins in general. Life had dealt him the worst hand, a hand that could have easily been my own, and he'd let that fuel his warmth rather than smother it.

"Where are we going?" I asked. I didn't much care so long as he kept holding my hand along the way. But the atmosphere was so heavy that I had to break it with words.

"Just wait and see. You're going to love it," he said.

I love you. I nearly choked on the unspoken confession. My face heated, and my heart ached. *No. No way. That's not allowed.*

"What do you think?" he asked, releasing my hand and gesturing to a fountain.

My hand felt empty and strange without his.

He glanced at me expectantly, completely unaware of the life-changing turmoil churning within me.

The fountain was more like a pool at that time of year; they hadn't drained the water from the basin for the winter. At the center was the statue of a puck with a grapevine wreath atop his head and a jagged dagger at his waist.

As far as fountains went, I'd seen more impressive ones though I did think the likeness was particularly detailed. I shrugged, trying to wrestle my mind into a state capable of easy conversation. "It's nice. Does it shoot water in the summer?"

"It's nice! Don't you know who that is?" Aodh asked in disbelief.

"Should I?"

He scowled. "No, I suppose not. If anything, they probably wouldn't want you to learn about him. This is

Robin Goodfellow, the greatest goblin king Goblintown has ever known. He's the reason I'm proud to be a goblin."

I looked more closely at the statue. "Ahh. I see. What did he do?"

That seemed to be the question he was waiting for because he launched into an enthusiastic lesson about who the puck had been.

"He was the best—smart and cunning. He helped all those who needed it, goblin or otherwise. There was a lot of corruption at the time, and he shut it all down. He taxed the rich, who had become heavy with the gold they exploited from others, and made sure the poorest among us always had food and shelter."

As he spoke, I took in the sight of him. His eyes were bright with hope and admiration. I wondered if he would ever look at me that way.

He turned to me. "Pretty great, right?"

I nodded. "What happened to him?"

"He reigned for as long as he could and eventually died at a ripe old age." Aodh pointed down a tree-lined road. "The goblins built him a tomb. It's watched all the time, and there's an eternal flame kept alight. They say he took one final edict to his grave, and the goblins will know of it when it's most needed."

"Why all the mystery, though? Hasn't anyone gone in there to get it?"

Aodh shook his head. "Plenty have tried, but it seems he had a series of traps made to ensure only the worthiest could access it. That's why there are guards. Goblins kept dying while trying to retrieve it."

"But if it's that important, why did he hide it like that?"

He pursed his lips in thought. "I don't know. We probably won't ever know until we actually read it."

I nodded, approaching the fountain and looking into the basin. A thin layer of ice had formed on the top. I reached out and touched it. The ice bobbed beneath my fingers, and cold water dripped from my hand.

I shivered. "Oh! That's cold."

Aodh snorted. "Well, that was obvious just by looking at it. Why did you touch it, then?"

"All right, saucy." Leaning over, I splashed some of the water his way though only a few drops hit him.

His eyes widened, and he grinned. "Oh, yeah?"

Before I could even move, he'd lifted me into his arms— one arm beneath my knees and the other at my back.

"One more peep out of you, and you'll be taking a swim."

I squealed, locking my arms around his neck and cringing into him as I squeezed my eyes shut. "Don't! Don't! Please, I'm sorry."

He laughed and made as if to throw me, but he kept me firmly in his grasp. "All right," he said soothingly, stepping back from the fountain. "But only because you asked so nicely."

Sighing in relief, I lifted my head from his chest.

His playful grin slid from his face as his eyes met mine.

For a moment, the world stopped. And the only thing I knew was his breath on my face, his heartbeat pounding against me, and his lips mere inches from mine.

His arms held me firmly to him. But as his eyes widened and his face flushed, they seemed to lose their strength.

"Oof!" The air rushed out of me when I hit the hard ground where he dropped me. A cloud of jasmine scent exploded around me, and I realized I'd landed on the drawstring pouch I'd purchased earlier that night.

~

A gentle knock on my bathroom door pulled me from my memories, announcing Eithne had returned to scrub my back. I sat up in the tub and leaned forward while calling for her to come in.

Her scrubbing was more gentle than usual, but when she spoke, it wasn't Eithne's voice I heard. "You should wash your hair as well," my mother said. "It glistens so when it's freshly washed. We should make sure you're at your best when your future husband comes for you."

My aching heart warmed at her softly spoken words, and tears welled up in my eyes.

"I'm sorry," she whispered. "I thought I was protecting you. No parent wants their child to have a hard life. And among the paths before you, you have chosen a difficult one. I hope you're prepared for what lies ahead."

"I know," I murmured. "If my heart would have allowed me any other choice, I would've taken it."

"You know, you're giving up becoming a banshee. You'll never be able to do magic without coupling with a sidhe," she reminded me gently.

"He's worth it."

She paused, digesting my response, then sighed. "It will take us time to fully adjust to the idea, but I want you to know we will help and support you in whatever you decide. You were right about showing kindness and compassion to the goblins. I hope all we've taught you will help you serve them well as their queen."

I looked back at her, placing my hand over the one she rested on my shoulder. "Thank you, Mum… I'm sorry if this has messed up Dad's plans at court."

She gave me a tender smile. "Your father will adjust.

Certainly, he won't have as much influence as if you'd become the royal mistress, but I'm sure he can find a way out of it. He was able to delay sending you to Sifra for the last five years already."

"Is he still angry?"

She frowned. "He's worried, dear. You know he could never truly be angry at you."

I nodded.

"If you want to be worried about someone's wrath, it should be King Lorccán's."

My mouth went dry, and it took effort for me to swallow. I crossed my arms over my naked chest. "Surely, the King will not be too upset. He can have anyone for his mistress, human or otherwise."

I peeked over my shoulder to see my mother shaking her head seriously. "I think you underestimate what a man with wounded pride will do."

My chest tightened. I knew Lorccán wanted me; he'd practically publicly declared as much the last time we'd met. And though I didn't feel the same way about him, I couldn't believe he would hold a grudge. He'd never force me into something I didn't want. He might be disappointed, but I had to believe he would make the wise decision and let me go. He would find someone else to bear his heir. It was every human woman in Tír's dream.

"I believe in His Majesty," I said. "Still...tell Dad I'll be the one to inform the King. It will hurt him less coming from me."

My mother's silence made me a little nervous, but I pushed the feeling away. I had to believe I was right in this; otherwise, I would feel guilty for putting my father in a tough position and maybe even scared at what Lorccán might do.

My mother dropped it, changing the subject. "So…tell me how you did it, my clever girl. How did you become the goblin queen? Was it awfully romantic?"

I could hear her forced tone, but I appreciated the effort. She was trying to make this normal in her own mind. I told her how I'd stolen his ring, conveniently leaving out the details of Graeme's involvement. I frowned as I recalled Aodh's reaction to the theft. "He wasn't pleased."

My mother shrugged. "What man is pleased when he's outsmarted by a woman? But I warn you, my dear, you have your work cut out for you. Your battle has only begun. If that's how he reacted, he won't accept you easily."

"Do you think I'll ever be able to tell him who I really am?"

She was silent for a while. She'd never been happy with how my father had gone about assuring Aodh would never know I was Mischief. Then again, she'd never really tried to convince my father to find a way to break the spell either. "Your father said those words in fear and desperation. He didn't build in a contingency to break the spell."

"So there's no hope?

"There's always hope, my dear. True love conquers all. If you can win his heart, you may be able to break the binding."

"May" isn't exactly a sure thing. Still, winning his heart again was already my goal.

She leaned over and kissed the top of my head. "I wish you luck, darling. You're going to need it." After standing from her stool, she headed for the bathroom door. "Wash your hair and get some sleep. You'll need to be well-rested for what tomorrow will bring."

CHAPTER
ELEVEN

The following afternoon, I sat playing cards with Graeme in the drawing room. I'd finished packing and was only trying to fill my time until Aodh came to get me.

Eithne rushed into the room, her piskie eyes bright with excitement. "He's here, my lady! His carriage is coming up the drive now."

My heart leapt, racing as I jumped up from my seat. I vaguely heard Graeme follow me as I sped from the house.

He really came. I couldn't stifle a grin as I watched the Goblin King's open carriage make its way up the hill. But that smile left even quicker than it had come as the carriage neared the house.

"What's wrong?" Graeme asked from beside me.

"That's not Aodh," I said flatly.

The kelpie who sat in the carriage was not at all whom I'd expected to see. He was handsome as most kelpies were— in their human forms as he was now but also in their horse forms—with skin that shimmered like the sunlight off rippling water. His flowing, sandy hair had seaweed plaited into it.

My parents joined us on the front step—my mother wrapping a cloak around my shoulders—just as the vehicle came to a stop. The carriage was simply painted, the goblin king's seal on the side. It wasn't at all how I remembered it.

The kelpie stepped down and dipped his head at us though his expression conveyed he was not pleased to be there. "I am here for Lady Melody Píobaire at the Goblin King's behest. I am charged with bringing her to Goblintown."

My father sucked in a breath. "What disrespect! Is this the treatment we should expect our daughter to receive at the hands of the Goblin King? Even King Lorccán went to retrieve his queen personally from her family home."

The kelpie blinked his seawater eyes blandly at my father's outburst. "Perhaps the Sidhe King had nothing better to do."

I winced. *So this is how he's going to play it, is it?* I raised my chin, ignoring the choking sound coming from my father as I said, "I'm glad to hear the Goblin King takes his duties to his people so seriously, and I am pleased he has sent for me so promptly. It displays his eagerness to make me his queen."

The kelpie's eyes slid to mine, and the blood drained from my face at his unrestrained glare. I blinked in surprise, but when I looked again, it was gone, replaced by that same bland expression.

"If you will just wait a moment, sir," I requested. "I'll have my things brought out, and we can leave shortly."

"There's no need for all that. One small trunk will suffice. You will be home before you know it," he replied.

I tilted my head. "Why so?" *He's mistaken if he thinks I'll give up that easily.*

"Don't fret, my love," my mother said, resting her hands on my shoulders. "There isn't much room in this carriage anyway. We'll pack the carriage and send Eithne with your things and Tadhg this evening."

At my mother's firm squeeze, I could hear her unspoken words of encouragement. She'd said the path wouldn't be easy, but she'd raised me to handle things properly.

I turned to my parents, pushing the kelpie's presence from my mind. "You'll come to visit once I'm settled?" I asked.

My mother smiled and pulled me into a hug. "Of course, my darling. Don't forget to write, and let me know if you need any help planning your wedding or coronation."

I assumed Aodh would have people who handled things like official events, but it was good to know I could ask for help if I needed it.

Turning to my father, I hesitated. His eyes were the saddest I'd ever seen. He was utterly defeated, no fight left in him. I wrapped my arms around him, resting my head on his chest. "I love you, Daddy," I murmured.

The air rushed out of me as my father squeezed me. "You come home anytime. I won't say a word."

My heart swelled. I wasn't going to give up, but I appreciated knowing I would always be welcome to return.

Finally, I turned to Graeme, who gave me a sheepish smile, then said, "I guess this is it. We did it. You're off to your husband's house."

Hugging my brother, I whispered, "It's not over quite yet. I still may need your help."

I felt him nod. "Anytime."

Emotion welled up inside me as I turned my attention to

the kelpie. It was what I wanted, but that didn't stop the moment from being bittersweet. Perhaps if Aodh was welcoming me with open arms, I wouldn't feel so nervous about leaving the people I knew would support me no matter what. But as it was, I left my childish anxieties behind and climbed into the carriage.

After joining me, the kelpie signaled to the driver we could leave. I waved to my parents, then watched my childhood home get more and more distant until it was out of sight.

Settling in my seat, I faced the kelpie. His seawater eyes watched me, carefully analyzing me for gods knew what. I analyzed him right back. His clothes were simple, not at all what I'd come to expect from those who worked closely with kings.

"What is your name, sir? And what do you do for the Goblin King?"

He frowned, clearly unhappy with having to make conversation. "I am Selwyn, the Goblin King's closest adviser."

I didn't fail to notice his lack of respectful address. "I will be seeing much of you, then."

"Not likely."

I bristled. I didn't like his tone at all. And though I normally wouldn't press the issue, the man was getting under my skin. "Hadn't you better at least address me properly?"

He stared straight into my eyes. "I apologize, my lady." His tone said he wasn't sorry at all for his disrespect.

"That's 'Your Majesty.'" I held up my hand to display the goblin king's ring still on my finger.

"Not yet it isn't, *my lady*."

I suppressed my irritation. It was too early for me to lose

my calm. I had a long way ahead of me, and I hadn't even reached Goblintown yet. I plastered a smile on my face. "You're right, of course, Selwyn." I continued to smile until he looked away first.

TWELVE

S elwyn wasn't keen to make conversation, which suited me just fine.

As we entered the streets of Piskishire, we earned some curious gazes from the piskies gathered outside. They knew me by sight and likely didn't understand why I'd be in the Goblin King's carriage. It was surreal being on the receiving end of such an exchange. I thought about the first time I'd seen the carriage with Aodh.

~

"Can you see?" Aodh asked, looking down at me as we tried to peer through the crowd to the street.

It seemed the Goblin King was going somewhere that evening, and the goblins had gathered for a glimpse of him.

I shook my head to answer his question. He frowned and glanced around us. "This way." He took my hand and pulled me after him.

His thin fingers were warm in mine, and my heart

fluttered. That sort of touch seemed so natural to him as if it meant nothing at all. But for me, it had only gotten more difficult to bear.

Aodh led me to a closed vegetable stand up against a nearby building and pointed to the wooden roof. "We can sit atop. Here, I'll give you a lift."

I eyed the structure. It looked solid enough. Then I put my foot in Aodh's clasped hands and hefted myself up. Leaning over the ledge, I offered him a hand and pulled him up to sit beside me.

A murmur in the crowd told me we were just in time. From our higher vantage point, I could easily see the Goblin King's open carriage turn into the street. The carriage was painted white with intricate gold ornaments fixed to the side, which sparkled in the flame-light from the torches and lanterns. The goblin king's crest was cast in gold and featured purple gems, expertly cut and set.

But as ornate as his carriage was, the Goblin King himself was even more extravagant. The selkie simply dripped with jewels, precious metals, and fabrics of the most sumptuous sort. His silver hair and large, dark eyes bespoke his other form, and I wondered if he adorned himself so richly when he donned his pelt and shifted to his seal form.

I'd seen kings before. I'd recently been officially presented at the Sidhe King's court, and my father often met with the leaders of other countries. I'd met the Dragon Emperor as well as the All-Father of Asgard before the age of ten. And none of the rulers I'd met or seen in my life were as ostentatious as the Goblin King.

"Where is the Goblin King going so dressed up?" I asked Aodh.

Aodh shrugged. "Who knows? But it must be someplace important because he hardly ever leaves the palace."

I nodded my acknowledgment.

"I won't be anything like that when I'm the goblin king."

My eyebrows rose. "Are you going to be the goblin king?" I laughed. "How's that? Are you hiding some secret ancestry I don't know about?"

But my joking tone dried up when I saw his face darken at my teasing.

"That's not how someone becomes the goblin king."

My stomach clenched at the unhappy look on his face. "Oh? Tell me how it works," I requested eagerly, hoping to cheer him up a little.

"The goblin king is chosen by the people by popular demand."

"Like a democracy?"

He shook his head. "More like a public outcry, nothing so formal as voting. When the goblin ruler dies or retires—a few have retired—a sort of competition begins. It can take months, but the goblins all decide who they believe exemplifies what it means to be a goblin. He or she has to be clever, courageous, steadfast, and persistent."

"Are there tests or something to determine who has all those qualities?"

He turned to me, and I was glad to see his earlier dejection was gone. "Tests can be devised, but usually someone does something to prove themselves before that's necessary."

"So what kind of king will you be, then, if you won't be like him?"

He pursed his wide lips. "I won't use my wealth for myself. So many in Goblintown need help. And my palace door will always be open to the public. I'll listen to the people. I know I won't have much power in Tír, and none at all in Faerie as a whole, but I want to use what I have to help those I rule."

I smiled at him. "Like Robin Goodfellow. It sounds like you'll be a very good king."

His dark eyes slid to mine, and they held all the warmth I'd come to expect. He cleared his throat as his face flushed. "How about you help me?"

I tilted my head. "Help you become goblin king? Is that allowed?"

His blush deepened. "Help me by being my goblin queen."

Heat bloomed on my cheeks and neck—even my ears felt hot. I could hardly hear my voice over the sound of my pounding heart. "Is this a marriage proposal?" I tried to make my voice light, but I didn't quite pull it off.

He dropped his eyes to the little bit of space between us. "I mean, you must like me at least a little. You've kept coming around these last few months after all." His nonchalant tone was much more convincing than mine had been.

Disappointment wiggled its way into my heart, but it made my lie much smoother. "Yes, to buy potion ingredients."

His expression sagged a little, and hope pushed the disappointment aside. "W-well, you did kiss me that time."

I could see it now, and I smiled while my heart rang as a bell struck. "Yes, to thank you for saving me."

All of his confidence, his bravado, crumbled away as he turned his gaze back to the dispersing crowd.

"Do you know what you're asking me to put aside?" I wondered aloud.

"I'm sure your parents have picked some rich and

powerful sidhe out for you," he said bitterly. "Is that what you want?" His question was quiet, uncertain.

Thoughts of guilt toward my family and Lorccán were long forgotten. My hand trembled when I reached out and rested it on his, and his eyes flicked to mine.

"They have. But even so, when you become the goblin king, I'll be your goblin queen," I murmured.

"You will…? You promise?"

"I'll promise if you do."

He laced his fingers with mine. "What would you have me promise?"

I leaned closer to him. "Promise that when you become the goblin king—when you're the most powerful goblin in Goblintown—you won't fail to come for me."

"Why would I?"

"Who knows how long it'll take for you to become goblin king? Perhaps you won't want me anymore after the world is in your grasp."

He scowled. "That's not possible. I'll always want you."

I hesitated. *But you don't even know I'm human.* "What if you find out I'm not who you think I am?"

"I know everything I need to know about you."

I analyzed him. He'd made that pronouncement with such confidence that I believed it to be true. Warmth spread through me as I gazed into his dark eyes. "Shall we seal it?"

He faltered only a moment before closing the few inches between us. His kiss was soft, almost hesitant, at first. My heart sang as a scorching heat kindled within me. Was this what it was like for Aodh to touch me? It ached. It burned. I needed more. I squeezed his hand tighter, pressing my lips harder against his.

Lifting his free hand to my face, Aodh urged me even closer. I trembled against him, losing all reason when his tongue met mine. As I lost myself in him, I knew this was what I'd wanted all along. From the moment he'd saved me from that unspeakable fate. With every smile he'd given me, every careless brush of the hand—this was what I'd longed for. My heart would never forget this moment. At that instant, I was branded as his.

Aodh pulled away slightly—his breath heavy and uneven —and I knew my face was as flushed as his.

"Now"—his voice was low and thick—"I've made my vow. What is it you think I can't accept about you?" His eyes held no accusation as his thumb stroked my cheek.

He'll accept me. I opened my mouth to tell him everything—that I was human, that I was a foundling, that my real name was Melody, that I was promised to the future king of Tír. But I shut it again without a word. *Will he believe me when I look like this? It will be easier to explain if I show him.* I gave him a smile to tell him I wasn't brushing him off. "I'll tell you next time. I should be getting back to Swonghilder's before my brother finds me missing."

෴

The Goblin King's carriage—lacking all its gold and jewels now that Aodh sat on the throne—bumped as it went over a hole in the road. Glancing around me, I realized we had entered Goblinwood without me marking our journey.

THIRTEEN

Grateful for my mum's thoughtfulness, I pulled my cloak tighter around me. It was not yet the summer half of the year and was still a little too chilly for an open carriage ride to be comfortable. I watched the trees of Goblinwood drift by. It was a path I'd walked many times before, and it hadn't changed much in the last ten years. But when the forest started to give way to city streets, I saw the same could not be said for Goblintown.

I'd never seen Goblintown in the bright light of day; I hadn't expected it to be so cheerful. The derelict houses, while still old, were no longer falling. Thatched roofs had been tiled, ill-fitting doors had been straightened and secured. The road beneath our carriage wheels was still uneven and riddled with holes, but it was no longer wet with whatever they used to throw out of windows.

The goblins, who upon seeing their king's carriage stopped what they were doing to watch our passing, seemed happier somehow. The colors of their diverse clothing appeared brighter in the daylight. Nowhere in Tír would such a gathering of fae occur but in Goblintown. Besides the sidhe, who ruled different areas of the country, the fae tended to stay within their own distinct communities. If I hadn't come to Goblintown with my brother so many times before, I might have only ever had extended exposure to sidhe and piskies since my family was put in charge of managing Piskishire.

I could see them quite clearly, the curious eyes of drakes, elves, pucks, gnomes, and so many others, watching as their new queen passed by on her way to the palace.

Will they accept me?

In general, fae had mixed feelings about humans. They could see me as an inferior being who couldn't even use magic. They could see me as useful in that it was far easier for humans to carry a child and give birth than it was for a fae. I was valuable for that reason alone. I hadn't met very many fae who saw humans the way my parents did—as just another living creature, the same as everyone else.

I sat up a little straighter and tried to meet as many eyes as I could with a kind smile. I knew Aodh didn't want me to be queen. Winning over the goblins would not only make it easier to govern them, but it would go a long way toward getting him to accept me.

As the carriage bumped and jiggled along, my stomach rose and fell. I clenched my teeth against my nausea, wondering if it would be inappropriate to ask to walk the rest of the way. But as we started up a hill, the pavement smoothed out, and I sighed in relief.

I could feel Selwyn's steady gaze on me at the little sound that had escaped my lips. *What is his problem?*

I ignored him in favor of looking for my new home.

Everyone had always referred to the goblin king's residence as a palace, so I was a little surprised when it was nothing of the sort. It was certainly bigger than anything I'd ever come across in Goblintown, but it was about the same size as my family's country manor. A mansion compared to where most people lived, but nothing I would call a palace. Then again, I had been to only a few sprawling, glittering palaces in my twenty-five years.

Still, it seemed a clean and cozy place, quite respectable, with a lush green lawn before a stone manor house. It was pleasant to the eye—symmetrical with three, evenly-spaced peaked roofs, grey walls, and square windows.

After passing through a guarded gate set in a stone wall, the carriage turned up the round drive and stopped before the simple painted door.

I stared at the entrance to my new life, at the door to the greatest challenge I'd ever faced, as Selwyn climbed down from the carriage. With a deep breath, I stood to follow him. He began walking without even looking back at me.

I cleared my throat loudly enough that he couldn't ignore it. He halted and turned back.

"If you wouldn't mind, Selwyn." I held out my hand. I could have easily climbed down from the carriage without assistance, but as long as the kelpie insisted on defying proper manners, I would continue to enforce them. I already had enough to worry about. I didn't need Aodh's closest adviser undermining me.

He frowned severely and practically stomped back to where I waited.

"Of course, my lady." He offered his hand to assist in my descent, smiling as a glint entered his eyes.

His expression made me hesitate, but it was too late to back down. I placed my hand in his. A cool sensation shot up my arm the moment my skin touched his like the refreshing caress of water on a hot summer's day. And for a moment, my mind was full up with thoughts of Selwyn. I couldn't seem to remove my hand from his, nor did I ever want to.

In the next breath, the feeling was gone as if I'd imagined it. The only trace anything had happened at all was Selwyn's haughty smile. "My lady?"

I pursed my lips and descended the carriage, pulling my hand from his the moment I was on stable ground.

I'd been warned of certain fae growing up though I'd never encountered a fae who dared to bespell me—other than my father, that was. Kelpies, like some other fae, could have great power over humans, power to influence our desires.

I glowered at Selwyn. He was a more formidable opponent than I'd expected. *I can't underestimate him.*

"This way," he instructed, still smiling that irritating smile.

Lifting my chin, I walked past him when he opened the front door, ignoring his presence as if the wind had blown it ajar.

CHAPTER
FOURTEEN

We entered an antehall, which had a door on either side and another straight ahead. The room was rather plain with a black-and-white chessboard floor—benches on either side, the backs up against dark wooden walls. The sculpted, white ceiling was the only relief from the severe decor.

Selwyn led me through the opposite door without a word.

We entered a long cloister, one side opening into an immaculately manicured garden. Symmetrical brick paths crisscrossed through low hedges, rose bushes, and lush grass. A fountain at the center shot water into the air, making a lovely tinkling sound when it returned to the basin.

On this side, I could see the house was U-shaped rather than rectangular as the front façade suggested.

Selwyn didn't slow down to allow me to admire the space but sped on into an anteroom. Again, the walls were dark wood, and I began to feel as though I were in a hunting lodge. There seemed to be a lot of empty space on the walls as if something—a painting or a tapestry—had once hung there. The only real color in the room came from a round table at the center, where a glass vase of yellow primroses—no doubt from the glorious garden—seemed to shimmer in the harsh monochrome.

From the anteroom, Selwyn led me into a library. My pace slowed. I wanted to stop and look. What sort of treasures did Aodh house in that temple of knowledge? There was more than enough to keep me occupied for the rest of my life; tall shelves covered every wall, broken only by a fireplace, around which crowded a collection of couches and chairs.

Because of my desire to linger, Selwyn was far ahead of me, well on the other side of the room before I'd taken five steps. I rushed to catch up when he exited a door at the far end. He did not look pleased with the delay when I entered the hall.

Turning right, he started up a rather plain staircase in that same dark wood that lined the walls. My boots scuffed on the naked stairs, and I began to wonder how cold the place would be in high winter. There were no rugs, no carpets, and no tapestries to stifle any draft that found its way in.

Upon reaching the upper floor, Selwyn spoke for the first time. "The west wing chambers are designated for the goblin queen"—he gestured down the hall to the left—"Over here, you will find the queen's reception room as well as a small bedroom for any of the honored guests whom you wish to keep...close."

My eyes snapped to his face. I didn't appreciate his suggestive tone in the least. Of course, I wasn't under any misconception all political marriages were the result of love. But to imply such a thing on the day of my arrival was just plain rude. Then again, I was realizing rude was unremarkable for Selwyn.

Turning right, I followed him down the hallway, which ended in another perpendicular hall with three doors.

"These are the queen's chambers," he said.

As if that were everything I needed to know, he turned on his heel and started back the way he'd come.

"Wait," I called after him. I had so many questions— When would I be meeting Aodh? Where were the kitchens? The dining room? The great hall? What about when Eithne arrived later? Would she be assisted?

But all those completely reasonable questions flew from my mind when Selwyn turned his seawater eyes on me.

"Where are the King's chambers?" I asked.

His bland expression soured. "The Goblin King can disclose that information to you if he sees fit. You may wait here until he summons you."

I clicked my tongue as he left without another word.

Standing where the two hallways met, I thought about wandering around by myself. I was to be the goblin queen after all. Who would censure me for getting to know my new home?

But I decided against it. *What if Aodh sends for me, and I'm not here?*

I opened the middle of the three doors ahead of me and entered what would be my bedroom from now on. It was quite unlike every other room I'd seen thus far. Delicate and pleasant, it was papered in a mint green and painted with white flowers and birds. The four-poster bed was draped in a pastel yellow, which matched the bedspread, the settee at its foot, and the nearby chairs. The ceiling was that same sculpted white, but a rug of rosy pink with sky-blue decorations lay on the floor.

Passing the bed, I opened the door on my right to discover it was a dressing room with more space than my clothes could fill. I saw another door farther in and assumed that was the bathroom. After closing the door, I crossed to the other side and entered a sitting room.

Large windows on the left and far side provided enough light that a lamp would never be necessary during the day. The walls were papered in a mossy green while the couches and chairs were upholstered in emerald velvet. The naked floorboards were a warmer wood than what was used in the rest of the house.

Closing the door, I couldn't help but scrunch my brow. *The queen's chambers are much warmer and more welcoming than the rest of the house. And while there's still a lack of art, they don't feel empty like the other rooms.*

My heart gave a little flutter. *Did Aodh prepare these rooms for me?* But then I shook my head. *Of course, he didn't. He wouldn't have had time to do that. Besides, all evidence proves he doesn't want me here at all.*

With a sigh, I lowered myself onto the settee at the end of my bed. *I'm already tired.*

A soft knock on my bedroom door made my heart leap into my throat. I jumped up from my seat. *Aodh!* But before I'd taken two steps forward to let him in, a high-pitched voice from the other side called out to me.

"Your Majesty? I've brought you refreshments."

My hope deflated. "Coming," I called.

CHAPTER
FIFTEEN

I blinked rapidly when I opened the door to find my visitor holding a wooden tray.

It was unusual to see imps in Tír, and I immediately wondered why she would have left Asgard and how she'd ended up in Goblintown. As far as I knew, no other countries in Faerie used the goblin model of outcasting "undesirable" community members. And they certainly wouldn't have sent them to Tír's Goblintown.

Her amethyst eyes brightened as she smiled up at me. Her pointed ears, the same lavender color as her face, seemed abnormally large as they poked their way out of her headkerchief, which managed to hide her horns.

"Good afternoon, Your Majesty," she said with a smile and small bow. "You must be hungry from your journey. I've brought you something to hold you over until supper."

Smiling at the imp, I opened the door for her. "That's very kind of you. Please, come in."

She scurried into the room. Whether she had her bat-like wings hidden under her dress, or something had happened to them, I didn't know. I couldn't see them when she passed me though I did notice her skinny, barbed tail peeking out from under her skirt.

"Oh, it's nothing at all, Ma'am. I'm just so pleased you're here." She placed the tray of bread, cheese, jam, and tea on the small, round table near the window. "I'm Odilie, and you can call on me for anything you need."

My earlier tiredness eased a bit as Odilie continued to smile up at me. "Thank you very much, Odilie. I'll do that. To that end, my lady's maid, Eithne, will be arriving sometime this evening. I expect she'll need help organizing and getting herself settled. Would you mind assisting her?"

Odilie looked as though nothing would give her more pleasure. "Of course, Ma'am. I will make her feel quite at home."

"Thank you."

With another bow, Odilie made as if to leave.

I called out to her to wait a moment, and again, she turned her eyes back on me. I hesitated as I tried to recall anything I'd been told about imp culture so as not to inadvertently offend her. If I remembered right, they had a particular fondness for humans though they didn't always show it in the kindest of ways.

"Yes, Ma'am?"

"You said you were pleased I was here. Why is that?"

"Ah!" she exclaimed, her already high-pitched voice nearly squeaking. "I should not speak as though I know, Ma'am. But, as for me, I feel the King will greatly benefit from finally having a queen. Many of us have been restless at his reluctance to take a bride, and there is too much to do for him alone. I can tell you, Ma'am, that he works hard for us, and a helpmate would only make things easier for him. I'm glad you've come, and I know many other goblins will rejoice at the news."

Aodh had been goblin king for one cycle already, a long time to have not taken a queen. The only ways to become the goblin queen were to outsmart him, the way I'd done, or be chosen by him the way he'd suggested two cycles ago.

Is he reluctant to get married in general? It's not just me, then? It's not just that I'm forcing his hand? But he asked me to marry him when we were young. He clearly wasn't against having a wife. Did something happen between then and now?

Guilt clenched my gut, and I felt the blood drain from my body.

Or does he no longer trust women? Did I break his heart so thoroughly? I thought he'd moved on, that I would have space to win his heart again even if he didn't know I was Mischief. *If he's so scarred from what I did to him, that could seriously affect my approach...*

"Is there anything else I can get you, Ma'am?"

I flinched, Odilie's question nudging me from my thoughts. I shook my head at the imp. "Thank you, Odilie. I appreciate the food."

She bobbed, acknowledging her dismissal. "Of course, Ma'am. Please let me know if you need anything else."

The meal Odilie had brought me was simple but filling. Sitting at the small table in my bedroom, I stared at the late winter sky out my south-facing window. It was so surreal to be nibbling cheese as I sat in the goblin queen's quarters. I had imagined this day so many times. But never had I been alone. My imagination was so full of daydreams, fuel for the fire of my resolve.

My stomach churned as I swallowed down my warm tea. *It's no wonder I've had a less than warm welcome from Aodh.*

Would it be worse if he knew I was Mischief? Not that I could tell him either way.

I thought about that fateful day, the day all my hopes and dreams for the future were shattered to jagged pieces.

~

I squeezed the vial of water tightly in my hand as I sneaked down the stairs. As long as I drank something, Graeme would be none the wiser that I wouldn't be glamouring my appearance tonight; my hood would ensure that.

The drawing room was dark, and I felt along the wall so as not to bump into anything. *Is Graeme outside already?* "Graeme?" I whispered. "Are you ready to go?"

I squinted against the sudden bright light of a lamp. "And where exactly are you going?" my father asked, crossing his arms as he stood in the middle of the room.

My mother frowned from the couch, pulling her hand back from the lamp.

My eyes widened as my heart raced. "What do you mean? I'm not going anywhere. Graeme is. I thought you were the one sending him on errands these last months."

My father's sea-glass green eyes glinted with displeasure. "Is that so?"

I nodded despite my mouth going dry.

"Is that what you wear to bed these days, then?" my mother pressed, gesturing toward my attire.

I looked down at my simple dress and apron. My hood wasn't pulled up, but she wouldn't have missed its presence either.

I cursed internally, and before I could think of a better lie, Graeme entered the room.

"Hey, are you—?" His question died on his lips as he took in the scene before him.

Our mother shook her head in disappointment.

"Is this how you act when given freedom?" our father growled. "I trusted you with an important task. I thought you were ready to take on some of the responsibilities of being earl."

"I-I am," Graeme argued. "I've done exactly what you've asked of me. You know how many goblins we've gotten out from under Lord Kelpania."

"You've done far more than what I've asked you!"

"How could you?" our mother said softly, her voice emotional. "How could you take Melody to such a place? You know how dangerous it is, for humans especially."

"I used a potion to glamour my appearance," I stepped in to defend my brother. "Anyone who saw me would think I'm a sidhe."

Our mother frowned. "That's hardly the point, Melody, and don't think I don't know you must have pressured your brother into taking you with him."

I lowered my eyes.

"She just wanted to buy potion ingredients. I didn't think there was any harm in that. I only take her to the most reputable shop."

Our mother scowled as if no such place could exist in Goblintown.

"So how is it you manage to get everything I ask of you completed and take your sister shopping in one night?" our father demanded.

There was no getting out of that trap. He'd taken me ingredients shopping before, and he knew I could spend hours in one shop alone.

Graeme averted his gaze.

My mother gasped. "Not only did you bring her with you, but you left her *alone?*" Her voice grew louder with every word, and she was practically in hysterics by the end of the sentence.

We lowered our heads. It was not a time to fight back. We'd both known that if our parents found out, we would be in trouble. If we just listened quietly and answered only when necessary, we could get out unscathed.

"Melody, go upstairs," my father ordered. "We will deal with you momentarily."

I slowly turned around to leave, wanting to hear the rest.

"Graeme, if it wasn't for the fact we have made promises to some people there, you would not be going tonight. Do not think this discussion is over—"

The sound of their conversation cut off as I shut the door behind me. I lost no time, racing up the stairs to my bedroom as fast as I could.

When I burst into the door, Tadhg's glow pulsed in surprise. But I didn't have time to reassure him. I rushed to my writing desk and grabbed a pen and paper.

Dear Aodh,

I can't explain everything right now, but I don't know when I will be able to see you again.

My parents found out I've been sneaking out, and I fear it will be a long time before I'm free of their watchful eyes.

Still, I want to tell you what I promised in case something unexpected happens. The truth is I'm human. My sidhe parents found me abandoned as a baby and took me home to raise as their own.

I was hoping to show you myself, but this will have to

do. With the help of my brother, I glamoured my appearance to look sidhe because he thought it was too dangerous for a human to go to Goblintown.

I hope what you said before was true—that you already knew everything you needed to know about me. I hope this doesn't change your mind.

No, I know it won't. You aren't like that. If it's a very long time until I see you again, just know I took our promise seriously. I will be waiting for you to come make me your goblin queen.

I love you, Aodh.
Lady Melody Píobaire
Your Mischief

I heard the front door close much louder than usual and ran out onto my bedroom balcony.

Graeme trudged toward the carriage house.

"Pssss," I hissed at my brother, who looked up at me. "Graeme, please. I was supposed to meet someone tonight. It's very important. I'm sorry I got you in trouble, but will you give this to him? He'll be at an old watchtower on the southeast side of the city near the edge of Goblinwood."

Graeme frowned.

After folding the paper into quarters, I dropped it. It fluttered to the ground, and Graeme picked it up and put it in his pocket.

"Thank you," I whispered before going back inside.

I closed the balcony door not a moment too soon.

My mother entered first, stern disapproval written all over her face, and my father followed her in. "I want you to be honest with me, Melody. How long have you been going with your brother to Goblintown?"

I clasped my hands in front of me, trying my best to look contrite. "A few months," I answered softly.

My mother closed her eyes and sighed heavily. "Even you couldn't spend all that time looking for potion ingredients in one shop. What were you really doing?"

"Please don't blame Graeme, Mum. I really did just want potion ingredients. But then I made a friend. I was perfectly safe. My friend grew up there, so he kept me out of trouble."

My mother raised an eyebrow. "He...?"

"Yes, an elf boy."

She turned her head to meet my father's eyes. "A goblin boy," she whispered aghast.

My father nodded, his expression severe and resolute. "Tomorrow, you will pack your things. We all will. I've been offered an ambassadorship to Olympus on behalf of the King. I wasn't going to take it. I have much too much going on here with this Kelpania situation. But my daughter's safety and reputation come before that. I will write to the King in the morning and tell him I accept his appointment."

I couldn't have been more shocked than if he'd slapped me across the face. My mouth hung open, and I forgot to breathe for long enough that I started to feel dizzy.

I sucked in air, and tears welled up in my eyes. "Dad, please. We don't need to do all that. Don't be upset. I'll let you meet him. I promise he's a nice boy. You'll like him."

My mother raised her chin. "You lied to us, Melody. You sneaked out of the house to meet someone we don't know— a goblin at that. You could have jeopardized your entire future with the Crown Prince. If this goblin is such a nice boy, then why is my daughter acting out to see him? If he's such a nice boy, why not invite him here as you would anyone else?"

I bit my lip. *Because I would have had to admit I'd gone to*

Goblintown to meet him. Because you won't accept me even being friends with a goblin boy. Because he doesn't know who I really am.

"Don't gnaw on your lip like that," Mum scolded. "It's unladylike."

I stepped forward. "I'll invite him next time. It's not his fault. I didn't even tell him I'm human. He thinks my name is Mischief. He doesn't know my real name."

My father's eyes turned stormy—the way they always did when he performed magic. "And he never will," he pronounced.

My mother stiffened, her head snapping toward my father. "Eirian, what did you do?"

As a human, I couldn't detect whatever my mother had felt, but her alarm was enough to make dread pool in my gut.

"Anyone with the knowledge that Melody is Mischief will be unable to reveal it. This family is bound to secrecy."

I stared at my father. Surely, if he saw how much it hurt me, he wouldn't do it. "Dad, please don't do this."

"Pack your things, Melody," he pronounced before leaving the room.

Tears left hot tracks on my face, and a sob rose in my throat. My chest ached as if someone had cracked each of my ribs to get at my heart.

My mother walked to the door, then looked at me over her shoulder. "You will soon forget this pain. You will forget him and live a happy life with the Crown Prince."

~

My chest tightened in an echo of the agony I'd felt that day.

She'd promised me it wouldn't last long, that my feelings for Aodh would fade with time.

But the time we spent apart only worsened my pain. It may not have been as sharp as it once was, but it was deeper and constant.

I loved my parents, and I had long reconciled their reasons for what they did to me that day. But I didn't think I could ever forgive them for it.

CHAPTER
SIXTEEN

Eithne arrived with my things before supper. She and Odilie bustled into my room. They were followed by one of my trunks, carried by a trow and a gremlin —his green face a few shades too dark with effort and his large eyes bulging as his spindly-fingered hands struggled to keep a good hold.

Before I could relieve them, Eithne took charge, pointing and organizing with a clear vision of what she wanted.

Tadhg bounded in after her in the form of an otter, the form he used most often when he was feeling playful or excited. He chittered happily at me, dodging my hands, too enthusiastic to sit still long enough for me to pet him.

I giggled at his antics, feeling lighthearted for the first time since leaving Maplecrest. With familiar faces around me, I wasn't quite so alone anymore.

As the trow and gremlin went back for more things, Eithne turned to me. "I will have this place tidy in no time, my lady. Don't you worry."

"Don't overwork yourself, Eithne. We have time enough to unpack, I think," I cautioned.

Eithne frowned. "You know how uncomfortable I am with uncompleted work, my lady."

I snorted. "I'll just leave it in your hands, then."

She nodded in satisfaction, and I could practically hear her say, "As it should be." Then she went about her task of unpacking.

As Odilie moved to help her, I called to her.

"Yes, Your Majesty?" she said, her amethyst eyes alight at all the activity.

"Odilie, it is getting rather late. At what time does the Goblin King sup?"

Odilie lowered her gaze—even her ears seemed to droop.

My chest tightened at her expression.

"Oh…the King asked that we bring him supper in his study this evening. He seems quite busy as he has been there all day. I asked my superiors if he was aware you had arrived, but…"

Of course, he's aware.

She brightened her tone, but it seemed to take her effort to do so. "Perhaps he will visit you this evening, Ma'am. Surely, he must leave his study at some point. I'll keep an ear out to give you proper warning, shall I?"

I tried to smile at her, but the motion felt wrong as it tugged on my cheeks. "I'm sure you're right, Odilie. If I don't see him tonight, perhaps tomorrow at breakfast."

She nodded encouragingly. "If you're hungry, I'll bring you supper. The kitchen made roast chicken and vegetables tonight."

My stomach rolled with turmoil. I was hungry. I wasn't used to eating that late. But I wasn't sure I could keep it down. "Yes, thank you. That sounds delicious."

Set with purpose, Odilie skittered from the room.

Frowning, I moved over to the window. The sun had sunk and approached the trees beyond the garden. I'd waited all afternoon for Aodh to call for me. I could have been acquainting myself with the house, the grounds, and the staff. But instead, I waited. Then again, I was used to waiting for him. How could it hurt to wait just a little while longer? At least he was within reach now.

That was what I told myself as I tempered the urgency in my belly with the patience I'd long since cultivated. But after I choked down my supper, when the tray had been taken away and the sun had long set, I couldn't seem to soothe that feeling any longer.

He's doing this on purpose. He thinks he can ignore me— simply brush me aside? He didn't come for me himself at Maplecrest, he didn't greet me upon my arrival, and he didn't even have supper with me. Well, I'll show him something he can't ignore.

I stood from the table and scanned the room for one of the trunks I'd packed my potions away in. It didn't take me long to find the trunk I wanted. Carefully, I read the vial labels, grinning as I found the one I was after.

Among all of the things I owned, it was the most precious. Not because it was the rarest or most valuable, which it was, but for the reason I'd acquired it.

I held the vial up to the light, the rosy-red liquid shimmering in the most pleasing of ways. I closed my hand around it and shut the lid of my trunk.

Walking with purpose, I crossed my bedroom and popped my head into my dressing room, where Eithne was still organizing.

"Have you unpacked my nightgowns yet, Eithne?"

She looked over at me. "Not all of them, my lady. But I did set one out on the bed for you already."

I knew without looking she'd not set out the one I wanted. "Where are the rest?"

After Eithne gestured toward a trunk in the corner, I went to rummage through it. "I want you to do something for me, Eithne." I didn't look up from my search.

"Yes, my lady?"

"Please find Odilie and bring her here."

"Yes, my lady."

I smirked as my hands closed around the garment I was after. Gently, I pulled it from its fellows.

I could still recall what Chrysanthe had said to me when we'd found it in that Olympus market. I was hesitant to purchase it, but she'd convinced me. *It's perfect. Which of the two of us was an attendant to Aphrodite? I know what I'm talking about. No man could resist such a thing.*

In shape, it was similar to my other nightgowns—long with belled sleeves at the elbow. But the fabric was a delicate white silk, luxurious on the skin with a cloudy transparency when held up to the right lighting. The neckline dropped in a still-modest V, and there was scalloped lace on all the hems.

I quickly changed into it and stood before the mirror in my dressing room. The white of the gown was enhanced by the dark waves of my hair, tumbling over my chest and shoulders. I was glad my mother had insisted I wash it the night before because it shined in the lamplight. My turquoise eyes, which usually leaned on the blue side, seemed greener somehow though still nothing close to the sea-glass green of a sidhe.

I wondered where Eithne had put my kohl; it would set off my eyes that much more. But when I heard someone enter my bedroom, I pushed away that desire and slipped a robe over my nightgown.

Returning to my bedroom, I was met by Eithne and Odilie.

"You asked for me, Your Majesty?" Odilie said.

"Yes," I answered. "I want you to show me to the Goblin King's bedchamber."

CHAPTER
SEVENTEEN

Eithne's mouth fell open at my request of Odilie. "My lady…" she gasped.

I ignored her, focusing on the imp, who frowned. "I don't know when the Goblin King will return to his chamber, Ma'am. You may be waiting quite a long time."

Eithne stood up straighter, her piskie cheeks flushing. "It is not proper—"

"For me to go to my future husband's bedroom?" I cut her off. It wasn't like I didn't know that. But Aodh had yet to call for me, and I needed to take the initiative if I wanted to get the desired result.

Eithne pressed her lips together, silencing her protests. She had leave to speak, but that didn't mean I had to follow her advice.

"I will wait," I told Odilie. *I've waited over ten years already; a few hours can't be worse than that.*

Odilie dipped her head. "Very well, Ma'am." With a lamp in hand, she turned on her heels and started down the hall. I left Eithne to unpack and worry over what I was about to do.

Odilie led me past the guest bedroom and the stairs we'd taken that afternoon.

I clicked my tongue when we entered an anteroom and saw another set of stairs—this one elaborately carved. *He took me up the service stairs.*

Through the anteroom, we came to a long gallery. It had a high ceiling with dark wooden walls on one side and windows on the other. Our steps echoed off the undecorated surfaces. Halfway down, a short hallway branched off.

"What's down there?" I asked quietly, worried my voice would carry in such a large space.

She glanced over at where I'd indicated. "Oh, the dining room is on the left."

"And on the right?"

"There's nothing on the right, just the upper part of the grand hall."

I nodded.

When we reached the other end of the gallery, I didn't need to ask Odilie what rooms were around us. She seemed to understand I wanted to know.

She gestured ahead of us when we entered an anteroom. "That's the king's reception room, where he meets with important guests. There's also a guest bedroom attached."

Turning right, we entered a hallway with another set of service stairs on the left and a door on the right.

"This is another guest bedroom," Odilie said.

I pursed my lips. *For those guests the goblin king wants to keep close, I suppose.*

Just like in the queen's wing, the hallway ended in three doors.

"The King's bedchamber is just ahead, Ma'am. Shall I

leave the lamp for you? I don't know if they've lit the king's chambers yet."

Taking the lamp she offered, I thanked her. With a wish I have a goodnight, Odilie said her goodbyes and headed for the service stairs.

I stood in the hallway, listening to the sounds of her footsteps retreat as I faced Aodh's bedroom door.

How I found myself in that situation, I almost couldn't fathom. I knew what I needed to do, but no matter how much Chrysanthe—a nymph well-versed in the art of seduction—had walked me through it, I still wasn't sure I had the nerve.

Swallowing hard, I lifted my hand and knocked on the door before me; the sound seemed to echo throughout the entire house.

As expected, there was no answer.

I can do this. I've wanted this for so long. I'll just have to take the lead.

I felt a mixture of relief and disappointment when I found the door unlocked. With a deep breath, I slipped into Aodh's bedroom.

The space was dark, the only light coming from my lamp and the dim specks of stars out the far window.

What I could see of the room was a skeleton of my own. There was the same four-poster bed, the same settee, the same table and chairs—though they were all upholstered in red rather than yellow. The walls were painted cream with none of the decorations mine had. There was also no rug.

I frowned. *There's no way this is how it looked during the previous goblin king's reign. This whole place is void of decoration and splendor. Given how much he seemed to like the finer things, I have a hard time believing he lived in a place like this.*

Without thinking, I went about lighting the space, removing the chimney of my lamp to share the flame with other lamps and candles.

When all was done, I was pleased with the result. The room seemed much cozier than before.

But my smile faded as I stood awkwardly at the center of the space. *How should I greet him?* My eyes shifted to the bed, and I could feel my face heat. *That's too bold even for me.*

Settling into a chair at the table near the window, I sat up straighter to present the most flattering lines.

I placed the rosy-red vial on the table and looked down at myself, biting my lip. I'd specifically worn my special nightgown, but now that I was there, I felt shy about it.

Clicking my tongue, I stood, removed my robe, and laid it on the settee at the foot of the bed before returning to my chair.

And then I waited.

The minutes ticked by as I looked around the space.

Aodh sleeps here. He's slept in that bed for over five years now.

Warmth spread through me as I pictured him there, his limbs stretched out under the sheets. *I wonder what kind of nightclothes he wears.*

My heart thumped when I wondered if he wore nightclothes at all. I averted my eyes from the bed.

There weren't many things in the room that could tell me anything about who he was now. I thought about looking in his dressing room. Surely, there would be clothes, a comb, something personal that belonged to him.

I mean, I'm here already. I might as well take a peek.

But just when I stood from my chair, I heard the doorknob rattle as it began to turn.

EIGHTEEN

Aodh's eyebrows scrunched, and he tilted his head as his gaze landed on the robe I'd laid on the settee. But then his dark eyes found me.

My heart drummed out an uneven rhythm as I stared at him in the intimate glow of the candles and lamps.

His hair appeared more red than usual, set off by the decor and the flame-light. His eyes seemed to swallow the light, and I couldn't quite make out the secrets they hid.

I struggled to speak. *Why did I think this was a good idea?*

But as his gaze traveled down my body, his face flushed. I recalled the blush he wore in the past each time I'd kissed him, and that gave me courage.

"G-good evening, Your Majesty."

He stepped fully into the room without a word.

"I know you were quite busy today, so I thought I would come to see you myself. I've brought you a gift, my wedding present to you." I gestured toward the vial I'd brought from my room, which still sat on the table. "It's nectar from

Olympus, enough to cure any ailment or illness. I hope we can live long and healthy lives together."

With every word I spoke, his blush deepened, and the response encouraged me. *He's just as nervous as I am. I needn't have been so self-conscious. It's Aodh after all.*

But when he snatched up my robe and held it out to me, I looked more closely at his expression. His flushed skin wasn't from arousal or embarrassment. He was angry.

"Put this on, and get out," he said, his voice soft with barely restrained rage.

My stomach quivered, but I stood my ground. "I apologize if I've overstepped my bounds. But surely, you'd like for us to get to know each other better before we are wed."

His eyes snapped to mine, and I flinched at his glare. "Tell me, *Lady* Melody. Are all humans as indecent as you are? Or am I just unlucky?"

Even if my mouth hadn't gone too dry to respond, he didn't give me the chance.

"Did you truly believe I would be pleased to have you appear before me in such a state uninvited? I am not looking for a broodmare. Have you no pride? No modesty? Do you believe this is how the goblin queen should conduct herself? I'm embarrassed for you and ashamed you are the person I find myself stuck with."

Every unfeeling word was a stake in my heart. I trembled in shame and self-pity under his ruthless stare. I could feel tears welling up inside me.

"Get out of my sight, and do not appear before me again until I send for you." He threw my robe toward me, and it fluttered to the floor a few feet away.

My knees wobbled as I moved to pick it up, and my hands shook so much I had trouble putting it on.

The only blessing I found in the exchange was that I managed to get out of the room before I burst into tears.

I ran down the hall, blindly following the path I'd taken earlier with conviction and hope.

It seemed that once the Goblin King had retired for the night, the lamps in his wing were extinguished. I was not yet familiar with the layout of the house. And though I made it down the hall unscathed, I ran into a table in the middle of the anteroom that led into the gallery.

The clatter of the table toppling over was followed by a crash of something breaking. Pain shot through me as I landed on the broken shards of whatever had adorned the table. I hissed and tried to examine my palms through the dark and my tears.

I didn't know how long I sat sobbing at the pain in my hands and heart. Through my tears, I eventually saw a glowing blue orb floating toward me. My mind didn't register the light at first, but as it morphed into a dog and licked my face, I realized Tadhg had found me.

For a moment, I cried even harder, fully releasing what I'd managed to hold back now in the presence of someone who cared for me. But when Tadhg whined in sympathy, I tried to calm myself.

It wouldn't do to show up in front of Eithne hysterical. I already looked a mess and was injured. That would be hard enough to explain with a clear head.

I nuzzled Tadhg as best I could without touching him with my bloodied hands before rising to my feet.

The walk along the gallery was long, but at least I could see by the light of Tadhg's glow.

Was Aodh always so unfeeling? Even if he didn't want me there, he didn't have to be so cruel.

Looking down at myself, my robe and nightgown

smeared with blood from my cut hands, my mind went to a different place.

Maybe I misjudged him. I thought he wouldn't mind the fact that I'm human. Or maybe I'm just not to his taste. I'm sure I was much prettier as a sidhe.

I'd thought under the circumstances I'd done remarkably well following Chrysanthe's instructions. But perhaps seduction was too advanced a technique for someone as inexperienced as me. She'd told me it wasn't that difficult—that once he felt it, he would likely take over from there.

Well, he obviously wasn't feeling it.

I hated how he had made me feel. I felt dirty and not just because my clothes had been soiled with blood. He'd rejected me so thoroughly that I questioned whether I'd ever had any right to consider myself attractive.

Have I made a mistake in coming here? Maybe I should just become Lorccán's mistress. He's never made me feel this way.

CHAPTER

NINETEEN

Eithne was irate at the state in which I returned to my room. She cried out in shock and asked what he'd done to me before pressing her lips into an angry line. She didn't speak again through the rest of our exchange.

I didn't tell her the whole story. I only said the King had not wished to be disturbed, and in my foolishness, I'd forgotten my lamp and fallen on my way back.

From the furious glint in her squinting eyes, I knew she didn't believe my story even though it was true on its surface.

Still, she carefully removed the few shards of glass stuck into my palms, cleaned the wounds, smeared on some healing salve—which I'd made myself—and wrapped my hands in bandages.

She helped me change into a fresh nightgown and climb into bed before taking my bloodied clothes with her as she withdrew to her quarters.

The salve numbed my wounds, so I couldn't lie to myself and say they were why I cried myself to sleep. At least a glowing blue dog was the only witness.

My eyes were red and swollen the next morning when Eithne arrived with my breakfast. She quickly brought me a cool rag, but I didn't much care how I looked at the moment. All I could think about was Aodh's wrathful expression and cruel words. Perhaps I wasn't as strong as I gave myself credit for. I knew he wouldn't be pleased, but his heartlessness made me question whether what I'd set out to do was even worth it.

He's changed so much. Two cycles is a long time. Maybe this new Aodh isn't someone I want to be with.

Despite Eithne's urging, I didn't even change out of my nightgown. I just sat at my little table, thinking about what I should do as I stared out the window at the garden.

At some point mid-morning, a gentle knock sounded on my door. Eithne opened it, and Odilie scurried in, a tray in hand.

I tilted my head at the cup on her tray. *Apple juice?*

Odilie dipped in a quick curtsy and crossed the room to place the beverage on the table.

"Good morning, Your Majesty," she greeted. Her tone was gentle as if she were talking to an invalid. "How are you feeling?"

I glanced at Eithne, who shrugged her shoulders to tell me she hadn't said a word.

"I'm fine, Odilie. Thank you."

"I've brought you something special this morning. It's what we drink at home to lift our spirits and promote healing."

She could indeed have noticed the bandages on my hands once she'd entered, but if Eithne hadn't mentioned it, how would she have known to bring me a healing draft?

"Thank you, Odilie. May I ask how you knew I would need such a thing?"

Odilie smiled, her amethyst eyes sparkling. "His Majesty, of course. This morning, he sent for me especially and asked me to deliver you some. I often serve it to His Majesty as well. The staff was a-flutter this morning about what might have happened last night. We found a table knocked over, a vase shattered to pieces, and traces of blood. We cleaned it up but had no idea who had been injured. But then His Majesty sent for me, and I knew it must have been you. I'm glad to see you're feeling all right."

Aodh asked her to send me a healing tonic? My mind spun at this new information. While it wasn't incongruous with the Aodh I'd once known, it certainly wasn't behavior I would have expected from the man I'd encountered the night before.

Movement from the corner of my eye caught my attention, and I turned to look out the window as Aodh and Selwyn appeared on the garden path.

In the full light of day, Aodh looked as though he'd been born to be king. His ruddy blond hair shimmered in the sunlight. And though his clothes—a simple tunic, belt, and trousers—were not nearly as ostentatious as the previous goblin king's, he wore them as if they were the most luxurious.

He stood up straight as he walked—his confidence bespoke with every stride—listening carefully to what Selwyn was saying to him.

Selwyn, for his part, appeared almost a different being from whom I'd come to expect. His expression was smooth and easy, and I couldn't help but notice how much different he looked when he smiled.

Selwyn reached out and rested a hand on Aodh's shoulder, and they both halted. I stiffened at the reminder of what Selwyn's touch had done to me. His kelpie influence wouldn't work on Aodh because he wasn't human, but it would continue to present a danger to me unless I did something about it.

Turning back to Odilie and Eithne, I said, "I need to go into town."

Odilie blinked at my abrupt change in conversation, but Eithne shook her head, crossing her arms.

"It's too dangerous," Eithne opposed. "You've never gone alone before, and—" She glanced over at Odilie.

And I've never gone as a human. Not to mention, I could be in more danger as the goblin queen. That remains to be seen.

"Then you can come with me," I told her.

Eithne paled at my suggestion. "W-wander around Goblintown?"

Did she not think we would ever have to deal with actual goblins moving here?

"Surely, Odilie would be a better companion on such an outing. She would be more familiar with the area," Eithne argued.

Odilie shrugged. "I don't mind going with Her Majesty into town, but I still have my own work to do."

Eithne waved away her concerns. "Oh, don't worry about that. We can swap. I'm no stranger to cooking, cleaning, building fires, or whatever else you do."

Odilie eyed her as if trying to determine whether there was some insult in her words. If there were, she decided to let it go. "Very well, I'll make you a list of everything I need to do today and whom you should talk to."

Eithne smiled in relief. "Wonderful. I'll assist Lady Melody in getting ready while you prepare it."

Carefully balancing the cup Odilie had brought me between my two bandaged hands, I took a drink. Then I coughed as the sweet tang of mead danced over my tongue. My face started to feel hot as it always did with even the slightest taste of alcohol. *I didn't expect that.*

CHAPTER

TWENTY

I wasn't sure how much I wanted to disguise myself before going out into Goblintown. I didn't want to advertise I was the new goblin queen. But if someone happened to figure it out, I needed to be prepared to act as such. I wouldn't be removing my ring after all. I'd take no chance in Aodh reclaiming it.

Eithne and Odilie had a long discussion about what was most suitable for me to wear on the outing, and they presented me with two choices: a blue wool tunic with an undyed apron or a dress of green velvet.

I raised my eyebrows at Odilie's choice. Velvet wouldn't be much of a disguise at all. But then again, Eithne's was too plain.

I quirked my mouth, staring at the two outfits. "Get me the red linen dress I wore to the market last time," I told Eithne. *It's a good middle ground.*

Even so, I pulled an umber cloak over it before saying goodbye to Eithne.

Once in the hall, I hesitated about which way to go. I

could have Odilie lead me out a servants' entrance, or I could boldly walk out the front door.

Straightening my spine, I chose the latter. It was my house now, too. I didn't have to sneak around.

I took the main staircase down to the first floor, rather than the service stairs Selwyn had shown me. My boots made little sound on the floors as I passed through the anteroom and out into the cloisters.

I glanced over at the garden, but Aodh and Selwyn were no longer there. *No matter. I'm not yet ready to face Aodh again. I need to reconsider my approach.*

Heading back inside, I walked through the entrance hall and out the front door, Odilie a few steps behind.

Once on the front lawn, she asked me where I wanted to go.

"I know where I'm headed," I told her, pulling my hood up. *Something like this can only be found on Redcap Row.*

It had taken me a while to return to the hidden street after the fright of my initial visit. But when I went again, Aodh had gone with me. By then, I was much more comfortable in Goblintown in general, and he had imparted some of his canniness to me. Besides, I was never afraid when he was by my side.

It was much too long a walk from the palace to Redcap Row, but we started in that direction.

A few blocks away, I saw just what I was looking for. I approached a leprechaun, whose ox-driven cart was being unloaded into a bakery.

"Excuse me," I said to him as he held his ox in place.

He tilted his head back to look up at me from under his wide-brimmed hat. He didn't say a word, nor did his expression welcome me to speak.

I smiled regardless of my reception. "When you're

finished making this delivery, might I hire you to take us to the other side of town?"

His red nose twitched in his grey face, and I showed him the coin I would use to pay him. He flicked his eyes toward Odilie, then bobbed his head without a word.

After all the flour had been unloaded from his cart, and the leprechaun had been paid for his delivery, he motioned for us to hop on. We climbed into the bed of the cart, our legs dangling off the back.

"Please take us east," I requested.

And with a click of his tongue, we began rambling down the uneven street.

Though I was never very good at riding backward, and the uneven road didn't help, the steady ambling pace of the ox made the journey bearable.

I glanced over at Odilie as she clung to the side of the cart—her lighter weight making her shift and bounce as we went.

"Do you mind if I ask you something, Odilie?"

"Of course not, Your—" She cut off her respectful address, glancing over her shoulder at the leprechaun.

"How did you end up in Goblintown? How did you end up in Tír for that matter?"

She nodded with a sad smile. "I suppose I am a curiosity in these parts, not many imps out this way."

"You don't have to answer if you don't want to."

She shook her head. "Oh, I don't mind. It's only thoughts of my community make me homesick sometimes." She sighed heavily, then glanced over at me. "Would you believe I did it for a man?"

I blinked at her. Given how I'd spent the last ten years of my life, I couldn't judge her.

Her sad smile returned. "It's true. Just as in Tír, our

communities are pretty isolated. Imps tend to stick with imps, dwarves with dwarves, and so on. But we have much more trade in between. My family did a lot of business with the elves. And he happened to be in Elfheim visiting the same time I was there—the elves of Tír are distant relatives of those of Elfheim, you know."

I didn't know that, but I didn't interrupt her to say so.

"He was a charming fellow; I found his accent most attractive. And somewhere along the way, he convinced me to come back to Tír with him. Of course, what I didn't know was he was involved in some shady business, and it wasn't long before the elves here had him arrested. His infraction was pretty minor, but he was sentenced to time in prison. And what was I to do—an imp living in Elfton? So, while he was serving his time, I came to Goblintown."

"Couldn't you have gone home?" I asked.

She shrugged. "Sure, but I was a stupid girl in love. I was prepared to wait for him. So much the pity. Once he got out and came to Goblintown, he didn't want anything to do with me anymore—blamed me for him getting caught, you see, not that I knew anything about the whole business."

I clenched my teeth. *What a prick.* "But why did you stay after that?"

She smiled cheerfully at me. "Well, I'd already made a life for myself by then. I had good friends, and I felt like I was making a difference for the goblins. I was working for the Goblin King. He has a way of making you feel seen, our King—even me, a lowly kitchen maid at the time. He knew I was going through heartbreak and took special care to ask after me."

My heart warmed while my chest ached. I turned my attention toward the road, glancing around to see what I could recognize.

As I'd noticed before, the streets seemed much cleaner, and the buildings had been renovated. Still, it wasn't difficult to recognize the old landmarks.

I tilted my head when my gaze landed on someone who happened to be going in the same direction as us. He had the flowing green hair and sand-colored skin of most water elementals, but something about him seemed familiar.

I lifted my chin in his direction. "I think that undine over there is following us."

O dilie followed my gaze to the undine I indicated. "Oh, him? That's just Charlie."

"You know him?"

She nodded. "Of course, he works at the palace. He's one of the unofficial guards."

"Unofficial guards?"

Odilie shrugged. "We don't have official guards anymore. The Goblin King said he didn't need protection from his own people. He thought the guards were a barrier between him and the goblins. But he also didn't want to dismiss those who already worked there, and the guards were very upset about him being unprotected. So he gave them other duties but allows at least one to accompany him when he leaves the palace."

I made a sound of understanding. *Then what's he doing following us? Did he take it upon himself to guard the Goblin Queen?*

I thought about calling out to him, telling him he didn't

have to follow so far behind. But then I thought better of it. I'd likely only draw more attention to myself if he joined us.

Glancing around again, I called out to the leprechaun to stop the cart. We were a few blocks from the entrance to Redcap Row.

I thanked him again and paid him what I'd promised. He was silent to the very end, only lifting his hand to the brim of his hat in farewell.

I looked over my shoulder at Charlie, who still followed at a distance, while we started walking. *Is he here to protect us or spy on me?*

I frowned at the thought. It didn't much matter. While the idea made me uncomfortable, I didn't have anything to hide.

The area was not much different than I remembered it. Perhaps it had been fixed up a little, but the changes in scenery could have just as easily been the cheeriness of daylight compared to how I was used to seeing it.

I did, however, mark an increase in goblin activity in the area. Previously, the neighborhood around Redcap Row had been fairly quiet, other than the tavern, until I stepped into the shadowy alley. But now it seemed just like any other part of Goblintown.

Ahead of us, a piskie swept the front stoop of what appeared to be a tenant house. Farther down, a gnome was restocking flowers on his shop cart. At that moment, Goblintown was as peaceful as any other city in Tír.

I found the tavern with the clurichaun painted on the sign with ease as if I'd only been there a few days before. I didn't hesitate to walk right into Redcap Row.

But with every step, I slowed. By the time I was a good ten feet into the alley, I came to a stop.

There was nothing there. There were no tables, no tents, even the permanent pet shop was missing as though it had never been there. I blinked in confusion. *Is it because it's still daytime? Does the market only operate at night?*

"It's not here anymore, Ma'am," Odilie explained without me having the chance to ask. "One of the Goblin King's first acts was to shut it all down."

My mouth dropped open.

Odilie nodded. "He ordered that anyone who trafficked in people or acted as a contract killer would be tried and put in prison, same as everywhere else in Tír."

"What about the other merchants? There was a human realm pet shop and potion ingredient shops and all manner of other things that aren't legal in Tír. Did he shut those down as well?"

"Oh, no. He said he didn't much care for the sidhe king's laws. The only thing he cared about with those businesses was that they could prove their wares had been ethically sourced. If they could do that, he had no problem. He even allowed them to set up shop in abandoned storefronts."

My heart warmed, and I couldn't help but smile.

But as proud as I was of what he'd accomplished, I couldn't deny the pain I felt at being left behind. He hadn't known who I really was or where to find me, but I should have been with him. I should have been by his side, helping him help them.

And as I stood in the alley where we'd first met, I felt a resurgence of purpose flow through me. I'd win him over if it was the last thing I did, but what was even more important was helping those we ruled.

Aodh had wanted to be goblin king to help the goblins, and I'd just wanted to be with him. And that was still the case. But Odilie had said he was overworked and needed a helpmate.

This position was more than just a marriage. It was service to Goblintown and the goblins who inhabited it.

I'd failed to seduce him. And though I would continue to try to rekindle his love for me, there was still something I could do. I could help the goblins to the very best of my abilities.

I looked down at Odilie. "Do you know where I could get seaweed from a kelpie's bed?"

She frowned in thought, then shook her head. "I don't know much about potions, I'm afraid. Perhaps we could ask Charlie."

I turned back toward the way we'd come, but Charlie was nowhere in sight. "Excuse me, Charlie?" I called to the empty alley.

The undine appeared out of nowhere as if he'd been the very moisture in the air. *Maybe he's part sylph.*

"Yes, Your Majesty," he said with a bow.

Now that he was closer, I saw he was quite tall with ocean-blue eyes and a smile that would capture any mortal's heart.

"Do you know where I could get seaweed from a kelpie's bed?" I asked.

He tilted his head at my request but then nodded. "Yes, Ma'am. Please, follow me."

As we trailed after him, his green hair rippling behind him, I wondered whether it was a good idea for Charlie to have been the guard to follow me.

Undines had the dangerous habit of falling in love with humans. If the objects of their desires didn't return that feeling, or if their human lovers were unfaithful, they would die. It was an all-or-nothing kind of love, and undines who were smart stayed away from humans altogether.

Aodh wouldn't have put one of his guards in unnecessary danger, would he?

"Here we are, Ma'am," Charlie said, gesturing toward a small, windowless shop called Seabottom Treasures.

CHAPTER
TWENTY-TWO

A bell chimed as I opened the door, but it was low and distant like the bell on a ship rather than the light tinkle of a shop bell.

Seabottom Treasures was rather small and dim for my human eyes. Candles back-lit large, transparent bowls lining the shelves; their flickering flames, eerie and distorted by water, provided the only light. At the center, a long table covered in bowls of various dried sea creatures—everything from shells and starfish to sand dollars and fish bones—spanned the space.

An undine looked up from the book she was reading from where she sat behind a counter at the far end of the shop. "It's been a while," she said with a smirk, her eyes on Charlie.

Charlie approached her with an air of familiarity. "How are you, Kathleen?"

I left them to their conversation, and Odilie stayed with me. Staring into each of the clear bowls I passed, I tried to discern their contents because they weren't clearly labeled.

"I've been better," Kathleen answered. "But what about you? Glad to see your king allows you out to get some fresh air once in a while. Auntie has been complaining she hasn't heard from you."

My ears pricked at the curious way she mentioned Aodh, and I peeked sidelong at them from under my hood.

"He's your king too, cousin," Charlie said seriously.

Kathleen shrugged. "Is he? He's not exactly living up to his promises. Might be time for a new king, one who can keep his word."

Odilie's eyes widened, and I could tell by her lavender face turning plum that she would give this undine a piece of her mind. I reached out and rested my hand on her shoulder, shaking my head slightly when she looked at me.

Charlie, for his part, stiffened at his cousin's words. "Show some gratitude," he censured. "You're only in this shop because he gave you a safe place to sell your wares. Would you rather have your sad little cart in Redcap Row?"

Kathleen seemed completely unperturbed by Charlie's scolding. "Sure, I'm grateful for my shop space. But, on the other hand, I was doing much better at my 'sad little cart.'"

I stepped forward slightly and kept my tone curious and neutral. "May I ask—why do you blame the Goblin King for that?"

Kathleen's ocean-green eyes shifted to me. She clearly had no qualms stating her opinions even to a stranger. "Now that he's outlawed the goblins' more nefarious trades, we get fewer visitors from outside Goblintown. And goblins had less money to spend than outsiders as it was. He said he was going to increase trade with the other communities, but that hasn't happened. He said he was going to fix up the city, improve our schools, recruit better healers. He hasn't done any of those things."

"He is fixing the city up. He's hired out-of-work goblins to renovate buildings," Charlie countered. "Don't tell me you haven't noticed that."

Kathleen nodded. "Sure, but the roads are still shit. I can hardly get supplies delivered without half my stock spilling on its way here. And that's not even mentioning how he said he would lower our taxes. He's been the king for over five years already, and my taxes have stayed the same. I bet he's just like King Conrí, charging us above what the sidhe king requires to lavish himself in gold and jewels."

"That's not true!" Odilie snapped. "King Aodh is completely different from King Conrí. He's not keeping anything for himself. He's even sold off paintings and tapestries from his palace walls to pay for public works."

Kathleen tilted her head, then turned to Charlie. "Who have you brought with you today, cousin? I appreciate the business, but I won't be yelled at in my own shop."

Squaring my shoulders, I removed my hood.

Kathleen's eyes widened. All the calmness she'd displayed while talking politics disappeared. "What's this? A human? Don't tell me you've risked taking a human lover, Charlie. Auntie will lose her mind. What if she's unfaithful? Is she really worth dying for?"

Charlie scowled at his cousin's assumption. "This is the future goblin queen."

Kathleen's ocean-green gaze slid back to me, analyzing me more carefully now. "A human, huh? I suppose he's even more base than I thought. Looking to start himself a dynasty, is he?"

I didn't flinch at her comment. She wasn't saying anything I hadn't heard before. It wasn't a secret male fae wanted human lovers for our ability to give them children. And many female fae weren't happy about that.

"I can assure you I've earned my place as goblin queen. I was not chosen by King Aodh. But more importantly, I have heard your concerns today. I know His Majesty is always open to hearing the worries of his people. And I will bring these issues up to him myself. You are free to voice your opinions, of course. But perhaps, in the future, might you bring them to us directly rather than sow unwarranted discord within the community?"

Kathleen stared at me for a long time, and I wondered if I hadn't just made things worse. Finally, she grinned. "Outsmarted the Goblin King, did you, human? I look forward to seeing this play out."

"You should address her properly," Odilie muttered.

Kathleen tilted her head playfully. "The day she proves herself worthy of her title, I will gladly curtsy and call her 'Your Majesty.' But until then, what can I get for you, miss? Is there anything in particular you're looking for?"

Fair enough. "Do you carry seaweed from a kelpie's bed?"

She nodded, all business as if I'd only just walked in. "Of course, both fresh and aged. Which do you prefer?"

I'm not looking to harm him, only keep him at bay. "Fresh please."

Kathleen walked over to a bowl near the front of the store. "How much would you like?"

I frowned. *How long will the salve last if I use it every day? I should get enough for a big batch, unless...* "You don't happen to have any kappa head-water, do you?"

She watched me, clearly wondering what I might be using those two things together for. It wasn't exactly a common recipe, and I was certainly improvising with ingredients. But, if in nothing else, I was confident in my potion-making.

"That's a rare ingredient, indeed—expensive too. I do have some though not very much."

"All right. Then just a leaf of the seaweed and a half dram of kappa head-water."

Kathleen nodded her acknowledgment and stuck her hands into the kelpie bed bowl to retrieve my seaweed. She placed the seaweed in a jar with water from the bowl to preserve freshness, then returned to the counter, where she pulled out a small bottle of kappa head-water.

Raising her palm near the mouth of the bottle, she deftly waved her hand, magically flowing some kappa head-water from the bottle into a half-dram vial before corking it.

She wasn't kidding about the price though I'd been prepared already. Kappa head-water had to travel a long way to get to Tír.

As the distant ship's bell clanged when I opened the door to leave, Kathleen called to her cousin to visit his mother or else.

TWENTY-THREE

With Charlie's added presence, it took us longer to find a ride back to the palace. We were eventually let off a few blocks away.

Odilie grumbled to herself about me missing lunch, and I was quite hungry. But I'd had enough adventures in my life and skipped more than a few meals.

I glanced over at the straight-faced undine as we walked. I knew it wasn't the best idea, but I couldn't stop myself from asking. "Why did you follow us today, Charlie?"

Worry crept into his ocean-blue eyes. "Please don't tell anyone you caught me following you, Your Majesty. I was ordered to not let you find out."

My mouth went dry, and I tried hard to swallow. *He was sent to spy on me, then.* "W-who ordered you to follow me?"

He hesitated, and dread crept into me. *If Selwyn ordered him to spy on me, then Charlie will tell him what I bought today.*

"I won't know who to hide it from if you don't tell me," I urged.

Charlie nodded slightly. "The King. He said it still wasn't quite safe in Goblintown for a human, so he asked me to follow you without being seen—just to make sure nothing happened."

I stopped walking, his words so shocking that my brain couldn't even execute that simple motion. My heart raced as I forgot how to breathe. *Aodh sent him to protect me? Why? From his reception, I would've thought he'd be glad to be rid of me, however it happened.*

I bit my lip. *It would be a political problem if something happened to me while I was here, I suppose. I'm the adopted daughter of an influential sidhe house. And since I haven't broken the news to Lorccán yet, I'm still technically the King's promised mistress—not that Aodh would know that... Aodh may want me to leave of my own accord, but that's not the same as me being hurt or killed under his watch.*

My lungs started to burn from lack of oxygen, and I sucked in a breath. *Could it be Aodh's soft heart is still hiding under the cold mask he's showing me? I know he cares about the goblins at least. Does this mean a small part of him cares for even me?*

"Your Majesty," Charlie said low. "I'll just trail behind from here so as not to get caught."

I blinked and nodded to Charlie, giving him leave to do as he willed. He let us move farther on without him.

My steps sped up as my mind whirled.

Regardless of Aodh's motivations, the only thing I was sure of was that Aodh was still a kind man. I only needed to figure out how to get him to show me some of the kindness he so freely gave to others.

As soon as we stepped inside, Odilie scurried away to parts unknown. I glanced around. At that time of day, I could hear the sounds of a busy kitchen staff. Though I didn't know where the kitchens were, they had to be nearby for my human ears to hear them at work.

I started toward my rooms, wondering how many goblins worked at the palace and how they managed to stay so unobtrusive. I'd hardly met any of them so far, but then, I'd been in my room much of the time.

Eithne was not in my room when I arrived, likely executing Odilie's duties as promised.

I pursed my lips and stared at the trunks Eithne knew not to unpack. *I need a workroom, and where I sleep is not a good choice.* Some of the ingredients I dealt with could linger and didn't make for pleasant smells when sleeping.

Laying my cloak on the settee, I crossed my arms before nodding to myself.

I opened the door that led to my sitting room and went back to move all my trunks. It wasn't the ideal place—too many windows—but it would do for now.

After dragging all my workroom things into the space, I rearranged the furniture to better suit my needs. My palms were sore and itchy beneath my bandages from the effort, and I took off the bandages to make sure I hadn't broken open any of my cuts.

I left them off for dexterity, closed the drapes, then lit the lamps. There was only one table high enough to safely work on though I preferred a table I could stand at.

Before beginning, I flipped through a book of potions recipes just to make sure I remembered correctly. Then I started pulling things from my trunks. I grabbed a flat dish, a few glass tubes, a glass container with a lid, a bottle of sun oil, and vials of petitgrain and black pepper oils.

The traditional solution to neutralize a kelpie's influence called for a salve that one would have to keep applying to the skin when it wore off. A kelpie's power was exercised through skin contact.

The recipe called for seaweed a kelpie had slept in, sun oil charged at both equinoxes and solstices for a whole year, beeswax, and equal amounts of petitgrain and black pepper essential oils.

But I wasn't going to follow that exactly.

I moved all my equipment and ingredients to the small round table and sat before it. I would have to work quickly if the experimental method had any hope of being effective, so I removed all the corks from the oil bottles and placed the glass tubes in them.

Carefully, I pulled the seaweed leaf from the jar Kathleen had put it in—the salt water stinging my wounds—and placed it on the shallow dish. If it dried out even a little, it would be useless, which was why the beeswax was so important in the original recipe; it preserved it in just the right way.

Directly onto the leaf, I carefully released a single drop of each of the three oils then I hurriedly covered it in kappa head-water.

There were many magical qualities of kappa head-water, but the one I was after was that it never evaporated because it was essentially part of a kappa's life force.

Thus, instead of concocting a salve I would have to keep applying and make more of, I could create a reusable patch.

I watched the dish carefully in the lamplight. The seaweed changed from a fresh green to a bright yellow to a dark green. The scents of sea salt, spicy pepper, and sweet and tangy orange wafted into my nose before settling into something soft and unobtrusive.

The salve would have smelled much stronger because it

called for more oil, but this could easily be covered with perfumes or even the smells of my soap or shampoo.

I pushed my long hair to one side and gently peeled the seaweed from the dish. Then I smoothed it onto the back of my neck. It felt a little slimy at first, but as my skin warmed it, I knew I would soon get used to it. In any case, I didn't have much choice. If it ended up bothering me later, I could always make the salve.

"Well," I muttered to myself, replacing the corks on my ingredient bottles. "Let's hope it works."

TWENTY-FOUR

When I returned to my room, Eithne was looking out the window. Tadhg sat by her side in the form of a fox—the form he took when he was feeling inquisitive.

He bounded toward me, and I pet him thoroughly. "Where have you been, Tadhg? Have you been exploring?"

Eithne turned toward me. "He has indeed. He's been following me around all day, meeting the other servants and taking a good look around."

Her face was flushed as if she'd been running.

"Eithne, are you unwell?"

She shook her head. "No, my lady. I merely haven't performed work like that in a while. It seems I'm no longer used to it. I've brought you lunch." She gestured toward a tray, which she'd set on the table. "When I saw your trunks moved, I knew you must be working on something, and I didn't want to disturb you."

"Thank you." I moved over to the table and sat. "What

did they have you doing?" I asked before taking a bite of buttered bread.

She puffed out her cheeks and sighed heavily. "What didn't they have me do? I built fires, whisked meringue—I can hardly lift my arm—they even had me fetching water. I feel a hundred years older."

I smiled. "Regretting not going with me?"

She pursed her lips. "I still prefer this."

I couldn't help but laugh. "Well, why don't you rest for a few hours? I won't need anything for a while."

"Thank you, my lady. I will do that as soon as I treat your wounds and rewrap them." Her tone held a hint of disapproval. But I'd never been good at keeping bandages on, so she didn't even bother to scold me.

After I finished my meal, Eithne sat in the chair near me and began applying more healing salve.

"Your cuts are looking better already, my lady. Perhaps a little raw from you overusing your hands, but they should be fully healed in a few days."

I heard her words, but I had other things on my mind. "Eithne, do you happen to know where the Goblin King is at the moment?"

"Last I heard, he was in the study. I built the fire myself before he arrived."

"And where is that?"

"It's on the first floor—directly on the other side of the cloisters, next to the drawing room..." She stilled in her wrapping. "My lady?"

I looked up to meet her eyes.

"You will be careful?"

I smiled at her. "I won't be running through the dark and knocking over any more tables if that's what you mean."

She nodded, but she didn't look reassured as she started bandaging again.

"Everything will work out, Eithne. You know how long I've waited for this. I'm not about to let him slip through my fingers."

Tying my bandage off, she didn't look up from my hands. "I know how much you've longed to be reunited with your first love, my lady. But people change. I know better than anyone your stubborn personality. I just don't want to see you get hurt by holding on to someone who no longer exists."

As always, she knew exactly what I was worried about. My heart squeezed as she voiced my own fears. "Well"—I swallowed hard when the word came out too thick—"it's too early to know just yet."

I wasn't ready to follow that thought—to make a plan on what I would do if Aodh was no longer someone I could love or someone who could love me.

She lowered her head in acknowledgment. "Yes, my lady. Should you need me before supper, you can send the first servant you see to fetch me."

"I'll be fine, Eithne. Go have a rest." As soon as she was gone, I turned back to Tadhg. "What do you say, Tadhg? Do you want to meet the Goblin King?"

He answered with that excited little half-scream half-bark foxes make.

I chuckled, petting his ears. "All right, then. Let's go."

In truth, I felt lighter having Tadhg with me. I had a solid plan, but his presence always seemed to make things easier.

He trotted alongside me as I headed downstairs and into the cloisters.

We made quick progress until I entered the anteroom on

the other side. To my far left was a door and then another elaborately carved staircase. Just ahead was a second door, which from Eithne's directions, I assumed led to the study.

I took a deep breath, looking down at myself to see if I needed to fix my appearance at all, then glanced at Tadhg, whose shimmering blue eyes watched me. His fox form blurred as he morphed into a large dog, clearly sensing my nervousness.

I smiled at him, patting his head. "I'll be all right," I murmured.

He didn't look convinced.

Straightening my shoulders, I lifted my bandaged hand and knocked on the door.

I listened hard but heard nothing until the doorknob rattled.

I raised my head and arranged my features in a serious but pleasant expression.

All that effort was wasted when Selwyn stepped into the anteroom. I immediately dropped any trace of friendliness.

"I was told this was where I could find the Goblin King," I said.

His expression was just as displeased as mine. "The King is busy at the moment. I believe I instructed you to wait in your room for him to call you."

Anger bubbled in my gut at his patronizing words and tone. "I believe a queen doesn't take orders from anyone. And might I remind you that you have, yet again, failed to address me properly?"

"Regardless, *my lady*, the King is too busy to deal with any of your petty concerns. Direct any issues you have to the staff. He has far better things to do."

I stepped closer to him, glaring up into his face. "I doubt very much the King finds the concerns of his people to be petty. I have important matters to discuss. Not that it's any of your concern as a mere adviser. Hadn't you better announce my presence? Who are you to decide whether I can see my future husband or not?"

I moved to push past him, but Selwyn grabbed my arm. He smiled that knowing smile, and a tingle ran over my skin as he tried to use his magical influence on me.

Tadhg growled a menacing warning.

But Selwyn's nasty little grin faded when I continued to glare at him. And I smiled at the triumph of my potion-making skills.

"Remove your hand," I demanded, too pleased at my win to sound as angry as I should have.

But before he could get over his confusion enough to comply with my demand, the door to the study opened farther.

CHAPTER
TWENTY-FIVE

The moment Selwyn saw Aodh's dark eyes on us, he released my arm, and Tadhg stopped growling. But the displeasure in the Goblin King's expression wasn't aimed at Selwyn.

"Why am I not surprised?" Aodh said flatly. "A commotion at my door could be caused by no one else."

My face flushed at his unfair statement. I wasn't causing a commotion—Selwyn was. And even though I was using it as an opportunity to speak with him, I did have legitimate business.

"Selwyn, wait inside for me."

"Aodh—" Selwyn murmured.

Aodh's gaze didn't leave mine. "I won't be a moment."

I clenched my jaw as Selwyn retreated to Aodh's study. *He doesn't even address the Goblin King properly. Are they that close? Is he that trusted? That doesn't bode well for me.*

Aodh crossed his arms. "What is it this time?"

I raised my chin. "When I went into town this morning,

I heard some concerns from the citizens I thought you ought to know about."

Aodh raised an eyebrow. "Did you go into town this morning?"

I snorted. *Is that how you want to play this? You know I did. You sent Charlie to protect me. Are you so desperate to appear indifferent toward me?* I nodded my answer.

"That was very foolish," he said. "Though I have tried to make Goblintown safer since becoming king, nowhere in Faerie is completely safe for humans."

Normally, the scolding would only annoy me. How had I survived twenty-five years in Faerie without his sage advice? But this time, it didn't annoy me because I knew where it came from.

I couldn't stop my small smile, so I lowered my face as I dipped in a curtsy. "I appreciate your concern for my well-being, Your Majesty."

He scowled at me, but the irritation behind it only made me smile more. "I believe I instructed you last night to not appear before me until I send for you."

I flinched at the reminder of his harsh words. "I believe the concerns of the people outweigh our personal grievances, Your Majesty."

He frowned, but it was not as severe as before. "That well may be, but I still do not have time for you right now. You may wait for me to send for you, or—if it is truly so pressing—you may write a report and submit it to Selwyn to give to me."

He turned to head back into his study.

"But—"

He cut me off without looking back. "Patience is another quality a queen needs. Would you prove yourself unworthy in yet another way?"

"Fine!" I huffed, clenching my jaw. I wanted to stomp my foot, but at least I had the self-control not to act like a child. Tadhg nudged my hand with his nose; it felt cold and wet though I knew the sensation was only in my mind.

While I looked down at him, patting his head in reassurance, my thoughts didn't support the action.

He thinks I don't have patience? I've waited for over ten years to be here! He's the one without patience. If it's a waiting game, I will surely win.

But what I didn't count on was that waiting countries away for a man who loved me and would surely come for me was vastly different from waiting in the same house for a man who could take or leave me.

I'd had such faith in him before, but now I had no basis to have that sort of faith in him again. I was nothing to him. He clearly didn't want a wife—or at least he didn't want me.

I waited for him to call for me over the next few days. Some of the time, I waited in my room. I tried multiple times to write my letter to Lorccán breaking the news to him. But when ink hit the page, I couldn't seem to find the right words. Eventually, I put it off in favor of exploring the house and grounds, trying to recall what unflinching faith in Aodh had felt like. But the only thing I could remember was when that faith had crumbled.

~

Lying in the shade, the cicadas chirping in a rhythmic cadence, I stared at the newssheet in my hands. The paper was worn and soft from over-handling, and every crease and crumble was reflected in the state of my heart.

Tears blurred the headline on the page, not that I needed to see it anymore to know what it said.

Elf Steals Robin Goodfellow's Dagger,
Declared Goblin King.

The story detailed how Aodh had sneaked into Robin Goodfellow's tomb, how he stole his iconic dagger with the amethyst blade, what Robin Goodfellow's last edict was— which was that whomever retrieved the dagger was even more worthy than him to rule the goblins—and how the goblins had named Aodh king with unprecedented numbers.

I'd read it and reread it nearly every day for the last five years and five months. When it first arrived from Tír, I thought it would only be half a month at most before Aodh sent for me. Aodh knew my name after all. I'd written my letter before my father's binding. It wouldn't take him long to find out who my father was and that he'd been sent to Olympus as an ambassador.

And as days turned to months turned to years, I still had faith in him. He'd promised. There was just something keeping him. I was sure he had a lot to take care of and learn as the new goblin king. He'd come for me as soon as he could.

Tears streamed down my face not because I didn't have faith in him but because I missed him. I wanted to see him again, to talk to him; I wanted to kiss him and congratulate him on what he'd done.

What did he look like now? Was he tall? Was he lean or muscular? Was his hair short or long? Did he smell the same? Had his voice deepened at all? He'd been a boy of fifteen the last time I'd seen him, and he was a man of twenty-five now.

"Is this what you're doing again today?" Graeme asked, approaching me from the direction of the house. "Weren't you supposed to meet Chrysanthe and Glykeria at the market?"

I glanced up at where the sun was in the sky and realized it was well past the time I was supposed to meet my friends. Chrysanthe would forgive me, but Glykeria would be hissing mad. She had little tolerance when it came to my mooning over Aodh.

I didn't make a move to get up. It was much too late now. I would apologize to them later.

Graeme frowned. "Haven't you had enough of this?" He sat down beside where I lay in the grass. "It's already been five years since you were supposed to become the royal mistress. King Lorccán doesn't have unlimited patience even if he would prefer you come to him of your own accord. Dad can only say you aren't ready for so long before it becomes dangerous."

I tried to give a reassuring smile though I wasn't in the mood to pull it off. My brother loved me, and I knew these remarks were coming from a place of concern. "I told you. I'm never going to want to be the royal mistress. I still love Aodh. I know Mum said I would forget my feelings for him with enough time and distance. But it has been nearly ten years since we left Tír, and still, all I can think about is him. How is he doing? Is he happy? Does he miss me as much as I miss him? When will he finally come for me?"

Graeme lowered his eyes and bit his lip. "H-he won't be coming for you."

My heart leapt into my throat, and I sat up. I searched my brother's face but found no answers there, only guilt.

"How could you say that? How do you know?"

He didn't meet my eyes. "Because...I never gave him the letter."

It felt like all the blood drained out of me, his words crushing me. "W-what?" I blinked rapidly, trying to make sense of what he'd just said, trying to keep hold of my last and only hope.

Finally, Graeme's eyes met mine. "I didn't deliver it."

My mind whirled as I absorbed his meaning, my heart pounding like a foreboding drum.

"You gave it to me in such a hurry that you didn't seal it. I was curious about who you had been meeting and why. You were always at Swonghilder's right where I left you, and you'd been lying to me for months. I was angry. But when I read the letter, I realized you were in trouble. You'd fallen in love with a goblin boy." He shook his head "I knew he wouldn't be good for you, and I knew our parents would never allow it. So I just…threw it away."

I gasped, tears filling my eyes as I brought a trembling hand to my lips.

"If he never got it, he wouldn't know where to find you. He thought you were a sidhe, and he didn't know your real name, so he couldn't find you even if he wanted to. I thought…" His eyes tensed as if in pain. "I thought that you'd get over it. That there was no way this kid would become goblin king, and even if he did, you'd have forgotten him by then. You'd have been with King Lorccán by then. But now, I see that's not going to happen. I don't want you to waste any more of your life. So let him go. He's not coming for you."

Agony pulsed through me with every heartbeat. Aodh wasn't coming for me. I'd promised to meet him, and I'd just never shown up. I'd disappeared. And my brother, one of the people I loved most in this world, had betrayed and lied to me. He'd snuffed out my potential happiness much more thoroughly than our parents had.

"I'm sorry, Melody. But I thought it was for your own good."

A sob managed to climb its way up my tight throat. I didn't have the wherewithal to be angry at Graeme just then though that certainly would come later. The only thing I could think about was how Aodh had thought I'd abandoned him and how I'd never see him again.

CHAPTER
TWENTY-SIX

On the morning of the first day of Certaigidré's dorchae, four days after Aodh had told me to wait yet again, my patience was starting to fray.

The sun was bright outside my bedroom window, and I wondered if it would be warmer again today. The last few days had held the sweet promises of summer though it was still half a month to Samcenn.

I'd done as I'd been told. I hadn't sought Aodh out at all. And while I did sneak a few glimpses of him as he walked in the garden every morning, I didn't attempt to approach him.

But the waiting game was getting ridiculous in my opinion. I knew he was being forced to make space and time for me in his life. But surely, he wasn't so overloaded that he hadn't planned to see me in the six days I'd been in the palace.

I gnawed on my lip, pacing before the window like a caged animal. *How long does he expect me to wait?*

A knock sounded on my bedroom door, and I called for whoever it was to come in.

Eithne and Odilie entered with arms full of bed linens.

Odilie greeted me for the first time that day, and they went about the task of stripping and remaking the bed.

I continued to watch out the window. "Do either of you know where the Goblin King is this morning?" I'd observed it was his habit to walk in the garden in the mornings, but it seemed later than the time he normally showed.

"Oh, he'll be in the great hall any moment, Your Majesty," Odilie answered. "He always accepts public petitions on the first day of the solus and dorchae of every month. Goblins have already started gathering downstairs."

My lips stretched into a grin almost before my brain could tell them to do so. *Public petitions? So anyone might bring their concerns directly to the King?*

The idea wasn't foreign though it was in its particulars. The king of Tír also accepted petitions. Of course, they were petitions from the lords who were supposed to bring the concerns of the people.

Moving quickly to my sitting room, I went directly to my stationary box where Eithne kept all my writing supplies. It was still sitting on the table from when I'd tried and failed to write Lorccán. I sat and wrote all of the things Kathleen had said at Seabottom Treasures—leaving out where I'd heard them. I also added my personal request to formally choose the date of our marriage and my coronation as goblin queen.

After signing the petition, I rose from my seat and looked down at myself.

If I were going to Lorccán's court, I would be seriously judged for wearing a simple linen dress. But I knew Aodh preferred the plain to the ostentatious. He'd probably scold me if I showed up in something expensive, especially with him having sold all of King Conrí's costly things to support the goblins.

I decided to appear as I was rather than change into something else.

Eithne and Odilie were gone by the time I returned to my bedroom, only Tadhg greeted me—his cat eyes blinking at me from the settee. He meowed as soon as he saw me, beckoning me to cuddle him.

"I can't right now, Tadhg. I have something important to do."

His shape blurred into that of a fox, and he hopped down to follow me.

"Very well, you can come along. But you better behave yourself. No biting."

He barked a little half-scream, and it gave me no reassurance.

The closer I got to the great hall, the louder the commotion. Voices echoed off the high ceilings as goblins talked among themselves, waiting for their king to appear. As I walked through the cloisters, I worried the antehall would be packed, but it was nearly empty when I opened the door.

A gremlin named Dáire, whom I'd met the day before while roaming the house, stood near the open door to the great hall. His huge eyes widened in his green face when I entered the antehall. He brought one spindly-fingered hand to his chest as he bowed to me.

"Your Majesty, we were told not to expect you today. We have not set a chair out for you. I'll hurry and tell Cináed to prepare—"

I waved my hand at the steward. "There's no need for that, Dáire. I won't be staying." I showed him my rolled-up petition. "I'll deliver this and leave."

Dáire's ears wiggled up and down in a gesture of confusion, but I smiled to set him at ease.

Before he could worry anymore, Selwyn's voice rang from the other side of the grand hall. "His Majesty King Aodh!"

The crowd, gathered on either side of a center aisle, hushed as Aodh appeared on the opposite end of the grand hall. He was dressed in a well-made but simple tunic with an amethyst-bladed dagger hanging on his belt. He also wore a crown of grapevines atop his ruddy blond head.

As he settled into a carved, tall-backed chair, he gave the goblins a small but kind smile, greeting them as they lifted their heads from bowing.

I straightened my back and raised my chin, stepping forward with my petition in hand.

In his hurry, Dáire's voice cracked. "Her Majesty Queen Melody."

I winced. His words weren't technically accurate. Though I hadn't bothered to correct the goblins who'd addressed me as queen thus far because my coronation was a formality at that point—and I'd even pushed Selwyn to address me as such—I'd been raised in proper courtly manners. I smoothed out my expression, brushing off Dáire's inaccuracy.

If it wasn't common knowledge that King Aodh was finally going to have a queen, it certainly would be after that.

Gasps and murmurs ran through the crowd. Some goblins were so shocked at Dáire's announcement that they didn't even have the wherewithal to dip their heads—not that I much cared.

In truth, I hardly even noticed their reactions. As I walked down the center aisle, Aodh glared at me from his throne.

CHAPTER
TWENTY-SEVEN

I couldn't hear the echo of my footsteps on the expanse of the black-and-white chessboard floor as the murmurs of the gathered goblins bounced off the high walls of the great hall.

Ahead of me, Aodh sat looking more displeased than I'd ever seen him. For once, Selwyn had no malice for me in his gaze as he stood near Aodh—but then he was looking at Aodh's reaction.

Tadhg bounded forward, shifting to a cat mid-hop. He showed no hesitation as he approached Aodh and jumped right into his lap.

My smooth strides faltered, and I stopped some ten feet from where Aodh sat, squinting at Tadhg's familiarity.

For his part, Aodh broke eye contact with me to look down at the spunkie. The tiniest of smiles quirked in the corner of his mouth.

When did they become friends?

But any amusement or kindness Tadhg had elicited

seemed only for him. Aodh looked up at me coldly, despite stroking Tadhg's luminescent fur.

"What brings you here today, my lady? Now is the time for me to hear from my people"—Aodh gestured toward the crowd—"the people who have waited to see me and whom you have so ceremoniously jumped in the queue."

At his words, the crowd hushed.

I could feel my face get hot, but my voice was clear when I declared, "I have a petition for the Goblin King."

Aodh raised an eyebrow, and I had to admit he was good at looking uninterested. "Do you indeed?"

He waved his hand toward me, and a young drake, maybe seven or eight, approached me where I stood at the edge of the crowd. His blond hair glowed like a warm fire, and his eyes were the color of a blue flame. Out of all the goblins there, he seemed to be the only one who didn't understand the magnitude of my presence. He simply gazed up at me expectantly and held out his hands.

After I gave him the petition, he crossed the distance to hand it to Selwyn.

Aodh turned in his chair toward his adviser, whose eyes widened in surprise when Aodh held out his hand for it. Despite the break from procedure, Selwyn gave my petition to Aodh without a word.

The heavy silence of the room pressed in on me, and I tried not to fidget. That wasn't how it was done, and I was feeling self-conscious as it was after he'd decried me.

Aodh read the paper before him while the minutes dragged out.

Finally, he looked up and met my eyes.

"So you believe yourself worthy to become the goblin queen? You have yourself declared as much in this official proceeding, and you petition to set a date for our wedding and your coronation?"

He's making a spectacle on purpose. Very well. Two can play that game.

I raised my chin. "It is customary that when a woman outsmarts the goblin king, and he is unmarried, she's declared the goblin queen. Is that not so?"

Whispers traveled through the crowd behind me.

"And did I not cleverly steal the ring of the goblin king directly off your finger on the last full moon, Your Majesty?"

Aodh smiled, and the little hint of mischievousness I remembered appeared in his eyes. "I freely admit you did. However, your behavior since then has made me doubt whether you are truly fit to serve these fine fae as their queen. Do you, a human raised by the sidhe, even know what it takes to be a ruler to the goblins?"

I put on the sweetest smile I could muster, the one I'd used when I had a cocky answer for my parents while growing up. "Of course, Your Majesty. Do you think I take this position lightly? The goblins admire and follow freely those who are clever, courageous, steadfast, and persistent."

His smile didn't slip, but I saw hesitation enter his gaze.

"I believe I have shown both cleverness in outsmarting you and courageousness in daring to steal the ring right off your finger."

Aodh snorted. "Cleverness, I will allow. But I would not call that courageous. You were in no danger." He paused for a moment. "You have asked me to set our wedding date. I will postpone that decision until you have proved yourself worthy of this office. You show me that you, as an outsider, can live by the principles the goblins hold dear before Bealtaine, and I will revisit your petition."

"If you'll excuse me, Your Majesty. But Bealtaine is less than a month away. How many opportunities will I have to prove myself courageous, steadfast, and persistent in that time? Perhaps the summer solstice would be more reasonable?"

He shrugged as if an additional month would make no real difference. "Very well."

I smiled again, that time genuinely. "I accept your challenge, Your Majesty. But might I make one further request?"

His sharp gaze analyzed my face. "You may though I reserve the right to refuse it."

I dipped my head. "It is but a trifle. You have suggested my behavior hasn't been what you would expect of your queen. However, you have been so very busy that you have had little time to get to know me. I request, from today until your final judgment, you give me a little of your time each day. You can hardly pass a fair judgment about whether I am fit to serve Goblintown if you're completely unfamiliar with who I am."

Aodh smirked, and I could tell he believed no matter how much time he spent with me, he wouldn't be swayed to accept me. But he didn't know what I knew. He didn't know that I'd won his heart once already, that I'd known him better than anyone else. I was confident all I needed was a little of his time to make him mine again.

"Very well, my lady. But I would ask for something in return."

"Yes, Your Majesty?"

"If and when you are proven unfit to serve as goblin queen, and I pass my final judgment, you will return my ring to me and go home without complaint."

My heart hesitated. Aodh didn't want a wife, and in this situation, he had all the power to make his determination. If I agreed to it, I'd be giving up the only power I had.

I bowed my head to him. "I know you are a fair and just king. I will abide by your decision."

CHAPTER
TWENTY-EIGHT

I felt a little dizzy when I stepped into the cloisters, and I blew all the air from my lungs as if I would explode if I didn't release the pressure.

I looked up at the blue sky, so like my mind at the moment. The sun was as warm as the promise of my allotted time with Aodh, but the thick, fluffy clouds threatened to blot it out. Did I just create clouds by agreeing to give up if I didn't pass his tests?

I shook the worries from my mind. This was my chance. He may be thinking he had all the power in the situation. But he'd be wrong.

I felt fairly optimistic the rest of the day. I watched the court proceedings from the little window on the second floor. The visiting goblins presented their petitions, which were collected by the drake boy and given to Selwyn, who stacked them neatly for Aodh's later review.

It was a pleasure to watch Aodh work, to see the open expressions he showed the goblins so freely—completely different from how he'd been with me thus far. I could tell he cared for them and truly wanted to help them, and I was glad he'd become the king he'd so wanted to be.

Late in the afternoon, when all the petitions had been collected, Aodh left the great hall, and I went outside to enjoy what remained of the afternoon sun.

I was sitting on the edge of the garden's fountain, watching Tadhg splash in the water in the form of an otter, when Eithne found me.

"There you are, my lady," she said, nearly out of breath. "The Goblin King has sent for you."

I jumped up from my seat. "He did?"

She nodded, her hand on her heaving chest. "He's requested you sup with him this evening."

As a thrill bubbled up inside me, I nearly laughed with joy.

She waved her hand at me. "Come, let's hurry. You don't have much time to change."

What Eithne meant was I had about an hour to get ready. But considering I would need to change my clothes, style my hair, and put on kohl and lip tint, I really didn't have much time at all.

I was the first to arrive in the dining room, and I was glad for it.

The space seemed at odds with itself. Neither the dark walls nor wooden floor held any decoration, but the ceiling was sculpted with geometrical patterns in white. The candles in the chandelier sparkled off the crystal facets hanging from it, but the candlesticks on the unclothed table were simply carved wood.

I frowned when I saw how far they'd put my place setting from Aodh's. There would be no way to have an effective conversation on opposite ends of the long table. Shrugging, I collected my plates and utensils and set them beside Aodh's. Then I moved my glasses and finally my chair.

I was sitting comfortably with my back to the fireplace when he arrived.

He hesitated, frowning slightly as his eyes flicked between me and where I should have been sitting.

I hope no one gets in trouble for this later.

I stood from my chair and nodded to him. "Good evening, Your Majesty."

He cleared his throat. "Yes." He sat down without another word.

I smiled pleasantly. He didn't look directly at me, but I could feel him watching me from the corners of his eyes.

"I appreciate you inviting me to dine with you this evening. I'm sure you have much work to do with all the petitions you received today."

"I will keep my end of the bargain. I trust you will keep yours when the time comes."

I continued to smile, not at all feeling the bite in his words. It had been so long since I'd seen him up close. So many years had I longed for him, I was just happy to be near him.

The door to the dining room opened, and some servants entered with trays of food. Rather than serving us, they placed the trays on the table and left.

As surprised as I was that we had to serve ourselves, I was just as happy. It meant there wasn't anyone listening to our conversation, and no one would interrupt us.

I waited for Aodh to take what he wanted from the platters, then followed suit.

He concentrated on the meal before him; the only sounds in the room were the fire in the hearth and the soft clinking of cutlery.

I took a sip from my water glass. "I read about how you became goblin king in a newssheet. That was very daring of you to enter Robin Goodfellow's tomb, knowing so many goblins had died before you."

His dark eyes met mine, and he stared at me.

I wondered what he was thinking as my heart skipped a beat.

"Is that when you decided to coerce me into marrying you?"

My mouth went dry, and I had a hard time swallowing. But he kept staring, clearly wanting an answer.

I lowered my eyes to my plate. The fish, which had been so delicious a moment ago, didn't seem appetizing anymore. "No, that was…more recent."

He grunted and returned his attention to his plate.

I frowned as a heavy weight pressed in on me. Had I had any better options, I would have taken them. "I'm sorry it happened this way."

"Why do something if you're only going to feel guilty about it later? Your apology is hollow, especially because you're still benefiting from your actions."

I winced, clenching my hands in my lap before glancing up at him. "Would you have said yes if I'd simply asked?" I could have taken that route, of course. I could have shown up at the palace and asked for him to take me as his wife and queen without him knowing I was Mischief. But if he refused, that would have been the end of it. Not only did the way I chose provide more time to win his heart, I proved right away I had one of the goblin virtues.

His eyes were harsh and cold when they met mine. "No."

"Then what choice did I have?" I murmured.

He dropped his utensils with a loud clatter and laced his

fingers together. "What do you want from this?" he demanded, glaring at me. "Your family has power enough being sidhe. You aren't a goblin. Did you really do all this just to be called queen? That is the only thing I could give you that you can't get from anyone else. Why are you here, Melody?"

My chest tightened. "I-I just want…you, Aodh."

I immediately regretted my whispered confession as Aodh's expression shifted from surprise to displeasure.

"Even if you pass this challenge and become goblin queen, that's the one thing you can never have."

I felt my lips tremble. "Why?" My voice shook on that little word. *Have I really gone through all this for something impossible? Can he not forgive me for forcing his hand?* I replayed his harsh rejection from a few nights before in my mind. *Am I so disgusting to him?*

The severe light in his eyes softened a little as he stared back at me while I fought to mask my emotions.

"It's—"

His response was cut off by a knock on the dining room door. Selwyn stepped into the room without a verbal invitation. "Forgive me for interrupting, but there's an urgent matter that needs your attention, Your Majesty."

Nodding once, Aodh stood from the table. "Until tomorrow, Lady Melody. Please, enjoy the rest of your meal."

Then he strode from the room.

CHAPTER
TWENTY-NINE

He'd left so quickly that I didn't even have the chance to stand from my chair. A flurry of emotions churned inside me. But as my surprise at Aodh's departure faded, anxiety took hold.

I laid my hands flat on the table on either side of my place setting, the feel of the cool wood under my palms steadying me.

Don't get upset. I knew this wouldn't be simple. I can't let my fear run wild. I don't know whether he's pushing me away more because he doesn't want a wife or because I forced his hand. I'll just ask him tomorrow and plan my approach from there.

My self-encouragement wasn't very effective. Sure, I didn't burst into tears. But I also didn't sleep well that night.

The truth was I wasn't very brave, and I knew it. When I came up with an elaborate plan to force Aodh's hand, I let my fear rule me—my fear of definitive rejection. Had I been braver, I would have just asked for him to marry me outright. And while his pushing me away still hurt, it wouldn't be nearly as bad as him rejecting me with no chance of winning him over.

Still, as the dawn lit the southern skies out my bedroom window the next morning, I told myself to have a little more courage. He said I could never have him and knowing exactly why could make all the difference in the success of my endeavor.

Eithne arrived with a tray, and I frowned. *I guess we won't be having breakfast together, then.*

"I've been sent word this morning that the Goblin King requests your presence in the garden mid-morning, my lady."

I was a little surprised our time today would be spent during his morning walk in the garden. From what I'd observed, he usually spent that time conversing with Selwyn. After last night, I'd assumed we would be sharing our meals. After all, he had to eat, and that was the easiest way to fulfill his promise without disrupting his day.

I nodded to Eithne and started eating breakfast while she went to my dressing room to select my clothes for the day.

Again, I arrived at our rendezvous point before him.

It was still a bit chilly outside—the sun having yet to warm the day—and I was glad Eithne had insisted on me wearing my cloak. The cool water from the fountain misted my face as I sat on its ledge.

Tadhg was not interested in the fountain today, instead sniffing around flowerbeds with his long, dog's snout.

We both looked up when Aodh stepped out of the door leading from his wing of the palace.

Tadhg bounded forward to greet him, and Aodh knelt to better receive his licks of affection.

"Good morning, my fine fellow," Aodh said.

I rose from my seat, bowing my head when Aodh glanced over at me.

"His name is Tadhg, Your Majesty," I informed. "He likes you. It usually takes him a while to warm up to new people."

Aodh stood from his crouch. "I likely endeared myself to him by giving him ham when he wandered into my study."

I chuckled. "That will do it."

We fell into silence. Aodh moved to stand by my side and gestured to suggest we begin our stroll. Tadhg trotted on ahead of us, amusing himself in the flowerbeds.

At first, the easy pace of our steps was pleasant. But the longer we didn't speak, the more strained the air became.

"Did you take care of the urgent matter Selwyn brought to you last night?"

Aodh's eyes snapped to mine. He held me in his gaze for a moment, then released me with little concern. He dipped his head by way of response.

There's no way around it. My stomach dropped and threatened to expel my earlier meal. I crumbled the fabric of my skirt in my fists. "Your Majesty, last night you said you were the one thing I couldn't have. I'd like to know why that is." I was pleased my voice was steady and sure though I didn't dare look into his eyes.

He sighed softly through his nose. "Let me ask you something, Lady Melody." He stopped on the path, and I did the same. "If it is not to be queen, why do you want me? As far as I know, we have never met. Are you the type of woman who would set her sights on a man she's only read about in a newssheet?"

"Of course not," I answered by reflex.

He nodded slightly. "I thought as much. Then we have met before."

I bit my lip and lowered my head in a nod as the familiar tug of my father's binding spell threatened to smother my words. How many letters had I tried to write Aodh since Graeme had confessed what he'd done? How many hours of a cramped hand or a spilled ink bottle had I suffered through? How many times had I tried to tell Chrysanthe and Glykeria the full story of why Aodh and I weren't together now—my words drowned before they'd ever had a chance to surface?

"When?" Aodh asked.

I cast my eyes around me, feeling closed in, but the clear path lined with flowers and shrubs was just the same as before.

"I will tell you my reason why you can't have me if you share when we met," he pressed.

I frowned miserably, crossing my arms.

His expression was curious but firm.

Despair clenched my heart. What I wouldn't have given to tell him the truth.

Aodh frowned in displeasure, and my guts twisted. "I don't understand how your secret could be more valuable than mine, but it's your decision."

If only it were.

He started down the path again, his movements stiffer than before. It was clear from the set of his mouth he was prepared to finish our meeting in silence.

I'm not making any progress. Whether it's because he doesn't want a wife at all or because I cornered him, I'm in the same boat. My exact approach might be different, but I can only show him who I am and let him decide to love me or not. "Your Majesty, surely, we don't need to continue on this way. You have set the terms of your challenge, and I have until the summer solstice to prove myself worthy of being queen. We are to meet every day from now until then. Even if you will not give me what I truly want, can we not be friends in the interim?"

Aodh grunted. "Is it your habit to force your friends into doing things against their wills? If you wanted to be friends, you wouldn't have forced me into this marriage. If you wanted to be friends, when I told you I couldn't give myself to you, you would have withdrawn."

I pursed my lips. "All right. Fine. I'm not a very good friend, then. You may not want a wife, but you could use a helpmate. At the very least, can I not help you with some of your duties while I'm here? It is my understanding you are overloaded trying to do everything yourself. If not friends, how about colleagues?" *Just give me an opening to get closer to you.*

Again, he stared down at me with those dark eyes of his. He'd gotten quite good at masking his thoughts. And I wondered if it was his skill or my lack of familiarity with the new him that made me unable to read him now.

"Very well, Lady Melody. Perhaps making use of you will keep you from any more of your clever schemes."

I flinched at his word choice. Though the dig was unnecessary, he wasn't wrong. Was my suggestion not another way to get him to let me in?

"Bealtaine is coming up. Why don't you plan a celebration for Goblintown? The goblins cannot attend the festivities in Sifra without being humiliated, and I have been too busy to plan such things since I became king."

My eyes widened. *The goblins haven't celebrated Bealtaine in that long?*

"There's no budget to speak of, but you may redirect whatever palace staff you require."

"I'll do it. You can count on me." I smiled up at him, pleased he'd entrusted me with anything at all.

He nodded, not even offering me a professional smile.

My mind whirled with possibilities. I had to do my very best. It was my chance to show Aodh what I could handle as queen, and I wanted to give the goblins as best a Bealtaine as I could.

I gazed over at him while we continued to stroll the garden paths. We still had time, plenty of time, to get to know each other again. He didn't want to be my husband; he didn't even want to be my friend, but he was letting me help him. He'd let me in a tiny little bit, and that was enough for today.

But just as I was about to ask if he had any special requests for the celebration, Selwyn rushed toward us.

"Your Majesty, something has come up that needs your attention."

Again?

"Please, follow me," Selwyn urged. But as he turned to lead the way, he met my gaze with a smirk.

I clenched my jaw.

THIRTY

Lifting my skirts to keep up with their quick pace, I followed them. *What is so important Selwyn used it as an excuse to interrupt us again?*

Aodh glanced back at me as we entered the antehall through the cloisters but didn't say anything.

Our hurried steps shuffled and squeaked off the black-and-white floor as we passed through to the front door.

When we reached the yard, we found the drake boy who'd accepted the petitions the day before.

Aodh frowned. "What are you doing here, Cináed?"

Cináed's eyes brightened upon seeing Aodh. But when Aodh crossed his arms and gave the boy a firm stare, he hung his head.

"I only agreed that you could work here during petition times. You're supposed to be in school. What did I tell you last time? If you skipped school again, you wouldn't be allowed to work here anymore."

Cináed's head snapped up, his eyes pleading with Aodh. "Please, Your Majesty. Don't dismiss me. I'm only here because I know how much work you have. There were twice as many petitions as last time. I want to help."

Aodh pursed his lips, but I could see the stern look in his eyes falter.

I smiled to myself. He clearly had affection for the boy and didn't want to stay firm with him.

Stepping closer to the drake, I bent to better meet his eyes. "Cináed, was it?" I asked with a smile.

Cináed turned toward me, nodding as he fought back tears.

"You admire the Goblin King. Don't you, Cináed?" Drakes were known to form strong bonds with those they admired.

"Yes, my lady," he answered in a hushed voice.

"So do I. But you want to know something? One of the things I admire most about him is how intelligent he is. Do you think he was always as clever as he is now?"

Cináed glanced up at Aodh, then looked back at me without answering.

"Of course not," I said. "He had to go to school to learn everything he knows now. Isn't that right, Your Majesty?"

Aodh nodded once.

"See? I know you want to help His Majesty. I know you're worried about him. But you will be far more helpful if you learn everything you can. Imagine how helpful you could be to him if you were even more knowledgeable than you are now. Wouldn't you like for His Majesty to turn to you when he needs something?"

The light in Cináed's eyes told me he could imagine it very well.

"Right. I'm sure His Majesty will forgive you this *one* time if you *promise* to study hard and only work on petition days."

Both Cináed and I turned to Aodh. His arms were still crossed, but I didn't miss the little quirk in the corner of his mouth as he fought a smile.

He nodded again. "Just this once. But you better show me top marks on your next exam. Deal?"

Cináed bobbed his head enthusiastically. "Yes, Your Majesty. I promise."

Aodh waved his hand, shooing the boy, then started back inside.

I grinned at Cináed. "There, you see? Now, go on to school before you miss something important."

Cináed's smile was all the thanks I needed as he scurried away without so much as a goodbye.

I sighed, crossing my arms and straightening while watching Cináed's retreat.

"I suppose you think that was cunning," Selwyn said.

I turned toward him. "What exactly is your problem? I haven't done anything to you. You've been hostile to me since the moment we met. I don't care whether you approve of me, but I am curious to know why you're acting this way."

Selwyn flattened his lips in angry silence.

I snorted. "You're brave enough to pick a fight, but not brave enough to come clean? Fine. What do you want?" I stood up straighter and stepped closer to him—my face inches from his—before lowering my voice as I continued, "How far does this go? Are you simply afraid my presence will give you less sway with the King? Or is it more than that? Are you coveting the crown for yourself? Worried I'll mess up some plan?"

Selwyn's face flushed, and his seawater eyes boiled. "You don't belong with him," he said, his tone hushed with barely restrained ire.

I raised my eyebrows. I hadn't expected that response.

"Selwyn, are—" Aodh reappeared at the front door, cutting off his words and coming to a full stop. After a tense moment, he continued. "We have a lot to do today, Selwyn."

I flinched when Aodh's dark eyes met mine.

"Until tomorrow, Lady Melody." His tone was chilly, back to how it had sounded before he'd agreed to work with me.

I cursed internally, and they left without another word.

As I made my way back to my room, I stomped my feet much louder than was necessary. *Fucking Selwyn. I knew he would keep getting in the way. If I don't do something, he's going to interrupt Aodh and me every day until the solstice. I need help. I can't very well spend time with Aodh and stop Selwyn all at once. I should send for Graeme. He's good at interfering.*

Deciding to write to my brother, I pulled up short when I found Eithne crying in my room.

She sat at the table near the window, a letter in her hands, with tears streaming down her face.

"Eithne," I said softly, closing the door. "What's the matter?"

She hurried to stand and wiped her face with her sleeves. "My lady, I'm sorry. It's nothing for you to concern yourself over."

I frowned, approaching her. "Come now, Eithne. Don't be like that. I might be able to help."

She lowered her face, staring at the letter. "It's my sister, my lady. She…she's pregnant."

Is she worried her sister will die in childbirth? "But she may be all right yet. It isn't always so dire when fae get pregnant. After all, my mother is still alive after giving birth to my brother."

She shook her head. "It's not that, my lady. I am worried, yes." She held up the letter without really showing me. "My sister just wrote to me that her husband died. Without his support, and because she's so upset at his loss, my little sister will likely miscarry the baby or die herself."

Thus, one tragedy is multiplied.

I reached out to Eithne and squeezed her hand. "Would you like to go to her?"

Eithne frowned. "Our father is with her now, so at least she isn't alone. But he won't be able to support her and the baby for long at his age. I would appreciate you allowing me to go to her when her time gets closer. For now, I think expanding my savings until then will be more helpful."

I nodded. "How about this, then? I'll write to my father and see what can be done for your sister. You've served us loyally for many years. Perhaps he'll take her in and give her an easy job until she's given birth. You can save more in the meantime and go when she needs you most."

Eithne gave me a watery smile. "Thank you, my lady. His Lordship takes good care of his staff. I know she'll be safe with him."

THIRTY-ONE

I wrote three letters to my family: one to my brother asking him to come with the plan of staying for a while, one to my father explaining Eithne's sister's situation and giving him information on where to find her, and one to my mother to assure her I was well so she wouldn't feel left out. As I was already at it, I tried to write my letter to Lorccán. But still, I couldn't bring myself to do it.

I handed the sealed letters to Eithne to post and asked her to bring Odilie with her on her way back.

As I waited for Eithne and Odilie, I thought about what I needed to do for Goblintown's Bealtaine celebration.

What aspects of Bealtaine are essential? Aodh said there was no budget. I could use my own money… Is that cheating?

I walked up and down my room, running through all the Bealtaine traditions in my mind.

Eithne and Odilie arrived not ten minutes later. I could feel their eyes watching me curiously as I paced the room. Finally, I turned to them.

"The Goblin King has put me in charge of this year's Bealtaine celebration."

Odilie squealed with excitement. "Oh, I haven't seen one of those since I left Elfton!"

I nodded and continued. "But we need to spend as little as possible. The most important part of Bealtaine, in my mind, is the balefires. I think we can safely burn them on the front lawn—one in the center of the round drive and the other to one side. It will be easier to go between them that way. His Majesty said I could redirect whatever palace staff I like, but I don't want to add work to those who are already laden. Odilie, could you gather a list of staff members who are willing to help?"

"Of course, Your Majesty."

"Good. I'm going to need people to go out into Goblinwood to gather wood for the balefires. That's our most important task. Secondly, I'd like a list of Goblintown's tailors, seamstresses, and fabric merchants."

Odilie tilted her head. "There aren't many tailors and seamstresses in Goblintown, Ma'am. Most goblins make their own clothes. But I will get you a list."

I frowned. "We'll just have to hope it's enough. I'd like to build a samcenn-pole, so we must find a suitable tree. Odilie, how many goblins are there in Goblintown?"

Odilie's eyes widened. "I have no idea, Ma'am. Can't be less than five thousand. The Goblin King would know that."

I bobbed my head. "I will ask him, then." *Even five thousand would be too many to feed properly.*

I turned to Eithne. "I know you don't want to go into Goblintown with me, so I'll keep your contributions to the palace grounds. I need you to gather as much fabric and thread as you can."

Eithne nodded once.

I stopped my pacing and faced them. "We don't have as much time as I'd like. Let's get to it."

While they scurried about their tasks, I went in search of Aodh. I tried his study first, rapping on the door with my knuckles.

As I waited for an answer, I glanced down at my palms. I'd been able to take my bandages off the day before, but I could not yet tell whether the wounds would leave scars.

I listened hard to the room beyond, wondering where else Aodh might be. But before I could turn to look for someone to ask, the door opened.

I smiled when I saw Aodh staring down at me rather than Selwyn and bowed my head.

"I apologize for interrupting, Your Majesty. I know this is not my designated time. But I need to know how many goblins reside in Goblintown to better plan our Bealtaine celebration."

"There are 8,364 goblins including myself at last count," he answered without hesitation.

I didn't know why I was surprised he knew without having to look it up. It was so like him to value every single goblin in his charge.

I bowed my head again. "Thank you. I'll see you tomorrow then."

I could feel his eyes on me as I crossed the anteroom. And when I glanced back at him upon reaching the door to the cloisters, I smiled to see he watched me curiously. The coolness in his gaze from earlier was gone. He looked at me as if trying to figure me out.

That seemed like progress to me, and my steps were light while I practically skipped down the cloisters to the antehall.

Turning left once in the antehall, I entered the pantry. The many shelves might have been filled with expensive dishes, crockery, and table linens at one time, but they were relatively empty now. What was left were common dishes—not enough for a large party by any means.

I moved through the pantry and entered the steward's office.

Dáire looked up from his desk, his eyes widening in surprise. "Your Majesty, I mean, my lady, I—"

I need to start giving him a fair warning, or he's liable to keel over.

I smiled at him. "Don't worry about it, Dáire. I'm only here to see the cook. Is she busy at the moment?"

"To see Gráinne? She should be starting on the midday meal soon," the nervous gremlin answered.

I nodded. "I'll make it quick."

I passed through the steward's office and looked over the upper walkway to the kitchen below to see Gráinne and Rosemary hauling ingredients up from the cellars. After crossing the walk, I descended the spiral staircase to meet them on the main floor.

Gráinne—a salamander I'd been told worked at the palace since the time of King Conrí—set down her load on one of the prep tables, which wrapped around a square pillar that supported the high ceiling at the center of the room. Rosemary, the piskie kitchen maid, did the same.

"What can I do for you, Your Majesty?" Gráinne asked with a warm smile, her eyes flickering like a mid-winter fire.

"I know you're about to start cooking, so I won't keep you long. King Aodh has asked me to plan a Bealtaine celebration. Odilie will be coming by to see if you'd like to volunteer any of your free time. But I have another question for you. I don't have the budget for a feast. Still, it seems wrong not to offer the people of Goblintown something to eat. So I'd like to make fresh butter and buttermilk. If we give all 8,364 goblins a knob of butter for their bread, how many gallons of cream will we need?"

"A little over one hundred and thirty gallons—one hundred and thirty-one if you want to be safe," Rosemary chimed in.

I glanced at the young piskie in surprise. "You must have a gift for numbers, Rosemary. That was very quick."

Rosemary curtsied, bowing her head at my compliment.

"That amount of cream won't be cheap, Your Majesty," Gráinne pointed out.

"How much is a gallon of cream?" I asked.

"Around eighteen copper coins," Gráinne answered.

"That's around twenty-three gold coins and six silver coins for the lot," Rosemary added.

I grimaced. Even as wealthy as my family was, my monthly allowance was only five gold coins, which was fifty silver coins or five hundred copper coins. *Maybe I shouldn't have bought that kappa head-water after all.*

Even if I'd wanted to, I didn't have that much to spend. I bit my lip.

"Perhaps we could make bannocks instead," Gráinne suggested. "Cream is quite expensive, but oats aren't nearly as much. We could probably make enough for everyone for maybe ten gold coins, less if the merchants give us a discount."

"But wouldn't that be more time-consuming?" I asked. "Making butter and buttermilk would be much easier than making bannocks."

Rosemary nodded in agreement. "We would need one thousand and forty-six bannocks to feed that many. If we started today, we'd have to make forty-six bannocks a day."

I frowned, shaking my head. "That's too much work to put on you."

Gráinne reached out and placed her red hand on my arm in a soothing gesture. "It's been over one cycle since we last celebrated Bealtaine in Goblintown—before King Aodh took the throne. I'm sure if we asked the goblins, they would be happy to help."

"There are nine bakeries in Goblintown," Rosemary said. "Why don't we ask them for help? Then we'd only have to make one hundred and five bannocks each."

"Do you really think they'd help?" I asked.

The cook and the kitchen maid nodded enthusiastically.

My disappointment evaporated. "All right, then. Please order the ingredients—submit the bills to me—and send word to the bakers they can pick up what they need here. Is that all right?"

When they grinned at me, my heart warmed to see their excitement.

THIRTY-TWO

I nearly crashed into Odilie when I exited the pantry to go back upstairs.

"Oh, Your Majesty!" Though she was gasping, she wore a bright smile. "I have that list of fabric suppliers for you right here." She handed me a sheet of paper. "But I'm still compiling your list of volunteers. Everyone seems very excited, and many of them would like to help. Charlie offered to lead the team to go into Goblinwood."

I nodded. "Excellent. Was Charlie busy? I'd like to go into town to talk to these merchants, but I don't want to pull you away from your task."

Odilie shook her head. "Not as far as I could tell, Ma'am. He was watching the front gate when I last saw him."

I thanked her before heading upstairs.

Eithne had also been busy with the task I'd given her. She'd gathered odds and ends of fabric and spread them out on my bed. There wasn't much of any particular pattern, but there was enough to get us started.

"Good job, Eithne. Is this everything?"

Eithne nodded. "That's all I had from the sewing kit I use to repair your clothing. But I'll also ask one of the maids if they have anything."

"All right. Why don't we move all this into my reception room so we have space to work? We're going to use this fabric to make the ribbons for the samcenn-pole. I know we won't have enough length to make long strips, so we'll have to sew them together." I held up my hand and drew my finger along the width of my palm. "Let's make them about this wide."

"Yes, my lady." Eithne started stacking the fabric to move it to the reception room.

"Oh, and when you find one of the maids, could you two get the guest room nearest mine ready? My brother should be coming to visit in the next few days."

Eithne's eyes brightened at the news. Despite Graeme's tendency to tease her, she did have a fondness for him. And I was certain she would be glad to have someone else she was familiar with in our new environment. "Yes, my lady."

"Thank you, Eithne. I'll be heading into town as soon as I grab my cloak. I don't know how long I'll be."

Apprehension crept into Eithne's face, but she didn't argue.

After pulling on my cloak, I went downstairs and out the front door.

Just as Odilie had said, Charlie was watching the front gate, leaning his elbows on the stone wall beside it.

This has to be a boring job, standing here waiting in case something happens.

"Hello, Charlie!" I called out to get his attention, and he turned toward me.

He bowed his head with a smile. "Your Majesty, Odilie

told me you're planning a Bealtaine celebration. I'd be happy to gather wood for the balefires and find a suitable tree for the samcenn-pole."

"Thank you. Yes, she already informed me as much. I'll leave it in your hands, then. You let me know if you're short-handed. I'll head into Goblinwood myself if necessary."

He frowned, looking quite disturbed by the suggestion. Still, he didn't protest.

"In any case, are you busy right now?" I held up the list of fabric suppliers. "I have some places to visit in town if you'd like to accompany me."

"Of course, I can ask another guard to watch my post. Shall I ready a carriage for you this time?"

I thought about his suggestion. Unlike before, having the goblins know I was on an official visit would probably help my endeavor. I nodded. "Yes, thank you."

"Would you prefer to wait out here or…"

A cool wind blew the hood from my hair. It seemed it wouldn't be warming up today. "I think I'll head inside to wait."

As Charlie went about his task, I returned to the antehall and the warmth it offered.

After a few minutes of waiting, I opened the door to the grand hall.

My footsteps echoed off the high walls of the empty space. It was almost a different room when it was void of people. Even the tall chair Aodh had sat in had been removed. I meandered to the far end, just passing time while I waited for the carriage.

The fire had not been lit, likely because there was no reason to be in there, and I rubbed my arms as the chill that hung in the air gave me gooseflesh.

Turning back toward the antehall, I'd only made it a few steps before I heard another set of shoes on the hard floor.

I spun around to find Aodh, with Tadhg trotting behind him in his fox form, entering the grand hall from the anteroom that connected to his study and the drawing room.

Aodh pulled up short, seemingly surprised at my presence.

"Good afternoon, Your Majesty," I greeted with a little dip.

He turned his head and looked at me out of the corner of his eye. "What are you doing here?"

Why does he sound so suspicious? What harm could I possibly do in this big empty room?

I gestured toward the antehall. "I'm waiting for Charlie to bring the carriage. I'm heading into town to see if any fabric merchants have scraps they're willing to donate so we can make ribbons for the samcenn-pole."

He nodded slowly, and I tried to decipher what he was thinking.

Is he pleased I'm trying so hard already? Does it annoy him because he wants me to fail his challenge?

"Did you meet Selwyn? I sent him on an errand a while ago, and he has yet to return."

I shook my head. *Thank my every blessing I did not.*

He stared at me for a heavy moment. "Very well. I'll ask Dáire."

Aodh continued past me, and Tadhg didn't hesitate to follow him. I smiled after them, pleased they got on so well. They reached the threshold of the antehall just as Charlie did.

I moved toward him, watching Aodh murmur something to Charlie before leaving.

Charlie hesitated when I turned to go outside. "You head out first, Your Majesty. I'll just be a moment. Excuse me."

I appreciated the delay once I saw the elf standing near the horses. She was the same driver who'd picked me up at Maplecrest.

I approached her with a smile. "Good afternoon. I don't believe we've officially met. What's your name?"

Her eyes widened, and she bowed. "Peony, Your Majesty. I work in the stables."

I nodded. "Nice to meet you, Peony. Thank you for driving us today."

"Of course, Ma'am." Her face flushed as she smiled back at me, pulling the lobe of one of her pointed ears.

I was explaining the list of places we needed to go when Charlie reappeared.

"I apologize for the delay, Your Majesty," he said as he closed the front door behind him. He carried a folded bundle in his arms. "Shall we?"

Unlike Selwyn, Charlie had excellent manners. He handed me into the carriage without being asked.

While I settled into my seat, he unfolded his bundle and offered me a blanket. "For your lap, Your Majesty. It's chillier today."

How thoughtful. I thanked him and laid the warm cloth over my legs.

THIRTY-THREE

Peony urged the horse on, and we started toward our first destination.

I glanced at Charlie sitting across from me. Even without knowing him well, I could see the anticipation sparkling in his ocean-blue eyes.

"I hope everyone will look forward to this celebration," I said.

He smiled widely, and a dimple appeared in his cheek. "It has been over five years since we've celebrated Bealtaine, and even before that, the festivals weren't very good."

"You've lived here a long time, then. Were you born here?"

Charlie shook his head. "No, I was born in Undine Bay, in the ocean nearest Selkby."

I nodded thoughtfully. *So he did something to be cast out.* "Oh, I just thought you might have been because your cousin and mother live here as well."

His smile took on a sardonic air. "I didn't break any laws if that's what you're wondering."

"I'm sorry. I didn't mean to pry."

He waved away my words. "Most goblins don't much like talking about how they landed in Goblintown; most want to forget their pasts and start afresh. But I don't mind talking about it. I didn't do anything wrong. It was my brother."

He turned his head and stared out the open carriage; his gaze seemed not to see the buildings we passed. "I'm sure you know undines have a soft spot for humans."

He didn't look over to confirm I knew. "There's a very powerful family in Undine Bay. Since the sidhe can't live underwater, this family acts as the fiefdom's proxy. My family had worked as huntsmen for them for generations. The second son of the proxy lord took a human lover. He kept her close by in Selkby. I don't know how my brother met her. But he found out she was being held against her will, and he returned her to the human realm."

I could see where he was going and nodded solemnly.

"Well, because the human he had given his heart to had left him, the second son died."

"And your brother was blamed," I finished.

"Yes," he murmured. "My brother was sentenced to death, but that wasn't all. His actions were seen as a betrayal of my entire family. None of us were jailed, but we were all banished from Undine Bay."

I sighed. Every new story I heard about the goblins was filled with tragedy though I supposed that was to be expected. I was likely one of the only beings there of my own accord.

"No wonder your cousin was so worried about the idea of you taking a human lover," I said. *That experience would add more weight atop the innate danger he'd face.*

Charlie winced, and his eyes flicked to mine.

Unease wiggled in my stomach.

"But I do have a human lover," he whispered. "That's why my mother was complaining I haven't been to visit her. I see my lover every chance I get."

My chest tightened at his words, but I didn't scold him. I was in no place to judge what others did in the name of love. "She lives in the human realm?"

He bobbed his head. "She says she'd like to come here, but I don't think it's a good idea... It's dangerous in Tír for humans and Goblintown in particular. But"—his gaze dropped to his lap, and I had to strain to hear the rest—"I feel like I'm losing her. Every time I visit, she seems a little more distant. Is it acceptable for me to put her in danger to save my own life? If I truly loved her, I would be willing to die to protect her."

A sad little sigh escaped my lips. I leaned forward, encouraging him to look up at me. "Charlie," I said gently. "I know you want to protect her. And, yes, it can be dangerous for humans here. I know that better than anyone. But if she's saying she's willing to take that risk to be with you, then you should bring her here. You're both suffering while apart. Together you will both be stronger and more able to deal with whatever challenges you encounter."

"You...you think so?" His eyes held a vulnerability that pleaded for me to affirm his hopes.

I smiled. "With my whole heart."

"She would love to see what we're doing for Bealtaine," he reasoned.

"Bealtaine is a time of new beginnings. But honestly, she would probably just be happy wherever you are, Charlie."

He leaned forward in his seat, bowing his head low. "Thank you, Your Majesty. I will discuss this with her."

"You do that, and when you bring her here, be sure to

introduce us. I haven't met many other humans in my life, and I'd love to meet her."

His dimple reappeared. "I will."

It wasn't more than a minute later that Peony stopped in front of a tailor's shop called Buttons and Spools.

Charlie hopped out of the carriage first, then handed me down.

Standing in the street, I could see my reflection in the small shop window and used it to fix my hair, which had been swept out of place during the ride. Then I straightened my cloak and skirts. It was my first official visit to town as the goblin queen, or prospective goblin queen rather; I wanted to present myself in such a way that would reflect well on myself, Aodh, and the goblins in general.

I smiled at my reflection, then turned to Charlie with a nod. "All right. Let's see what they have for us here."

THIRTY-FOUR

Rather than a bell ringing to announce our entrance into Buttons and Spools, a sort of hollow wood-on-wood sound clanked from overhead. I looked up to see wooden wind chimes swaying above the door.

The shop was similar in appearance to the tailor's shop my brother frequented in Piskishire. There were shelves with bolts of fabric along one wall, three angled mirrors at the back, and a counter—where a sylph clerk was accepting a stack of gold coins from a patron whose back was to us.

I tilted my head. As far as I could tell, no fabric on display would be so costly as to require that level of payment. But I brushed the feeling aside. *I should be glad this Goblintown business is doing so well. Perhaps this customer ordered a lot of things, and that's why his bill was so high.*

The sylph looked over at us, and his solid form flickered, turning wispy around the edges, as his grey eyes widened.

His gaze snapped from Charlie to me. "Why, Your Majesty." He bowed with an easy smile. "How honored I am the goblin queen has come to my little shop. What can I do for you?"

The customer who'd just paid the sylph shop owner glanced over his shoulder at me. He audibly gasped, and my chest tightened upon recognizing the sidhe.

"Melody?"

"Brochfael," I said at the same time.

A slimy smirk spread across his face, and I stifled my grimace.

"Well, well, Lady Melody Píobaire, what an interesting development. The goblin queen, is it? And to think, I almost didn't come to Goblintown today."

I hoped my expression was as stony as my cool voice suggested. "Viscount Hepsly, why *are* you in Goblintown exactly? I thought you only patronized the King's tailor in Sifra. I recall you making a big deal about it at the Winter Equinox Ball."

His pale face flushed. "Oh, this isn't for me. This is for our servants. You know how my father likes to support goblin-owned businesses."

I nodded. "Lord Kelpania was quite active in Goblintown in the past. But I had no idea he still was, especially after his unfortunate scandal."

Brochfael squinted his sea-glass green eyes at me. "Speaking of scandals, Lady Melody. I wonder what King Lorccán will say when he finds out you've become the goblin queen. From what I saw last month, I thought you were his mistress already."

I clenched my jaw, and Brochfael's smirk returned. Brochfael didn't know I'd long been promised to Lorccán, but there had been no mistaking the King's behavior when last we met.

"Or was the King not satisfied with your quality? You

couldn't hope to compare to the grace and beauty of Queen Lilliana, of course. But I would have thought you were qualified enough to carry the future king at the very least."

I snorted. That sort of insult would have really hurt me before I'd met Aodh. Now, I didn't much care whether others thought I was suited for Lorccán or not. "Your family has always been liberal with flattery. I hope the Queen appreciates your gilded words and that your tongue doesn't get tired from all the boots you've been licking."

He wrinkled his nose. "How I've missed you since you've been away," he said flatly. "But this is likely the last time we'll be seeing each other, isn't it? As the goblin queen, you have no place at court." He shook his head, clicking his tongue rapidly. "You could have held the highest status a human like yourself could hope for... How sad."

I smiled sweetly. "I guess that's a benefit I hadn't considered—I no longer have to tolerate you. Thank you so much for pointing that out to me."

Brochfael frowned. He'd never been good at getting the last word.

"Do give my regards to those at court," I said, clearly dismissing him. "I trust my friends will be as happy as I am at my new station."

With one last glower, Brochfael left without another word.

I held in my sigh. Brochfael wasn't wrong. Lorccán wouldn't be happy, and it would only be worse coming from someone else. I internally kicked myself for having not written that letter. How much time did I have before Brochfael opened his big mouth?

Lifting my chin, I turned to the shop owner, who'd watched the whole exchange with as much interest as one would expect.

He'd removed the gold coins from his counter while I'd sparred with Brochfael. *Why was Brochfael really here?*

"I've come in today to see if you have any spare fabric you wouldn't mind donating to make ribbons for the samcenn-pole. The Goblin King has charged me with planning a Bealtaine celebration for Goblintown."

"Ah." The sylph's expression opened with realization. His eyes flicked toward Charlie for a moment before returning to me. "If it's for such an honorable cause, I can do much better than just scraps. I'll give an entire bolt of whatever fabric you choose, Your Majesty."

I hesitated. *I know he was just given a lot of gold, but that's generosity bordering on suspicious. Kathleen had made it sound like Goblintown businesses were struggling though I suppose they're in different trades. Even so…* I waved my hand at him. "Oh, no. I couldn't ask for that. Just odds and ends are fine. I wouldn't want to hurt your business by taking too much."

With yet another glance at Charlie, the sylph dipped his head. "I appreciate your consideration, Your Majesty. Wait here for a moment while I gather what I can from the back."

The sylph disappeared in a puff of air, and I jumped—air elementals always disconcerted me when they did that.

I glanced over at Charlie, who frowned severely in thought. "What's going on?" I whispered.

His serious tone reflected his expression. "He's up to something," he murmured.

I nodded but didn't ask more. It wasn't a safe place to discuss it. One never really knew when air elementals were listening in.

THIRTY-FIVE

E ven without giving me an entire bolt of cloth, the sylph donated much more than I'd expected. I frowned at the basket of fabric sitting beside me in the carriage.

"What do you think is going on?" I asked Charlie while Peony drove us to the next location.

Charlie sighed through his nose. "Tac used to run his shop on Redcap Row."

I tilted my head. "Why would a tailor's shop need to do that?"

He shook his head. "We could never figure that out. We suspected he was also being hired as a contract killer, but we never had any solid evidence. Tell me, do you think this Viscount Hepsly would put a price on someone's head?"

I thought hard. *His family doesn't have any qualms about indentured servitude or bribery, but murder?* Even though Brochfael was Lord Kelpania's son, I couldn't imagine that a boy I grew up with would have someone killed. *Who would he even be trying to kill?* "I honestly don't know," I answered. "Let's both ask around and see what we can figure out."

Charlie nodded.

I replayed my exchange with Brochfael in my head, looking for any clues as to why he was really in Goblintown. I cringed at his reminder of the last ball I'd attended in Sifra.

~

The equinox moon shined through the crystal ceiling of the grand ballroom, bouncing off the golden walls in such a way it looked like broad daylight.

The day had been full of festivities, which were now culminating in a ball at the palace. It felt strange to see the equinox activities celebrated by all those around me. My family had kept up our traditions in our household, but I'd gotten used to the traditions of Olympus.

I stood against the wall, watching the sidhe dance in hypnotic circles around the room. Though it wasn't my first party since returning to Tír, I hadn't yet rekindled the friendships from my youth. Everyone was pleasant, of course, but we'd all grown and changed. We were essentially strangers.

Even above the music and chatter, I could hear my brother laugh. He was chatting with Lady Puckford and her daughter not far from me. Even at that distance, I could see Lady Fern's delight at his attention. I wondered if I would have a sister-in-law before long.

"Lady Melody," a smooth voice greeted, and I turned to acknowledge its owner.

My heart skipped a beat as Lorccán smiled down at me. I lowered my head and dipped in a curtsy. "Your Majesty."

"Are you enjoying the party, my lady? I noticed you have yet to take to the dance floor."

I lowered my eyes. "I fear my full belly from the generous feast you served has made me languid."

Lorccán reached out and lifted my chin with his curled forefinger. "Do let me see your pretty face, my lady. It is one of the perks of holding such an event after all."

My cheeks flushed at his compliment. After over ten years without seeing him, I was still taken aback by the change in his attitude toward me. Gone was the Lorccán of my childhood. Gone was that brother-like sweetness. He was more and more blatant with every conversation we'd had since my return. I met his gaze as directed. His nearly emerald eyes held a hunger I couldn't get used to.

"Your eyes are such a beautiful color. It's a shame they hold such sadness though I must admit wistful melancholy suits you as well. I was under the impression that whatever has kept you away for an additional cycle was over now. Will you tell me what troubles you?"

But for all his power and wealth, the sidhe king couldn't help me. The truth was, my heart was broken. Since Graeme had told me what he'd done, I'd been hopelessly drifting about my life. Aodh wasn't coming for me; he'd either forgotten me or hated me for abandoning him. And I couldn't seem to get over it. I was trying my best to move on as my brother had urged. I was trying to reconcile myself to what was expected of me, but my heart just wasn't letting go.

"I appreciate your concern, Your Majesty," I murmured.

He raised an eyebrow when I didn't answer his question. "Are we not close enough for you to share your worries with me, Lady Melody? It wounds me to think so."

I resisted the urge to squirm. His tone was friendly, perhaps a touch sad, even a little playful.

"I apologize, Your Majesty." I tried to give him a reassuring smile. "I'm fine. Really," I insisted, lowering my face again.

He stepped closer to me and hooked my chin with his finger. And when he lifted my head once more, his face was inches from mine.

My stomach fluttered as my heart jumped into my throat. I shifted my gaze to glance at all the fae who may be watching us.

"Look at me," he whispered gently, holding my chin in place.

I met his eyes—heated with an intensity I didn't know how to take from him.

"I'd like us to get a lot closer than we are. I thought we were close enough that you would tell me all your worries and fears. But it seems I must prove myself to you yet. You're a beautiful human, Melody, and I know you'll make an excellent mother. I hope it is not self-doubt that makes you pull away. I pray you know that with me, you will never want for anything."

I trembled at his words, at his gaze, at his touch. I licked my lips. "O-of course I trust you, Your Majesty. Thank you. I will endeavor to be all you expect of me."

He quirked his mouth in a smirk. "I understand your reticence. I have known you long enough to recognize when you're being shy." He trailed his fingers down my arm, his smile widening when it reached the bangle he'd given me on my thirteenth birthday. He lowered his voice to a gentle caress. "Don't be afraid, Melody. I will be gentle with you."

I couldn't help feeling this was all wrong. I wanted to be loved—not just desired. And as I stared into the sidhe king's eyes, I wondered if he could give me that. For all his promises I would need for nothing, was he even considering what I needed most of all?

"May I kiss you, Melody?" he murmured.

I frowned and nodded.

But when his lips brushed mine, everything within me screamed. *This is wrong!*

He smiled, clearly pleased. He'd effectively just announced to all present he would take me as his mistress. There was no need to hide our arrangement anymore.

I wanted to cry; I could feel the tears welling up inside me as my chest tightened.

"You're trembling," he said, a hint of concern in his tone. "I apologize for taking your first kiss in such a public way. I just couldn't help myself."

I didn't dare tell him that wasn't my first kiss.

Reaching up, he stroked the hair at the top of my head. "I will always take care of you."

Grabbing my hand, he pressed a more formal kiss to my knuckles. "Dream of me this night, Melody. Dream of me and all I can give you. I will make you a banshee. And as a woman of the sidhe, you will be given abilities beyond your imaginings."

I shivered at his words. Many times in my life I'd wanted the magical abilities of the fae around me. And, for most of my childhood, I knew becoming a banshee was my future. I knew one day I would be given abilities—even if just a small amount—through my connection with Lorccán. But as I stared into his lustful eyes, I no longer wanted them. If it meant letting a man other than Aodh possess me, if it meant letting someone else claim me as his own, I'd rather remain the powerless human I'd always been.

CHAPTER

THIRTY-SIX

The rest of our visits to tailors, seamstresses, and fabric shops around Goblintown went much more smoothly. One seamstress was reluctant to donate her scraps because she used excess fabric for patchwork hair ribbons, waistbands, and coin purses. But she did donate a few spools of thread. She also volunteered to organize music for the celebration. She knew many musicians in Goblintown.

Overall, the trip into town was a success. I was sure I had enough fabric to make ribbons for the samcenn-pole. But after the visit to Buttons and Spools, I couldn't get my mind off Brochfael and what he was doing there. Was he hiring Tac to kill someone? If so, whom? Would he tell Lorccán I had jilted him before I had the chance to tell him the truth?

Once we returned to the palace, Charlie helped me carry our donations up to my reception room.

The walls of the queen's reception room were the color of green gooseberries while the few chairs around the perimeter of the room and the two settees near the fireplace were upholstered in dusty pink.

We found Eithne in the center of the floor, fabric spread out in front of her as she cut it into strips. Charlie put down his load and left us to our task.

With a sense of urgency, I went to my workroom to write my letter to Lorccán—hoping against all odds it would reach him before Brochfael did. My stomach clenched, and I felt a bit queasy, but my discomfort at causing him pain was pushed aside by the fact that hearing it from Brochfael would be so much worse. Instead of addressing it formally with "Sir" as was expected when writing to the king, I chose the more personal approach I'd used in my past letters.

Dear Lorccán,

I take no pleasure in writing this. I pray you know I would never wish to do anything that might cause you upset. However, I can only live true to my own heart. The truth is I love another. The whole of the matter comes down to that. You have always been kind to me and treated me with great affection. I shamelessly ask that I might impose on that sentiment.

I know there are a great many in Faerie who would gladly take my place at your side. I wish only for your true happiness, and I hope you trust me when I say you will never find that with me as your mistress.

You have always been a good friend, and I know you wish for my true happiness as well.

I have the honor to remain Your Majesty's humble and obedient subject.

With the warmest of regards,
Melody Píobaire

After sealing my message with my father's family crest, I asked Odilie to post it.

Eithne and I spent most of the rest of the day and into the evening cutting all the fabric and piling the strips into sections so all we had left to do was sew. The busy work did little to put my mind at ease.

Odilie eventually delivered the list of volunteers, and I met with each one to assign them to help Charlie with gathering wood, help make the bannocks, or take some fabric to sew ribbons.

Despite my full and productive day, my sleep was fitful, my mind spinning with too many thoughts and concerns. I awoke late the following day, and though I was grateful to have finally rested, I was disappointed I'd slept past Aodh's walk in the garden. But as Eithne had not roused me, I assumed he had not called for me.

After dressing, applying my anti-kelpie patch, and eating breakfast, Eithne and I returned to my reception room, each taking a small pile of fabric to sew. Tadhg—in his cat form—had initially complained he couldn't sit in my lap, but he eventually settled on the settee beside me, taking the seat closest to the fire. We were working diligently when Aodh walked in without preamble.

We both started and rose to our feet. The fabric that had rested in my lap fell to the floor.

Aodh glanced around the room, taking in the many short stacks of fabric piled up and down the large space. "Odilie told me you have a lot of sewing to do, so I thought I would come to you for our daily meeting."

I smiled. "That's very thoughtful of you, Your Majesty. Would you please excuse us, Eithne?"

Eithne nodded and placed her unfinished ribbon on the table beside her before leaving.

Aodh crossed the room and sat on the settee Eithne had just left. I returned to my seat, picking up my dropped project and placing it back on my lap.

"You seem to have accomplished your goal from yesterday's trip into town," he said.

I smiled. "Would you like to hear about how the preparations are going for Bealtaine?"

His expression said he did not, but he nodded regardless.

"Actually, before that"—I placed the ribbon I was working on aside—"There are a few more important things I'd like to discuss with you."

He frowned. "More important than the task I assigned you?"

"As important as I believe bringing the goblins joy with this celebration is, yes, I think fulfilling their basic needs even more so. You did not address most of my petition the other day."

His expression turned from bland to cold. "I'm well aware of the promises I made to the fae of Goblintown. But improvements to roads, schools, and hospitals take money, which would require higher taxes. I cannot, in good conscience, raise their taxes knowing many of them have lost income."

"I'm not criticizing you, Your Majesty. I'm merely bringing the concerns of your citizens to your attention. I agree with you that the violent professions of Redcap Row needed to stop, but we must figure out a way to bring outsiders to Goblintown again or else request aid from King Lorccán."

Aodh scowled. "The sidhe king cares not for goblins. The only time he even acknowledges us is to collect our taxes."

"Does he take all the taxes you collect and give nothing back? Is that why you took to selling the palace's valuables?"

He wrinkled his nose. "Does my austere dwelling not suit your tastes, Lady Melody?"

"On the contrary, Your Majesty," I replied calmly. "I find it honorable and refreshing that someone in power would put his people before himself. What good are tapestries, paintings, and fine dishes if those around you are suffering?"

Aodh's dark eyes analyzed me, but I met them unflinchingly.

"Well, to answer your question, no. The sidhe king gives Goblintown nothing. And upon realizing this after a few years and many unanswered requests for aid, I have ceased paying taxes to him. Goblintown needs that money more than he does. If he will not provide for us, then we must provide for ourselves as best we can."

I can't imagine Lorccán refusing to help the goblins. There must be some misunderstanding. "I'm worried, Your Majesty. It does not seem to be enough and…" I hesitated.

He met my eyes again, and for a moment, I couldn't get air enough to finish. He was seeing me, waiting for me to speak as if he cared about what I would say.

"I fear violent criminality still lurks in Goblintown. When I went into town yesterday, Charlie and I may have witnessed payment for a contract killing."

Aodh leaned forward in his seat. "Tell me what you saw."

"We were at—"

A shuffling followed by raised voices outside my reception room door interrupted me.

There was a rapid knock just as Graeme burst into the room with the grin of a jaunty hero, Selwyn glowering over his shoulder.

My heart leapt at the arrival of my brother, and I rushed toward him. "Graeme!"

Tadhg looked up at my outburst, glanced over at my brother, and returned to his nap.

"Yes, dear sister, it is I," he declared, wrapping his arms around me when I reached him. "Come to see how you're settling into your new household."

"It has been only seven days since her arrival," Selwyn muttered under his breath.

As an overwhelming relief washed over me, I thought I might cry. I hadn't realized just how alone I'd felt until Graeme smiled down at me.

"Well?" my brother asked. "Where is this Goblin King you had your heart set on?"

I flinched. Graeme knew none of us could reveal I was Mischief. But knowing my brother, he knew exactly what he could get away with without tripping the spell.

Aodh approached where we stood, and the two men nodded to each other.

"I've heard much about you, brother-in-law," Graeme said, a bite in his tone despite his smile.

I nudged him in the side with my elbow.

Aodh glanced over at me, clearly wondering what I could have told my brother about him.

"I'll leave you to your guest," he said, his cool demeanor returning. "But I expect to continue this conversation later."

THIRTY-SEVEN

"So what's going on?" Graeme asked after he shut the door to his guest room. "I didn't think you'd need my help already."

I glanced around the space, so bare and unadorned compared to the other rooms in the queen's wing. Sighing heavily, I turned to my brother, who leaned against the mantel of the cold fireplace.

"Every step of this has been a struggle. Aodh doesn't want a wife; he's effectively rejected me in every way he can."

Graeme raised his eyebrows. "*Every* way?"

My face flushed. "I don't even want to talk about it. He called me out in front of an assembly of goblins, telling me I'm not worthy to be goblin queen. And now I only have until the summer solstice to prove I exude goblin virtues."

"Goblins have virtues?" he muttered.

I scowled at him. "I managed to negotiate a little time with him every day in exchange for accepting his challenge. But he isn't keen to open up to me."

"So what do you need me for? How am I supposed to convince him to let you in?"

I shook my head. "I've barely had a chance to spend time with him, and every moment we have together is interrupted by Selwyn."

"Ah, the kelpie with the grumpy demeanor."

"I suppose that's one way of describing him. I need you to stop him from interfering. I don't know how persistent he'll be, though."

A smirk spread across Graeme's face. "Not as persistent as I am. But why do you think he's trying to stop you? Is he worried about losing influence?"

I gestured toward my brother. "See! That's what I thought too, but when I confronted him about it, he said I didn't belong with Aodh. Whatever that means." I bit my lip in thought. *Does Selwyn hate humans?*

When my gaze met Graeme's, he smirked. "Perhaps I should get close to him and find out. He prefers men; I don't have a preference. I can easily distract him with a little tryst."

I sucked in a breath. "How can you be sure?"

Graeme's expression was one of amusement. "I'm sure, believe me."

I frowned. "But is seducing him such a good idea? I mean, as much as I want him to give us space, I don't want you to mess with his heart."

My brother rolled his eyes. "Give me a little credit, will you? I'm not going to force him to do something he doesn't want to. I'm just going to convince him to play with me. Besides, he's adorable, and I kind of like that grumpy expression. He's going to be a challenge." He shrugged. "And if I'm really not his type, then I'll distract him in other ways. Though, that would be far less interesting."

I thought about it for a moment, then nodded.

Graeme tilted his head. "Anything else I should know?"

I shook my head. "Ah! Actually, what's the news from Lord Kelpania and his family lately? I saw Brochfael in a Goblintown tailor's shop yesterday, and he gave the clerk a stack of gold."

Graeme squinted, sucking his teeth. "A tailor's shop? That's unusual. There's no way he'd buy clothes in Goblintown."

"And unlikely they'd cost that much if he did," I added. "One of the palace guards suggested he might be putting a contract out on someone."

My brother blinked in surprise, then his expression darkened. "I'll quietly look into it."

"Do you think we should tell Dad?"

Graeme didn't answer for a long time, his steady gaze fixed on the floor in thought. "Maybe. But we don't have much information just yet. Let me ask around first. Besides" —he looked up to meet my eyes—"Dad isn't really in a steady mood since you left."

My heart grew heavy. I'd never wanted to hurt my family. "Is he... Do you think he'll be all right?"

Graeme sighed. "I'm sure he'll be fine eventually. He's worried about what the King will do. But I think he just misses you more than anything. He was glad to receive your letter—glad you were relying on him for something."

I nodded. "Is he going to help Eithne's sister?"

"Of course, he is. Since we don't have any vacant positions, he sent a letter of inquiry to the King's household. He thinks he'll be able to secure her a position in the royal archives. Though, we don't know how much longer we'll have such influence once you tell the King what you've done... *Have* you told him yet?"

I dropped my head in a nod. "I sent him a letter yesterday."

My brother hummed. "Well, that should make the letter he sent you interesting reading, then." Graeme went to his trunk and pulled out a sealed paper, offering it to me. "It arrived yesterday morning."

Before I sent mine. My heart squeezed as I took the rough paper from my brother.

"Hey," he said, pulling my attention back to him. "Let's just worry about one thing at a time. You've got a goblin king's heart to win, and I've got a grumpy kelpie to seduce. Everything else is a later-problem."

I snorted. My brother never worried about anything that wasn't staring him in the face. I'd always admired his carefree attitude amid threats and turmoil.

"Well, I've already had my allotted time with Aodh today, but I suppose I should get back to sewing the ribbons for the samcenn-pole." I walked to the door and opened it before looking back at him. "Shall we meet for supper?"

Graeme smirked a suggestive little smirk. "If I'm not already busy with Selwyn by then."

"Pfft, even you aren't *that* charming."

THIRTY-EIGHT

Graeme was the only one to join me for supper in the dining room that evening, which didn't surprise me.

"Didn't have much luck with Selwyn, I take it?" I asked before bringing my goblet to my lips.

My brother snorted. "Probably more than you've had with your elf."

I let that comment pass as he continued.

"Busy little bee, that kelpie. He flitted here and there all day. I'm not quite sure what he actually does, to be honest. He paid me little mind, but worry not, I'll find a way in. What about you? What's your plan for getting closer to the Goblin King?"

I sighed. "The trouble is I don't know what the right approach is. We fell in love so easily before; it just happened naturally."

"As it usually does," Graeme chimed.

"In some ways, he's just the same as he was when we were younger. He's still kind—even if not to me. He cares about the well-being of the goblins. He's grown into the man he wanted to be."

"But?"

"In other ways, he's completely different—or at least it appears that way. Toward me, he's cold, adversarial, and cruel with his words. I'm certain much of his animosity is because I forced my way into the position of goblin queen. But it feels like more than that. He's been goblin king for over five years and—from what I'm to understand—has shown no inclination to take a queen. I'm worried that when I left him without a word, I hurt him so much he's distrustful and no longer interested in love."

He frowned, lowering the food he was about to put in his mouth. "You have an awfully high opinion of yourself. People fall in and out of love many times in their lives. Do you really think he's still holding on to that hurt after all this time?"

My heart panged at his words, and my answer sounded sad even to me. "Was I not holding onto him all this time? When I found out he wasn't coming, did I not fall into desolation? If he loved me even half as much as I love him, he couldn't have let go so easily."

His eyes filled with sympathy. "I'm sorry, Melody."

I gave my brother a sorry excuse for a smile. "I'm not looking for an apology, Graeme. I've told you already I know you did it out of love. I don't hold it against you, and I'm glad you're here to help me."

My brother nodded slowly.

"Right now, I want to show him how good I'll be as the goblin queen. It's not as romantic as I was hoping for, but until I can get him to open up to me a bit more, it's the best chance I have."

Graeme quirked his mouth. He'd never been a

proponent of the force-Aodh-into-marriage plan. He'd suggested I simply appear before him, ask him to marry me, and accept his response—whatever that response might be. But then, he likely would have been happier if I'd been outright rejected and forced to move on with my life. I wasn't willing to take that chance.

"Well, I'll try to help you by distracting Selwyn at least. Perhaps all you need is some uninterrupted time with him— time for him to get to know you for who you are."

If only it will be that easy. "Thank you."

Scraping the last bite from his plate, Graeme stood from his chair. "In light of that, I think I'll try to catch him before he leaves. Perhaps he'll allow me to escort him home."

I wished him good luck while he departed.

After my brother left, the dining room felt too large and empty. The crackling fire sounded soft and feeble despite its bright flames. It echoed the loneliness that swept over me. And I was reminded why I usually took my meals in my bedroom.

I rose from the table, my plate only half-finished, to retire for the night. Perhaps it was still too early. But my hands were sore from all the sewing I'd done that day. I felt a hot bath and my favorite book were just the cure for the ache in my heart.

After Eithne had drawn my bath, I dismissed her for the night, telling her I would ready myself for bed.

I soaked until the water turned cold, then hurriedly dressed in a nightgown and robe. Settling myself near the roaring fire in my hearth, I let the heat seep into me while I pulled a comb through my damp hair.

The room was quiet, and the only light came from the dancing flames. Leaning forward in my seat to better allow my hair to dry, I stared into the light.

How often had I sat just like that, longing for Aodh in a foreign land? And still, under the same roof, it was no different. He was no closer to me than he had been for the last two cycles, not really.

Was I just an idealistic fool to have thought his heart would recognize mine? What had I hoped for?

Despite the heat warming my skin, a shiver ran through me. My eyes caught Lorccán's letter, which I'd placed on the mantel. With a sigh, I retrieved it and broke the seal.

My beautiful Melody,

I cannot express how disappointed I was you did not attend the Duke and Duchess of Westcount's party on the full moon. I hope you are recovered from whatever ailed you. I asked your parents if they would allow me to send my court healer, but they assured me you were merely tired.

Has it truly only been a month since I saw you at the ball, since I tasted your sweet lips on mine? My heart still flutters to think of it.

Every night, when all is quiet in the palace, I think of how you trembled under my fingertips—how soft your skin was, how bright your eyes. My mind lingers on what I might do to please you.

I have promised to be gentle, and my word is good. But the longer I wait for you to come to me at last, the more my blood heats.

Please, if you have any affection for me at all, put me out of my misery. Agree to my proposal that you become my royal mistress this Bealtaine night.

Yours in sweet agony,
Lorccán

My face felt hot, and not from the effect of the fire, as I tried to remember how to swallow. I'd never received such an explicit letter from Lorccán before. It made me question whether he would accept my refusal at all.

A gentle knock sounded on my door, and I pulled my gaze from the page. *Did Eithne forget something?*

I rose from my chair and went to the door, my bare feet cold when pulled away from the fire's heat.

My heart nearly exploded when I beheld Aodh standing there.

He cleared his throat, his expression smooth and professional. "May I come in?"

CHAPTER
THIRTY-NINE

So shocked was I at Aodh's sudden arrival, and in my bedroom no less, that I didn't have the wherewithal to greet him properly.

His gaze traveled over me, taking in my damp hair, my robe, my bare feet, and the King's letter still in my hand. "Shall I wait until tomorrow?"

"No!" I flinched at my outburst. "Forgive me, Your Majesty. Please, come in."

He stepped inside when I held the door open, and I closed it behind him, hastily refolding Lorccán's letter.

My heart beat wildly as I turned to him. His strong back seemed much broader than I remembered from only a few hours before. The firelight brought out the red in his long hair, which was splayed over his shoulders.

He glanced back at me, and my face flushed when his dark eyes met mine in the intimate hush of my bedroom.

"I would like to finish the discussion we started earlier," he explained.

I took a steadying breath. *What had I been thinking he*

was here for? Lorccán's words must have muddled my thoughts. "Of course, Your Majesty. Would you like to sit?" Putting the letter on the chair I'd been sitting in when he arrived, I rushed over to the other chair by the window and lifted it to move it nearer the fire.

I didn't get two steps before Aodh took it from me, placing it facing mine. I angled mine to face his, then lowered myself into it, holding the letter in my lap.

But as the quiet firelight flickered beside us, I couldn't meet his eyes. I didn't know why I was so self-conscious to have him in my space, and I marveled I'd ever been bold enough to enter his.

"You said you saw something while in town with Charlie," Aodh prompted. His voice was steady and too loud in the hushed setting.

I nodded. "Yes, Charlie and I went to a tailor shop called Buttons and Spools." The more I talked, the more comfortable I became. "We found a sidhe paying the owner a large stack of gold coins."

When he didn't respond, I looked up to meet his gaze. He sat, thoughtful and passive. Then he frowned. "And so you thought something untoward was happening?"

"W-well, the fabric on display in the shop didn't look very expensive, and I know for a fact this sidhe wouldn't buy clothing from a goblin tailor."

His eyes sharpened. "You know this sidhe, then?"

I bobbed my head. "Yes, I've known him most of my life."

"And you don't believe he would frequent Goblintown?"

I hummed an indecisive sound. "It's not that he wouldn't come to Goblintown. It's that he wouldn't come here for clothes. He's sort of a gallant, and the last time I saw him, he made a big deal about only buying from King Lorccán's tailor."

"Did you confront him on this point?"

"I asked him what he was doing in town, and he said he was buying clothes for his servants."

"But you don't think that's the case?"

I was starting to feel like it was more of an interrogation and less of a conversation. "I think this sidhe and his family have never been up to anything good in Goblintown, and Charlie agreed something strange was going on. He's the one who told me this shop used to be on Redcap Row, that this owner was suspected as a contract killer, but it was never confirmed."

Aodh didn't answer for a while, and when he did, his tone softened a little, clearly trying to put me more at ease. "What was his family up to in the past?"

With that question, I lamented that Aodh and I had never gone into details about why my brother frequented Goblintown so many years ago. Then again, with my father's binding, would I have even been able to answer if it gave too much away?

"Did you hear anything about the scandal surrounding Lord Kelpania? It was a few years before you became goblin king."

Aodh considered my question, his eyes losing focus as he thought back.

"He's an earl, but he also owns a ship-building company," I said, trying to jog his memory. "He was hiring goblins at abysmal rates, effectively indenturing them."

His face lit with recognition. "Ah, yes. I recall now. There was some talk in town about a way to get out from under him, and he eventually stopped coming around."

I nodded. "At the time, my father tried to buy out as

many goblin contracts as he could and find them better places to work. In the end, Lord Kelpania was found out and fined a pittance, but he was never really brought to justice. The sidhe I saw at Buttons and Spools was Lord Kelpania's son, Viscount Brochfael Hepsly."

Aodh pursed his lips ever so slightly, and the expression distracted me from my story.

Warmth spread through me as I thought about the last time I'd kissed them.

"It sounds to me like your family and his are rivals."

I blinked at his implication. Was he doubting my information was sound? I snorted, and all trace of desire drained out of me. "I suppose you could put it like that. But that's the way of the sidhe court. All the sidhe are rivals for the King's favor. You could be best friends and undermining each other still. You could be poaching employees from each other while arranging for your children to marry. For all its glamour and polish, it's a savage place."

Aodh's dark eyes watched me carefully as if my defensiveness, my sharp tone, fascinated him.

"Is that what happened, then? Did your father poach his father's employees while arranging for you to marry him?"

I clicked my tongue. "My father didn't poach anyone. Most of the goblins he helped didn't work for us. And, no, I was never in talks to marry Brochfael."

Aodh quirked an eyebrow. "Your tone suggests you were in talks with someone else."

I bit my lip at his statement. *I didn't want to tell him this until he had warmer feelings for me, but I guess he should probably know sooner rather than later.*

"I wasn't in talks to marry anyone…but I was promised from a young age to the Crown Prince, King Lorccán now."

FORTY

Aodh's mouth dropped open. No longer did he wear his bland mask of indifference, and gone was his little glint of curiosity. He was clearly and plainly shocked.

But that shock didn't last long as he shot from his seat, taking two powerful strides away before charging back toward me.

"What is this?" he growled, gripping the arms of the chair I sat in while standing over me. "Why are you *really* here? Are you an agent for the sidhe king? A spy?"

I gasped, confused in the face of his animosity. "Why would I tell you he wanted me for his mistress if that were the case? Why would I offer that information?"

"Why would you choose to come here if the highest rank in Tír for a human was being offered you?" he snapped. "What? Are you using me to get out of an unwanted match? Sure, run off to live with the goblins. He won't want you after you've so sullied yourself. Is that it?"

"No! It's because I love you! I've only ever loved you.

And I would rather die than be another man's mistress." I breathed heavily, my heart pounding as I stared into the angry face of the fae I loved. "Cast a truth spell on me, an elf should have no trouble with a spell like that. Ask me anything you like. But don't"—my voice broke as emotion rose in my throat—"don't ever doubt my feelings for you." I finished in a hushed plea, gazing into his dark eyes, which blazed in the firelight.

His rage eased into uncertainty. "Why?" he murmured, his face mere inches from mine. "You don't even know me."

"I know everything I need to know about you." I repeated the words he'd spoken to me all those years ago, wishing without hope they would spark something inside him.

But he didn't seem to recognize them. He pulled away, sighing heavily. "How could one small human be so very troublesome?"

They don't call me Mischief for nothing. "My brother has expressed the same sentiment many a time, Your Majesty."

He sank back into the chair across from me. "Speaking of, how long will your brother be staying with us?"

My heart thrilled at his word choice—*us.* "I can't rightly say. He's quite protective of me. He just wants to ensure I'm healthy and happy. I'm sure he'll go once he confirms I am."

He met my eyes, and I could practically hear his questions. *Are you happy? How can you be when you're not welcome here? Hadn't you better just go home to your loving family?* But he didn't give any of them voice.

He sighed again, resting his forehead in his hand. "You realize you've brought trouble to Goblintown. The sidhe king is likely already displeased with me having not paid our taxes, and now he'll think I've stolen his mistress."

"I've written to him and told him in no uncertain terms that I'm in love with someone else. He'll let me go."

He eyed the letter still in my lap. "Is that his reply?"

I shook my head. "No. It is from him, but he wouldn't have gotten my message before sending this one."

"May I read it?"

I blinked in surprise.

"If you're truly not a spy, then you won't mind. Will you?"

"As you wish." I offered him the letter without hesitation.

With every passing moment, I saw Aodh's face get redder and redder. Finally, he cleared his throat, offering me the paper without meeting my eyes. "He doesn't sound like he will accept your refusal with grace."

"He will. He won't force me when he realizes I'll only ever be yours."

His dark eyes met mine in the firelight. "You say the most ridiculous things," he muttered under his breath.

"But," I continued as if I hadn't heard him. "I am sorry if I've brought trouble to Goblintown. I'll endeavor to be worth more than I cost."

Aodh stood from his chair, and I did the same. "Yes, well, in regard to this sidhe friend of yours who visited yesterday, don't worry about it. I'll talk to Charlie and look into what's really going on."

I nodded. "My brother also said he would make inquiries. It may help for him to look into what Brochfael is up to from his end."

Aodh paused before agreeing. "Thank you for letting me know what you saw, and I apologize for keeping you from bed."

"Feel free to visit me anytime you wish, Your Majesty. I'll always be happy to receive you." I bowed to him respectfully.

He turned without acknowledging my words and made his way to the door; I followed him. But as he opened it to leave, he paused.

Without looking back at me, he murmured, "You should not be here, Lady Melody. Goblintown is no place for a woman like you, and I…I'm unsuitable to receive your affections. I hope you will take this trial time to carefully consider the kind of life you would have here. I cannot give you what you wish for."

And with that, he left, closing the door behind him with a soft yet final thud.

His words, spoken so gently, seeped slowly into me.

So it is that he doesn't want a wife, then. My chest tightened. *If he thinks I'm too good for Goblintown, it must mean he's more upset at the idea of getting married than me forcing his hand.*

My breath rushed out of me as tears welled in my eyes. It was my fault for abandoning him. What had I done to the only man I'd ever loved? How had he suffered because of me? Even if I hadn't done it on purpose, even if it was the last thing I ever wanted, I'd abandoned him—I'd broken him.

I knew what I needed to do.

I would be the best wife, the most constant and true lover, that anyone ever had. I would try to be the best queen Goblintown had ever seen. And no matter what he said to me, or how he pushed me away, I would not let it daunt me.

As I crawled into bed that night, my heart sore at the pain I'd caused him, I vowed he would never doubt me the way he'd doubted Mischief. I would make myself worthy of him. I would be clever, courageous, steadfast, and persistent. I would exemplify all the goblin virtues. I would heal his heart from the damage I'd caused.

CHAPTER

FORTY-ONE

The following days were busy and full as I worked with the staff to get everything ready for Bealtaine.

I met with Aodh every day; we mostly talked about my preparations, but I did try to nudge him into talking more about himself. He wasn't nearly as forthcoming as he had been in the past, so I told him about myself instead—as much as the binding would allow.

It was the first day of Samcenn, and the goblins again gathered to submit their petitions to their king. I peeked into the proceeding as I passed to head out the front door.

The days were getting perceptibly longer and warmer, and excitement was building as Bealtaine approached. I hadn't seen much of my brother, except for mealtimes, since he'd arrived. But I hadn't seen much of Selwyn either, so it was worth it.

Since Selwyn was busy assisting Aodh with petitions, Graeme had nothing to occupy him. So I'd asked him to take me into town to complete the last bit of organizing I had to prepare before our Bealtaine celebration.

He waited for me in the buggy, staring at the piles of wood in the front yard. They grew a little every day as Charlie and his group added more dry wood, which they collected during the night.

With a cloth-covered basket in hand, I pulled myself up into the buggy beside my brother.

"So where are we going?" he asked.

I glanced over at him. "To the orphanage. It's not far from here. I'll tell you the way."

Graeme scrunched his brow but didn't say anything. He urged the horse toward the front gate.

Charlie was on gate duty again, and he opened it for us to pass, waving as we did so.

"So how's your conquest going?" I asked my brother. "Whatever you're doing, it's giving Aodh and me some uninterrupted time together."

Graeme sighed through his nose. "He's a hard nut to crack, that kelpie. He wasn't very open to talking to me at first. I offered to buy him a drink as an apology for being impolite to him upon my arrival. It took a lot of coaxing, but once he got some alcohol in him, he loosened up a little. He's a great bundle of emotions—anger, grief, and self-pity all rolled into one. Personally, I think he's repressed, and I told him as much."

I tilted my head. "Oh? And how did he take that?"

Graeme smirked. "Like an invitation."

"Wasn't it?" I said, huffing a laugh.

"Of course, it was, not that he accepted."

"So what? You two have just been drinking together?"

Graeme scowled at me. "That was only the first night. I just needed a way to get him to talk to me."

"And has he?" I pointed to the left to indicate the direction he should go as we approached a crossroads.

"A little."

I clicked my tongue at his lack of specifics. "So you bought him a drink, talked about nothing, made a pass at him—which he refused—and that's all? What have you been doing all this time? It has been nearly half a month since you arrived."

My brother glanced at me before turning back to the road. "Is this how you've approached your seduction of the Goblin King? No wonder you haven't made much progress. Not everyone is comfortable jumping right into bed. Some feel like they need to get to know you first. They want to feel seen, listened to. So that's what I'm doing. I'm listening. And he's told me a great many things in very few veiled words. That's how I can come to the conclusions I have."

I pouted. "Sounds like you two have just been sitting staring at each other and saying very little. I could have told you he was a bundle of negative emotions."

"A comfortable silence is sometimes more useful than empty words. And maybe you knew he's a bundle of emotions, but you don't know their source. You don't know why he's so hostile toward you."

"And you do?"

He shrugged. "I have my suspicions."

I waited for a full minute, but he didn't break the silence. "Which are?"

"I'll keep them to myself until I'm certain."

I sighed heavily. "Can you tell me anything at all?"

Graeme frowned. "I can tell you how he became a goblin."

I sat up straighter, listening carefully as the buggy's wheels rattled over the uneven road.

"He killed his father."

I gasped, my mouth dropping open in shock. "What?" I

whispered. "He's a redcap? How was he released from prison if he killed someone and his own father at that? Patricide is way too serious a crime for him to be wandering around even in Goblintown."

He shook his head. "He never went to prison."

I swallowed the questions that flew around my brain, waiting impatiently for him to clarify.

"His father wanted to die. He was sick and in pain, and the healers couldn't help him. He begged Selwyn to kill him."

I blinked in surprise as sadness weighed on my heart. I couldn't imagine how horrible a situation that would be. "Is euthanasia illegal in Kelpania?"

Graeme shook his head. "No, they follow Tír's laws on that point. In fact, for the kelpies, it's a child's responsibility if this situation arises."

"But then, if he euthanized his father as kelpie custom demands, why is he in Goblintown?"

"I told you; he's a bundle of complicated emotions. He wasn't ostracized or shunned from Kelpania. According to him, everyone there was sympathetic and supportive. It seems that's what hurt him the most. Despite it being part of kelpie custom, he feels guilty. He blames himself as if he committed a crime."

"Ah…" I finally saw what must have happened. "So he exiled himself to Goblintown."

Graeme nodded. "He's rather an interesting fellow, don't you agree?"

I frowned. It had been easier to dislike the combative kelpie when I didn't know anything about him other than his treatment of me—not that his past hurts excused his bad behavior.

Motioning toward a large house at the very end of a residential street, I told my brother to pull up in front of it.

FORTY-TWO

We gazed at the house. It was two stories of unpainted wood, wider than it was tall. The stone garden wall in front showed recent signs of repair, but the gate hung a little crooked.

It seemed a quiet, somber place from the outside, and I wondered how often the children played in the front yard.

"Are you certain you don't want me to come with you?" Graeme asked from beside me.

I shook my head. "No, it's all right. Go ahead and make your inquiries about Brochfael, and pick me up when you're finished."

My brother agreed and climbed back into the buggy.

The clip-clop of the horse's hoofs on the street as he drove away wasn't even loud enough to cover the squeal of the gate when I opened it. It shut with an even louder clang.

The air of the place washed over me—an odd mixture of the innocence and joy of childhood and the struggle of poverty with the pain of abandonment. At that moment, I keenly felt the loss of my birth parents, whom I never had the chance to know. Why did they leave me out on the moors? Was I so inconvenient? Were they too poor to care for me? Did I have too many siblings to feed already?

I had, of course, wondered about such things in the past. But then, my adoptive family loved me. Those children— and Aodh—hadn't been so lucky.

Taking a deep breath, I raised my hand and knocked on the front door.

And then I waited. I stood on the front stoop for so long that I wondered if the place was abandoned. But eventually, the door clicked and opened to reveal a puck.

She blinked her hazel eyes at me, then smiled a tight-lipped smile—likely trying not to scare me off by showing her sharp teeth. "Yes? How may I help you?"

The tufted head of a selkie peeked out from around her skirt.

I smiled at the little girl, then turned my attention to the puck. "Hello, is now a good time? I'm in charge of the Bealtaine celebration and would like to discuss something with you."

Her eyes widened. "Are you the human who's to be our goblin queen?"

"I'm hoping to prove myself worthy of that position, yes."

"Oh!" The puck grinned, no longer hiding her teeth, not that it bothered me. "Please, come in. Now is the perfect time. The baby is sleeping, and the older children are still at school."

She stepped aside, and the little selkie didn't move fast enough to stay hidden.

The girl was still very young—her long, white hair only

just starting to silver at the roots. Her large, dark eyes expressed a mixture of curiosity and shyness.

"Hello," I said softly, nodding to her. "What's your name?"

She lowered her chin, peeking up at me as her hair fell into her face. "Marina," she whispered before rushing behind her guardian's skirts again.

"That's a lovely name," I told her. "I'm Melody."

The puck looked down at the girl, kind indulgence in her eyes. "This lady is going to marry Aodh, Marina. She's to be our queen."

Her tufted head appeared again, her eyes more and more curious. I couldn't help but giggle, and the puck joined me.

"This way, Your Majesty. We can talk in here." She gestured to a door on the left. "Marina, why don't you go see what Conláed and Gwilym are up to?"

Marina hesitated, then scurried up the wooden staircase.

While the matron opened the door, I glanced around the entrance area. As stark and uninviting as the exterior had been, the inside was warm and welcoming. The entrance hall was a cheery pink with needlework pieces hanging on the walls. From the varied quality of the art, I was certain the children had embroidered them.

"Come in," she said.

I followed her into a study, which had a sturdy desk in the center of the room and a wall of bookshelves at its rear.

"Can I offer you anything, Your Majesty? Some tea perhaps? We still have a little while before elevenses, but I can ask Gaye to make you something early." She sat in the chair behind the desk, leaving the one in front of it for me.

"Oh, no, thank you. I wouldn't want to put anyone out. I'll have some with everyone else if I'm still here."

She dipped her head. "Very well. I'm Eulalia, matron of

Goblintown's only orphanage. You said you'd like to discuss something about the Bealtaine celebration?"

I set my basket on the floor beside me. "Yes, I know His Majesty was raised here, and this place is very special to him."

Eulalia's eyes warmed. "Aodh has been very good to us since becoming goblin king. He's made sure everything is fixed, and no one goes hungry. He even hired some of the older children to work around the palace, and that little bit of money gives them much hope for the future."

I wondered who, other than Cináed, she could be talking about. But I took her at her word. "As you know, lighting the balefires is a big part of the Bealtaine celebration. It starts off the whole thing. I was hoping, if it isn't too late in the evening for them, the children could light their candles with the eternal flame at Robin Goodfellow's tomb and walk to the palace to light the balefires. It isn't very far, and as long as they have supervision, they should be safe."

Eulalia beamed at the suggestion. "Oh, they would love that. Such an important job, and at the first Bealtaine since Aodh became king, too! Thank you so much for thinking of them."

My heart lightened at her enthusiasm. "I'm glad to hear it. How many candles should I have prepared?"

"Hmm, let's see. I think ten should be enough."

I nodded. "All right. I'll send further instructions with specific details along with the candles as soon as possible." Picking up the basket, I set it on the desk. "I've brought a little something for them as well, but I thought I'd ask you before giving it to them."

Removing the cover cloth, I revealed little vials of

brightly colored liquid. "They're just little potions meant to taste like different sweets."

Eulalia nodded with a warm smile. "Of course, I'll save some for the children at school, but you can give them to the younger ones now. Would you like a tour of the premises?"

I stood from my chair, excitement bubbling up inside me. "I'd love to see where His Majesty grew up."

FORTY-THREE

With a kind smile, Eulalia led me back into the entrance hall.

"We have made many improvements to the house since Aodh increased our funding," she said, lifting her skirts—revealing her furry ankles and hoofs—to head up the stairs. "We're saving to spruce up the exterior of the house next."

At the top of the stairs was a long hallway, which branched off on either side of the landing. The hall was lined with doors.

We stopped in front of the first door on the left. Fastened to the wood were two sheets of paper. One was carefully painted in rainbow stripes with "Conláed" written neatly in the center. The other featured a small handprint in shimmering gold; "Gwilym" was painted in a mixture of uneven upper- and lowercase letters.

"You would never believe the upstairs used to be one large room. It was Aodh's idea to section it off into smaller rooms. While he was here, there were just rows of beds with washbasins at the end of each."

She opened the door to Conláed and Gwilym's room, and we peeked in—not crossing the threshold. The walls were clover green, and bits of colorful paper—candy wrappers if I had to guess—hung from the ceiling on strings. There were two beds, scooted to the back corners, with wash basins beside them. The room was small to be sure, but I imagined it was far more comfortable than sharing one large room with many other children.

"We let them decorate their rooms as they like. The little ones have roommates, but the older children have their own. We like to give them a quiet space for their studies. Though I do wonder if the twins will ever want to split into their own rooms. They're so attached to each other. They each have their own beds, as you can see, but I often find them sleeping together when I wake them in the morning."

It's a blessing to have not been separated from each other, I bet. I didn't ask about the circumstances around which the twins had wound up in the orphanage. From what Aodh had told me when we were younger, they varied quite a bit—anything from abandonment to death to prison.

"Would you like to see the playroom?" Eulalia asked.

I smiled, hoping my expression didn't look too sad. "Yes, please."

The matron nodded. "Since the twins aren't in their room, they're probably in the playroom. Let me just peek in on the baby while you head that way. It's on the ground floor, across from my office."

I followed her directions and found the door to the playroom already cracked. It creaked loudly as I opened it the rest of the way, giving the children inside ample warning they had a visitor.

The room was a light yellow with a blackboard affixed to one wall—the alphabet written neatly in white. But the space wasn't just an early schoolroom; there were wooden toys—blocks and carved animals—scattered on the floor.

Marina lifted her chin, looking very proud of herself. "See?" she declared to the two leprechaun boys in front of her. "I told you so."

The boys turned to me, disbelief shining in their coal eyes. Their noses were red, and I might have thought they'd been rubbing them raw if I didn't know all leprechauns had red noses. Being as young as they were, their skin hadn't greyed yet. It was still as pleasant as fresh cream. Rather than the wide-brimmed hats most leprechauns favored, the boys wore stocking caps.

"Are you going to marry Aodh and become the goblin queen?" the boy with the green cap asked.

"That's what I'd like to do, yes," I answered.

Ignoring Marina's complaints that they hadn't believed her, they glanced at each other, then back at me. And I saw the unmistakable glint of mischief in their dark eyes.

I met the look with a grin of my own. "Oho! Are you planning some mischief just now? Why don't you let me in on it, eh? I could help."

They blinked at me, surprised by my attitude. No doubt the adults around them usually dreaded their shenanigans.

The boy with the green and white striped cap stepped closer to his brother and whispered, "But didn't Aodh say—"

His brother nodded. "He told us last time."

"Then she's not—"

The second boy shook his head. "He doesn't want to marry her."

My heart skipped a beat. How would these two small

children know that? Did Aodh tell them he never wanted to get married?

Their black eyes flicked to me again.

"But she seems—" the boy with the striped hat started.

His brother nodded.

The boys turned fully back to me as if I hadn't been aware of their little aside.

"I'm Gwilym," said the boy with the solid green cap. "And this is my brother, Conláed."

"We like you," Conláed added. "We're going to help you win Aodh over."

I nearly laughed. How could these small children help me win Aodh's heart? It was too sweet of them. Somehow, I managed to keep a straight face.

I crouched to their level, meeting each of their eyes seriously. "Thank you so much. I'm sure he'll love me in no time with your help."

The boys grinned at me, looking awfully proud of themselves.

"I want to help, too!" Marina protested.

I smiled kindly at her. "Oh, we wouldn't dream of leaving you out, Marina. Would we, boys?"

I glanced significantly at the brothers.

"Oh, no!" "Of course not!" they assured.

I grinned. "Let's seal our pact, shall we?"

The children's eyes gleamed. "How?" Conláed asked.

"With this." Lowering my knees to the floor, I uncovered my basket, revealing the vials of colorful liquids. "We each pick one and drink to our promise."

They eagerly chose their bottles of candy, and I took one I knew would taste like apples.

I helped them uncork their vials, and we clinked them together before downing the sweets.

I placed the empty bottles back in the basket. "And don't forget," I said in a hushed tone as I held my finger to my lips. "It's our little secret."

Their shining eyes told me this was the most exciting thing that had ever happened to them, and my heart warmed at the sight.

CHAPTER
FORTY-FOUR

W hen Eulalia found us in the playroom, Marina was proudly reciting the alphabet.

"Time for elevenses," the matron announced.

The children and I rose from the floor and filed out of the playroom. I handed Eulalia the basket of sweets, telling her I'd already given some to the little ones.

As I followed the children to the side of the stairs down a narrow hallway, we passed a door on the left and entered a doorway farther down.

The dining room was quite large, certainly the largest room in the house thus far. The small windows did very little to illuminate the space.

I blinked as I entered. Above the long table, yellow fae lights floated, providing most of the light in the room.

Fae lights are a creation spell, only a—

My confused thoughts were interrupted when a sidhe entered the room, a tray of biscuits in her hands. I blinked in surprise.

The sidhe placed the tray on the table among the tea things and sat beside Marina.

"This is Gaye, our cook," Eulalia introduced.

Though it was rude, I couldn't help but openly gape at Gaye. Sure, I wasn't an expert on Goblintown, but never once had I met a goblin sidhe. Any sidhe I'd ever met there was only visiting.

What could she possibly have done to end up in Goblintown? It's no secret the sidhe protect their own.

Gaye's eyes showed no irritation at my rudeness. "Good morning, Your Majesty." She dipped her head smoothly. "Please, enjoy our humble table."

I shook off my curiosity and put on a much-too-late smile. "Thank you. I shall."

The rest of the meal was occupied by us helping the little ones with their tea and biscuits and listening to their stories about their grand adventures with the other children. I heard about each of the older children as well. But as much as the conversation interested me, I couldn't help but take furtive glances at Gaye.

And though she pretended not to notice, she knew what was going on. As we rose from the table, she asked if I wouldn't like to see the kitchen, and I said that I would.

Making myself useful, I carried a tray of dirty dishes. We turned right out of the dining room and entered a door at the far end of the hallway.

The kitchen was modest but functional. Certainly not as large as the one at the palace, but large enough to serve a crowd. I placed my tray of dishes beside hers on the prep table at the center of the room.

She let loose a short sigh before meeting my gaze. "I can see you're curious about me, not many goblin sidhe around."

"I apologize if I made you uncomfortable. I was adopted by a sidhe family. I grew up among the sidhe, so I'm surprised to find you here."

She snorted, quirking a sardonic smile. "What could I have possibly done to get the sidhe to exile me, right? It's not like we don't get away with all kinds of crimes. We're the only ones who seem to go unpunished."

I dipped my head, waiting for her to continue.

"I'm not ashamed," she declared. Though she said so, she waited a long time to continue. "I was raped."

The blood drained from my face, and my stomach dropped. But before I could even voice my sympathy and shock that she—the victim—would be punished, she added, "And I had an abortion when I discovered I was pregnant with my rapist's child."

I took a shaky breath, pain echoing in my chest—a tiny fraction of what she likely felt.

"Well, you know how fae are about reproducing. It's so hard for us to get pregnant as it is. And the sidhe are particularly invested in furthering their bloodlines. But I wasn't about to risk my life for that monster or his child."

I couldn't argue with that. She very well could have died in childbirth like so many other fae.

She blew out a sigh as if blowing away all her old pain. "What a joke, right? I end up a goblin, and he inherits his family's title. The other sidhe even sympathized with him, sent him condolences and everything. Our system is broken."

I nodded. "There seems to be little justice in this world. I'm sorry you went through that."

Her expression warmed. "Thank you. I had a hard time for a long while, but eventually, Eulalia found me, nursed me back to some semblance of sanity, and gave me a job here. I do love it here." She glanced around fondly at her kitchen. "The real question is: what is a human who has been raised by sidhe doing in Goblintown? Why do you want to be Goblin Queen? Has the pool of sidhe bachelors diminished that much?"

I laughed. "Well, that's another question entirely. But the short answer is I want to marry the Goblin King."

I could feel her eyes analyzing me. I shrugged. "I love him. It's really as simple as that when you get right down to it."

Gaye pursed her lips. "And how is Aodh responding to that?"

I tried not to show my apprehension, my disappointment, the state of affairs between us. I was unsuccessful.

"Don't fret too much," she murmured. "He's…he seems tough on the outside, but he's very gentle, feels very keenly. If you feel as strongly as you say, if you love him unwaveringly, he will see that."

Hope bubbled inside me at her words. "But will it win him over?"

She frowned. "I couldn't say, but he'll see you for who you are and judge you fairly."

That much I knew already. I wouldn't have agreed to his challenge if I hadn't.

"Cheer up. Oh, I know. I'll let you in on a little secret. The boy has always had a sweet tooth."

I tilted my head. "Oh?"

She nodded. "Yes, his very favorite is greengage crumble."

Greengages won't ripen for a few more months. Maybe I can

have Gráinne teach me how to bake before then. "Thanks for the tip."

Gaye stretched her back. "Well, I better get to starting the midday meal. I'll be rooting for you."

I smiled at the cook. "Thanks, and…thank you for sharing your story with me."

"I'll tell the truth to anyone who will listen. People need to know how flawed our system is; otherwise, it can never be fixed."

"I agree. And for my part as the goblin queen, I'll do my best to bring justice where it's needed."

With smiles and nods, we bid each other goodbye, and I left her to her work.

I found Eulalia and the children in the playroom. She'd given them each an unlit candle, and they were practicing walking while holding them steady.

I knocked gently on the door. "I don't mean to interrupt. I just want to say goodbye before I leave."

The children made sounds of protest, but Eulalia gently hushed them.

"I'll see you all again at Bealtaine," I promised. "I'm entrusting you with a very important job, so I expect you to work hard, yes?"

They agreed. And as I turned to leave, I didn't fail to notice the glint in the twins' eyes as they held their fingers to their lips. I nodded to them with a smile.

Eulalia walked me to the door, and I told her I would have everything sent to her as soon as possible. I also thanked her for her help with the celebration.

Once outside, I found Graeme snoozing peacefully in the buggy at the front of the house.

"Don't you get enough sleep?" I asked my brother, nudging him awake.

"I would if I didn't have such a demanding little sister who wants me to seduce a certain kelpie."

"I never said to seduce him," I argued, climbing in beside him. "That was the route you chose."

He smiled. "Because that was the most enjoyable of my choices."

CHAPTER
FORTY-FIVE

I felt a little closer to Aodh after visiting his childhood home. He'd once shown me the orphanage from the outside, but that wasn't comparable to walking the same floors he'd once walked and meeting the people who'd raised him.

Since the night he'd visited me in my room, hope had grown within me. He hadn't said or done anything that told me we were getting closer. But somehow, it felt as though he wasn't pushing me away as hard.

I waited impatiently for our daily time together. As he'd heard petitions most of the day, we met in the evening—for a stroll in the garden.

The sun back-lit the surrounding trees as it approached the horizon, and it dyed the low-hanging clouds and half-moon gold.

"Everything seems to be coming along with your preparations," Aodh said from beside me.

I nodded. "Yes, only a few things left now. We still don't have enough wood for the balefires. I think perhaps I'll go with Charlie and the others tomorrow night. Even one spare set of hands could make a difference."

Aodh frowned. "Goblinwood is a dangerous place for those who aren't familiar with it."

As many times as I'd walked through Goblinwood, I wouldn't say I was familiar with it. Graeme and I had stayed on the road, except for the time I'd stolen Aodh's ring.

Still, I smiled. "If you're worried, Your Majesty, perhaps you should come as well. No one would dare mess with the goblin king in his own territory."

He snorted. "No one indeed."

"In any case, a bow and a quiver of arrows is no joking matter in the hands of an elf."

His mouth quirked in an expression of amusement. "Perhaps I will accompany the group. A walk in the forest sounds lovely. And at the very least"—his eyes slid to mine —"I can't have you robbing any passersby."

I laughed. But when I grinned over at him, he stiffly turned his head forward, and the sweetness of the atmosphere evaporated.

Leaning my head back, I gazed up at the sky. As the silence between us grew, I filled it as I'd been doing of late. "Where was I? I already told you about what it was like to grow up as a human in a sidhe household, what my family and friends are like, what I got up to in Piskishire, and what I did with my free time. There isn't much left."

For the past few days, Aodh had passively listened to me talk about my life. He didn't respond much though he did ask a few questions here and there.

I sighed. "Not much left at all..."

I could feel his eyes on me when I didn't continue right away.

"When I was fifteen, my father took a post as an

ambassador to Olympus. We spent over two cycles there and returned in Capallré."

"Is that all?" he asked after a long pause. "You've told me many details about your earlier life, but you sum up the last ten years in two sentences?"

Great sadness weighed down on me as I thought about my time in Olympus. I looked over at him. "I don't like to remember the time I spent away. Every day I wasn't in Tír was a day of suffering for me. Sure, I tried to make the best of it. I made friends. I ate and slept and did all the other things I was supposed to do. But I was just existing, floating in time until the moment I could return."

He didn't ask me why I was so sad about leaving. And though my heart screamed it was him I'd missed so much, he didn't hear it.

"And…now that you've returned to Tír, are you no longer suffering?"

Emotion welled inside me, and I smiled up at him. "I could never truly suffer at your side, Your Majesty."

Whether it was a trick of the sunset's glow or my words made the Goblin King's cheeks flush, I couldn't say. He seemed to have gotten used to my romantic declarations of late. And though I loved nothing more than to see him blush, I hoped it was a sign he was slowly opening himself to my feelings for him.

He broke eye contact and resumed walking. "And what of the sidhe king? Where does he fit into this narrative? You have yet to mention him."

I took a deep breath through my nose and sighed it all out through my mouth. "I met King Lorccán when he was still the Crown Prince. From the time I was eight until I went to Olympus, I saw him twice a year, and we exchanged letters at least once a month. He is five years my elder and has always treated me as a little sister."

Aodh snorted. "That is not how you write to your sister."

I glanced over at him. "Well, that came later—much later. I was supposed to become his mistress at age twenty, but my father kept pushing it back. It wasn't until we returned to Olympus that his attitude toward me changed."

Aodh's expression darkened, and the echoes of our conversation from days before rang in my mind. Would he tell me to leave again? Would he insist I was better off with Lorccán?

But my declaration of love must have made an impact because he didn't say any of that. He just frowned thoughtfully, watching Tadhg pounce at something in a flowerbed ahead of us.

We slipped back into silence, but it was comfortable and unhurried. He knew almost everything about me now, and I was grateful for the chance to have told him.

Halting, he turned to me abruptly. The sun was nearly set, and all was still in the struggling light.

"Won't you tell me how we met?" he asked, his voice hushed to match the dying day.

My breath caught in my throat, and it took me a moment to calm my heart enough to reply. "Won't you tell me why you're the one thing I can't have?"

At that point, I knew why he'd said that, but I also knew he didn't want to tell me. I'd told him nearly everything about myself, but he'd said very little about himself. He didn't tell me about the orphanage, how he became king, or his tragic young love.

But I couldn't answer his question, so I asked one I knew he didn't want to answer. Better that than refusing to tell him and appearing untrustworthy.

Uncertainty shone in his eyes, and I bit my lip. *Will he tell me after all?*

He sighed in defeat but didn't pull away from my gaze. "What will you do if I remember you on my own?"

I smiled sadly. "I guess we'll find out should that happen."

His brow scrunched. "I don't understand. Don't you want me to remember you? A meeting that left such an impression on you that you would declare yourself mine for the rest of your days, and you won't tell me?"

"I suppose it doesn't make much sense. But even if you don't remember, Your Majesty." I pleaded with my eyes for him to take my words to heart. "Please judge me fairly for who I am now."

"You would rather our first meeting be when you pickpocketed me?" He raised an eyebrow.

I huffed a laugh. "I was hoping your first impression of me would be a clever human who outwitted you. It might hurt your pride to admit, but I hope one day you'll come to admire that cleverness."

He frowned, but it was more thoughtful than displeased. "It's not the fact you outwitted me, nor my pride, that makes me unwilling to accept you, my lady. I've been a goblin all my life, and I know our customs and virtues. By our standards, you did nothing wrong. It's our practice that— should a spouse not be chosen by the goblin ruler—one might earn the place for themselves by wit and wile."

I held my breath, waiting for him to continue.

"I just"—he searched my face as if he would find some answer there—"I just wish you hadn't."

My heart panged at his rejection, but I didn't let it cow me. "To be honest, Your Majesty, I regret that this is the route I chose. I never wanted to hurt you. You wouldn't have accepted me any other way, so I felt it was my only choice. For me, it was to live my life in agony without you or to try to win you by the customs of your people."

He nodded slowly.

My heart jumping into my throat, I reached out and touched his hand lightly with my fingertips. "I don't know why you say I cannot have you, and I know—despite following goblin custom—I've upset you by thrusting this marriage upon you. But, please, Your Majesty...Aodh, won't you give me a real chance? I've accepted your challenge to prove myself worthy as goblin queen before the solstice. In that time, will you not also consider me as a woman and not just a queen?"

The sun had fully set now, and I had a hard time seeing Aodh, not a foot from me, with only the first quarter moon and stars for light.

His answer never came. Taking my hand and placing it on his arm, he said, "Hold onto me, or you'll fall on the way inside."

As he led me through the darkness toward the lights of the palace, I didn't let his lack of response discourage me. I'd said what I needed to say, and he'd heard.

FORTY-SIX

The following evening, as dusk lit the sky, Odilie and I went down to the front gate to meet the volunteers heading out to gather wood for the balefires.

Charlie had parked a cart and was talking with a few other guards.

Kirk, a gnome with a hat so tattered it was either his favorite or his only one, bowed deeply at my approach. Lottie, a drake with apple-red hair that fell into her eyes as she dipped her head, looked as serious as ever. And Darkweed, a piskie missing the point of one of his ears, gave me a sharp nod.

After lowering his head in respect, Charlie frowned, his eyes swimming with concern. "Will you be joining us, Your Majesty?" he asked.

I looked down at my practical work clothes. It was obvious he was only asking to try to discourage me. "I will. But don't worry about me, Charlie. I won't be any trouble."

"Oh!" Odilie exclaimed, the white scarf she'd wrapped

around her head like a hood slipped down as she turned back toward the house.

I looked in the same direction to see Aodh plainly dressed with a quiver over his shoulder and a bow in his hand. I'd have taken him for a huntsman before a king.

"Your Majesty," Odilie said. "Are you joining us as well?"

Aodh's dark eyes met mine. "Even one spare set of hands could make a difference, right?"

I silently smiled back at him.

"Here comes Peony with the other cart," Charlie announced. He waited for Peony to arrive before looking around at the assembled volunteers. "All right. Is this everyone?"

I couldn't contain my delight that Aodh had elected to come with us. We'd already had our scheduled time in the morning, so this was a windfall. And even better, Selwyn was nowhere in sight.

"We're going a little farther out today because we've scoured most of the nearby forest," Charlie explained. "We'll fill these two carts with dry wood and head back. Hopefully" —he glanced over at Aodh and me—"it will take less time with the added help. Hop in."

I moved to follow Odilie into the cart Charlie drove.

"Your Majesties," Odilie said seriously. "I think this cart is too full. Why don't you two go in Peony's cart?"

I smiled at the imp. She had stuffed herself into Charlie's cart with the other three guards. She grabbed Lottie's sleeve as Lottie moved to switch to the other cart with us, shaking her head severely at her.

I glanced over at Aodh, who didn't say anything before heading to Peony's cart. He lowered the latch and climbed up before turning back to offer me a hand.

His hands were colder than I remembered from our

youth as his fingers gripped mine tightly. But his arms were much stronger when he hauled me up into the cart beside him.

My heart skipped a beat as I met his eyes, his body so close to mine.

As usual, he looked away first, dropping my hand like it had burned him.

Without a word, I settled in for a bumpy ride, sitting cross-legged with my back to the side of the cart. After closing the latch, Aodh sat opposite me, stretching his legs out so his feet were beside me.

"All ready?" Charlie called.

Peony looked back at us and answered in the affirmative. Then she urged the horse forward, and we lurched into motion.

I didn't feel it necessary to speak as I watched the setting sun glimmer off Aodh's long hair. I'd always thought he was attractive, but I never could have imagined the man he would grow to be. I wondered how his lips would feel. Would he hesitate as he did before? We were no longer the impatient and irresponsible youths we once were—well, he didn't seem to be anyway. Had he grown bolder with the added years? Or would his inexperience make him clumsy?

With that thought, another darker thought occurred to me. How did I know he was still inexperienced? Just because I had waited for him didn't mean he had waited for me. And even though he didn't have a wife, that didn't mean he'd never had a lover. Even if he didn't want love, that didn't mean he'd never been physically intimate with someone else.

I frowned, my stomach curling in jealousy for a woman who may or may not exist.

"Cináed came by after school today." Aodh broke our silence.

I jerked to attention. It was a rare thing for him to speak to me first, especially in such a conversational way. "Oh?" I encouraged him to continue.

He nodded. "He asked me what your favorite flower is."

I tilted my head. What a strange thing to come all the way to the palace to ask. And why not ask me if he was curious?

Aodh's eyes watched me carefully. "He wanted it to be a surprise, but he told me the children at the orphanage are so excited to be included in the Bealtaine celebration that they wanted to thank you. Apparently, the twins begged him to come here to ask me because they want to make a flower wreath for you to wear during the celebration. I didn't know the answer, but I told them anything they could find would be fine."

I smiled fondly at this news. "That's very sweet of them. They need not go to such trouble. I'm just glad they're taking part."

Again, he analyzed me. "What made you decide to include the orphans?"

I blinked in faux surprise. I knew what he was asking. "Did I do something wrong, Your Majesty? You know, I'm an orphan—a foundling—myself, and I'm sympathetic to children who were not as fortunate as I was. I needed someone to light the balefires and thought they would be happy to be included. They're the children of Goblintown if nothing else, surely."

He shook his head. "You misunderstand my meaning, my lady. I'm not scolding you… You're right. Thank you for thinking of them. Cináed is thrilled to play such an important part in the celebration. I've been so worried about the physical needs of the goblins that I've neglected their spirits. I see that in how much everyone is looking forward to Bealtaine."

I lowered my head at his praise. "I only wish I knew how to do more."

"That means a lot," he murmured. "I grew up at the orphanage."

I looked up at him, my surprise genuine this time. I hadn't expected him to share with me.

"Eulalia and Gaye are as kind-hearted as they come. They did everything they could to raise us in the absence of our parents. And though we were poor, and we didn't always have enough to eat, we were happy."

I smiled kindly at him. "You loved each other. They're your family."

His answering smile held all the warmth in his heart. "Yeah, they are."

CHAPTER
FORTY-SEVEN

Once in Goblinwood, the surrounding trees muffled the sound of the carts' rattling wheels. Eventually, we stopped along the side of a road I'd never been on before.

Again, Aodh offered me assistance. I alighted, my hands clasping his, and met his gaze once my feet were securely on the ground.

Something in his eyes made my breath hitch, but then he pulled away as the others approached.

Staring at his face, I wondered if I'd been mistaken. Had he held onto my hands for just a moment longer than before? Had there been the hint of warmth in his eyes when they'd met mine? His expression gave no indication either was the case. I turned toward Odilie, the ends of her scarf fluttering behind her as she bounced toward me. *Did I imagine it?*

Odilie offered me a lantern, and Charlie handed one to Aodh.

"Don't stray too far alone," Charlie said to the group though his gaze lingered on me.

Oh, don't worry about that. I wouldn't squander this time with Aodh.

And even though I stuck close to him most of the time, we didn't talk much as we filled our arms with dry wood and broken sticks from the ground and piled them into the wagons.

For the task at hand, Charlie had picked a good spot. There was a lot of dead wood near the road, and the wagons were already half full by the time we needed to head farther into the forest.

We were about a furlong from the road—I was staring at the ground by the light of my lantern as I followed close behind Aodh—when the path seemed to become more illuminated.

I looked up and saw we'd entered a clearing. The moon, though only a day after its first quarter, was bright. I couldn't help but gasp at the beauty sprawled out before me.

Even at night, I could see the brilliant colors of the many wildflowers. The clearing seemed carpeted in blue, yellow, and white as the bluebells, lesser celandines, and wood anemones swayed in the breeze.

Some of the flowers at the palace had bloomed already, but nothing could compare to nature's vitality growing wild.

Aodh looked back at me, and I nearly dropped my lantern. I didn't know what I'd done in my life to deserve to behold such a beautiful sight. The moon sparkled in his dark eyes and shined off his hair. With a bow in his hand and the wildflowers behind him, I might have thought him Orion—loved by the goddess of the moon and kept forever with her as stars in the sky. I couldn't help but think how arrogant the sidhe were to claim to be the most beauteous of the fae.

"My lady?" Aodh asked, a curious expression on his face when he found me transfixed by him.

My body flushed, and it felt like the wind had been knocked out of me. A painful hunger clawed at my core. I wanted him. I didn't care that the others were somewhere nearby. If he would only say the word, give some indication he consented, I would claim him in every way possible.

"Aodh…" My voice trembled, my lips mouthing his name with little breath to speak it.

A deep growl rumbled through the air. The sound of glass shattering came from the trees on the other side of the meadow followed by a strangled scream.

I tore my eyes from Aodh to look toward the sound just as Odilie burst through the trees.

Her dress was torn at the back, her wings having ripped the fabric so she could fly. Terror shone in her amethyst eyes as her white scarf whipped behind her like a war banner.

Her gaze fell upon us, and she swerved in our direction, waving her arms wildly. "Run!" she yelled, her voice squeakier than usual in panic.

A dark shadow loomed behind her, taking shape as it stepped into the moonlight.

I froze while the hair rose on my neck and arms. A massive red dragon unfurled its leathery wings in the clearing. Its black eyes glinted like obsidian as it flicked its barbed tongue.

Aodh reacted so quickly that I barely registered the movement before he was aiming an arrow directly at the beast.

"Wait!" I shouted. *If he fires, his elf shot will kill it for sure.*

But he wasn't listening to me.

I rushed forward, putting myself between him and the dragon as Odilie flew toward us.

"Move!" he urged.

"You don't have to kill it!" I didn't dare look back at him as I positioned myself.

Odilie was nearly to us now, and the dragon's gaze followed her with unmistakable rage. But just as she flew past me, I snatched the end of her scarf.

She made a choking sound before spinning out of it and crashing to the ground.

With the scarf in my hand, I stepped forward, waving it to get the dragon's attention. Its eyes never left the garment. It growled a deep, guttural noise that made me question my sanity.

"Aodh," I said softly, trying not to anger the beast more than it already was. "When I throw this, I want you to shoot it. Make it go as far as possible."

I didn't look back to see whether he'd heard me. I rolled the fabric as quickly as I could and launched it into the air.

Aodh's arrow whistled, piercing the scarf and carrying it into the forest beyond the meadow.

The dragon turned to pursue it, not caring about us at all.

Quickly, I moved toward Odilie and picked her up in my arms. I took a few steps, my knees trembling in relief. "I'm sorry," I murmured to her.

She had a cut above her eye, and blood trickled down her lavender face. She would probably be covered in bruises later.

"Let me take her," Aodh said, holding his arms out. "It will be faster."

I nodded and handed the imp to him, picking up the

lantern he'd set down—mine having broken in my haste. We ran back to the carts.

Once there, Aodh set Odilie on the driver's seat, and I climbed up beside her.

"I'm sorry, Odilie. I didn't mean to hurt you," I told her, pressing my handkerchief to the wound on her head. "I just didn't have time to communicate what was going on."

"What *was* going on, Your Majesty? Why didn't it chase us? Why did it follow my scarf?" She shivered as the wind hit her exposed back.

"Hold this," I instructed.

She raised her hand to hold the handkerchief to her cut.

I removed my own scarf and draped it over her shoulders like a shawl.

"This time of year, the red dragons migrate to their breeding grounds," I explained. "They normally don't bother anyone, but they won't tolerate their enemies—the white dragons. I suspect, with the dragon's drive to mate amplified at this time, it saw your white scarf and just sort of went crazy. It wasn't trying to hurt you. It just didn't understand."

Odilie nodded. "That was very courageous of you, Your Majesty—charging ahead like that."

I chuckled. "I'm not quite sure about that. It felt foolhardy to me."

"Then why didn't you just let me shoot it?" Aodh asked in a curious tone.

I frowned. "The dragons are producing fewer and fewer hatchlings every year—red dragons especially. I just didn't want to kill it unnecessarily."

He stared at me for what seemed like a long time, then sighed. "I suppose you have the goblin virtue of courage after all."

CHAPTER

FORTY-EIGHT

I knew I should have felt ecstatic at his judgment. Courage was arguably the most difficult of the goblin virtues to embody and prove. After all, I only had steadfastness and persistence left, and as someone who'd faithfully waited for the same fae for over ten years, I didn't have a problem with those two.

But as I stared back at Aodh, I couldn't muster the feeling. He'd given a fair judgment as he saw it, but he wasn't happy about it. All the hope I'd cultivated since I'd confessed my love for him in my room flew away as effectively as Odilie's scarf with an arrow in it.

He saw me as worthy of being queen, at least in two out of four categories, but he still didn't want me as his wife.

I bowed my head more to hide my expression than out of respect. "Thank you, Your Majesty," I said softly to mask the emotion in my voice. "I will strive to always be as brave as I was today."

Whether it was lucky or not that Charlie and Peony arrived with arms full of wood at that moment, I didn't know. But at least their concern for Odilie and her telling of what had happened distracted me and drew Aodh's gaze from me.

Though we hadn't filled the wagons completely, we thought we should head back. So once Lottie, Kirk, and Darkweed had arrived at the cart, we began our return to the palace.

Everyone insisted Odilie sit beside Peony in the driver's seat. She didn't take up much space, and it wasn't a good idea for her to walk after a bump on the head. She must have been feeling pretty tired because she didn't protest even a little.

The walk back was nearly silent, the wood rattling in the carts as the horses snuffled every so often.

I was keenly aware of Aodh's presence beside me and the dejection coming off him. My instinct was to boost his spirit, but knowing I was likely the cause of his current mood, I hesitated.

Despite the sting of inherent rejection, I bolstered my courage. He wasn't necessarily feeling this way because he didn't want me per se.

"Your Majesty," I said. "I heard from Gráinne and Rosemary that the city is buzzing about Bealtaine. All the bakeries in Goblintown are helping them make bannocks for the celebration. I think all those who can come will come. I know we don't have a lot of time left, but with the help of Eithne and the other maids, I think we should get the ribbons for the samcenn-pole finished in time."

He nodded, my chatter not quite pulling him from his thoughts.

"Your Majesty, shall I tell you a secret?"

As his eyes lit with curiosity, he finally gave me his attention. "Will you tell me how we met?"

I laughed, shaking my head. "Something else."

He sighed through his nose. "Very well. What were you thinking about before the dragon showed up? You had a very strange look on your face."

I halted in the middle of the road, my cheeks heating as I recalled the moment he was asking about. He stopped a few steps ahead of me and turned to face me.

"I-I..." I dropped my head. "I'm afraid if I tell you, I'll undermine the respect I've earned thus far."

He cocked his head. "Why is that?"

My heart panged at remembering his harsh words when I'd tried to seduce him, and I couldn't bring myself to look up at him. "Given some things you've said before, Your Majesty"—I shifted my weight—"I'm sure you'll think I'm terribly indecent."

"What I said bef—?" He dropped his sentence mid-word.

I peeked up at him through my eyelashes. His face was as red as it had been that night, and I flinched, preparing for his anger.

"I'm sorry," he whispered.

My eyes widened as my head snapped up.

"I shouldn't have handled it that way."

I raised my hands. "You don't need to apologize, Your Majesty. I shouldn't have entered your space without permission. And if you...found me that repulsive, I'm glad you were honest even if I would've preferred a gentler rejection."

His eye twitched. "I have not been kind to you, Lady Melody. And despite that you still...you still desire me in that way?"

I frowned. "I know you would say I have no pride, but I desire you in every way."

He shaded his eyes with his hand, pressing his fingertips to his forehead as though his head ached. "Please," he nearly groaned. "Can you forget my words from that night? I have no grounds to ask you to do so, but I regret everything I said."

I blinked in surprise. *Is he un-rejecting me?* "You don't mind my lustful desire for you, Your Majesty?"

He glanced around as if shocked by my question and where it came from. The carts had slowly moved farther and farther down the road though they were still in sight.

Aodh cleared his throat. "I regret the way I handled your sudden appearance that night, my lady. You are free to feel how you wish, but I still can't indulge those feelings."

Disappointment bubbled inside me, but it wasn't even close to the despair I'd felt that night. I nodded once. "I see. Well, then I won't attempt to suppress my desires for you from now on."

He frowned, but he didn't protest. He simply turned to follow the carts.

I skipped to catch up and walk alongside him. "Do you know how many times I've wanted to kiss you since I've been here?" I asked, smirking as I glanced over at him.

His cheeks pinked, but he kept his expression neutral.

"I have to say, I thought you were handsome before, but you are infinitely more so now. I would've given you every inch of myself in that meadow if you had wanted me." I peeked at him again and grinned.

He'd effectively given me permission to speak openly, and I would let him know just how much I loved and desired him.

CHAPTER
FORTY-NINE

I was in a cheerful mood the following afternoon as Eithne and I continued sewing ribbons. I hummed to myself while I sat near the window, the sun warming my skin despite the still-chilly temperatures outside.

"Still at it, then?" Graeme asked.

I glanced back at him, not having heard him enter the reception room. "We're almost there. You can see we only have a few piles left."

"Why didn't you just buy ribbon again? Must you always do things the hard way?"

I frowned. "Even if I get an allowance from Dad for the rest of my life, I should try to live by the standards of my new household." I didn't tell him I'd pretty much spent my savings on bannocks for the celebration.

"Eithne, my love," Graeme said sweetly. "Would you be a dear and bring us some tea?"

"I've told you, my lord, you aren't my type," Eithne rebuffed.

"I'm everyone's type. Unless you don't like your men rich, handsome, and charming."

"I like my men earnest and reliable. Thank you very much."

"Boring, you mean."

I watched as they sparred back and forth, smiling at the familiarity of the exchange.

Eithne lifted her chin. "Would you like anything in particular, my lady?"

"The usual is fine. Thank you, Eithne."

She carefully set her half-made ribbon aside and left the room.

My brother plopped down on the couch across from where she'd been, a little under a rod from my chair by the window. Tadgh looked up at having been jostled, squinted his cat's eyes, and hopped down from the couch, slinking off to somewhere unknown.

"So you've made progress, then?" I asked, taking in Graeme's tired yet satisfied expression as he tilted his head back and closed his eyes.

"I said I'm everyone's type, didn't I?"

Even though I'd seen my brother's charm wear down many others in my life, I couldn't believe it had worked on someone as stiff as Selwyn. I was truly and plainly shocked. "No way."

He lifted one eyelid. "You doubt me, sister?"

I pursed my lips. "There's no way you seduced Selwyn so easily."

He frowned and took a deep breath. "In truth, he's difficult to get close to. I'll admit he has not yet been completely taken by me. But I've made significant progress."

I snorted. "You made it sound like you'd gotten somewhere."

"I got a kiss. That's more than you can say."

I raised an eyebrow. "Did you really?"

"I did."

I shrugged. "Well, I've made progress, too. I passed the challenge of courage last night, and Aodh apologized for throwing me out of his bedroom that first night."

Graeme sat up from his slouch to stare at me more directly. "Oh? How did you manage that?"

Now that his full attention was fixed on me, I bit my lip. *I shouldn't have bragged about that.* My brother would not be so impressed with my facing down a dragon. He was more likely to drag me back home than praise me.

"Hey, did you ever find anything out about what Brochfael was really doing at that tailor's shop?"

Graeme squinted at my abrupt change in subject but let it pass. "I've been using my time away from Selwyn to ask around. I tracked down some old acquaintances—fae I knew back in the day who used to take contracts or knew those who did. No one has heard anything. But last night, I met up with someone who said Brochfael had stopped in to see him."

I stilled my fingers—my needle halfway through the fabric.

"Apparently, Brochfael was looking to take out a contract, and he was nervous about it. My acquaintance turned him down; it seems your elf has made assassination a far less attractive career in Goblintown than it once was."

"Did this fae know who Brochfael was trying to have killed?"

Graeme shook his head. "He did not, but he seemed under the impression it was someone high up."

My chest tightened. *Someone high up could be anyone*

from aristocracy to government officials to a wealthy competitor of his father.

I stood abruptly from my chair and put my sewing aside.

"Where are you going?" Graeme asked while I strode toward the door.

"I'm going to tell Aodh what you just told me."

"What about tea?"

I shook my head and opened the door. "I'm sure Eithne will be happy to enjoy it with you."

At that time of day, it was more than likely Aodh was in his study, working on the petitions he had received two days prior. But as I hurried down the long gallery toward his wing of the house, I heard his voice coming from the anteroom that led to the king's reception room and the stairs.

"What has gotten into you these days? You were the one who offered to help. Did you not?"

I crept nearer the end of the gallery and the cracked door to the anteroom. Aodh's voice sounded strained, and his clipped words were a clear censure.

"I'm sorry," Selwyn responded. "I do want to help. I've just been distracted lately, and I haven't been getting much sleep."

I smirked, silently thanking my brother for doing such a thorough job of diverting Selwyn's attention.

"You're *distracted*?" Aodh snapped.

I flinched at the irritation in his tone.

"We're running out of time!" Footsteps thumped on the floor of the anteroom, and I couldn't tell if they were getting closer or not.

I lifted my hand to knock on the door. I wanted to hear more, but I couldn't risk getting caught eavesdropping.

"We have to—" Aodh's words were cut off by my rapping. "Who is it?"

At his question, I stepped into the room, being sure to arrange my face in a pleasant—and innocent—smile. "Good afternoon, Your Majesty." I spared a glance at Selwyn, smiling a bit wider at the thought that he was letting Graeme distract him. "Selwyn."

Aodh's gaze flicked to Selwyn before returning to me. He frowned. "Selwyn, continue to my study. I'll be there momentarily."

Looking cowed, Selwyn bowed his head and moved toward the stairs.

Once his adviser was out of sight, Aodh turned back to me. His eyes seemed tired, and his brow was wrinkled with worry lines.

"Is everything all right, Your Majesty?" I asked.

He frowned, then sighed through his nose. "No, my lady. Nothing is all right."

I clenched my fingers, my skirt gathering in my fists. "Did something happen?"

As well as I knew Aodh, I couldn't decipher the look he gave me at that moment. Was he sad? Angry? Was he hurt or simply exhausted? The only thing I knew for sure was something within him was looking to me to answer the question he didn't ask.

"The sidhe king has demanded our presence at court. He says it's about Goblintown's unpaid taxes. But given how he specifically asked you to attend and referred to you by your father's name rather than as the goblin queen, I'd say it's got more to do with you jilting him."

I winced. I hadn't heard anything from Lorccán since I'd sent my letter. I'd hoped his silence meant he'd accepted my decision.

"Oh, and he sends an ultimatum, too. We will be there on the dorchae of Samcenn, or he'll send an army."

FIFTY

After my initial shock lapsed, I frowned as I considered his news. *I knew Lorccán wouldn't be happy about me turning him down, but I didn't think he would do something spiteful.*

"Maybe it's a misunderstanding," I suggested. "I'm not yet the goblin queen; you still address me as an earl's daughter. Perhaps he's just being accurate."

Aodh raised his eyebrows. "And the army?"

I shrugged. "I mean, you said you were likely to get in trouble for the taxes, right? Sure, he's being excessive, but maybe he just wants to ensure we come."

He crossed his arms. "Do you have so much love for the sidhe king that it's blinded you? This is an act of hostility. Why are you so willing to believe he's acting in good faith?"

I scowled. "I try to have faith that people can be trusted until they prove otherwise." *You taught me that.* "King Lorccán has been nothing but kind to me. I have no reason to doubt him. I don't think we should jump to conclusions about his motives. This could be the opportunity you were hoping for. You said you reached out to him multiple times, and he never answered. Well, now you have an opening to negotiate on behalf of Goblintown."

The tension in his body didn't ease, but his mouth quirked. "I still think his motives are bad, but you're right I might be able to use this to my advantage. Even so, we need to be on guard."

I smirked. "I know one thing for certain."

His gaze met mine, and I could see his curiosity at what I would say.

"If he does have bad intentions, you and I can figure it out together. You're the greatest goblin king since Robin Goodfellow. And my courage and cleverness have already been acknowledged by such a great fae."

His dark eyes glinted, and the tiniest smile appeared in the corner of his mouth.

My chest warmed as the shared moment passed between us.

But then he looked away, and the atmosphere grew heavy.

"Well, you don't need to worry about it at this moment, regardless. The dorchae is still eleven days away, and Bealtaine is only five. Is that what you sought me out for, concerns about the celebration?"

"What?" I blinked. "Oh, no. Actually, Graeme just told me something I thought you should know."

He waited patiently while I ordered my words.

"That exchange at Buttons and Spools, where Brochfael gave the tailor all that gold? I think Charlie is right. I think he was taking out a contract on someone."

Aodh tilted his head. "What makes your brother think so? We've been keeping a close eye on Tac since then and haven't seen anything suspicious."

How could you tell with a sylph? They can literally turn into air. I glanced around the room, then back at Aodh. *Does Aodh have a sylph working for him? Only a sylph could see another sylph in air form. How careful should I be about the things I do and say?*

"Uh..." I shook the thoughts from my mind as he watched me expectantly. "Graeme said he ran into someone who used to take out contracts. I guess Brochfael approached him, but this fae refused. It seems your policies on that profession have made a change in Goblintown."

Aodh nodded seriously. "Does he know who your friend wants killed?"

I frowned. "He's not my friend, and no. I don't even know if this fae knows. But he seemed to have the impression it was someone high up. Which makes sense, given the amount of gold I saw change hands."

Aodh rubbed the side of his thumb over his lower lip in thought, his eyes losing focus. "Someone high up..." he muttered.

"It could be anyone," I continued. "It could be any aristocrat, influential government official, a wealthy merchant. It could be my father; it could be his father. It could be you or King Lorccán for all we know. I could make a better guess if I knew more about Brochfael's motivations."

"You've said you two have known each other for a long time, but you aren't friends. Are you friendly enough to earn his confidence?" Aodh asked.

I pursed my lips. "Not easily. I might have been able to ten years ago, but a lot has happened since then. Do you want me to try to get close to him and see what I can find out?"

Aodh shook his head. "No, not quite yet. It could be

more dangerous than we know. We need more information before we do something like that."

"All right, but how are you going to get more information?"

His eyes were calm and confident when they met mine. "Now that we have confirmed this sidhe was coming to Goblintown to take out a contract on someone, we have a reason to question Tac more directly."

I nodded.

"Thank you for bringing this information to me."

"Of course, Your Majesty. I want us to be partners after all."

"Partners, huh?" he commented thoughtfully. "I thought you wanted us to be lovers."

A thrill ran up my spine. "Be careful, Your Majesty," I responded with a sly grin. "Hearing you throw around words like that might make me think you're flirting with me."

I held his dark gaze in mine for a few rushed heartbeats before he looked away. "You are brazen, aren't you?"

I smiled because his words held no bite. *You want to see brazen?* I stepped closer to him, within arm's reach but not uncomfortably so.

With no windows in the room, the only light was provided by the lamps and the far window in the stairwell.

"You look very handsome in flame-light, Your Majesty. It brings out the red in your hair."

He didn't thank me for my compliment but didn't pull away either.

I smiled wider at the small victory. "May I kiss you?"

Because I was so close to him, I heard his soft intake of breath at my bold request. His face reddened again, and I prepared myself to weather his anger.

Even though he blew the breath from his nose in an

irritated sigh, and his expression hardened, he didn't snap or rage at me. He simply shook his head and said, "No."

Given the progress I'd made since coming to the palace, I took the small rejection in stride. He wasn't ready for that yet, but I would keep trying until he rejected me completely by throwing me out of his house or he gave in.

I sighed as if in great disappointment. I'd asked him for a kiss more to get him used to the idea than in the hope he'd actually give in. "Well, I suppose I should go back to my preparations for Bealtaine, then." I took a few steps toward the long gallery, then glanced back at him. "Shall we take a stroll in the garden this evening, Your Majesty?"

He nodded once, and I left.

CHAPTER
FIFTY-ONE

The next five days blurred together as all Goblintown prepared for Bealtaine. My fingers were sore from frenzied sewing, but I knew it would be worth it once I saw the ribbons streaming from the samcenn-pole.

Even though Aodh had told me not to worry about our trip to Sifra, he didn't seem to take his own advice. Our short time together each day was plagued with thick silences and pensive expressions. When I tried to ease his tension, he would put on a more pleasant mask. But I could still see the apprehension in his eyes.

Since the night of the dragon incident, Charlie and his volunteers had taken to collecting wood during the day and completing their work tasks at night.

So as the sun set on Bealtaine, they were adding the last cartfuls of wood to the piles on the front lawn of the palace.

I placed my hand over my heart, hoping the gesture would ease its racing speed as I stood watching from my reception room window.

Beyond the front wall, the goblins had begun to gather.

The many blurred into one mass, their faces aimed in my direction. Their lanterns pulsed like stars in the sky. In truth, they were probably just facing the proceedings as it wasn't likely they could see me in any detail.

Don't be nervous. Everything has been meticulously planned. I can only do so much now if something goes awry. The bannocks are made, the samcenn-pole is ready to be erected in the morning, Eulalia can handle the procession, the—

"There you are," Aodh said.

I turned toward the door as Aodh entered.

My breath caught in my throat when I beheld him. His tunic was the color of lush evergreens, and his hair was long and loose down his back. The cut of his tunic made me very aware of just how wide his shoulders were and how solid his chest.

He wore his amethyst dagger and crown of grapevines, and he'd painted a bold but elegant pattern across his forehead and down one side of his face with kohl, the design bringing an entirely different dimension to his face.

My breath hitched at the sight of him, and any hope of my heart calming was lost. He looked mysterious, like a stranger I very much wanted to know.

My skin warmed as his dark gaze traveled over my green, linen dress—much lighter in color than his tunic. With his eyes on me, I was glad I'd chosen a dress that accentuated my bosom so well.

"Your Majesty," I whispered. I took a deep breath to continue at a more suitable volume. "You look stunning. Anyone in Goblintown would wish to share your bed this night."

His dark eyes—finished with their journey down my body—found mine. And at that moment, something passed between us like the charged air before lightning strikes. My heart thumped in my ears.

"Don't wear that dress when we go to Sifra," he said.

My face flushed.

"The sidhe king may very well uncouple my head from my shoulders if he thinks I've had you."

It took my mind a moment to catch up to what my heart understood immediately.

"You can, you know," I murmured, unable to gather real boldness in the face of his steady gaze and charged words. "You can have me however you want me… Surely there's no harm in coming together on Bealtaine night."

Given how the holiday was a celebration of fertility and the beginning of the growing season, all Tír would be feeling the stir of passion that night.

But I never got to hear Aodh's response because just as he looked about to speak, the sound of drums and pipes rose from the crowd outside. The sun had gone down, and the goblins were getting excited to start the celebration.

"It's time to make our appearance," Aodh stated. "The children will be setting out from Robin Goodfellow's tomb any moment."

To my surprise, Aodh held out his hand to me. I blinked stupidly at the gesture before my heart swelled. Hurrying to him, I placed my fingers in his.

I must have looked giddy to the point of silliness to him because, as he tucked my hand into the crook of his arm, he smirked an indulgent smile.

Feeling like the true queen of Goblintown for the first time, I raised my chin and squared my shoulders proudly as the Goblin King escorted me downstairs, through the cloisters, down the antehall, then out the front door.

The full moon had yet to rise, so the only light came from the stars and the braziers that lit the grounds.

The moment we stepped into view, the gathered goblins burst into cheers.

I smiled at their enthusiasm and joy as we continued toward the gate. Upon reaching the garden wall, Aodh dropped my arm and climbed atop. The goblins approved of his antics with loud whoops.

After a few waves, Aodh turned back toward me and held out his hand. My eyes widened, but lifting my long skirt, I took his offer, and he pulled me up to stand beside him.

Looking out at the crowd, smashed into the streets between buildings like clotted cream and jam between a halved scone, I almost couldn't believe how much energy rolled off them.

Aodh let out a loud, sharp whistle, and his subjects quieted to hear what their king would say.

"I can't tell you how glad I am to see all of your smiling faces!" he shouted. "Before we begin, I want you to thank Lady Melody Píobaire for organizing our first Bealtaine celebration in over five years!"

He gestured toward me, and the crowd roared their approval. Despite my smile and wave, my heart stung at him not referring to me as the future goblin queen.

Once the goblins had quieted down again, Aodh glanced at me. "Go ahead," he encouraged. "Tell them what to expect."

Taking a deep breath, I tried to project my voice as if I were calling Tadhg home when he had wandered off somewhere unknown.

"Thank you so much for coming! I'm proud to have been trusted with such a task by our great Goblin King!"

I paused as cheers erupted at even the mention of Aodh.

"Tomorrow, we will have dancing, music, and bannocks for all! But tonight, the children of Goblintown are going to light the balefires with flames from Robin Goodfellow's tomb! They should be on their way now, so please, dowse your lanterns and make a path for them!"

In short order, the goblins extinguished their lanterns, the darkness rolling outward as if the gods were blowing them out in one huge breath.

Before the last brazier was extinguished, Aodh hopped down from the garden wall and offered me his hand again.

As my feet touched the ground, we were plunged into darkness, the stars above hardly visible while my eyes attempted to adjust. I blinked rapidly to help them along.

With one sense suddenly gone, I was keenly aware that Aodh still held my hand. So I didn't miss it when he stroked my knuckles with his thumb before pulling away.

FIFTY-TWO

I peered into the darkness in Aodh's direction. *Is he teasing me?* But because I couldn't see his face, I couldn't tell if his gentle touch had been a joke, encouragement, or a small indulgence on his part.

My heartbeat pounded in my ears, and I thought about whether I should reach for him in the dark. If he were teasing me, then he was asking for retaliation. If he were encouraging me, then he wanted me to make a move. But if he was indulging some small part of himself that wanted to let me in, then it might be better to let it go unmarked.

It was the first time he'd initiated something with me. But it was too slight an action to ascribe an intention to it. If some part of him felt the need to reach out to me on his own, then standing still would only fuel more of that desire.

Chasing him had produced very modest results. But enticing him to chase me—if such a thing was possible— would be much more effective.

I gnawed my lip, my knuckles still tingling where he'd

stroked them. I wanted to reach out and grab his hand; my fingers twitched with their desire to do so.

But I clenched my fist instead. I didn't know the reason behind his action. I clamped down on my instinct to forge ahead and see what happened, instead fostering the hope that he would do something even more next time.

As I wrestled with my inner turmoil, tiny specks of yellow light appeared far away, and the goblins began to murmur.

My gaze fixed on the flames, smiling as they slowly but surely drew nearer.

It didn't take long before I saw the children's glowing faces.

Cináed was in front, leading the others—all dressed in their holiday best—in a line. Each child walked slowly, carefully balancing the long candles in their hands.

Their smiles were brighter than the flames they carried, but none were as bright as Marina's. She was the last child in the line, followed by Eulalia. Instead of a candle, Marina carried a crown of flowers in her small hands.

Finally entering the gate, Cináed stopped before us and bowed his head.

"Well done," Aodh congratulated them, pride shining in his eyes. "Let's light the balefires."

He gestured for half of the children to follow him and the rest to accompany me.

I walked to one of the giant piles of wood—the twins, Marina, and two other children trailing me.

"All right," I told them. "Touch the flames to the kindling there at the bottom. Be careful now."

I supervised the task, watching to be sure they pointed the flames away from themselves and didn't get too close. As soon as the kindling caught, I urged them to step back quickly.

Charlie and the other volunteers had done an excellent job of building the fires. The dry sticks went up easily, and a rush of heat blasted us.

I smiled down at the children as their eyes glinted in the light of the balefire.

"Your Majesty," Marina said seriously.

I met her expressive gaze. "Yes, Marina."

Her small brow puckered. "I wasn't very good at holding the candle steady, so Eulalia said it would be better if I gave you this instead."

The selkie held the crown of flowers above her head. The wreath was bursting with color as if they'd tried to fit every spring flower they could find in it.

"For me?" I asked the child, who nodded. "That's very sweet of you all. Thank you! But could you do something for me?"

Wonder sparkled in Marina's eyes.

I knelt to her level and bent my head. "Would you put it on for me, please?"

Very carefully, as if the task took the utmost concentration, the child placed the crown of flowers on my head.

I looked up to see her wide grin. "Thank you so much, Marina. May I give you a hug as thanks?"

The little girl nodded, and I drew her tiny body close to mine. Warmth spread through me as her short arms wrapped around my neck.

I patted her back. "Bealtaine blessings upon you, child."

The twins, who stood nearby, stepped up behind Marina when I released her.

"May we have a hug, too, Your Majesty?" Gwilym asked.

I smiled at the boys and opened my arms to them.

They both hugged me at once, laying their capped heads on each of my shoulders as I gave them a squeeze.

Before I knew it, the rest of the children, some more self-conscious than others, had queued up for an embrace. I thanked each of them in turn and put names to the faces of the ones I'd only heard about.

"Are you ready?" Aodh asked.

I glanced up while the last child stepped back into the group, and my heart swelled as Aodh smiled warmly at me.

"Shall we lead the procession?" He offered me his hand.

Tingles ran up my arm when my fingertips touched his, and that charged atmosphere surfaced between us again.

I rose to my feet, holding my breath as I stared into his dark eyes.

"Come," he whispered, and I shivered as he laced his fingers with mine.

My head spun; I felt too giddy to breathe.

As he pulled me along beside him, leading the procession of children between the two balefires, I couldn't believe I'd lived to see this day.

It had been only a month since I'd stolen his ring. And the rage the full moon had reflected in his eyes then was nothing like the look he gave me now.

Cheers rose from the crowd of goblins when we reached the front steps and turned back to them. They started to file in through the front gate.

They, too, would pass between the balefires, receiving the season's blessings before lighting their lanterns from one of the fires to rekindle the dead flames of their hearths.

After the children wished us goodnight, they headed back to their beds. And as we watched the goblins make their way around the drive before leaving to go about their

Bealtaine night revelries, Aodh unlaced his fingers from mine. Then he lifted my hand to his lips and pressed a gentle kiss to it.

"Happy Bealtaine, Lady Melody," he murmured before letting go.

That was all I would get from him tonight. But even as I trembled from the need for more, I still smiled at him. *This is enough for now.* "Happy Bealtaine, Your Majesty."

CHAPTER
FIFTY-THREE

I told myself over and over to be grateful for what he'd given me. A kiss on the hand from one who'd spurned me not long before was progress indeed.

But as I watched couples smiling and making eyes at each other while they headed off into the night, I couldn't help but be a little envious.

It seemed so easy for them to find someone to celebrate Bealtaine with while I'd spent every Bealtaine since my sixteenth year thinking of the elf beside me.

Though they didn't celebrate Bealtaine in Olympus, they did have fertility holidays, and some of them were quite exuberant.

I'd never once been tempted to indulge in such practices akin to what happens all over Tír on Bealtaine night with the few who'd asked me to do so in Olympus. Never once had the spark of the season gotten into my blood. Never once had I felt the unbearable yearning that swelled within me now—so close to the fae I'd waited for.

As the last of the goblins lit their lanterns and passed

between the balefires, as the full moon shined brighter than what remained of the flames, I looked at Aodh.

Does he feel the same ambiance I do?

His dark eyes slid to mine, and a tingle ran up my spine. "You did well, my lady."

I bowed deeply, leaning slightly forward as I did so. "Thank you, Your Majesty."

Aodh's gaze landed exactly where I wanted it to. "And now, I think you ought to sleep. For you will need your rest once the sun rises and the goblins return."

"I fear I will find no rest tonight." I lifted my eyes to his.

My heart pounded as he stared back at me.

"But I will go to my bed… Should you need me, Your Majesty, you know where to find me."

I swallowed with difficulty and turned to enter the front door. I would not wish him goodnight in the slim hope it would not be the last I'd see of him that Bealtaine night.

My bedroom was quiet and empty when I entered. Eithne had the night off. And I didn't know where Tadhg was half the time anyway.

Slowly, I readied myself for bed—the fabric of my dress sliding off my tender skin made me quiver. Even as the cool air raised the hair on my arms and legs, I flushed with inner heat.

My nightgown felt too constricting. I took it off a moment after I'd put it on and simply slipped my robe over my bare skin.

The hearth was cold and dead when I left my dressing room. It would be lit again in the morning from a flame taken from one of the balefires. Only the single candle in my hand lit the chilly room.

I placed the candle on the table beside my bed, removed my robe, and quickly slipped between the cool sheets.

My muscles shivered, but I didn't find the sensation unpleasant.

Staring at the pale-yellow curtains of my bed, pretty and soft in the candlelight, I knew there was no way Aodh would come to me. Still, I couldn't make myself snuff out the light.

My mind wandered—too charged to even attempt to sleep. *What is Aodh doing right now?*

Would he have already changed out of his green tunic? Again, I wondered what he wore to bed.

Would he have already washed the kohl from his face? It had looked so lovely on him, and I wondered if he'd done it himself.

What would he be doing this Bealtaine night? Would he work? Would he take a break? Perhaps read a book? Or would he simply sleep?

I could almost imagine his sleeping face lying beside me in bed, his long hair catching the light of the candle as it splayed over the pillow. I smiled at the thought.

Would he breathe softly and evenly, or would he snore? Did he like to cuddle, or did he like his own space?

I ventured to guess he would take up much more of the bed than I'd expect.

I wondered if my staring at his sleeping face would wake him. Would he tell me to go to sleep? Or would he smile at the thought that I liked to look at him even then?

"Aodh," I whispered to the phantom who wasn't there. "How can I tell you how much I've longed for you? Words aren't enough."

I felt the echo of his lips on my fingers, so much closer than the memories of our first kiss, and shivered.

Closing my eyes, I could still see the warm glow of the candlelight through my eyelids. But silencing one of my senses only seemed to amplify the others.

I could hear the wind whish in the chimney, sending specks of soot into the cold fireplace. The blankets pressed on my body, and I could almost imagine they were the weight of the elf I loved.

My body flushed, warming the space in which I lay.

No, Aodh would not be coming that night. And if I had any hope of rest, I would need to relieve the pressure within me.

My eyes shut to reality, I pictured Aodh atop me, pressing his warm weight against me. I could still see the charged look he gave me in the reception room only hours before.

I brushed my fingertip ever so gently against my neck, and I could almost tell myself it was his lips on my skin.

I huffed out heavy breaths, trembling as he kissed down my neck and along my collarbone. I shifted my weight beneath him, undulating as he reached my breast. Running my thumb over one nipple, I gasped at the jolt of pleasure.

An ache started in my core and continued to build as I stroked and gently pinched my nipples. A slick heat trickled, and I spread my legs.

I whimpered as if begging the phantom to relieve the sweet pain.

Trailing my hand down my torso, I slipped my fingers inside, tensing as a pulse of pleasure ran through me.

I slid my wet fingers up to my clitoris and stroked. My head grew fuzzy, and I no longer had the presence of mind to accurately imagine Aodh with me.

His phantom faded in and out, sometimes there—his heavy breathing matching my own—and sometimes just a thought.

As the pleasure built, and my limbs began to shake, I couldn't help but call out his name.

CHAPTER

FIFTY-FOUR

As the breath rushed out of me, Aodh's name still hanging in the air, a soft thump emanated from outside my bedroom door.

I gasped, my heart leaping into my throat. "Who's there?" I called.

But there was no answer.

Throwing the blankets from my naked body, cold air slamming into me, I hurriedly pulled on my robe and grabbed the candle from my bedside table.

My bare feet thumped on the floor as I walked to the door. "Yes?" I asked, opening it.

Only the dark and empty hallway greeted me. I blinked and squinted into the blackness, holding my candle higher to see if there was anything lurking in the shadows beyond the flickering light.

Taking a step forward, I cringed when my big toe squished into something. I retreated a bit and knelt to see what I'd stepped in.

There in the darkness, near the threshold of my bedroom door, was a tiny pool of dull beeswax—maybe two or three drops—the swoops and swirls of my toe's print pressed into it.

Was someone here? The wax had been soft enough to have not completely hardened but not so fresh it was still liquid.

I peered into the shadows again. *But there's no one here now—not even the flicker of a far-off candle—and it didn't take me that long to answer the door.*

I frowned, shaking my head. *I'm over-thinking it. It's chilly out here. The wax was probably from my candle and hardened faster than I expected.*

And with that conclusion, I returned to my room and bed.

I was relieved all the tension that had built inside me had been released. As I snuffed out the candle and closed my eyes to sleep, I hoped I would have more presence of mind around Aodh—perhaps I wouldn't be so very distracted by his sexual appeal as I had been of late—now that I wasn't wound so tight.

I was awakened the next morning by cheerful birdsong and opened my eyes to see Tadhg in his cat form staring intently at me.

I scrunched my eyebrows at him. "Where have you been? Out with the spunkie girls all night, were you?"

He didn't even blink.

"Ah, right. Eithne is off today, so you're probably hungry. You want food?"

His ears swiveled at the word he recognized very well.

I chuckled. "Let me put something on."

I slipped on the nightgown I'd worn for only a moment the previous night and pulled my robe on over it; I didn't bother applying my anti-Selwyn patch. It was still too early in the morning after Bealtaine night, with the sun only just peeking over the horizon, for anyone to be up and about. If they weren't sleeping off their night of revelry, they were indulging in one last bout of lovemaking before the day of festivities. So I didn't think it necessary to fully dress just to go down to the kitchen to feed Tadhg.

The house was still and quiet while Tadhg and I made our way downstairs. I found it to be pleasant. The day would be bursting full of energy and celebration, so it was nice to have a silent moment of tranquility.

The feeling was shattered when I reached the walkway on the upper level of the kitchen and heard the hiss of water on fire. I looked down to see Aodh hanging a pot over the fire.

"Good morning, Your Majesty," I said with a smile, announcing my presence.

He jumped and looked up at me. From what I could see, he hadn't slept well. He had dark circles under his eyes, and his face seemed to sag with exhaustion.

His expression tensed, then he winced and turned his back to me. "Good morning," he muttered.

I scrunched my eyebrows. "Are you unwell?" I asked as I descended the spiral staircase.

"What brings you here?"

I tilted my head at his question but gestured toward Tadhg, who was already approaching Aodh to greet him. "Eithne is off today, so I came down to feed Tadhg. And you?"

He stared fixedly into the pot of water he had put over the fire. "Breakfast," he muttered.

Uncertainty coiled inside me. *Why is he being so distant? I thought I'd made progress.* Despite my frown, I tried to make my voice light. "Shall I help, then?"

His eyes slid to mine, and my heart skipped a beat at the intensity I found there. My face flushed. He looked like he was about to take me right there in the kitchen. "Do you know how to cook?" His tone didn't match the mundane nature of his question at all.

I trembled, attempting to breathe enough to answer him. "H-how hard can it be?"

And then he looked away, and my knees nearly buckled as if his gaze had been holding me up.

"Sure," he said. "Why don't you slice some bread and cheese while I make the tea?"

I nodded though he didn't look at me to see.

It seemed whatever relief I'd found the night before, the same could not be said for Aodh. Whether it was the energy of the holiday or something else, I couldn't say. But as I sliced a few pieces of bread from a loaf on the worktable— thick and uneven slices due to my unpracticed hand—I wondered why he hadn't just taken care of himself the way I had.

I glanced over at him. The energy was rolling off him, and he seemed to take up much more space than usual as he prowled around the kitchen looking for whatever he was looking for.

Tadhg let out an insistent meow, and I shifted my eyes to him as he stared up at me from the floor. Grabbing the wedge of cheese, I broke off a hunk and put it on the floor for him.

But when I straightened, I found Aodh standing before me. My breath hitched, and I stepped back, my bum bumping into the worktable behind me.

He reached out, gripping the ledge of the table on either side of my hips as he stared down at me with an intense and unreadable expression.

I could feel the heat of his body, not a foot from mine, and I swallowed with difficulty.

The feeling coming from him was fierce but confusing, and I didn't dare move in the chance it was arising from a place of anger.

"Your Majesty?" I whispered unsteadily.

CHAPTER
FIFTY-FIVE

"Stop." His order was hushed but firm.

My mind spun to think of what I'd been doing to so offend him.

The ferocity of his gaze wavered, and he seemed to wince. "Stop making me…"

My heart panged in sympathy. I didn't know what he was trying to say, but I didn't like to see him struggling. I lifted my hand, reaching toward his face in an instinctive need to comfort him. "What—?"

He snatched my wrist before I could touch him. His fingers burned with heat, and his pulse pounded against the sensitive skin of my wrist.

"Don't," he growled.

I stilled, watching him carefully as sadness welled up inside me.

He let out a long, stuttering sigh, closing his eyes. "I don't…want…" His words trailed off.

"What don't you want, Your Majesty?" I asked softly.

He winced again as if the very sound of my voice caused

him pain. Opening his eyes, he fixed me with a steady stare. "I don't want to want you."

I held my breath, a thrill running through me.

"So stop it." With every word he spoke, his tone turned from a fierce demand to a hopeless plea. "Stop doing whatever it is you're doing to get inside my head. I was just fine before you showed up, and I don't want this."

An odd mixture of feelings swirled inside me. It was clear everything I'd done thus far to earn Aodh's favor had worked to some degree. And that should have made me beyond happy. But I couldn't really feel joy when he looked so miserable. He clearly wanted me—perhaps not enough to indulge in such a feeling but enough that he felt a pull.

I blinked slowly before gazing into his eyes. "Very well, Your Majesty."

I won't tell you how much I love you anymore. I won't say how my body yearns for yours—even if those were the answers to questions you asked me directly. If this is what you want, I think my point has already been made. But do not take my silence as any indication those unspoken things are no longer true.

Though I gave in to his request immediately, he did not move away. He stood, hovering over me with my wrist still in his hand. If he thought my yielding to his demand meant I would push him away, he was mistaken.

"Good," he said, his tone a little surprised and confused that it had been so easy.

I gave him a small, polite smile to show we were in agreement.

He stared down at me for another moment, that analytical gaze of his sweeping over my face. Then he released my wrist and stepped back. The shadow of regret flitted over his expression before he turned away.

I watched while he made his way to the pot of boiling water and pulled it out to ladle some into a teapot.

There was no space in me to feel regret that he had effectively rejected me yet again. I was too full of sympathy for the pain his desire was causing him, joy that somewhere within him he still wanted me, and, of course, my never-wavering hope.

And I wasn't discouraged by my agreement to no longer openly express my feelings toward him because I knew I didn't need to. He could tell me to stop doing what I was doing, and I could stop with my overt actions. But that wouldn't help him. I would still be me. Those declarations I had so boldly made weren't who I was. And if he actually wanted me, then that wouldn't change by me simply silencing my speech.

The atmosphere between us as we breakfasted off the kitchen worktable was thick and silent. I could feel the heavy energy coming from him, but it didn't dampen the light in my heart. I ate contentedly as though the world belonged to me. And so it did with every furtive glance Aodh took at me.

For his part, Tadhg seemed to take the greatest advantage of this unusual meal, alternately soliciting food from both Aodh and me before slinking off to do whatever it was spunkies did most of the time.

After all the food had been eaten and the tea drunk, we lingered at the table.

I would not be the first to leave his side, and so I waited for him to either depart or dismiss me. But to my delight, he seemed to hesitate.

Finally, he stood up straighter and dipped his head in a formal bow. "The goblins will be arriving again soon." He eyed my robe. "We best get dressed for the rest of the celebration."

"Thank you for the company, Your Majesty, and for the tea." I smiled warmly.

He watched me for a long moment, then nodded. "You head up first. I'll take the dishes to the scullery."

"Would you like some help?"

"No, thank you. Go on ahead."

I smiled again before doing as he urged.

As I ascended to my bedroom, I wondered how likely it would be for Aodh to give in to his desire for me. Would he be able to overcome his reservations on his own? Could I quietly do something to help him along? Was it time to push him to have a real conversation about why he was so reluctant to begin with? I couldn't let him know I was Mischief, but asking why he didn't want to want me was a completely reasonable question. If I left it alone, would he release his doubts before the summer solstice deadline?

I was deep in those thoughts when I stepped into the hallway that led to my chambers, but they were pushed to the background when I saw Graeme arriving at the guest room door.

My eyebrows rose as I took in his disheveled appearance. His hair was tangled with elf locks, and his shirt was torn.

"Graeme?" I called.

He turned to me slowly. I was relieved to see he didn't have a black eye.

"What happened to you?" I studied him to make sure there wasn't blood anywhere.

He snorted, and a languid smile spread across his face. "Selwyn."

CHAPTER

FIFTY-SIX

My eyes nearly popped out of my head.

Turning the knob of his bedroom door, Graeme gestured with his head. "Come in. I've figured some things out."

I closed the door behind me as I entered the space.

Graeme removed his jacket and shirt, then made his way to the water pitcher and basin on the washing table.

He poured the water, which was now likely quite cold since it had been filled for him the previous night, and thrust his hands into the basin.

I eyed my brother's shirtless form. There were red marks on his chest. "Did you two fight? You look terrible."

Graeme splashed water on his face, then dried it with a towel. "You're too innocent for this world, little sister."

I pursed my lips, taking his comment as an insult.

"No, we didn't fight." He looked down at the marks. "Oh, he really got me, didn't he? These are love bites."

I crossed my arms. "So you got what you wanted, then? You finally bedded Selwyn?"

My brother turned to me, frowning. "In a manner of speaking." Moving toward the luggage pushed up against the wall, he knelt and started to dig through it.

"What does that mean?"

Finding what he was looking for, Graeme threw clean clothes onto the bed and turned toward me. "I had sex with him, but he didn't have sex with me."

My eyebrows scrunched together. I didn't have the patience for riddles.

He held up his hand to silence me before I could voice my complaint. "He asked me to glamour my appearance"— he frowned seriously—"to look like your elf."

My mouth dropped open. "What?" My volume was much louder than I intended. "H-he—"

Graeme nodded. "It seems that grumpy kelpie is in love with the Goblin King."

I reached out, steadying myself before sinking onto the bed. "So that's what he meant. That's why he hates me so much?"

"Yep." Graeme punctuated the word with a loud pop of his lips. "I suppose the good news for you is that not only does your elf not know about it, but he's also not interested in males at all—at least according to Selwyn."

I sighed. "So he was just jealous of me being with Aodh? Was it really that simple?"

Graeme shrugged. "Seems so."

I looked up at my brother, frowning in realization. "Oh, but Graeme... How could you do that to him? Don't you think indulging in that kind of request will only hurt him more in the long run?"

Graeme seemed to consider my words carefully before answering. "I'm not sure. It really could go either way. Perhaps by having what he wanted even in his imagination, it will be enough for him to let go. Perhaps you're right, and the farce of it all will only hurt him more deeply. But whether it hurts him more or not is not really the question."

"What is, then?"

"Will he let go? The fact is this one-sided love of his is truly not going anywhere. And in order for him to live the rest of his life, he needs to let it go. So whether this will hurt him more, I couldn't say. But this will force him to come to terms with that inevitable fact one way or the other, especially since…"

I waited for him to continue.

"Especially since I told him I would only do it the once."

I looked carefully at my brother's expression. "You didn't want to do it to begin with, did you?"

He met my eyes, then averted his gaze. "Well," he said lightly. "It did hurt my pride a little to have the fae I was trying to seduce ask me to be someone else, but…I couldn't refuse when he begged me so piteously."

Silence hung in the air as if Graeme could still hear Selwyn's pleas.

"Are you all right?" I asked gently.

My brother flinched and glanced at me in surprise. "Me?" He smiled softly. "Yeah, I'm fine. I suppose we can all stand to be brought down a peg now and then. Besides, it's not as though I'm in love with him or anything. But…I do want to help him."

An old sadness, one I'd seen far too often, entered his gaze as he looked at me. "I've seen what a heart's longing can cost someone, and I don't want him to go through that any longer than he has to. I may have started this to help you and for a bit of amusement, but now I see some good can come of it. I'd like to help him heal if I can."

I rose to my feet and closed the distance between us,

embracing my brother around the middle as he rested his chin atop my head. "My sweet, soft-hearted brother," I murmured, patting his bare back. "You—" I pulled away from our hug.

"I, what? Keep going. I love it when you compliment me."

"You stink like sweat and…"

"Selwyn juice?"

I cringed. "Ugh, ew! Why would you say that?"

He laughed the way only teasing brothers can. "You're the one who wanted to give me a hug before I properly bathed."

"You should have warned me," I complained.

"But then I wouldn't get to see your reaction, and it's hilarious. Plus, I'll never say no to my little sister showing me affection."

"Blegh," I gagged. "Gods, you're so gross. Go take a bath already. I have to get ready for the rest of the celebration."

"I love you, too!" he called after me as I exited and shut the door behind me.

I rolled my eyes and huffed my annoyance before shaking it off and going to my room to dress.

CHAPTER
FIFTY-SEVEN

I couldn't think about how alluring Aodh looked in the morning sunshine or how solid his arm felt beneath my fingertips as he led me out into the palace grounds.

There was much too much going on to hold onto those thoughts.

Charlie was directing a trio of guards where to plant the samcenn-pole as the ribbons we'd worked so hard on fluttered in the breeze.

Rosemary and Lottie were carrying a table toward a long row of tables that had already been set out while Gráinne directed the bakers as they arrived with their baskets of bannocks.

A group of musicians was already settling in not far from the samcenn-pole, and they struck up a lively tune just as Odilie approached us.

She bowed to us. "Bealtaine blessings, Your Majesties."

I smiled at her. "And to you, Odilie."

But her amethyst eyes said she had not come merely to wish us a happy holiday. "Um, I fear there are too many bannocks and not enough people to pass them out, Your Majesty. I worry the crowd will get impatient. Shall I ask a few citizens if they wouldn't mind helping?"

"Let's not take from their celebration unless absolutely necessary," I said. "I'll help pass out bannocks myself."

Her eyes widened. "You, Your Majesty?"

"Of course, why not?"

"B-but wouldn't you rather enjoy the festivities? You worked so hard to organize the whole thing."

I nodded. "Therefore, it's my responsibility to see it goes smoothly. Besides, the faster we pass out the bannocks, the quicker we can all enjoy the party."

She smiled up at me, and I pulled my hand from Aodh's arm.

"If you'll excuse me, Your Majesty," I said.

"I'll help as well," he offered, following us before we'd even taken two steps toward the tables.

I grinned. "Your help is much appreciated. Thank you."

He stared at me silently for a moment. "All the better to pass them out quickly, right?"

As surprised as Odilie had been that Aodh and I had offered to help, Gráinne nearly toppled over when Aodh asked her where she wanted him.

With everyone's hard work, we were ready when the goblins began to arrive at the front gate.

And once they were on the grounds, everything became a blur of music, swirling dances around the samcenn-pole, and laughter. Even from my vantage point at the bannock tables, I could see just how much the goblins were enjoying themselves.

People ate and drank, told jokes, and sang songs. And it wasn't just our bannocks for fare either. Some of the local restaurateurs, innkeepers, and tavern owners had brought along food and drink to sell. But even more goblins had packed meals from home and openly shared with those around them.

I shook my head when I saw Tadhg in dog form doing tricks for scraps.

The children of the orphanage were thrilled to receive their bannocks. Aodh and I even earned a smile of approval from Kathleen when she came to the table though I knew all this only went a short way in addressing her very real concerns.

At one point, I saw Charlie dancing with a human, her bronze curls shining in the sunlight as he spun her around.

Toward the end of the line, when we began running low on bannocks, I spotted my brother approaching Selwyn, who sat in the grass not far from the samcenn-pole. Selwyn didn't seem keen on whatever Graeme said to him. But in that playful way my brother had, he bumped him with his shoulder, and Selwyn smiled. It wasn't the sly or nasty smile I'd seen from him either; it was warm and genuine.

I couldn't help but grin when they both stood up and took a twirl around the samcenn-pole.

"What are you looking at?" Aodh asked from beside me.

I pointed to Selwyn and Graeme as the song ended and they collapsed in exhausted laughter. "Has Selwyn gotten a bannock yet?" I asked Aodh.

Aodh frowned. "Not that I saw."

I took one from the small stack still on the table. "I'll be right back."

Making my way through the crowd and winding between laid out blankets, smiling at those who greeted me, took longer than expected even though Selwyn and Graeme weren't that far from me.

I approached them, and Selwyn's eyes widened as they both looked up at me. Then his face tightened.

I knew he didn't like me, and I could understand why. I couldn't even blame him. Aodh had a way of making people fall for him after all. But I didn't want to fight with him anymore if I could make peace. I tried to adopt my friendliest smile.

"I noticed you didn't come to get your bannock, so I thought I'd take the liberty to bring you one." I held it out to him, but he didn't move to take it.

"Where's mine?" Graeme asked.

I clicked my tongue at my brother. "You aren't a goblin, so you aren't allotted one."

I ignored my brother's grumbled response and knelt to better speak to Selwyn. "Don't you want it?"

A storm seemed to brew in his seawater eyes, and disappointment coiled in my gut as I prepared for him to snap at me.

"Not from you," he said, brushing my hand aside.

I stood with a sigh. "Well, there's one for you even if you don't take it from me." I gestured toward where Aodh and Gráinne, who was the only baker who'd refused to leave her post until all the bannocks were gone, still stood.

His eyes followed my gesture, and his face reddened upon meeting Aodh's gaze.

With a deep frown but no more words, he snatched the bannock from my hand and passed it to my brother.

I suppose it will be like this for a while yet. Without saying goodbye, I turned back toward the tables and made my way there.

I found Aodh's gaze easily across the crowd. His frown was as deep as Selwyn's had been, and his eyes glinted with displeasure. I tilted my head. I would have thought he'd be happy I was trying to get along with his most-trusted adviser though I supposed it hadn't exactly worked out for me.

I was nearly halfway to him when Charlie intercepted me, his fingers laced with those of the bronze-haired human.

"Your Majesty," he said with a bow of his head. "I'd like you to meet Aoife."

I turned to the woman, whose blue eyes sparkled as if it was the happiest day of her life. "It's a pleasure to meet you." Her pale face reddened. "I'm still a bit awkward, can't quite believe I'm here. How should I address you?"

I'd met very few humans in my life, and none who had lived in the human realm for any great amount of time. "You're Charlie's human lover?"

Aoife's blush deepened, and she nodded.

My cheeks ached as I smiled widely back at her. "That's wonderful. I'm glad you're here...to stay?" I glanced at Charlie, who nodded. "You can just call me Melody. Welcome to Goblintown! Please let me know if there's anything you need. Perhaps, once things settle down, you would like to come to tea and let me know how you're doing?"

Aoife grinned. "I'd love that. Thank you."

I nodded. "Of course. I look forward to it. Please, enjoy the festivities."

As Charlie led Aoife away, I glanced back at the tables, and my smile faltered. Aodh was no longer there.

CHAPTER
FIFTY-EIGHT

I reached Gráinne just as she was gathering baskets in her arms.

She smiled. "They're all gone—every one."

I nodded. "Wonderful. Now you can enjoy the celebration as well."

"I'll just pop these back into the kitchen first."

"All right. Before you go, do you know where His Majesty went?"

Gráinne tilted her head. "Oh, he didn't tell me where he was going. He just thanked me for my contribution. But I think I saw him go around the house."

"Thanks, and yes, thank you for all your help, Gráinne. We couldn't have done it without you."

The salamander beamed with pride, her fiery eyes glowing all the brighter.

As she headed back into the house, I began walking around the side.

The afternoon sun was warm though still only offering the mere promise of high summer.

While I continued down the side of the palace, I was surprised at how quiet it got. I could still hear the merriment in the front yard, but it sounded remarkably far away.

When I finally reached the garden, I found Aodh immediately.

"There you are," I said.

He looked up from his seat at the fountain's edge, and I nearly stumbled. The sun glistened off the flowing water behind him, and his hair fluttered gently in the breeze. The look on his face was melancholy, and wistfulness swam in his dark eyes. No one in any realm could look as beautiful as him, and my heart skipped a beat.

"Why are you out here all by yourself?" I asked, brushing aside my reawakened desire for him.

He shrugged slightly, and I knew he wouldn't tell me.

I forced a bright smile. "Well, if there's no reason, why don't we go back? We haven't taken a turn around the samcenn-pole. Would you dance with me, Your Majesty?"

He met my gaze and frowned. "No, thank you," he responded coolly.

I blinked, surprised by his tone. *What's going on in that head of yours?*

"Very well," I replied lightly.

He didn't even look at me when I sat beside him on the fountain's ledge.

Silence settled in between us, and it was anything but comfortable. I thought of some way to pull him from this pensive mood.

I grinned. "What about a little mischief?"

He flinched and looked over at me, his eyes searching my face, and my heart squeezed. *Did that trigger something in his mind? Will he recognize me?*

But when he spoke, there was nothing in his tone or words that indicated as much. "What sort of mischief?"

I forced a grin, tempering my disappointment. "I have just the thing. Follow me." Standing, I held my hand out to him.

And after a moment's hesitation, he took it. I tugged him along after me, dropping his hand and lifting my skirts as I ran on ahead.

He jogged to keep up while I rushed through the cloisters and into the anteroom.

"Come on! Hurry up!" I called, racing up the stairs.

I was much farther down the hallway that led to my bedroom when he reached the landing.

He hesitated upon seeing the direction in which I was headed.

I shook my head at him with a laugh. "Don't worry. I won't do anything untoward to you, Your Majesty."

Down the hall, I entered the door on the left, the one to the sitting room I'd converted into my workroom.

"What's this?" Aodh asked from the doorway.

I glanced over my shoulder as I opened one of my potions chests. "Oh, I needed a place to make my potions more than I needed a room to sit around in. I hope that's all right."

He didn't say one way or the other but approached where I was setting things out on a table. "What are you doing?"

I smiled. "What's your favorite flower, Your Majesty?"

He frowned at the question. "Jasmine."

I froze, my breath hitching. It took me a moment to recover. I met his eyes in the shining sunlight streaming through the large windows.

"My lady?"

I forced a little laugh, trying to cover my surprise. "What a coincidence. Jasmine is my favorite as well."

Ignoring the nagging feeling that seemed to creep under my skin, I concentrated on the task before me.

"Once, when I was young, my father met with the Dragon Emperor." I filled up the space with my words as if talking would cover the ache in my heart at hearing jasmine was his favorite.

I carefully cut a square of fabric and a length of cord.

"Well, he was quite impressive, of course. But the discussions he had with my father weren't terribly interesting to a young child."

I uncorked a wide-mouthed jar and took out one incarnadine luan feather.

"One of his aides found out I was interested in potions" —I pulled the feather's barbs from its rachis and sprinkled them onto the cloth—"and he showed me how to make this."

Opening my jar of penghou ash, I shook a generous amount over the disassembled feather.

"And what is it you're making exactly?" Aodh asked.

"If I told you, it wouldn't be a surprise," I answered with a smirk.

Returning to my trunk, I pulled out a large jar of carefully preserved white flowers. It had once been full, but only a precious few remained.

As I removed the lid, the intoxicating scent of jasmine wafted toward me. I breathed deeply, sweet memories of Aodh swirling in my mind.

I offered the jar to Aodh, placing it near his nose for him to enjoy the fragrance. Despite saying it was his favorite flower, he winced and shied away from it.

My stomach soured. I dumped the remaining flowers

into my hand before crushing them in my fist and brushing their remnants onto the cloth.

Gathering the corners, I used the cord to tie the lot into a sachet.

The bundle clenched in my hand, I raised an eyebrow at Aodh. "Any idea how we might get up to the roof?"

CHAPTER
FIFTY-NINE

Curiosity played in Aodh's eyes, but he didn't ask. He simply nodded and led me out of the sitting room to the service stairs.

The service stairs continued upward, ending at a door, which Aodh opened and stepped past.

My heart skipped as the fresh wind blasted my face and the landscape sprawled out before me.

We weren't terribly high, but Goblintown was still a sight to see from up on the hill.

As I gazed out at the many homes and the goblins still enjoying the Bealtaine festivities, I could feel Aodh's gaze on me.

I thought he was merely being impatient, but when I glanced at him, he didn't appear so. He simply looked at me with that inscrutable expression of his. I wondered if he was admiring or condemning me in his mind.

"Just like last time," I started. "I'm going to throw the sachet into the air, and I want you to hit it."

He frowned. "I didn't bring a bow and arrow. And in

which direction are you going to throw it? The arrow will have to come down eventually, and it could hurt someone."

I shook my head, holding up a small glass vial. "You'll hit it with this."

He held out his hand for it.

"Be careful," I told him. "It's not very stable."

He took the vial from my hand, gazing through the liquid as he held it up to the light. "What is it?"

"Sea fire."

His eyes widened, and I thought he was going to drop it in panic. "Sea fire! What are you doing with a thing like that? You can't just keep that lying around."

I clicked my tongue. "It's only a little bit. It's not enough to cause any real damage...I think."

He grunted in disbelief as his mouth fell open. "You *think*?"

I rolled my eyes and shook my head. He was starting to sound just like he had when we were young and he thought I was doing something dangerous. "Yeah, yeah," I said like I had a million times before.

He stopped, falling silent, and I looked at him. I knew that quality of his, and I'd expected him to continue for some time.

A line formed between his eyebrows, and he tilted his head as if he heard something I couldn't, a sound he couldn't quite place.

"Are you going to do it, or what?" I asked since I had an opening. "I can throw both, of course. But your elf shot will definitely hit the target while my chances are...not as good."

He sighed through his nose. "You're sure no one will get hurt?"

I scowled. "Do you think I care so little for the goblins

that I would risk their injury? There are children down there. My brother is down there."

He shrugged. "I don't know how much you like your brother. This could all be a plot to eliminate him for all I know."

I let out a disbelieving laugh and made as if to shove him.

"Hey! Hey! Sea fire here. Sea fire in my hand. Let's not horseplay while I'm holding explosive materials, shall we?"

I tensed as if to do so anyway. "Yeah, well, maybe watch who you insult while you're holding explosives. They're dangerous, you know."

He shook his head. "Yeah, all right. Let's get this done so I'm not standing here with something that could burn me alive."

I smirked. "Well, I wouldn't want to ruin that pretty face."

His eyes shot me a reproof, and I held up my hands in surrender.

"Sorry. Force of habit."

He pursed his lips but didn't say anything.

Readjusting my grip on the sachet, I moved closer to the ledge of the roof, staring down at the goblins gathered on the front lawn.

"You ready?" I asked him.

"Ready."

I threw the sachet as hard as I could, and it sailed upward and over the crowd. With elven accuracy, Aodh hit it dead on with the vial of sea fire.

The sachet flashed as it burst into a quick puff of flame, then sparked and fizzled.

"Is that it?" Aodh asked, turning to me with one eyebrow raised.

I pointed toward the air. "Look!"

Luminescent green vines spread through the air like lightning, bursting in flashes of white as jasmine flowers made of light bloomed. The vines traveled over the crowd, the goblins gasping at the breathtaking sight.

With one final pop, the vines and flowers shattered into specks of glittering magic, sprinkling the scent of jasmine over the onlookers and onto the breeze.

As the light faded and the scent drifted away, the goblins roared with cheers. I smiled and turned to Aodh.

"Well?" I asked him. "That was a pretty good surprise, right?"

Shaking his head, he huffed a laugh through his nose. The smile he gave me was warm. And, if I wasn't mistaken, I could have sworn admiration shone in his dark eyes. "You do seem to be full of surprises."

My heart swelled as if it would burst. I knew that look. That was the same look he'd given me all those years ago when he'd told me he knew everything he needed to know about me—when I'd agreed to be his goblin queen and he'd kissed me and promised to always come for me.

I never thought I would see him look at me like that again, and I nearly broke into tears.

But when I met his eyes once more, I saw he'd replaced the expression I'd so longed to see with the pensive look I'd become familiar with.

That's right. He doesn't want to want me. But he doesn't seem to be able to help it. Whether something inside him recognizes something inside me, or he's simply attracted to the same qualities I've always had, his heart will always want me.

Turning to me with a much more reserved smile, Aodh nodded. "You did well, Lady Melody. Thank you for giving the goblins a Bealtaine to remember."

Is this enough? He's fighting it, but there's no mistaking that look. Does he love me yet?

I desperately searched his eyes, swallowing my racing heart as giddiness overtook me. "Your Majesty, I have something to tell you. The truth is—" The air rushed out of me, and my throat squeezed. A moment of panic was followed by utter disappointment. *The binding is still in place.* I sighed heavily and bowed my head to him. "Thank you, Your Majesty."

CHAPTER
SIXTY

Given everything that had transpired between Aodh and me that Bealtaine day, it should have been one of the happiest days of my life. I even got to spend most of the day with him instead of the odd hour or two.

All my efforts to attract him were working. And even though he was resisting his urges, I had a reasonable hope he would give in to them eventually.

But as the sun began to set, and the goblins headed back to their homes, the pervading feeling in my heart was still disappointment.

And it continued to weigh on my mind. Why did I feel so discouraged when my efforts were bearing fruit? I'd waited for so long already. Could I not wait just a little longer?

In my weaker moments, I even thought that perhaps he wasn't going to give in after all. He'd rejected me time and time again, and it was possible he would continue to do so. We didn't have much time left before the summer solstice.

He could certainly resist me until then, especially because I'd promised to not provoke him.

Those were the thoughts occupying my mind over the next two days.

We were preparing to leave Goblintown to answer Lorccán's summons to Sifra. But that didn't require much effort on my part.

Eithne ensured I had everything I would need, giving me more than enough time to wallow.

The night before our departure, I was trying to distract myself in the library. I wasn't doing a very good job at it; I mostly just stared at the page without absorbing any of the text.

I jumped when Aodh and Selwyn entered and stood from my seat near the fire.

"This should answer any questions you have on the subject," Aodh was saying as he grabbed a book near the entrance. "It's the same as any other time. Just accept them on my behalf, and assure them I'll address their concerns upon my return."

Aodh's gaze flicked in my direction, and he blinked in surprise at my presence.

I bowed. "Good evening, Your Majesty."

Aodh nodded to Selwyn, dismissing him after handing him the book.

Selwyn frowned but left.

"I haven't seen you yet today, my lady. I apologize, but I've been busy preparing Selwyn to handle things while we're gone. I can sit with you now if it's convenient."

"Is Selwyn not coming with us?" I was a little surprised. Eithne was accompanying us, so I'd just assumed Selwyn would as well—not that they had the same job. But the goblins submitted their petitions on the dorchae, so someone needed to accept them while we were at Lorccán's court. It made sense Aodh would appoint Selwyn to do so.

Aodh's face stiffened, and his dark eyes glinted in the firelight as he approached me. "Is that a problem?" he asked flatly.

I stilled, confused by his suddenly displeased tone. "No, why would it be?" *If anything, I'm thrilled to not have to deal with him.*

Aodh crossed his arms. "That's what I'm asking you."

My brow wrinkled. "I don't think I understand what you're asking."

"Is that so?"

"Yes, that is so," I said firmly.

With every moment the conversation drew out, Aodh looked angrier and angrier. "So you're telling me, with that innocent expression, you don't know what I'm insinuating?"

I spread my hands, palms up. "I haven't the foggiest. Do you perhaps think I find Selwyn unequal to the task of accepting petitions on your behalf?"

He scowled as if I were the stupidest creature alive. "I'm going to ask you something, and I want your honest answer."

My stomach clenched.

"Are you having an affair with Selwyn?"

I felt like I'd been slapped in the face, and I couldn't help but laugh at the ridiculousness of this situation. "What?"

My laughter did nothing but annoy Aodh further. "Do you deny it?"

"Of course, I deny it! What would even make you think such a thing were possible?"

"There's more than enough evidence to make me think so," he spat.

"Such as?"

"At Bealtaine, you went out of your way to deliver Selwyn a bannock."

"I was trying to be nice." *All the good it did me.*

"But when he glanced over at me, he looked guilty of something. And since that day you have been…distant."

You tell me to keep my distance, then complain when I do as you ask? But I knew that wasn't what he meant. Since the rooftop, I'd been wrapped up in my own thoughts. Any attention Aodh had paid me only made me feel more despondent because it wasn't the type of attention I wanted. To him, that very well could have looked like me pulling away.

"In fact, he's been acting strange since the moment he retrieved you from your parent's estate—distracted, irritable."

I flinched. I knew exactly why Selwyn would be acting that way. "Well, I can't speak to that. That sounds like something you should take up with him. But offering your closest adviser a bannock on a holiday doesn't even come close to suggesting we're having an affair."

"You didn't offer me one," he grumbled.

And finally, though it seemed quite obvious after the fact, I realized this argument was coming from a place of jealousy. Aodh was jealous. All the irritation drained out of me as my chest warmed. "I apologize, Your Majesty. I would've fed you a bannock with my own hands had I known I would cause such a misunderstanding."

His face flushed, but he wouldn't be distracted so easily. "The way you look at him is very…heated."

With dislike.

"What about the day I came into the yard to find you two nose-to-nose?"

I thought back to when he was talking about. "He was

quite literally telling me I wasn't good enough for you. You want to know how I feel about Selwyn? I dislike him immensely. He has been nothing but rude to me since the moment we met. I tried to smooth things over the other day, but it didn't work out. I wager he dislikes me even more than I him."

I took a few steps nearer to Aodh, meeting his eyes and urging him to feel the truth of my words. "Rather than worry about us having an affair, it would be more prudent to worry we might get into a brawl."

He snorted. "Is all that true?" I could see in his eyes he very much wanted to believe me.

I nodded. "You're placing me in a very difficult situation, Your Majesty. You order me to temper my words, but then you question my feelings for you." I lowered my voice to an intimate hush. "Did I not tell you I would rather die than be another man's mistress? If words aren't enough, I could show you in whatever way you need."

He stared at me for a long time, turmoil flickering in his eyes.

My heart sinking, I moved to step away from him.

"Don't," he whispered, reaching out and grabbing my forearm.

When I met his gaze, my soul cried at the pain I saw there.

"Don't pull away from me."

I trembled at his words; I dared not move. "What would you have me do, Your Majesty?" If I spoke any louder, I wouldn't have the breath to carry my voice. "One moment, you tell me to stop moving toward you, and the next, you tell me not to move away. Would you have me simply stand still?"

His eyes fluttered closed, and he winced. "No." His voice caught. He cleared his throat, releasing his hold on me with a heavy sigh. "No, of course not. That wouldn't be right."

"Because I will," I told him. "I will stand still and wait

for you to decide. I will be the predator if you're too meek to act or the prey if you want to give chase. I'll be however you want me to be if it means I can be by your side."

I knew Aodh was only wrestling with indecision because of me. He was never so conflicted in the past. So if this was what he needed to heal—to return to the person he was before I'd made him so uncertain of his own heart—then that was what I would do.

My eyes filled with tears, knowing the whole situation was entirely my fault. I wanted to tell him. I wanted nothing more than to tell him that I was Mischief, that I hadn't abandoned him, that I'd held onto my love for him all that time. My lips trembled as the truth of who I really was died before the words could be formed.

Slowly, he lifted his hands to my face, gazing at me with deep regret. Leaning down, he gently brushed his lips to my forehead.

"Do not wait for me."

I could feel his hands shaking as his breath caressed my skin.

"I know you would. I'm sorry I doubted you."

Hot tears spilled down my cheeks.

"But don't," he murmured.

I looked up at him, his face blurring as my eyes filled again.

He smiled sadly, wiping my wet cheeks with his thumbs. "I have no heart to give. I'm not who you take me to be. And you shouldn't waste your youth on someone fragmented like me. You're a fine woman, Melody. And someday, when you've forgotten all about me, you'll make someone a good wife."

My chest ached, and I felt as if I couldn't breathe. "Never." I tried to make my voice firm and resolute, but it only came out small and sad. "Even if all of my memories were spelled from my mind, I would feel the hole inside me where you once lived."

He winced.

"If you say you cannot love me, that you have felt nothing for me in this last month, then that's a different matter. But do not reject me—do not throw me away—for some misplaced noble gesture."

"Melody—"

"Tell me, truly." My sniffling undermined the steel I tried to inject into my tone. "Did I never sway your heart? Can you honestly say that since the day I showed up here, you have not once wanted me?"

He shook his head and moved to pull away. "It doesn't matter."

I grabbed his hands, halting his retreat. "Tell me it isn't so, and I'll never bother you again."

The knob of his throat jumped as he swallowed, and his hands shook in mine. "I didn't. I never wanted you."

The air rushed out of me as if I'd been kicked in the chest. I clenched his hands tighter, struggling to breathe. "You're lying."

He took a deep breath, standing up straighter as he pulled his hands from mine. "I never once wanted you, Melody."

My head swam, and I wobbled with dizziness. "Y-you—you would send me away with such falsehoods? I thought you were an honorable fae."

"You forget, my lady. I'm a goblin." With every word he spoke, his voice grew colder and more distant. It sounded like the voice of a stranger. "But as the daughter of a noble house, I expect you to keep your word. You will accompany me to Sifra to attend the sidhe king. And when we return, you will pack your things and return to your parents' house. Or perhaps you'd like to stay in Sifra? From what I gathered from his letter, you've already given the sidhe king more than just a taste."

He turned his back to me, and my knees buckled.

The numbness of disbelief had taken me. I was only barely aware that the floor was cold beneath my hands.

He glanced back at me sitting on the floor only to avert his gaze forward again. "I trust you'll behave in a way that brings credit to Goblintown while we're at the sidhe king's court. It's the least you can do for what you've put me through."

With steady, even strides—and without looking back— Aodh left me there alone on the floor. The only thought that existed in my mind was that this was what I deserved. This was how he'd felt so many years ago, and now I knew what I'd done to him.

CHAPTER
SIXTY-TWO

I didn't know how long I sat on the floor of the library, tears pouring down my face.

I was pulled to my senses when Odilie bustled into the room. "Are you still in here, Your Majesty? I've come to refresh the fire. Is she gone? None of the lamps are"—she halted her approach—"Oh! Your Majesty, are you all right? Why are you sitting on the floor?"

Looking around, I saw the room was quite dark. The fire had burned low, and the sun had long set. I wondered at the state of my face and if the light was dim enough to hide that I'd been crying.

Odilie crept toward me. "Your Majesty?"

I cleared my throat, but still, my voice didn't come out as evenly as I would've liked. "I haven't corrected you until now, Odilie, but as I'm not the goblin queen, my proper title is still 'lady.'"

The imp blinked at me, but I didn't have the wherewithal to try to discern her reaction. "If that's what you prefer, my lady. I simply always saw you as the goblin queen."

At least someone did. Rising to my feet, I was grateful my legs supported my weight. "You need not refresh the fire in here for my sake. I'm headed to bed."

Odilie bowed her head. "Goodnight, my lady."

"Goodnight, Odilie."

As I drifted to the goblin queen's room, my feet finding the way on their own, I was a ghost. I saw no one, and no one saw me.

I didn't know where Eithne was—perhaps packing her things—but the goblin queen's bedroom was uninhabited when I arrived.

As I entered the dressing room, I caught my reflection in the mirror. Her face was red and puffy, and her turquoise eyes were dull. She was someone I knew quite well.

Turning away, I continued into the bathroom. The small wash-pitcher still had water in it. The gentle splash as I poured it into the basin sounded far away.

As I cupped my hands in the water, something inside me recognized it was cold. *Good. It will soothe my swollen eyes. Perhaps Eithne won't notice when she returns.*

I splashed my face with the water before holding my breath and plunging my whole face into the basin. I kept it there as long as I could before coming out and gasping for air.

While I dried my face, I realized too late I'd failed to pull my hair back—the front locks were dripping wet. I patted them dry with the towel as best I could.

Returning to the dressing room, I changed into my nightgown and removed the patch from the back of my neck. With any luck, I would be asleep before Eithne returned to help me.

I stood before the mirror again. The cold water had refreshed my face. My eyes were still dull but not nearly as puffy. Taking a deep breath, I rearranged my features, forcing my lips into a polite smile. The practiced action returned to me too easily.

A rapid knock sounded on the bedroom door.

Fixing the contented expression on my face, I went to answer it.

"I hear you're heading to Sifra tomorrow," Graeme said the moment I opened the door.

I turned my back to him and retreated into the larger room as he entered. "Yes," I confirmed. "King Lorccán has summoned us."

"Well, I think I'm going to stay. You won't need my help, right? You can use the trip to get closer to your elf"—I flinched—"and I'd like to use this time to help Selwyn make more progress."

I nodded.

"Are you going to stay at the townhouse? Mum and Dad will be there."

"I didn't plan on it."

"Really? How are you going to get away with that? It will be a good chance to show them what you see in your soon-to-be. You know how much they miss you, and they'll be hurt if you don't stay with them. I'll write to them and tell them to expect you."

My heart ached, and at that moment, I wanted nothing more than my mother's embrace. "Thanks," I murmured.

"Hey," my brother said. "Look at me."

Steeling my nerves, I faced him.

"What's wrong? Did something happen?"

I stretched my lips into a tired smile and shook my head.

"I'm fine. I'm just nervous about going to court. I don't know what to expect."

Graeme frowned, analyzing my face. "Yes, the King is likely not pleased about you choosing another, especially when he made such a show of claiming you at the equinox."

I nodded.

Approaching me, my brother rested his hands on my shoulders. "Don't worry too much though. You didn't do anything illegal. He can't really come after you. And besides, Dad will be there with you, too. He still holds some sway at court."

Graeme wrapped his arms around me, patting my back gently.

It was all I could do not to burst into tears at his loving embrace.

He pulled back to look at me again. "You're trembling. Are you that scared?" His brow scrunched in concern. "I think I'll come with you after all. I'll go pack my things now so I'm ready in time."

I grabbed his hand when he started to leave. "No"—I tried for my most convincing smile—"stay here and help Selwyn. I'll be fine. As you said, Dad will be there, and I've known the King a long time. I should trust him. Plus, A-Aodh will be with me."

My brother pursed his lips. "Are you sure?"

I nodded. *I don't know if I can keep up this farce for two days with Graeme watching me so closely.*

"All right, if you say so. Then you better get to bed. I'll see you off in the morning."

"Goodnight."

After wishing me goodnight, he left.

The moment the door closed behind him, burning heat

began to build behind my eyes. I clenched my eyelids closed to stop the tears, then took a deep breath. I could do it. I'd done it before. I only needed to do it for the rest of my life.

CHAPTER

SIXTY-THREE

By the time Eithne returned to my room, I'd already slipped into bed—Tadhg in dog form curled up beside me. I heard her soft knock, then she stuck her head in. I shamelessly pretended to sleep so she would go away without me having to talk to her.

I honestly couldn't say whether I slept that night or not. My instinct said I didn't, but those twisted imaginings—where I replayed that evening's interaction with Aodh over and over in my mind—very well could have been dreams.

The early morning sunshine brought no warmth with it though I didn't know whether that was reality or my mood.

Eithne arrived shortly after dawn with my breakfast, and I was ready for her with a false smile and a prepared excuse of not having slept well.

While I forced down the food she'd brought, she filled the bathtub. It would be a two-day journey to Sifra, and I didn't know where we'd be stopping to rest along the way. At least I'd be able to bathe again at my parents' townhouse before presenting myself at court.

It seemed I needn't have worried so much about fooling Eithne as to the state of my mind because she went about her duties with a skip in her step and a hum under her breath. She was clearly excited to be leaving Goblintown. *At least one good thing will come from me being turned out. Eithne will be happy to return home.*

Even though it was getting warmer every day, Eithne bundled us both up, insisting it would be colder than I thought riding in an open carriage.

The Goblin King's carriage was already waiting at the front door when we stepped outside. Eithne went to see that the trunks were properly mounted while Peony chatted with Kirk and Lottie, the two guards accompanying us.

"All ready to go?" Graeme asked, stepping into the morning light.

I nodded as he slipped his arm around my shoulder.

"I've already sent a message to Mum to expect you, so don't try to change your mind now."

I rested my head on my brother's shoulder.

"Don't be scared," he murmured, squeezing me. "You've done far more dangerous things in your life."

I let him believe he'd comforted me. Standing on my toes, I kissed him on the cheek. "You're right." *About everything.* "I should always listen to you."

Graeme chuckled. "I'm glad you're finally starting to appreciate the wisdom of your big brother. Remember that the next time you decide to do mischief."

With another squeeze, Graeme released me. He held out his hand and helped me into the carriage. Before letting go, he gave me an encouraging smile and patted my hand.

Everyone turned toward the door when Aodh and Selwyn exited the house, and I was glad their attention was not on me. My stomach lurched to see the morning sunlight shining in Aodh's hair.

Directing my gaze to my knees, I took a steadying breath.

Aodh's voice was confident and smooth though I hadn't the presence of mind to hear what he said. After a few minutes of talking, the carriage lurched as he climbed in across from me.

I didn't dare meet his eyes.

With everything ready, Peony and Eithne climbed into the driver's seat, and the two guards mounted their horses.

At least I managed to wave to my brother as we started to pull away. While we moved toward the palace gate, I gathered all my inner fortitude. All eyes would be on us as we made our way through Goblintown.

Despite the pain in my heart, I took a deep breath and raised my head. The smile that pulled at my mouth was a comedic mask, and I only hoped I was as good an actress as I thought I was.

I waved at those who stopped their morning chores to watch us drive by, and their bright faces were worth the effort.

But as soon as the carriage entered Goblinwood, the smile slipped from my face, and I clenched my hands in my lap.

"You're quite good at pretending," Aodh said, no doubt marking my sudden change in demeanor.

I met his eyes and immediately regretted that decision. My chest tightened as though it were trying to crush my heart.

He sat across from me as beautiful and as cold as the night when we were reunited—when I had stolen his ring and he'd demanded its return.

Had I imagined we'd gotten closer since then? Was all that had transpired between us some great machination on his part? Did I think I was in control when I was only playing into his plan all along?

He'd told me that night that I hadn't known what I was getting myself into. He didn't want a wife and was furious I'd forced myself into his life. Did he somehow convince me I was winning him over just so I would make some statement like the one I'd made the night before?

The terms of our agreement had already been set. If I proved to have the goblin virtues, he would accept me as queen. But if he could get me to wager my leaving against something he had complete control over, then all he had to do was answer accordingly.

I had the goblin virtues. Did he know that from the beginning? Was he only buying himself time? Or had he expected me to fail? Was that his plan all along, or did it form when he saw how eager the goblins were to accept me?

My heart told me none of that was true—that he felt something for me and was lying about it. But as he met my gaze across the small space of the carriage, his dark eyes holding no warmth, I wasn't sure anymore.

"So are you," I replied.

CHAPTER
SIXTY-FOUR

In the carriage, it didn't take very long for us to pass through Goblinwood.

Even so, it felt like an eternity. Since the moment we'd met, Aodh's existence had taken up a large space in my mind. His physical presence was not something I could ignore. Even if I didn't look at him, everything in me was aware he sat across from me.

My sadness—like the many tears I'd shed for him—seemed an ocean, and I was a shipwrecked sailor, clinging to the plank of what once had been.

If the place I found myself now was the result of his masterful machinations, I couldn't even be angry about it. Had I not manipulated him to try to win his favor? Why should he not manipulate me to get rid of what he never wanted?

The truth was I honestly didn't deserve him. Had I not lied to him since the very moment we'd met? Perhaps our love was always destined for disaster. Perhaps it was never real at all. How could love be real if its foundation was lies?

As the thick trees of Goblinwood began to thin, Peony slowed the carriage and came to a stop outside of Tally's inn.

I glanced around the familiar area. It was still morning, and I could hear the chickens clucking happily near the stable.

Aodh rose from his seat and descended to the ground, not bothering to offer me a hand. I frowned, even that small neglect made my heart pang.

Climbing down on my own, I looked around the place. I'd never been there in daylight. It was far bigger than I'd thought. There was the inn, of course, and the stables. But there also seemed to be a corral beyond, where goats grazed.

Without a word to me, Aodh moved toward the entrance. The pathetic creature that I was, I followed him.

As we entered the familiar space, I was surprised at how very empty the inn was at that time of day. The long tables were normally crowded after dark. But that morning, only two other patrons sat near the fire.

Tally came out from a back room when the bell over the door announced our arrival and smiled broadly, bowing her head in respect. "Welcome, Your Majesties. I have to say, I almost didn't believe my girl when she said the Goblin King's carriage was outside."

Aodh nodded to her. "I know it's still early, but could we order a midday meal?"

"How many will I be feeding?" Tally asked.

"Six," said Aodh.

She crossed her arms. "Well, the stew isn't ready yet. But if you lot will settle for a simpler fare, I can make it work."

"Whatever you can manage is fine," Aodh assured, placing the payment on the bar.

Tally nodded and gestured to the empty tables. "Sit

wherever you like. We've got nothing but space this time of day."

I was curious about why we were stopping so early. By the road we were traveling, we would pass near Piskishire by midday. There were plenty of fine restaurants, even roadside inns, we could stop at.

But as Aodh started asking Tally about how things were at the edge of his territory, I figured he just wanted to check in on her.

After a short conversation, Aodh turned toward me to head to a nearby bench; his eyes didn't even seem to register my existence. The heavy weight, which had pressed on me since the previous night, pushed harder.

Silently, I sat across from Aodh at the table. Even in my current state of anguish, I would rather have been near him than not.

Eithne, Peony, Kirk, and Lottie joined us just as Tally brought out the food. Our midday meal consisted of bread, plum preserves, cheese, and a boiled egg.

The others ate quickly, but I was having a hard time forcing the food down. Somewhere in my mind, I knew it tasted good. I just wasn't hungry.

After ten minutes, the others excused themselves from the table, leaving Aodh and me alone again.

While I struggled to swallow the last bite, I glanced at Aodh's plate, which was still half full.

I looked up at him; he stared intently at the meal before him.

He's even beautiful while he's eating. I averted my gaze, my stomach too recently filled to take such a shock. "Thank you for the meal." I stood from the table before fleeing outside.

Peony was leading the horse back toward the carriage when I reached it.

"Allow me, Your Majesty," Kirk said, offering his hand to assist me into the carriage.

I smiled at the gnome. "Thank you, Kirk." I took his hand and climbed in.

Before I'd fully settled into my seat, Aodh exited the inn. After a short conversation with Kirk and Lottie, he mounted Kirk's horse, and Kirk climbed up beside Peony. With a smile, Eithne took Aodh's seat across from me.

"What's going on?" I asked her while Peony urged the horse forward.

Eithne pulled some knitting from her bag and looked up at me when I spoke. "Oh, it seems the Goblin King merely wants to ride for a while. I can understand why. Long carriage rides always leave my back sore."

I frowned. *Yes, I'm sure it has nothing to do with him trying to put more space between us.*

Still, with the cheerful mood Eithne was in, I would likely only find relief in her company as opposed to Aodh's.

"What are you making?" I asked the piskie.

With a smile, she held up the wide square of fabric, striped in yellow and white. "I'm finishing a baby blanket for my sister's baby. I hope I can get it done before we get to Sifra."

"Oh, right. Your sister works for the royal archives now, doesn't she? How is she getting along?"

Eithne dropped her gaze to her knitting needles. "From what I can tell from her letters, she's doing quite well. But I'll be glad to confirm as much for myself once we arrive. I'll be sure to thank His Lordship before I go to see her."

"Will you be staying with her while you're there?"

Eithne blinked. "Is such a thing possible, my lady? I thought you would need me to prepare you for court."

"I'm sure Reannon wouldn't mind helping me get ready.

I don't think my mother will be coming to court with us, so she shouldn't have to help her. You should spend as much time with your sister as you can."

Eithne beamed at me. "Thank you, my lady! That's very generous of you."

At least I still have the power to make you happy, Eithne.

SIXTY-FIVE

As the carriage continued toward Sifra, I watched the landscape go by without paying much attention. The flat fields and farms outside of Goblinwood begin to climb and dip into the foothills and valleys around Piskishire. Summer had indeed returned to Tír, and shoots of green waved in the cool breeze.

I felt as though I were sleeping, as if all that happened in those hours would be forgotten the moment I awoke.

At some point, I blinked and looked around myself, confused. We'd been on the road to Piskishire but had somehow avoided going through the city altogether. And now we were past the town and climbing steadily toward the pass through the Starless Mountains.

Did I miss it? Was I paying so little attention to the journey I missed all of Piskishire? Did we go around?

Whatever had happened, I knew I wouldn't miss Gnomeburgh—the outside part at least. There was only one public pass through the Starless Mountains, and there was no way the gnomes would let us through the mine road without prior permission.

While the daylight still had many hours left, the sun had dipped behind the mountains. I shivered in its shadow, grateful yet again for Eithne's forethought as I pulled my thick cloak tighter.

I stared up at the misty clouds that always hung low over the mountain peaks, the fog that gave the mountains their name. I'd traveled that road many times before, and I never got used to the sight of the sky bearing down on me.

At that moment, I missed the open skies of Olympus. As much as I'd complained of the baking sun, I longed for it now. I closed my eyes, but I couldn't call forth the feeling of that sunshine.

When the carriage slowed and came to a stop, I opened my eyes to see what was happening. We were still half a mile from the opening of the pass and another mile to the nearest inn atop that.

Peony had turned onto a narrower trail—only wide enough for our carriage—which likely headed into one of the many entrances to the caverns and mines.

To one side of where we'd stopped, there was a small clearing in the trees. Peony hopped down from the driver's seat and went about unhitching the horse.

"There's a stream not far from here where we can water the horses," Kirk said.

Aodh and Lottie dismounted and handed their horses over to Peony and Kirk.

"Lottie, Eithne, gather some wood for a fire," Aodh ordered.

Eithne's eyes widened, and her gaze flicked to mine. I nodded to bid her do as he asked.

Then Aodh looked up at me from beside the carriage.

"Let's go," he said before turning and heading toward the mountain pass.

I scrambled out of the carriage after him, trotting to catch up with his long stride. "Where are we going?" I asked, huffing a bit at the exertion to keep up.

"To get food."

I frowned, looking around me. *Where are we going to get food out here? Does he think we're going to hunt for it? Surely, Peony—being a fellow elf—would have been a better choice if he needed a hunting partner.*

He sighed as if he'd heard all my thoughts and was annoyed at having to address my questions. "We're the least likely to draw attention. We can't all go. Two elves, a drake, a gnome, a piskie, and a human? Nothing says 'goblins' quite like that combination."

But why should that matter? We're traveling by orders of Lorccán. Besides, we have to pass through this way with the carriage; they'll certainly know we're goblins by the crest painted on the side. But I didn't argue with him. If he wanted to hide the fact we were there, I was in no state to argue that point. I simply tried to keep up with him as we hiked down the road.

When we neared the edge of Gnomeburgh, Aodh slowed his pace. I sighed in relief, wondering how sore my legs would be from sitting all day and then practically running for a mile and a half.

"Listen," he said low. "Don't address me as the goblin king while we're here. We're going to go to the inn, get some food, and leave quickly. If anyone asks, we're travelers simply buying fare for the next few days."

"That inn?" I asked, pointing to the warmly lit building at the edge of town.

He nodded.

I shook my head. "It's not going to work."

"Why not?"

"Because they know me at that inn. That's where my family stays whenever we're going to or from Sifra."

"Well, then, what would you suggest?" he snapped.

I raised my chin and straightened my cloak. "Just follow my lead."

He frowned but didn't argue.

The inn was just as it had always been for as long as I could remember. It was much larger than Tally's, with many more rooms to accommodate the numerous guests who used the pass every day.

The tavern on the ground floor was packed with locals—there to enjoy the excellent food and drink—and a few travelers, who were just passing through.

Devan, the gnome innkeeper, looked up from pouring a drink to mark our arrival. He grinned widely. "Lady Melody Píobaire! I was wondering when I'd be seeing you again."

I approached the bar with a friendly smile, Aodh trailing after me.

"I saw your parents just before Bealtaine. I asked after you and your brother, you know. But they were so tired from the journey and weren't up for a chat."

"How are you, Devan, and how's Gemma? Did you two have a nice Bealtaine?"

He nodded. "Oh, yes, Gnomeburgh may not have as large a celebration as Sifra, but we know how to throw a good party. Gemma is fine. She's around here somewhere. Shall I bring her out? I know she'll be happy to see you."

"Perhaps, if there's time. I'm just popping in to get some food to take with us if you don't mind."

Devan's gaze flicked to Aodh, and he tilted his head. "Who's this? Don't think I've seen him before. Are you in some kind of trouble, Lady Melody? You've never traveled in the company of anyone other than your family if I recall correctly."

I forced a toothy grin. "Of course, I'm not in trouble, Devan! Goodness, who would have the gall to threaten me? This is my husband, just married, you know. A childhood friend of mine owns a little cabin up in the mountains, perfect place for a secluded honeymoon, don't you think?"

How many times had I dreamed about referring to Aodh as my husband? The sweet words left a bitter taste on my tongue.

Devan's eyes widened. "Just married? You don't say. Congratulations, my lady! And to you, sir." He offered his hand to Aodh for a hearty handshake. "We don't get many elves out this way, what with Elfton being on the other side of Sifra. You're most welcome! What a pleasure you came to Gnomeburgh for your honeymoon of all places. Oh, Lady Melody, married already! It seems only yesterday you were coming this way to visit Sifra for the first time. I can't wait to tell Gemma. She won't believe it. I'll go find her."

"A-actually, Devan, before you do that, do you mind putting in an order with the kitchen? We're keen to get back before dark."

He grinned. "I bet you are, my lady. What can I get you?"

My face flushed at his implication. Devan and his wife had always been a bit on the bawdy side. "We don't need much, really. Maybe just a few loaves of bread, some cheese, some fruit and veg if you have it."

He nodded enthusiastically. "Of course! Nothing would be easier. I'll have them make you up some baskets, and then I'll go find Gemma."

CHAPTER
SIXTY-SIX

As soon as Devan had scurried away, I began to squirm. I could feel Aodh's eyes on me. But really, there was nothing else I could've said. It wouldn't have been proper for a lady to travel with a man she wasn't related to, especially if not chaperoned. If he'd wanted to avoid attracting much attention, he should've brought Peony. Two elves, even out that way, would've still been less conspicuous.

I peeked up at him, hoping he wasn't too angry at my tactic.

His expression was bland, but I couldn't mistake the pity in his eyes. He redirected his gaze away as if he hadn't cared to look at me to begin with.

"My lady!" Gemma squealed, boldly rushing to embrace me. "I can't believe your news! Congratulations." She pulled back to analyze me. "What a surprise, and your parents didn't say a word about it. Must've been a quick one, eh?"

Her gaze dropped to my stomach, and I instinctively covered it with my hand as if she could somehow see inside.

Her eyes glinted, and I shook my head. *You misunderstand, Gemma. There's nothing there, and there never will be.*

"How did you two fall in love? Where did you meet? You haven't been long back from Olympus," she said.

At her questions, tears began to burn the back of my throat. I coughed in the hopes of keeping them at bay. "Oh, it feels like I've always loved him."

The gnome didn't push for specifics but grinned.

"Here you are, lovebirds," Devan announced, placing two bursting baskets onto the bar.

Aodh stepped forward to settle the bill as Gemma motioned me closer.

"He's a handsome one, my lady. I bet he's as good as he looks, eh?"

I flushed, and she chuckled, reaching out and taking my chin in her hand.

"You want to know the secret to a good marriage from someone who knows?"

I have a feeling you're going to tell me whether I do or not.

"Honesty," she nodded seriously. "Tell him what you want and when you want it. Tell him when he's doing good and tell him when he's fucking up. And be specific. These fellas aren't good with subtlety, you know." She tapped her nose knowingly. "You do that, and you might just be as happy as Devan and me one day."

I swallowed back tears while forcing myself to smile. "That's all anyone can hope for."

The cool evening air stung my lungs as we stepped out of the inn. I slowed my pace so Aodh would walk in front.

Tears burned my nose and silently spilled down my face. For once, I was grateful he didn't want to look at me. I was barely holding it together. If he looked back at me, I would surely sob as loudly as my heart screamed inside me.

I tilted my head back, staring up into the thick clouds again. I wished they would just swallow me whole.

Aodh didn't speak as we walked back to the carriage. He carried the baskets and watched the road ahead. As dusk approached, the mist seemed to descend to the path. Our quiet footsteps sounded too close as if they were the only sounds in the world.

Lights appeared in the distance in a curve leading into the mountains. I wondered what was up there. Now that the mist had made my wish come true, perhaps I could just disappear.

I could follow the lights to someplace unknown. No one would ever know where I'd gone. *The Goblin Queen who never was just disappeared one night on the mountain pass. They say on nights when the mist is particularly thick, you can still hear her calling for her king though he never comes.*

My fanciful daydreams drifted away as one particular light grew brighter and brighter. It wasn't long before I realized it was the fire from our camp.

Aodh set down the baskets and started to parcel out food to the others, who sat around the fire in a cozy picture of adventurers on a trek.

I didn't say much while sitting beside Eithne. The ground nearest the fire was dry, but the mist was starting to make everything else feel damp. I might have thanked Aodh for the food he passed me—bread with cheese and sliced mutton—but if I did, it was in a voice that got lost in the surrounding fog.

After everyone had eaten, they started pulling out their blankets.

Eithne didn't look happy about the idea of sleeping outside, but she must've been told beforehand because she, too, readied a place for us near the fire.

"There's room for both of you in the carriage," Aodh said, staring down at the blankets Eithne was arranging for us.

"Then where will you sleep, Your Majesty?" I asked. If I was to sleep in the carriage, it only made sense he would, too. He wasn't making an exception for Lottie or Peony, so he wasn't simply being chivalrous to the womenfolk.

"I'll sleep on the ground with the rest of the goblins," he said.

I flinched. *There he goes, drawing that line again.* "Then so will I." I lifted my chin. "I'm no better than anyone else here."

Eithne frowned. She clearly would much rather sleep in the carriage than on the cold, damp ground.

Without a word, Aodh snatched up the blankets Eithne had laid out and stomped over to the carriage. Then he threw them onto the seats.

Everyone eyed him silently, not quite knowing how to deal with his outburst.

"Must you always be so difficult? Can you not, just once, do as you're told?" he demanded exasperatedly.

My face flushed. He needn't have done all that in the presence of others. I sharply sucked air in through my nose. "Very well."

He watched me as if he hadn't expected it to be that easy. "All right, then."

"Fine," I answered.

"Good."

"Good, indeed."

With a grunt, he settled into his blankets.

There was no hiding the fact that something was going on between us now. I could feel the others watching to see what I'd do. But I simply walked over to the carriage and curled onto the seat, covering myself in the blanket he'd thrown there.

With the matter seemingly settled, everyone else crawled into their blankets. We would have a long drive ahead of us if we hoped to reach Sifra by the following night. The carriage jostled as Eithne climbed in and laid down across from me.

I rolled onto my back, bending my knees and staring up at the grey carpet of clouds overhead. *What was that all about? Why does it matter where I sleep?*

It wasn't long before everyone else was asleep. Eithne breathed quietly across from me while Lottie filled the camp with quiet snores—smoke puffing from her mouth with every exhale. I sat up and looked around.

The fire had burned low and was only barely illuminating the four goblins sleeping around it.

As quietly as I could, I alighted from the carriage, wrapping my blanket around me to combat the chill. I crept toward the fire and carefully placed more sticks on it. They hissed gently while they caught.

As it flickered back to life, I stared down at Aodh. His sleeping form was just as I'd imagined it, and I sat beside him to get a better look.

My heart ached to see him in such an intimate way. I'd longed to watch him sleep beside me for so many years, and this was the only chance I'd ever have to see him thus.

Lowering myself to my side, I lay my head on my bent arm and just looked at him.

As the dim light of the fire cast glimmers and shadows on his face, I tried to memorize every dip and curve.

But despite my wanting to make the moment last as long as I could, my eyes grew heavy. I hadn't slept the night before, and I couldn't fight it anymore.

CHAPTER
SIXTY-SEVEN

"You just do whatever you want, don't you?" Aodh murmured. His distant words were harsh, but his tone sounded almost indulgent.

I squeezed my eyes tighter as if I could force myself to stay asleep. If I tried hard enough, he would still be with me, even for just a little longer.

The waking world crashed into me as Lottie yawned loudly.

I winced and sighed, giving in to reality as I opened my eyes.

Despite how uncomfortable the ground was, I'd slept hard. I hissed as I sat up, my body aching from not having moved enough in my sleep. Still, I was rested. My mind was clear, which wasn't necessarily the best thing when I was trying to come to terms with the love of my life rejecting me.

Glancing over to where Aodh had lain the night before, I frowned in disappointment. Both he and his blanket were gone.

It seemed Aodh, Kirk, and Peony had been up and about for at least a little while. Kirk had refilled our water skins, and Peony was leading the horses back to camp—I assumed from watering them at the stream.

Aodh was digging through the baskets, a slice of mutton hanging from his mouth. I might have laughed at how silly he looked if the very sight of him didn't make my chest hurt so badly.

The mist from the night before had lifted though it still hung low as it always did in the Starless Mountains. I wondered if the gnomes ever saw the sun or if they even knew what they were missing.

As Lottie sat up and rolled her blanket, Eithne gasped and looked around frantically. Her gaze landed on me, and she sighed. Her pursed lips told me she knew exactly what I'd done, and I only hoped she wouldn't nag me too much for it.

We ate a quick breakfast before getting back on the road. That time, Aodh rode with me in the carriage, and Eithne again sat beside Peony.

It was no easier to look at him that day than it had been the day before, but something inside me urged me to do it anyway.

He wore that same cool expression as he stared out the carriage. But the closer we traveled to Gnomeburgh, the tighter his jaw seemed to get.

As we neared the inn, his eyes flicked to me. I flinched at his sudden attention.

"Pull up your hood," he ordered, his voice tense.

I complied, swallowing my questions.

It was a quiet morning in Gnomeburgh, the same as many others I'd seen. Gnomes went about their business—

sweeping their steps, talking to neighbors, and opening their shops.

But as the Goblin King's carriage passed through their town, the pleasant atmosphere soured.

It started with a low hiss that gathered into boos and jeers.

"Oi! Get out of here, you damn goblins!" someone shouted.

"Yeah! We don't want your kind here!"

My eyes widened, and I turned my head to look at who could yell such a thing.

Aodh leaned forward and grabbed my hand. Meeting my eyes, he shook his head. And that was when someone threw something.

Whatever it was thunked against the side of the carriage. Eithne yelped, cringing into Peony. But Peony didn't even flinch.

Kirk and Lottie rode close to the sides of the carriage, blocking any projectiles as best they could.

Something wet and dirty hit Kirk in the head, and I jumped to my feet to come to his defense.

Aodh quickly switched seats and pulled me down next to him.

"Don't," he murmured, replacing my hood. "You'll only make it worse. Just keep quiet, and we'll be out of here soon enough."

With every insult hurled at us, with every clump of dirt, I became more and more enraged. I trembled with fury, and the only thing keeping me in place was Aodh's steady gaze.

His dark eyes said nothing at all. He wasn't angry. He wasn't sad. To him, this was just how it was for goblins outside of Goblintown.

By the time we reached the other side of Gnomeburgh, we were much worse for the wear.

Once he was sure there wasn't anyone for me to throw something back at, Aodh returned to his seat and directed his gaze out toward the wooded mountain pass.

We rode in silence for a long time, my anger sharpening with every minute. That was unacceptable. Was that how it was for everyone before they came to Goblintown? Was that what it was like before they left their own communities? How could I make it better? What could I possibly do?

Eventually, at Kirk's directions, Peony stopped beside a small mountain lake. Kirk and Lottie dismounted their horses and went to clean the muck off them as best they could.

Aodh got out to see if they were injured, and I went to check on Peony and Eithne.

For her part, Eithne was still shaken. She'd buried her face into Peony's shoulder, clutching at her as if the slight elf were her personal shield. Peony patted Eithne's back.

"Are you all right?" I asked.

Peony nodded, and it didn't look like she'd been hit by anything at least.

Eithne released the elf and turned toward me. Her face was streaked with tears. "My lady!" she cried. "What a horrible experience. How can you want to be goblin queen after that? Is this what will happen to us anytime we leave that horrid place? I can't do this!"

I frowned. I knew Eithne didn't like being in Goblintown, but I also knew she wouldn't be there for long. As soon as we returned, we would be going back to Maplecrest. Still, it wasn't a good idea to say such a thing in front of the goblins. They didn't know Aodh had rejected me, and I still had to make a good showing on Goblintown's behalf at court.

Reaching out, I patted Eithne's hand, hoping that would be enough to soothe her.

CHAPTER
SIXTY-EIGHT

If the first half of the journey had been tense, the rest was solemn. While the goblins showed no reaction to the incident in Gnomeburgh, their lack of emotions told me everything I needed to know.

Once we left gnome territory and crossed into Trowstead, we again moved off the main road. I understood why we'd gone around Piskishire now. I didn't recall anyone acting so hostile when Selwyn had driven me through Piskishire that first day, but then, the piskies knew I was the earl's daughter. Still, better to be safe.

I hoped we would get through trow territory without incident. The foothills and forests were as beautiful as always, but I was alert to every sound in case some trow decided to pick a fight.

When midday came and went without us stopping to eat, I didn't complain. My parents would have more than enough to satisfy our empty stomachs when we arrived.

The sun was making its slow descent toward the horizon, and we were nearing the edges of Sifra when I finally spoke.

"Did my brother tell you where my parents' townhouse is?" Now that I considered it, I wondered if Aodh had ever been to Sifra before. I thought it unlikely.

He nodded without looking at me. "Peony knows where to take you."

I frowned. "Take me? Will you and the others not be staying with us?"

When his dark eyes found mine, I saw only coolness there. "Why would we?"

Leaning forward, I dropped my voice. "I thought you were the one who wanted to keep up appearances until after we returned."

His answer was at a normal volume though I didn't know if anyone else heard. "I'm certain your parents would prefer if you were to visit without us."

I bit my cheek. *He's probably not wrong about that.* "But what about going to court? Will you really present yourself before the King and all his nobles travel-worn?"

"I am as I am," he said simply.

"Can you not be as you are after a bath?" I sighed, trying to find the words to convince him even as I saw the stubborn set of his mouth. "Look, everyone at court already doesn't like you, right? They're going to judge you harshly simply because you're a goblin. I'm not saying you have to change who you are. But they'll be far worse if you don't at least clean up a little. And if they're too distracted by your appearance, they won't be listening to your case. It will only hurt Goblintown if you don't make a little effort. Besides"— I gestured toward the others—"don't you think they would also like to clean up properly?"

Aodh glanced at Kirk, who hadn't quite gotten the muck off his well-worn hat. He pursed his lips but gave a single nod of ascent.

Though he gave in to me, I didn't feel I'd won. The truth was I had no idea how my parents—my father, in particular —would receive him. They would, of course, provide food and beds to the goblins, but I couldn't really count on anything else.

I stared into the distance, and it wasn't long before the setting sun illuminated the gleaming white walls and towers of Sifra. I tensed in my seat, hoping the sidhe wouldn't act as openly hostile as the gnomes had.

Apprehension weighed down on us. Eithne seemed the only one to perk up as we approached. Glancing at Aodh, I saw his hands were clenched into fists. The urge to reach out and lace my fingers with his made my heart twinge. But he wouldn't appreciate the gesture even if it was meant to comfort.

The closer we got to the city gates, the larger and more imposing the walls became. This was a new sensation for me. I'd always felt relief and excitement upon nearing the gates to the sidhe city.

The sun had already set, and the many fae lights that illuminated Sifra after dark had been brought to life by the time Peony pulled up to the gate.

"What in the Morrigan's ass feathers is this?" one of the guards said as Peony came to a halt.

I winced at his curse. This wasn't getting off to a good start.

Peony didn't seem fazed. She held out a folded sheet of paper. "We have a summons from King Lorccán."

The guard snatched the paper from her hand and unfolded it. He snorted. "The Goblin King, is it, then? This summons is for the morrow." He threw it back at her. "Come back then."

With a click of my tongue, I shot to my feet. "Guard!" I

snapped. "What is the meaning of this? As you can see, I was also listed on that summons—Lady Melody Píobaire. If my father—the Earl of Piskishire—means to house my companions for the night so we might answer the King's call on time, who are you to say no?"

The sidhe glanced behind him at his compatriot. As a sidhe, he wasn't used to taking orders from a human, and he was from one aristocratic family or another by the very nature of his race. But he was either from a family without great influence or was so far down the family tree he was practically a peasant himself, else he wouldn't be a guard to begin with.

His comrade motioned him closer and whispered something to him. The first guard's sea-glass green eyes widened as he looked back at me.

Without another word, he gestured for the gate to be raised. I took my seat, and Peony urged the horse on.

The spotless streets of Sifra had always seemed a paradise to my young eyes; they didn't look so now. The shining storefronts, the neat houses all in tight rows, the sweet scent of flowers on the breeze, the arched bridges over clear canals where otters happily played—it was all the same. But that night, the fae lights didn't seem to reach as far; there were many more shadows than I remembered.

Every sidhe we passed on the street looked positively scandalized. Some looked downright enraged. Whether it was luck or the fact that they thought too highly of themselves, we managed to reach my parents' townhouse without further incident.

Peony pulled up outside, and I stood. "Eithne, would you mind showing Peony where she can store the carriage and help the others get settled in the servants' quarters?"

"Yes, my lady," she answered softly.

I hopped out of the carriage first, not allowing Aodh to slight me in front of my family's home. Still, I waited for him on the pavement.

He stared up at the building—modest compared to the goblin king's palace—and I could not discern his thoughts.

All I could think about while we climbed the front steps was that this wasn't how I'd wanted their first meeting to go. It should have been a happy occasion. My parents were meeting the fae I loved.

As I twisted the knob of the front door, I might as well have been wringing my own heart.

CHAPTER
SIXTY-NINE

Removing my cloak in the front hall, I called out. "Hello? Mum? Dad?"

The clatter of a cup wobbling in a saucer came from the sitting room to my left, and my mother appeared in the doorway a few moments later.

She smiled, joy sparkling in her eyes as she rushed to embrace me. "My daughter! You're finally here. I've missed you."

I clutched her, clinging to the warmth I'd so needed the past few days.

"Do you have one of those for your dear ol' Dad?" my father asked, emerging from the same place.

I smiled and released my mum to hug him. He patted my head, then stroked my hair affectionately.

"So this is him, then?" Mum asked, assessing Aodh with her keen gaze.

My father eased his embrace to an arm around my shoulder.

Aodh bowed his head to her in the exact proper manners

that were her due. "Lady Piskishire"—then he did the same to Dad—"Lord Piskishire."

"Oh!" Mum blinked in surprise at his impeccable greeting. "It's nice to finally meet you, um… What shall we call you?"

"Well, I can tell you one thing," Dad grumbled. "I won't be calling him 'majesty.' What is your name, boy?"

I winced. "Dad!"

But Aodh maintained the same respectful composure. "My name is Aodh, my lord."

"Aodh? Is that all? Have you no family name to accompany it?"

I squirmed out of my father's arm. "Dad, that's enough."

Aodh frowned. "My mother's family was called Silfurmune."

Dad raised an eyebrow. "And your father's?"

"Mr. Silfurmune," Mum said with a smile, stepping between Aodh and Dad. "I speak for everyone when I say welcome to our home. You've had a long journey. I know I'm always tired when we arrive from Maplecrest, and Goblintown is even farther. Why don't you clean up a bit and have a rest while I make sure your attendants are being properly cared for? Supper should be ready shortly."

Mum turned to me. "Melody, please show Mr. Silfurmune to your room."

I blinked at my mother. "My room? Then where am I to sleep?"

Mum tilted her head at me. "Melody, I am not a child. Do you want me to believe you have lived over a month with your betrothed, and you're still too shy to share a bed?"

"I protest, Siwan," Dad said. "They're not yet married."

Mum scowled. "Oh, Eirian, don't be daft. What's the difference now?"

"I agree with Dad," I interjected. "We have more than enough space to have our own beds."

Mum's eyes sharpened, but she shrugged. "Very well. If you feel so strongly about it. But still, lead him to your room for now so the maids can prepare the guest room."

I glanced at Aodh, embarrassed by everything that had transpired thus far. *If he didn't want to marry me before, he certainly never will now.*

"Follow me," I murmured, starting up the stairs.

As he trailed after me, I couldn't shake the surreal feeling of his presence in my family home. It was as if the part of my life in which he existed was another world from the one where I was with my family—and ne'er the two shall meet. I pushed away the instinct to reconcile my two worlds. One would soon be erased, and I would only feel more pain if I missed his presence in this space, too.

Leading him down a long hall, I entered the last door on the right.

My bedroom in Sifra was not nearly as large as the one at Maplecrest. But it had everything I needed: a bed, a washing table, and an armoire. Though my father stayed in the city for long periods of time, the rest of the family was only there for short stints—mostly for festivals and balls and my visits to Lorccán.

"There's a bath down the hall for after supper, but you can clean up here for now," I told Aodh.

He nodded by way of an answer.

"I'll uh…leave you to go first, then." But as I turned toward the door, I hesitated. "Are you all right?" I asked. I glanced back at him when he didn't respond. "I don't know what has gotten into my father. I assure you, he doesn't normally act that way."

His eyes met mine. "He loves you," he said softly. "And he wants what's best for you."

My guts clenched at his unsaid words: *And he knows it's not me.* "Yes, well"—my voice sounded hollow even to me—"I suppose it doesn't really matter whether my father approves of you or not, does it? As you never wanted me to begin with."

In the overhead fae light, he didn't look away. He didn't even make a move. His eyes were unfocused and empty. And at that moment, I believed I'd been mistaken all along. Whatever I'd thought I'd seen, whatever I'd thought he felt, it had never been there. He didn't want me. He'd never wanted me, not as Melody anyway.

I didn't know whether it was some elaborate plan on his part or I'd just been severely wrong. Perhaps I was very good at lying to myself—at seeing what I wanted to see.

But whatever else, this elf who stood before me wasn't the Aodh I'd once known. He was a stranger, and my heart wrenched as if the boy I loved had died.

Tears welled in my eyes, and I turned my back to him. "Right," I whispered, my voice breaking at the end.

Stepping into the hallway, I closed the door behind me. *I need to pull it together.* I wiped my face with my sleeves as errant tears escaped down my cheeks. *Dad is likely to turn everyone out if he sees me upset.* I sniffed hard and straightened my spine.

Pushing my emotions aside to process later, I descended the stairs and went in search of the other goblins to make sure they were settling in all right.

I found Eithne fastening her cloak in the back hall, a large bag on the floor beside her.

"Oh, Eithne, are you off to see your sister?" I asked.

The piskie turned to me, and she wore all her troubles on her face.

I frowned, her words in Gnomeburgh resurfacing in my mind. "Are you…coming back?" I inquired softly.

Eithne sucked in a shuddering breath through her nose. "I don't know, my lady. I need to think on it."

I wrestled with the notion of telling her we would only be in Goblintown for a short while longer. But before I could come to a decision, she dipped her head.

"Please excuse me, my lady. My sister is waiting." And then she left out the back door.

CHAPTER
SEVENTY

The atmosphere at the dining room table was strained, and only the sounds of our cutlery broke the silence.

"How are things at court these days, Dad? I'd like to know what I'm walking into," I asked before bringing a slice of carrot to my mouth.

My father frowned. "Tense. But what can you expect when the King was jilted by his promised mistress?"

I sighed, exasperated at his suggestion. "Surely, King Lorccán isn't so petty as to throw the whole court into turmoil over one insignificant human? Is there really nothing else?"

"Don't call yourself insignificant, dear," my mother scolded gently as if I'd forgotten to place my napkin on my lap.

"Kelpania has stepped back a bit now that young Brochfael has come of age," my father admitted. "Boy seems to be doing well for himself. He's spending as if he owns a mine."

I tilted my head in thought.

"He summoned me, you know," Dad said.

"Brochfael?" I asked surprised.

He shook his head. "The King. He didn't believe it when young Brochfael told him you'd run off to Goblintown."

I lowered my head, staring at my food. "What did he say?"

"You hurt him, Melody. Hurt his heart and bruised his pride. I wager it's not too late if you want to change your mind."

My head snapped up, and I looked at my father, then Aodh—who quietly continued to eat.

"What say you, *Goblin King*?" Dad asked. "Do you think it prudent to keep my daughter with you when the King has long claimed her?"

"Dad!" I censured.

"Oh, Eirian!" Mum scowled.

Aodh slowly lowered his fork and met my father's gaze seriously. "Your daughter is free to make her own choices."

Except the one I want.

Silence strangled the room again, and I just let it happen.

"How was your Bealtaine, dear?" Mum cheerfully changed the subject.

"Why didn't you come for my daughter yourself?" Dad demanded, glaring at Aodh across the table. "You would have her hand in marriage, but you couldn't be bothered to make the short journey from Goblintown to Maplecrest? My daughter deserves better."

Aodh didn't even flinch under my father's fury. "I agree," he said simply. Removing the napkin from his lap, he placed it beside his plate. "Thank you for the meal. I think I'll retire for the night. Don't trouble yourself. I'll get someone from downstairs to show me to the guest room."

"Eirian!" Mum scolded the moment Aodh left the room.

"What? Shall I sit silently while my daughter is disrespected?"

"There are better ways," she argued.

I rose from my chair as well. I was exhausted. All I wanted to do was take a bath and go to bed. "I'm going up, too. I'll see you in the morning."

After my parents wished me goodnight, I retreated upstairs.

I was drying my hair from the bath near my bedroom fire when a knock sounded on my door. I flinched, remembering a similar situation not long ago.

But it was my mother, not Aodh, who'd come to check on me. After I opened the door for her, she sat on my bed.

"Come here, and I'll plait your hair for bed," she said, patting the blanket in front of her.

I crawled up with her and handed her my comb.

We were quiet for a while as her fingers gently untangled my hair.

"What's really going on?" she asked.

I didn't answer but huffed a sad little sound. *I don't know why I thought I could hide anything from her.*

"You can tell me honestly. I won't hold it against him," she urged.

"He doesn't want me, Mum," I murmured. "I thought I could win him over, but he's rejected me at every turn."

Her deft fingers smoothed and twined my hair slowly.

My throat began to burn with tears. "He said that once we're back from Sifra, he wants me to leave Goblintown. He even suggested I stay with King Lorccán." My voice broke with a sob, and I heaved when another followed close behind.

My mum leaned me back, wrapping her arms over my chest. She shushed me softly, her mouth close to my ear. "I know, my darling. I know it hurts. I'll not tell you time will heal this pain. You're very special, and you love with everything you have."

She rocked me gently from side to side. "But don't forget you are strong, my girl. You have the strength to see this through. And when you're done, you can come home to those who love you. You can come home, or I'll take you wherever you want—anywhere in all of Faerie."

I cried in my mother's arms, and she continued to whisper how much she loved me until I was out of tears.

Then, wiping my face, she laid me down and tucked me under the covers. Crawling in beside me, she took my hand —kissing my fingers as she hummed the song she'd sung to me all my life.

She reached out and petted my head while my swollen and bleary eyes strained to see her in the dim light.

"Go to sleep, my darling," she whispered. "I'm here, and I'll be here when you awake."

With the soothing sound of my mother's soft hum and the warmth of her loving presence, I drifted off into an exhausted sleep.

SEVENTY-ONE

When I awoke the following morning, Mum still lay beside me, her hand clasping mine.

The ache I'd felt since that night in the library still hollowed out my chest, but it didn't seem to sting so badly now.

I propped myself up onto my elbow and kissed my mother softly on the cheek. As I slipped out of bed, I wondered how long she had stayed awake, watching me to ensure I slept soundly.

Quietly, I went to my armoire, where Reannon had put away my things, and stared at the dresses Eithne had packed for me.

I frowned at my choices. Though it was understandable, she'd chosen the finest silk I had that was appropriate for the occasion. Beside it was a much simpler linen travel gown for the return journey.

I took out the linen. It was proper for me to present myself in finery before the sidhe king. But it would not help my cause. If I knew Aodh at all, he would wear something simple and clean if he even owned anything so fine as my silk dress.

Aodh would be making the case for why he hadn't paid Goblintown's taxes, and showing up in expensive fabrics would only undermine him.

That day, I was the goblin queen, and I needed to act accordingly.

By the time my mother stirred from my bed, I was already dressed. She appeared in the mirror over my shoulder, a gentle smile on her face.

"How should I wear my hair?" I asked her.

"Loose," she suggested, adjusting a lock she'd deemed out of place. "With that silver circlet you bought me with your first allowance."

I nodded.

She squeezed my shoulders. "I'll go get it."

As I waited for her to return, I applied kohl to my eyes.

"Here," she said.

I turned to face her, and she placed the circlet over my hair, the metal cool against my forehead.

"Lovely." She smiled.

Looking back in the mirror, I nodded. I didn't look quite like a queen, but then I wasn't one really.

"Let's get some breakfast in you before you head out," Mum said, rubbing my back in a slow circle.

The mood in the dining room that morning was much the same as it had been the night before. The only difference was Dad had already said his piece, and we were all very clear about his feelings regarding the whole business.

Aodh had dressed as I'd expected him to though I was a bit surprised to see him carrying Robin Goodfellow's dagger. He did not wear his crown of grapevines.

Dad left before us in his carriage. I imagined the entire court would be assembled well before our appointed time.

As Aodh and I waited in the front hall for Peony to pull up the carriage, my mother took my cloak from Reannon and fastened it around me herself.

"Remember what I said," she told me softly. "Do as you've always done. Follow your heart."

I nodded, swallowing down my nerves.

As we stepped out into the morning sunshine, my heart pounded like the executioner's drum. I had no idea what I was heading into, and I could only hope we would make it out unscathed.

Peony must have spent part of the night before cleaning up the carriage because it had no traces of our Gnomeburgh confrontation. Kirk and Lottie, too, looked refreshed and worthy to escort the Goblin King.

To my surprise, Aodh handed me into the carriage, but I didn't take it as a sign of anything other than what it was.

I bit my lip while we trotted smoothly toward the palace. *Trust your instincts. Lorccán is an honorable fae. If he cares for me as much as Dad says, he won't hurt me. I know he wants to be a good king. He won't risk looking petty and spiteful in front of all his nobles.*

Whatever Aodh was thinking, he didn't say. And his expression said even less than his silence. Perhaps he was going over his case. Perhaps he was singing "The Piper's Pretty Petticoat" in his mind; I really didn't know.

As soon as the palace came into view, my eyes fixed on it. Had it always been so close to our townhouse?

The crystal roof winked in the morning sun, and the golden walls glimmered so brightly I had to shield my eyes.

I could hardly hear the sound of the wind over my own heartbeat as Peony stopped the carriage before the marble steps of the sidhe king's palace. How many times had I been there in my life? I'd never been so nervous.

Seemingly unperturbed, Aodh gracefully climbed down from the carriage and offered me his hand again.

"Will you be all right?" he asked me in a hushed voice, tucking my hand into his arm when I reached the ground.

"Worry not, Your Majesty," I answered in kind. "Today, I act on behalf of Goblintown. If you believe nothing else, believe I have only their best interests at heart."

When he didn't reply, I glanced over at Aodh to see him frowning. *There's really no way for me to please him.*

With slow and measured steps, Aodh led me up the stairs and into the main entrance.

The guards posted on either side of the grand entrance didn't even seem to register our presence.

Immediately upon entering the door, we were in the grand hall. Gold and marble columns twisted toward the marble ceiling, two for each of the three hallways. The floor was covered in a lush red rug, and marble statues decorated the corners.

Aodh hesitated, but I gently led him through the hallway on the left.

Farther down the hall, the red carpet continued, climbing up the grand staircase, which led to the upper floor.

Our footfalls made no sound on the rug, and with every step, the chatter coming from upstairs grew louder and louder.

Once on the landing, the large anteroom opened before us. Oversized paintings of King Lorccán and Queen Lilliana hung on either side of the far doorway, staring down at us as if our fates were already decided.

Every step closer to that door seemed heavier than the last.

I swallowed with effort as Aodh handed the steward our summons. The young sidhe glanced at the paper, then raised his voice in a clear shout that cut through all the commotion.

"The Goblin King and Lady Melody Píobaire, daughter of the Earl of Piskishire!"

CHAPTER
SEVENTY-TWO

The nobles on either side of the long path through the throne room hushed at the steward's announcement.

As Aodh slowly stepped forward, I lifted my chin and tightened my grip on his arm.

Staring straight ahead, I fixed my eyes on the sidhe rulers sitting on their thrones of twisted marble and gold.

My peripheral vision saw the stares of the many sidhe around us, and I marked my father not far from the entrance. *Has he been so demoted that he's that far away from the King?*

Queen Lilliana's bright eyes flashed, and her frown sent a shiver up my spine. I couldn't recall having ever offended her. In truth, we'd never exchanged more than a few passing words, but it was clear she found our presence distasteful.

Compared to Lorccán, the queen's countenance appeared measured and composed.

He wore the same heated expression he had the last time

I'd seen him. His gaze traveled over me as if to check my condition, to ensure I was not damaged in any way.

But when he looked at Aodh, his nose wrinkled as though he smelled something foul. A deep hatred burned in his eyes, and for the first time, I truly feared whether we would get out of this alive.

Upon reaching the end of the aisle, I released Aodh's arm and curtsied deeply. Beside me, Aodh bowed.

The moments drew out as we held our positions, waiting to be released by one of their commands.

"You may rise," Lorccán said.

We did so, my legs burning at having had to hold the awkward position for so long.

"The Goblin King," Lorccán called, a smirk on his face. "That is what you call yourself, isn't it?"

Aodh's expression was calm, much calmer than those of the sidhe rulers. "That is what the people of Goblintown call me, Your Majesty, as their chosen representative."

"And how exactly do you represent them?" Lorccán asked.

I clenched my jaw at the question. He knew very well what Aodh's job was meant to be, but he was trying to trap Aodh into insulting the Crown.

"Unlike the rest of Tír, Goblintown has not a sidhe to govern it. I simply do what the aristocracy does elsewhere."

I could feel the crowd tense around us. They did not like being compared to a goblin.

Lorccán smiled with venom—the expression on his face thoroughly foreign to me. "But you have not done as my fine nobles have, have you *Goblin King*? Every one of those gathered here pays taxes to the Crown. You have not done so in three years."

Aodh didn't even flinch. "And in return, the territories

under their care are given public aid. The goblins are not afforded the same privileges."

"And why should they be?" Lorccán demanded. "They are but criminals and outcasts. Should they be given the same rights as citizens of good standing?"

Aodh's eye twitched, and his measured tone slipped. "Anyone who committed a crime has already paid their debt to society."

"Your Majesty," I said, drawing Lorccán's attention to me. "As a wise and honest king, I know you want to ensure the welfare of all your citizens, goblin or otherwise. Surely, we can negotiate a better plan for Goblintown. The Goblin King would be happy to pay your taxes if he had the funds he needs to help his people."

"Don't call him that," Lorccán snapped. "He is no more a king than I am a goblin."

I bowed my head, swallowing the lump that rose in my throat from him using such a harsh tone on me. "I apologize, Your Majesty. I merely meant to say Mr. Silfurmune would happily comply if you would but ensure those living in Goblintown weren't suffering so. I'm certain this is all a simple oversight. For I know you to be the kindest of all the fae."

Queen Lilliana scowled, but Lorccán's rage eased a bit.

"Do you truly?" he asked.

I nodded. "I have said so to Mr. Silfurmune before. Have I not?" I looked to Aodh.

Aodh frowned, and his dark eyes seemed to burn like glowing coals. "Lady Melody has expressed such sentiments to me."

Lorccán smiled, and something inside me told me I'd been mistaken about him. "Very well, I have a solution, then. It is my understanding you are not yet married?" He lifted an eyebrow.

My stomach soured, but I answered him with a nod.

"Leave Goblintown and become my royal mistress, and I will forgive the goblins' debt and extend your father's territory to include Goblintown. Then we shall have no more of this business of not paying taxes, and the goblins can be administered to as the earl sees fit."

A murmur ran through the crowd, but my heart pounded too loudly for me to make out what anyone was saying. I glanced over at Aodh.

His gaze met mine, and for a moment, I saw the Aodh I remembered. He looked as vulnerable and self-conscious as a boy of fifteen asking the girl he loved for a future promise.

I tried to swallow, no moisture in my mouth to execute the motion properly.

My legs shook, and my lips trembled. "I-I can't," I breathed.

Dropping to my knees, I prostrated myself before the throne. "Please, Your Majesty, ask for anything else, I beg you. I cannot forsake the man beside me. I can give my heart to no other for it has only ever been his."

The room went completely silent, and I dared not breathe.

Lorccán's face flushed, and his eyes bulged.

"Your Majesty," someone called from the crowd near the throne, "if I may."

The Duke of Westcount stepped out of the crowd and into the aisle in front of us. "You are quite right. The goblins have been running amok for far too long. To properly manage them, we should appoint one of our own. But I caution against a hasty choice. Lord Piskishire may live nearest Goblintown, but let's not forget Lord Kelpania's land also borders Goblintown."

The duke gestured toward Lord Kelpania and Brochfael. "I humbly request you think carefully before making such a serious decision."

Lorccán frowned.

"My father is right, my love," Queen Lilliana said in a quiet and soothing tone. "You need not have a mistress who is so prone to girlish fancies. Let her have her goblin. I can give you an heir myself."

The gathered nobles gasped and whispered among themselves.

Lorccán's eyes still blazed, and he lifted his lip in a sneer. "Very well. I will think carefully about who to appoint as lord over Goblintown. I expect you"—he leveled a glare at Aodh—"to assist my chosen governor in a smooth transition."

Aodh bowed deeply before kneeling beside me. Wrapping his arm around my shoulder, he lifted me to a stand.

"Get out of my sight," Lorccán spat. "Go back to the muck where you belong."

CHAPTER

SEVENTY-THREE

"I'm sorry," I panted, unable to gather enough air in my lungs to speak any louder.

"Not here," Aodh hushed as he led me through the anteroom toward the grand staircase.

My mind whirled at the implications of the decision I'd made. How much worse would it be for the goblins? There was no way my father would be put in charge of Goblintown after that. What level of damage could Lord Kelpania do with direct control?

We flew from the palace as if Aodh thought Lorccán would change his mind and hold us prisoner.

"Go," he ordered Peony after practically lifting me into the carriage.

"I'm sorry," I said again.

He stared outward, refusing to look at me.

"I-I know I should have just given in. You told me as much yourself, but—"

He held up his hand to silence me, and I bit my lip.

I couldn't tell from his side profile what mood he was in,

but given I'd just cost him his position as goblin king, I couldn't imagine it was good.

As soon as Peony stopped in front of my parents' house, Aodh rose to his feet. "Prepare to depart at dawn tomorrow."

He didn't help me out of the carriage but went over to say something to Kirk and Lottie.

My mum came out of the sitting room as we shut the door behind us. "So? What happened?"

Aodh climbed the stairs to the upper floor, and I watched him go before turning back to her.

"The King gave us an ultimatum: If I agreed to be his mistress, then he would give Dad dominion over Goblintown and forgive their back taxes."

Her gaze looked up the stairs to where Aodh no longer stood. "And you said?"

I shook my head, lowering my eyes to the floor. "I couldn't do it, Mum."

My mum sighed but pulled me into an embrace. I knew what she would have wanted me to do. Aodh was sending me away anyway, so why did I need to be loyal to him? My parents had always planned on me becoming the King's mistress.

But she didn't say any of that, not that she needed to. She just patted my back. "We'll talk about it when your father gets home."

Not long after, the cook called that the midday meal was ready. Mum and I headed into the dining room, but Aodh didn't join us. The meal was slow and silent, and I was grateful the food was a simple stew and bread.

After we finished eating, I took a tray up to Aodh's guest room. I knew he was angry with me, but he still needed to eat.

Knocking softly, I called out to him. "Your Majesty? I've brought you some food."

I listened carefully, but there was no response. Balancing the tray in one hand, I opened the door with the other. No one was inside.

I frowned. *Where could he have gone?* Taking the tray with me, I descended to the kitchens, where I found Peony eating with the rest of the servants. Aodh was not with them.

"Do you know where the Goblin King is?" I asked her.

She shook her head. "He took Kirk and Lottie somewhere, but I've no idea where they went."

Where could three goblins in Sifra even go?

I left the servants to their meal.

He went without a word. Did he abandon me here? No, even if he would have left me, he wouldn't have gone too far without Peony. Even though I knew that was the case, I couldn't help but feel lonesome, like a child who'd lost sight of her parents in a crowded market.

When I entered the sitting room, my father was telling my mother what had happened at court from his perspective. I sat in a chair and lowered my head, preparing to get scolded.

"I'm sorry, Melody," Dad said.

My eyes widened as my head snapped upward.

"I didn't know you felt so strongly about your goblin boy. To say no to the king of Tír in that situation, knowing what it could cost you... I'm proud you followed your heart, and...I'm sorry... We shouldn't have taken you away all those years ago. I shouldn't have cast that binding. If I could break it now, I would. Can you forgive this foolish old sidhe?"

I smiled sadly and rose to embrace my father. It didn't

matter anymore, but I appreciated that he finally understood me.

"Don't give up," he encouraged as he stroked my hair. "Even if you aren't going to be the King's mistress, I have a solid case to manage Goblintown. Historically, the lands belonged to the piskies. I'm not going to give in to Kelpania so easily."

That's something, I guess. But my father's words only made me feel marginally better. The fact was that all Aodh ever wanted to be was goblin king. And instead of helping him as his goblin queen as I'd promised, I ended up knocking the crown from his head.

It was true that if Goblintown was going to be brought under direct sidhe control like the rest of Tír, the goblins would do far better with my father than with Lord Kelpania —someone who had no problem indenturing them not so many years before. But I couldn't imagine anyone in Goblintown would be happy about giving up their sovereignty.

Aodh still wasn't back when we sat down to our evening meal. And though my father had expressed his regret to me, I wasn't sure he was prepared to express the same sentiment to Aodh.

I turned in early that night. Aodh had said we would leave at dawn, and I would be ready even if he meant to abandon me to my parents and send my things back to Maplecrest separately.

CHAPTER
SEVENTY-FOUR

The following morning, I was awakened by Eithne as she shuffled around my room while packing my trunk.

I squinted at the lamp flickering on the bedside table. "Eithne?" I asked, sitting up. "You came back?"

The piskie turned to me, and I nearly gasped at the look on her face. She was as pale as a ghost, and there were dark circles under her sharp eyes.

"What's wrong? Is everything all right with your sister?"

She shook her head. "She's in grave danger, my lady."

"Is her pregnancy that bad? Do you want to stay with her even though she isn't that far along yet?"

"Yes," her voice trembled. "I will come back to her, but I need to return to Piskishire first."

I nodded. "All right. Whatever you need, I'm here for you."

Eithne burst into tears. "Oh, my lady!"

Rushing to her, I wrapped my arms around her as she

heaved great sobs. Eventually, she seemed to calm down a little.

"Why don't you wash your face?" I said gently. "I'll finish packing up, and then we can go down to get a bite to eat."

Eithne looked even worse after crying, and my heart ached for her. I hoped her sister and her baby would be all right.

After changing into the linen gown I'd worn the day before, I finished packing the rest of my things into the trunk, then went downstairs.

It was still too early for my parents to be up, so I popped into the kitchen for a simple breakfast. I also asked the staff if it wouldn't be too much trouble to fill the baskets we'd gotten in Gnomeburgh with something for midday.

By the time I returned to the front hall, the sun was just starting to light the eastern windows. I was pulling on my cloak when my parents descended the stairs, still in their dressing gowns.

My mum embraced me. "I'll see you in a few days," she whispered, squeezing me harder by way of encouragement.

As she released me, Aodh entered the front door, and we all turned to him. My parents no doubt wondered where he'd been as much as I did.

I hugged my father next, and he promised to do the best he could in the coming days.

For his part, Aodh bowed to my parents as he had when we'd arrived. "Lady Piskishire, Lord Piskishire, thank you for accommodating my staff and me."

"Have a safe journey," Mum said.

Dad nodded. "Take care of my daughter."

Aodh hesitated, staring at my father for a moment, then bowed again.

The others were already set by the time we climbed into

the carriage. Eithne had ensured the trunks were secured and was sitting beside Peony on the driver's seat. Kirk and Lottie were mounted on their horses.

I gave my parents a little wave as they bid us goodbye from the doorway, and then I faced forward for my last journey to Goblintown.

Our departure from Sifra did not cause as much stir as our arrival had, but that had more to do with the time of day than anything else. The streets were fairly empty, so we were outside the city walls before anyone really knew the difference.

I watched Aodh as he sat across from me while he gazed out the carriage.

It still hurt my heart to look at him. He was as beautiful as he ever was and far more out of reach than ever before. I'd taken everything from him. I didn't deserve to say I loved him.

How could I make such an outrageous statement when I'd done nothing but hurt him and steal his dreams? If that was what it meant to be loved by me, I should dedicate myself to a virgin goddess the first chance I got.

He didn't speak to me, didn't even look at me, until we were nearing the pass through the Starless Mountains. And then it was only to tell me to pull up my hood again.

I almost welcomed the jeers of the gnomes this time around—not for the others, but for myself. If Aodh wasn't going to curse and yell at me, at least someone would.

Just as we had before, we pulled off the road to make camp.

The place where our fire had burnt only two nights before was still blackened. Our stack of firewood remained. Without being told, I climbed out of the carriage and started to follow Aodh toward the inn. We'd eaten the food the cook at my parents' house had packed for us at midday, so we would need to get more for supper and tomorrow's breakfast.

Even though I trailed not far behind, his every step away from me sent echoes of agony through me.

"I'm sorry!" I shouted, stopping on the side of the road. "I know it's not enough, but I'll say it just the same. I'm sorry that, because of me, you'll no longer be goblin king. You've worked so hard for the goblins, and I just—"

"I'm sorry." His softly spoken apology cut me off. He turned back toward me, but I couldn't see the expression in his dark eyes as he hung his head. "I'm sorry you were put in that position because of me. Even for Goblintown, I wouldn't want you to sell yourself. I wouldn't want you to be forced to bear that sidhe's children."

My heart skipped a beat, and I took a step forward. "But your position…"

He shook his head. "You think I wanted to be goblin king to be the foremost goblin in Goblintown? I thought you'd know me better than that by now. I wanted to be the goblin king to help the goblins. We've always been part of Tír yet still outsiders. That's not what we wanted. Do you think every single goblin who lives in Goblintown wouldn't return to their own communities if they could?"

He sighed heavily. "King Conrí was a horrible goblin king. He taxed us twice as much as was required and kept most of it for himself. I only ever wanted to see the goblins prosper, and I knew I could make that happen. If giving up my made-up title can make Goblintown really a part of Tír, then it may be worth it."

Even as I couldn't believe what I was hearing, I still wasn't surprised. My heart swelled. This was the fae I loved even if I had no right to. He was good and righteous, and he cared more about others than himself.

He met my gaze. "I won't stop fighting for the goblins. I won't give up trying to make their lives better even if it means working for some sidhe lord. So don't apologize to me."

His dark eyes seemed to caress my face, and warmth spread through me.

"I would never force you to be with someone you don't love. Just because I will not claim you for my own doesn't mean I would have you suffer. I wish for your happiness even if I cannot give it to you."

CHAPTER
SEVENTY-FIVE

As the clouds of the Starless Mountains descended around us, I gazed into Aodh's eyes. *You would wish for my happiness even after everything I've done to you? After I stole your ring and forced you into a marriage you didn't want? After I made you uncomfortable by throwing myself at you almost daily? After I took your crown?*

My chest throbbed as if my heart were a drum shaking the walls of a living cavern. "I didn't think it possible to love you more than I already did," I whispered. "But you just keep becoming more honorable, more wonderful, and more unobtainable with every day. I will not ask you to love me, but I will never stop loving you. With my dying breath, I will whisper your name."

I closed my eyes and took a shaky breath before starting forward again. I didn't look at his face as I passed. I couldn't handle his rejection just then.

The inn was as lively as it had been two days before, and Devan and Gemma greeted us with the same enthusiasm.

"The lovebirds are back for more sustenance, eh?" Devan chuckled.

I put the baskets on the bar, and he took them to have them refilled.

"You missed all the excitement," Gemma said. "Though I suppose you were having some of your own, eh?" She winked at me. "Goblins came through here."

I could see Aodh stiffen from the corner of my eye.

"Can you imagine?" she continued. "Not once, but twice! Well, we didn't see them ourselves, what with working the inn, but it's all anyone can talk about. I guess it was the very Goblin King himself, riding around in his own carriage like he's something special. They won't be coming back anytime soon, I wager. From what I heard, Gnomeburgh gave them the right welcome they deserve." She nodded sharply.

My stomach sank. She was a fae I'd known much of my life. Sure, we weren't close, and I didn't see her very often, but she had always been kind, friendly, and cheerful whenever I did. The fact that she could tolerate—even approve of—what the gnomes had done to us was simply heartbreaking.

Aodh rested his hand on my shoulder. I didn't know whether he was trying to comfort me or if he thought I was about to fly into a rage and was reminding me he didn't want our identities revealed. Either way, his touch had the same effect it always did—forcing my entire world to focus on him as everything else fell away.

Devan returned not long after, and as Aodh released me to pay the bill, the sounds of the inn surged into my ears.

I might have muttered a goodbye when we left, but I really couldn't say. I was simply glad to leave Gnomeburgh behind while we hiked back to camp.

Again, silence reigned between Aodh and me, but then I suppose there wasn't much left to be said. He knew how I felt. I knew how he felt. And when we arrived in Goblintown tomorrow, I would be sent away as soon as possible.

After we all ate our simple fare, we settled in to sleep. I didn't argue about sleeping in the carriage that time around. And as I lay on the bench, curled onto my side, I couldn't remember why it had been such a big deal the first time.

Still, I didn't sleep nearly as well in the carriage as I had on the ground beside Aodh. I awoke, groggy and sore, to find the goblins packing up camp.

"Where's Eithne?" I asked, holding the side of my head, which throbbed as I sat up. I winced, but once I was properly sitting, the pain subsided.

"She'll be along," Peony assured. "She was just at the stream filling the water skins."

By the time Eithne had returned, I'd eaten what was left in the baskets—everyone else having already breakfasted— and we were all ready to leave. She gave everyone's filled water skins to them. I frowned as she offered me mine. She looked awful as if the last few days had taken years from her life.

"Would you like to sit beside me the rest of the way, Eithne?" I asked her. "You look like you could use more sleep, and that will be far easier in here than on the driver's seat."

She shook her head. "No, thank you, my lady." Her voice was weak and tired, hardly above a whisper.

I didn't press though I wished she'd chosen otherwise.

As we restarted our journey, my eyes clung to Aodh. It was my last chance to see him for any great amount of time.

For his part, he stared out at the landscape, looking the very portrait of beauty and indifference.

I took a drink of water, my mood making it taste bittersweet. A shiver ran through me as the icy water hit my stomach, and I pulled my cloak tighter around me.

My mood only sank lower with every silent moment that passed.

Once we were out of the mountains, the sun shined brightly down on us—not a cloud in the sky. But I did not feel its warmth.

In fact, with every step closer we took to Goblintown, I felt more and more numb.

Eventually, we came to a fork in the road; one direction headed around Piskishire. We stopped as we turned off the main road through the city.

Eithne climbed down, her bag clutched in her hands, and I got out to say goodbye.

I hugged her tightly. "Take care of yourself, Eithne. Thank you for everything. I want you to know there's always a place for you with me. Please, write to me and tell me how your sister is doing or if you need anything at all even if it's a reference."

Tears spilled down Eithne's face, and I gave her a sad smile. "Go on now," I said to her. "You'll want to reach town before dark. I'm sorry we couldn't take you the entire way, but you understand."

She dipped her head and whispered, "Goodbye, my lady." Then she turned away and started walking down the road into town.

CHAPTER
SEVENTY-SIX

The emotional blow of the loss of my trusted and loyal lady's maid and the impending loss of the love of my life on the same day was far too much to bear. A chill I couldn't seem to shake settled into me as I climbed back into the carriage.

I shivered and took up the blanket I'd slept with the night before, pulling it over my chest and shoulders.

By the time we neared Tally's inn at the edge of Goblinwood, my head ached, and I had to close my eyes against the brightness of the setting sun.

Though we weren't far from the palace, we'd skipped our midday meal, so we stopped at Tally's for supper.

I could hear the crowd inside, already loud and rambunctious, and I winced at the thought of going in.

After climbing down from the carriage, Aodh looked back at me. "Aren't you coming?" he asked.

I shook my head, but even that small gesture sent pain shooting through me. "No," I whispered. "I have a headache, and it's too loud. I'll wait out here."

Aodh frowned. "I'll have Lottie stay with you."

"No, it's all right. I'll be fine on my own for a little while."

"Would you like us to send something out to you?"

"I have no appetite. Perhaps just a cup of willow bark tea."

He nodded and headed in, asking Peony to hold off on taking the horse to the stables until he returned.

It wasn't ten minutes before he reappeared with my tea, bringing his supper with him and dismissing Peony. But as I sat up to take the mug from him, my head spun, and my stomach lurched.

"Lugh's spear! Your hands are freezing!" Aodh exclaimed when I reached out to take what he offered. "I think you should come inside and warm up by the fire for a while."

The thought of standing and walking even a few steps made me want to vomit.

"I'll be fine," I assured though my voice didn't sound very convincing. "The tea will warm me."

Somewhere inside me, I knew I should be pleased he was even showing me that much concern. But I wasn't feeling well enough to appreciate it.

I closed my eyes, and I must've drifted off to sleep because when I opened them again, we were pulling up the palace's round drive.

Tears welled in my eyes. *I wanted to be with him during our journey at least. Why did I waste time sleeping?*

My brother's voice, loud and cheerful, rang out as the carriage stopped. "Dear sister, you've returned! I can't wait to hear what happened at court."

My vision was blurry, but I saw him approach the carriage.

"Melody?" His voice wasn't nearly as cheerful anymore. "What happened?" he demanded.

"I don't know," Aodh replied. "She said she had a headache."

"Melody," Graeme said. His hand burned me as he touched my face. "She's as cold as ice. Melody, can you hear me?"

I blinked slowly, but I couldn't seem to clear my vision. "Yes," I breathed.

Without another word, Graeme scooped me into his arms.

I clenched my jaw against my nausea when he hopped out of the carriage.

The warm glow of the lamps and candles seemed too bright as we entered the drawing room.

Kneeling to the floor, my brother placed me near the fire. I could barely feel its heat.

"Look at me, love," he urged, his head close to mine while I leaned against him.

I squinted against the fire's light to try to look at him.

"Can you see me?" he asked. "Her eyes are dilated."

"Blurry," I answered.

Tadhg whined close by me. I knew he was in dog form when he licked my face.

"She's freezing. Her lips are purple. Stick out your tongue for me, Melody," Graeme encouraged.

I opened my mouth and showed him my tongue.

He gasped, and I was vaguely aware something bad was happening.

"What?" Aodh demanded.

"Her tongue is white… She's…been poisoned." My brother's voice broke, and I wanted to comfort him, but I couldn't form the words to do so.

"What? No! That can't be possible. We've all eaten and drank the same things as her. And we're all fine."

"I don't know what to tell you," Graeme snapped. "But she's ingested asrai venom. There's nothing else it could be."

My brother hugged me closer to him, rocking me as he pressed his lips to my forehead. Tadhg howled a mournful sound that seemed to echo in my very soul.

"So you're just going to sit there?" Aodh said, his tone thick with disbelief.

"There's no antidote," Graeme whispered.

My teeth started to chatter, which only caused my head to hurt more. "I'm cold," I told my brother.

"I know, love." His voice broke with a sob.

I drifted off as blackness took me, and I was relieved to have the pain dulled.

I didn't know how I'd gotten there, or for how long I was out, but when I opened my eyes, I couldn't see anything at all. I still felt cold, but I was aware I was lying somewhere soft, and a heavy weight lay atop me.

"Come on, Melody," Aodh urged.

I didn't know what he wanted me to do, but I would have gladly done it to make the anxiety in his tone disappear. "Aodh," I whispered.

He opened my mouth and poured something into it. The liquid was sweet, far too sweet for my tastes, and I wrinkled my nose.

"Swallow it," Aodh said.

I didn't want to, but it took less effort to swallow whatever it was than to spit it out.

"There you go," he praised. "Good girl."

I felt pretty good about myself just then. I didn't know what I'd done that earned me such warm words from the fae who'd rejected me more times than I could count. But I would do it again just to hear him speak so kindly toward me.

"Will it work?" Aodh asked.

"I don't know," Graeme answered.

And the blackness took me again.

CHAPTER
SEVENTY-SEVEN

When I awoke again, my headache was gone, but the rest of my body was sore. I felt exhausted, likely from shivering for so long. The room was quiet, and I could hear a fire and gentle breathing.

I felt heavy, and as I tried to lift my hand, I realized every blanket in the house had been piled atop me.

I tried to open my eyes but gave up when the effort required was too great.

There was the sound of a door opening followed by footsteps on the carpet.

I must be in the goblin queen's bedroom.

"It wasn't him," Selwyn said in a hushed tone.

"It had to be," Aodh replied. His voice was thin and tired.

"He said he was hired to kill the sidhe king. He hadn't even heard there was a contract out on her."

A long silence answered Selwyn's statement, filled only with the crackle of the fire.

Finally, Aodh sighed. "Find the piskie. She has to know something."

"And what of the sidhe king?" Selwyn asked. "Should we not warn him someone is trying to have him killed?"

"He can suck a salamander's burning cock for all I care," Aodh growled. "He's behind this somehow, mark my words. Find the piskie, and make her talk."

I heard footsteps retreat, then the door shutting gently.

My heart pounded in my chest, and I was happy just to be aware of it. I had enough wherewithal to gather something big had happened but not enough to piece it all together. Whatever energy I had, it wasn't enough to speak, and I soon gave up, opting to sleep some more.

I was awakened by the cheerful sounds of birds singing outside. With a sharp intake of breath, I stretched under the many blankets and cracked my eyes open.

The goblin queen's bedroom was filled with sunlight, and I blinked rapidly to adjust my eyes to it.

Glancing around the room, I saw my brother lying on the settee at the end of the bed, his head leaning back at an awkward angle I was sure would result in a neck ache later.

Aodh had pulled a chair near the side, and the top half of his body rested on the bed. His hair looked golden in the morning sun, and he seemed tired even as he slept.

Tadhg stood beside me in dog form, wagging happily when I turned my head toward him. His blue aura glowed brighter, and he started licking my face enthusiastically.

I sputtered and laughed, my hands trapped under the blankets, unable to push him away.

Aodh looked up at the sounds of my losing battle, blinking before his eyes widened in surprise.

"You're awake!" he exclaimed, his shout alerting my brother.

Graeme jumped up and rushed to the other side of my bed, shooing Tadhg off. For his part, Tadhg growled from the floor; he would not soon forget this insult.

With effort, I managed to slip one of my hands out from under the blankets. Aodh seized it in his immediately.

"How are you feeling?" he asked, his dark eyes analyzing my face.

"Sweaty," I said. "Why are there so many blankets on me?"

"Let me see your tongue," Graeme instructed.

I stuck my tongue out at my brother as I had so many other times in my life.

He sighed in relief and smiled. "It's normal." But his relief soured as his smile slipped. "Don't you ever do that to me again. Do you hear me? I nearly died of fear. What would I have told our parents?" His face paled. "I can't even think about it."

"All right," Aodh hushed my brother. "She's still recovering. Why don't you go see about getting her something to eat?"

Graeme didn't seem to like Aodh telling him what to do, but he leaned over and kissed my head before warning me, "Don't think this is over." Then he left the room.

I wanted to sit up and stretch my back, but I didn't dare move. Aodh still held my hand, and if I drew his attention to it, he might pull away.

The moment Graeme was gone, Tadhg jumped back onto the bed and settled beside me.

"What happened?" I asked Aodh.

He frowned. "We can discuss that later. How are you feeling, really? Are you cold? Do you have a headache?"

I shook my head. "No, I'm really warm, too warm, actually. My head doesn't hurt at all."

"Are you still tired?"

"No, I slept like the dead."

"Quite nearly," he said, his face paling.

I frowned. "Won't you tell me what happened?"

He squeezed my hand before letting go. "I will. I promise."

He started folding down the blankets so I would have an easier time getting up. Tadhg jumped back down as the blankets moved under his feet.

"But I think you ought to eat something first, and I'm sure you'll feel even better after a bath," Aodh suggested.

I felt as light as a sylph on the wind as I slipped out from under the covers. Looking down at myself, I saw I still wore the linen dress I'd worn to court and on the return trip. "Yes, a bath is just what I need, I think."

I was happy to find my legs were strong, and my knees did not wobble when I stood up. Aodh appeared just as satisfied.

After a sharp knock on the door, Odilie let herself in, a tray of food in her hands. Her lavender face looked tired, but her amethyst eyes shined as brightly as polished stones.

"My lady, I'm so glad to see you better," she said. "I'm sure you're starving, but I brought you only porridge for now. You don't want anything too heavy after your ordeal."

I thanked Odilie for her efforts.

When Aodh made to leave, I called out to him, my voice sounding desperate in my rush. "Your Majesty, won't you stay for a little longer?"

He gave me a gentle smile, one that made my heart soar. "I'll be back in a while. I've some things to take care of."

As soon as he was gone Odilie said, "I've never seen the Goblin King so angry as he was last night, my lady. I thought he'd burn the whole city down if anything happened to you. Well, you just sit down right here, and I'll start drawing your bath, shall I?"

As usual, Odilie scurried about her business.

While I blew gently on the porridge, I considered her words. *Was Aodh really worried about me that much?*

SEVENTY-EIGHT

When my brother returned to check on me, I was tying my hair after a bath. I didn't much feel like drying it completely, so I just got as much moisture out of it as I could with a towel, then plaited it.

He watched me seriously, analyzing me to make sure I was really as all right as I seemed.

"Will you tell me what happened?" I requested. "I asked Aodh before, but he just insisted I eat and bathe first."

Graeme sighed, pressing his hand to his forehead. "I don't know much either. I was hoping you could tell me. All I know is you were poisoned with asrai venom, and you were already fading fast by the time you arrived."

My stomach lurched, and I was glad I'd only had porridge to eat. "Asrai venom? But…how am I alive?"

Graeme shook his head. "Your elf." He snorted. "I never would have believed he'd have a vial of nectar just lying around. I have to say one thing for him: He gave it to you without a moment's hesitation. I don't know how he got something so precious to begin with, but he isn't likely to be able to get more."

I didn't respond. My brother had no way of knowing I'd given Aodh the nectar as a wedding gift. I couldn't believe he'd used something so valuable on me.

"You really don't know how you were poisoned?" Graeme asked.

I shook my head, stroking Tadhg's cat fur as he purred on my lap. "I don't make a habit of going around licking every asrai I meet."

"Did you meet one?"

"No."

He stared at me so long I started to question whether I'd met one and didn't know it. "That was a close one, Melody. I'm sure glad your elf was here to save you."

I frowned.

"Well"—Graeme patted me on the head—"it's been a long night for me. I think I'll go sleep in a proper bed. I'll catch up with you more later. Shall I?"

I nodded and wished him a good rest.

My mind whirled with questions. Who could have poisoned me? After my showing at court, there were any number of fae who could have wanted me dead. But I didn't eat at the palace. I'd only eaten at home and in Gnomeburgh before I'd started to feel unwell, and Graeme would have told me if anyone else had died.

And they would have died, the venom secreted from an asrai's skin was a nasty toxin. If an asrai so much as touched another creature, the wound would never feel warm again. But to ingest it? The victim would freeze from the inside out.

I shivered just to think of it, and I didn't wonder why my brother had been so upset. If Aodh hadn't given me that nectar, I would be dead.

As the hours ticked by, I came back to the same question —who could have actually poisoned me?

Around midday, Odilie came to my room again, bringing me more substantial food.

"Do you know where the Goblin King is?" I asked her. He'd promised he would return and tell me what had happened, but he'd yet to appear.

"He and Selwyn left the palace, my lady. He bid me tell you—if you asked—that he would not fail to visit you when he returned."

I sighed but thanked her. When she left, I bid her take Tadhg with her. He hadn't left my side all day and needed to be fed.

With my mind too full of questions and no way to get answers, and with nothing for me to do but wait, I decided to make myself busy.

Eithne was not there to help me, and now that I was feeling better, Aodh would be wanting me to leave Goblintown soon. So I started to pack my baggage. I didn't know where Eithne would have put what, but she wasn't there, so she couldn't really complain.

I was rather proud of myself. I managed to fit all my things into the space I had though I'd had to get awfully aggressive with one of the trunk's lids for it to latch properly.

I sighed heavily, looking over the work I'd completed. *Perhaps I won't get another lady's maid right away. There's something satisfying in doing things myself. And it's not like I won't have plenty of reason to distract myself once I'm gone.*

Another knock on my door announced a visitor, but when Odilie didn't bustle in with my supper, I went to open it myself.

I wasn't too surprised when Aodh stood in the doorway,

not as I might have been any other time. His expression was solemn, and I knew he bore serious news.

"Come in, Your Majesty. I've been waiting for you." I moved farther into the room, and he followed me.

But as he stood near the fire, dusk making the room glow, he seemed at a loss for how to begin.

"Do you know who poisoned me?" I asked.

He nodded.

"Was it the sylph Brochfael paid?"

He shook his head. "No, he was paid to kill the sidhe king."

My eyes widened. *Why would Brochfael want Lorccán dead?*

"It was Eithne," Aodh whispered. "She put asrai venom in your water skin."

I gasped. "W-what?" I could hardly get enough breath to speak. "Why?"

Aodh's jaw tightened, and it seemed to take him a lot of effort to keep speaking calmly. "The King told her that if she didn't, he would kill her sister and her unborn child."

A great sadness washed over me. *Poor Eithne. I can't imagine how horrible that was for her. No wonder she was so upset.* "What will happen to her?"

"She'll be prosecuted in Goblintown. I still have the authority to do that until the sidhe king—or whoever replaces him—appoints a governor."

My brow scrunched. "Whoever re—why would anyone replace him? Aren't you going to tell him Brochfael is trying to kill him?"

Aodh's dark eyes turned cold. "Why would I do that? He's the reason your lady's maid tried to kill you. And for what? All because his pride was hurt when you rejected him?"

I understood where he was coming from. Of course, I did. I was the victim, after all. And I was angry Lorccán would go that far. But I stepped closer to Aodh, gazing up at him, hoping to make him understand. "We can't just let them kill the King. Whoever takes over after him will either be his murderer or propped up by his murderer. There's no way Brochfael is acting alone in this."

Aodh squinted at me. "How can you *still* defend him? Why do you *always* defend him?"

I sighed. "I'm not defending him. I'm defending us! Think about it. If we save the King's life, even after he tried to have me killed, then he can't come after Goblintown. And if we don't, we may end up with someone even worse— worse for Goblintown and worse for Tír."

He stared at me silently.

I huffed out a breath. "Look, I know I'm not goblin queen, but I care about the goblins. There's no reason for you to risk what's best for your people for someone who isn't even going to be here by Samcenn's end."

He closed the distance between us, hovering over me, his chest nearly touching mine. I flinched at the intensity in his gaze and readied myself to weather his ire.

"Do you think," he whispered, "after a speech like that— after knowing what you're willing to do for my people—I could still send you away?"

CHAPTER
SEVENTY-NINE

I blinked rapidly as if the gesture would help me understand his incomprehensible words. "What—?"

My question was cut off as he lifted his hand and ran his thumb along the edge of my lower lip. His eyes blazed with a purpose I couldn't mistake. And I didn't dare breathe while my heart pounded.

Dipping his head, he slowly lowered his face toward mine—his eyes watching my reaction closely. His lips were soft, and I whimpered and trembled as he kissed me gently.

At that first sound from me, he crushed me to him, pulling me closer with a more insistent kiss.

I gasped, need shooting through me while my body flushed with fever. I clenched my fists, his tunic's fabric rough in my hands.

His palm felt heavy as it traveled down my body before grabbing my bum roughly.

A surprised sound squeezed out of me, and my eyes popped open.

Is this really Aodh? Is this the same fae who rejected me over and over? Was he really lying when he said he didn't want me before?

Releasing my lips, he dropped his head to kiss my throat, each one burning me like a brand.

I could hear my breath, ragged and labored, but it sounded as if it was coming from someone else. Surely, I couldn't make such a lewd noise.

Opening his mouth, he flicked his tongue on my throat, sending a hot jolt through me.

"Ah!" I bit my lip, quieting the sound. I grew dizzy, and my knees wobbled, but he held me firmly against him.

Pulling back only slightly, he gazed down at me, his face flush with desire. "Be as loud as you like, my lady. I want to know when I'm doing well."

My cheeks heated at his words, said with such a straight face. Was this really the boy I once knew?

With thoughts of how he used to be, my wherewithal resurfaced. If he really wanted me to stay in Goblintown, could I tell him the truth? Did he love me enough for the binding to have dissolved?

He watched me closely. "Have you changed your mind, my lady?" He started to loosen his arms around me, but I tightened my grip on his tunic.

"Never," I vowed.

A smirk played in the corner of his mouth. "That's good. That would've made things rather awkward."

Again, he pressed his lips to mine, and my mind started to lose its grip as I was pulled deeper into him.

His lips on my mouth, his breath mingled with mine, his hard body pressed to me, every bit of him demanded my attention.

Grabbing me again, he lifted my feet from the floor and took a few steps toward the bed.

"Wait," I breathed, breaking our kiss.

"What is it?" he whispered into my ear before nibbling my earlobe.

I huffed as a tingle ran through me. "I..." My voice was breathy and carried little weight. "I...need to tell you something."

He lifted me onto the bed, sitting me on the edge as he stood between my knees.

Slowly, watching me the whole time, he unbuckled his belt. It slid to the floor with a thunk. Then he pulled his tunic off over his head.

I quivered at the very sight of him. Taking my hands in his, he pressed them to his toned abdomen—his flesh hot and firm beneath my fingertips.

He reached out and gently lifted my chin so I would look up at him.

"If you don't mind, my lady. I would ask that you tell me later. I've waited long enough."

As he hovered over me, I leaned back until his hands rested on the bed behind me.

"Do you still want me?" he whispered, his lips close to mine.

I breathed heavily, and I hardly had enough sense to answer. "Always."

He rewarded me with a kiss that burned up whatever was left of my reason.

"Tell me how much," he said, moving his hands to my thighs on either side of his hips.

"I...I've never wanted anyone but you," I told him.

He smiled and lifted my skirts a few inches up my legs.

I trembled, an aching need building in my core. "I'd give up everything I have if I could only have you."

He raised my skirts some more.

I closed my eyes, trying to swallow to form more words.

"Is that all?" he asked.

"P-please," I whimpered. "You know I would do anything for you."

"Hmm," he hummed, lifting my skirts only a little more. "I'm not sure you want me quite enough yet."

I trembled, this time in frustration, and tried to sit up. "Am I so easy to disregard?" I demanded.

Aodh smiled wider. "I like you far better with that fiery expression than when you're begging."

I pursed my lips. He was teasing me, but he was wrong if he thought he would win.

I squirmed out from under him and got to my feet. Pulling off the tie at the end of my plait, I unbound my hair.

Since I'd had to dress myself that morning, I wore a gown that fastened in the front. Meeting Aodh's gaze defiantly, I slowly loosed the laces of my gown.

His dark eyes sparkled with appreciation.

"And you, Your Majesty, the Goblin King?" I slipped my dress off my shoulders, and it tumbled to the floor at my feet. "You still haven't admitted to wanting me."

He smiled, taking in the sight of me in my chemise.

He took a step closer, but I took a step back.

"I believe you told me you never wanted me even once. Is that true?" I raised an eyebrow at him.

He tensed and pounced at me, catching me easily at the hips—his hands burning me through my chemise.

"What fool would turn away a beauty such as you?" he asked, pulling my hips toward him until I felt his stiff manhood through his trousers.

"A fool, indeed," I agreed, wrapping my arms around the back of his neck. "But will you not say all those words I have spoken so freely to you?"

"I prefer actions," he replied, sweeping me up into his arms and placing me back onto the bed.

This time, he lowered his weight atop me, and it was much better than I'd imagined on Bealtaine night.

He was solid and heavy, and his bare flesh heated me to my very soul.

My head swam, and my body shook with need. "Aodh," I whispered into the now dark room where only the fire glowed.

He pulled back from kissing my collarbone and met my gaze in the dim light.

"Don't tease me anymore. Give me what I want," I demanded.

"I will make you forget you've ever known the touch of another," he promised.

I blinked, confused. "I haven't. Lorccán took a kiss and nothing more."

Aodh scowled. "Speak not that name to me. Even a kiss is too much for the likes of him."

I smiled. I liked that he would be jealous even over a simple kiss. Reaching out, I stroked his face with my thumb. "I have only ever been yours. My heart, my body, my soul— claim what belongs to you."

With a heated smile, he trailed his hands up my outer thighs, pushing the skirt of my chemise as he went. The sensation of his hands on my skin, the brush of the fabric, and the cool air where he exposed me to him sent a flush of anticipation through me.

He made short work of unfastening his trousers before lowering his solid weight atop me again.

I could feel the blunt tip of his cock against the slick heat of my core, and a moment of panic shot through me as I wondered if it would hurt.

"Relax," he murmured, not in any rush as he tickled my thighs.

I giggled, and my tense muscles eased.

A loud hiss escaped my lips when he slowly inched into me, and I felt the stretching pain as my body tried to accommodate him. His brow puckered in concern, and he froze.

"Kiss me," I huffed.

He pressed his lips to mine in a feverish hope.

And the more he kissed me, the more of him I wanted inside me. "Deeper," I urged.

He slid in farther, inching in slowly until he was fully inside. I shuddered, and a low moan escaped his lips. Looking at his face, I took in his expression—tight with the pleasure I was giving him.

At first, it felt strange and foreign to have him inside me as if he didn't belong there. But as he slowly pulled out and pushed back in, and the pain turned to pleasure, I fully embraced his presence. This was how he became mine, how I finally became his. This was how we became one.

"Deeper," I moaned into his ear.

His ragged breathing and labored grunts only heightened my gratification.

With every thrust of his hips, I got closer and closer to my peak.

"Look at me," I whispered, his head lowered to the side of mine.

He did as I asked, his gaze meeting mine while he continued to fill me with only him. I looked deep into his dark eyes, trying to push myself into his heart.

"I love you," I told him.

And as he stared back at me, his face twisted in pleasure, something in his eyes broke. But he did not look away.

"Aodh!" I cried out, euphoria warping his name.

Thrusting deep inside me, he shuddered as he filled me with proof of his desire for me. And still, he did not look away.

CHAPTER
EIGHTY

I awoke in near darkness—the fire in the hearth having burned down to embers. I groaned. My body ached, and I wondered how long I'd slept.

Given the evidence of our lovemaking was still wet on my inner thighs, it couldn't have been very long. I reached out to where Aodh had lain beside me and sat up when I found he was no longer there.

I frowned, but I wasn't worried. He'd proved that he wanted me, and I could handle anything else in the world.

Rising from my bed, I added some wood to the fire and lit a lamp by its flames. Then I went to the bathroom to clean myself. Sex was a messy business, despite its many pleasures, and it took me a little while to feel refreshed.

Passing through my dressing room, I put on a nightgown and a robe before leaving to search for my goblin king.

It couldn't have been very late because the hall lights were still lit. As such, I left my lamp on my bedside table for when we'd return together.

My legs were sore and shook when I tried to stand up

straight. I hoped that wouldn't be the result every time we came together because I imagined that would get cumbersome after a while. How was one supposed to go about one's business if sex made it difficult to walk afterward?

I shook my head at myself, thinking it was likely only because I wasn't used to it, and I thought about asking my mum the next time I saw her.

Down the hallway, I peeked into my reception room though I didn't really think that was where Aodh would be. It was far more likely he'd wanted to change, or—at the most—he'd wanted to start on the petitions Selwyn had accepted on his behalf.

As I rounded the corner from the anteroom to the long gallery, I saw him not far from me.

I smiled. He was staring out the windows at the garden below, and he looked beautiful in the moonlight.

A sound escaped him, and my heart jumped. I looked more closely at his expression and saw the tears trailing down his face, glistening in the light of the moon.

"I'm sorry," he said, his whisper traveling to me with ease. "I can't do this anymore."

Lifting his hand to the glass, he leaned his head against it and let out a sob.

My heart sank. Never in my life did I want to see him in such pain.

And I knew it had to be my fault. Whether he wanted me or not, I couldn't say for sure at the moment. But one thing was clear, being with me was tormenting him. And I would rather have had the soul ripped from my body than have ever been the cause of the misery and shame I saw in him now.

I watched silently, standing in the shadows, unable to comfort him but unable to look away.

After a few more agonizing minutes, Selwyn appeared at the other end of the gallery. He crept closer, clearly not wanting to disturb Aodh but equally needing to.

"What is it?" Aodh asked, his voice still thick though he'd wiped his tears away.

Selwyn kept his head down, and I guessed the sight of Aodh's pain hurt him as much as it hurt me. "I've drafted the warning to the sidhe king. Do you want to look at it before I send it?"

Giving one hard sniff, Aodh straightened his spine and nodded. "Yes, let's go to my study."

I watched them head in the other direction, Aodh's long hair catching the moonlight shining through the windows.

As I turned back toward the goblin queen's quarters, I knew my heart was fully broken. But this time, I had no tears.

I'd gotten what I'd always wanted, and it had only caused the fae I loved pain. I should never have come to Goblintown from the beginning. His life would've been better from having never met me.

I drifted toward the guest room and knocked gently on my brother's door. He took a few minutes to answer, and when he did, his hair was disheveled from sleep.

"Melody, what is it?" he asked.

I didn't know what expression I was wearing, but it clearly alarmed him.

I met his eyes, swallowing back my tears. I wouldn't cry anymore. "I want to leave, Graeme."

His brow scrunched. "Right now?"

I nodded. "Without delay. Will you take me home?"

He stared at me silently for a moment longer before nodding. "Of course. Are we trying to take your things with us?"

I shook my head. "No, you can come to get them later. I'll go change and grab what I can carry."

"All right, I guess I'll dress and meet you outside, then."

Doing just as I said I would, I returned to the goblin queen's dressing room and changed into a traveling gown.

I hesitated as I reached for one of the bags I'd packed earlier. The goblin king's ring—the ring that had begun the entire farce—caught the light from the lamp. With a heavy heart, I slipped it from my finger. The soft clunk it made as I set it on the bedside table seemed too quiet for how significant the action was.

Turning to Tadhg, who'd slipped into the bedroom while I'd been changing, I called for him to follow me. Then I grabbed two bags and left the room that had never truly belonged to me. I couldn't even remember what I'd packed in the bags I took. I only chose them because they were easy to carry.

I didn't have to wait long out front before my brother pulled up his buggy. Handing him my bags, I climbed up and settled beside him with Tadhg sitting comfortably in my lap.

"Are you sure about this?" Graeme asked.

I looked over at the goblin king's palace. I knew somewhere inside the fae I loved was suffering because of me. Staring straight ahead, I nodded.

Neither of us said a word while we made our way through Goblintown, the wheels of Graeme's buggy clattering over the unkempt roads.

By the time we reached Goblinwood, I already knew

what I would do. Mum had said she would take me anywhere I wanted to go. And just then, I wanted nothing more than the bright skies of Olympus. I really hadn't appreciated it the last time I was there.

By the end of the day, my mother and I would be on a boat to Olympus.

EIGHTY-ONE

I stood beside Chrysanthe as Glykeria stared seriously at the jars of olive oil. To my human eyes, they all looked the same. But the gorgon took all decisions very seriously. Her feathery wings ruffled as she readjusted them —even the snakes on her head seemed tired and limp.

Chrysanthe threw her arms wide, not an intimidating gesture for someone who would forever appear as a girl stuck just outside the fullness of womanhood despite being well beyond my age. "Come on already!" she demanded, squinting her cow-like eyes.

Glykeria's snakes hissed to life when she glanced over at us. "I waited a solid hour for you to decide what sandals to buy, you can give me five minutes."

Chrysanthe brushed her long red hair off her shoulder. "It hasn't been five minutes. It has been ten. And it's not as if you're comparing olive oil merchants. This is the same stall. All the oil is the same!"

I tried not to laugh at their bickering. It was situations like these that reminded me of how much I'd missed my old friends while I'd been in Tír. "All right, now. We won't rush you, Glykeria. We're just going to look right over there." I pointed to a nearby stall where sunlight was winking off copper and bronze jewelry. That would keep Chrysanthe occupied long enough for Glykeria to decide which oil she wanted.

The gorgon nodded as I led the oread away.

Chrysanthe was immediately appeased as we approached the merchant's stall, which had a selection of bronze and copper bracelets, broaches, and torcs set out on green wool.

I frowned and reached out to stroke one of the broaches, the design familiar.

"You've got a discerning eye, my lady," the satyr behind the table said to me. "These are all from Tír. Got a connection with the pucks out that way."

Chrysanthe smiled prettily at the satyr. "Oh? Well-traveled are you, then?"

I stifled a sigh as they made eyes at each other. It was a wonder nymphs and satyrs could even hold civil conversations. For her part, Chrysanthe had never met a satyr she didn't like.

The satyr puffed out his hairy chest with pride, his hoofs scraping on the stones of the street as he stood straighter at Chrysanthe's attention. "I've been around." He grinned.

"I'll bet you have," Chrysanthe giggled.

"Just got back from Tír earlier this week, in fact."

"Is that so? My friend here arrived from there not a month ago." Chrysanthe gestured toward me though the satyr hardly spared me a glance.

"Place was in a right uproar, what with the King being deposed and everything. I'm surprised they got things under control so quickly."

I flinched. "What do you mean the King was deposed?" I demanded.

He blinked at me, frowning that I'd pulled his attention from Chrysanthe. "Oh, yeah. The pucks gossiped about little else while I was there. Apparently, the sidhe king went mad —or so his nobles thought—something about an obsession with a human woman. Then he suddenly attacked the Queen and her father as well as a few of the nobles—the pucks didn't know why. But they did know the nobles gave him an ultimatum: abdicate or be deposed."

I brought my fingertips to my lips, my eyes wide. "What happened?" I whispered.

The satyr shrugged. "What was he to do, lose his head? He stepped down—retired to some far-off castle—and his younger sister took the throne. Queen Mairead, I think it is."

Lorccán was replaced by his sister after he attacked Queen Lilliana and her father? Brochfael did mention her when I saw him in Goblintown, and the Duke of Westcount pushed for Lord Kelpania to be put in charge of Goblintown. My father said Brochfael was spending money like he owned a mine. Was it the Queen and her father who had him hire Tac to kill the King? "Is that everything you heard?" I asked.

The satyr frowned and shrugged. "I didn't know I was going to have to give a full report upon my return."

Chrysanthe leaned forward, pouting her lips suggestively. "Aw, don't be like that. My friend is just looking for news of her home. Surely, you've heard *something* else. Hmm?"

His grin returned, and he leaned closer to her over the table of forgotten jewelry. "Now that you mention it, I did hear some uproar about goblins."

I hardly had breath enough to form words. "What about goblins?"

He didn't look at me as Chrysanthe reached out and tickled his chin. "I guess some elf who called himself the goblin king was made a lord or something. Apparently, an elf earl is something to be shocked about. And the pucks weren't happy about Goblintown becoming officially recognized as part of the Queen's realm."

My heart squeezed as it did every time I thought about Aodh, which was most of the time. *Aodh's an earl? That's unheard of in Tír! The Queen must have rewarded him for saving her brother's life. At least he's still in a place to help the goblins.*

Though I ached in my very soul, I was happy to hear everything had worked out for Goblintown—glad to hear Aodh was still doing well without me.

"So what are you doing for the solstice?" the satyr asked Chrysanthe.

She rolled her delicate shoulders, batting her long eyelashes at him. "What are *you* doing?"

"You if you want."

Chrysanthe giggled. "All right."

"I'm positive I got the best one," Glykeria announced, grinning widely at her success as she walked up behind us.

EIGHTY-TWO

I bent to retrieve the ball Vissarion had tossed to me, which I'd missed. The satyr at the market had invited us to his party. And as I was the only one not particularly interested in making merry, I entertained the children with a game.

The sounds of joyful lyre music and boisterous singing floated all around. It was the night before the summer solstice—when those in Olympus celebrated the new year. The wheat harvest had been plentiful, and everyone was in the mood for revelry.

As for me, I was glad the sun had finally set. The day had been long and hot, and the cool night breeze was just the relief I needed.

"There you are," I heard someone say from inside the garden wall I knelt beside.

My heart squeezed, and I looked up to behold Aodh standing there.

I blinked, unable to believe my sight.

His dark eyes smiled down at me in the torchlight. He'd

cut his hair since I'd seen him nearly a month ago, the ruddy locks hanging about his chin.

"How—?"

He tilted his head. "How did I find you? Oh, it wasn't easy. Your family was very reluctant to tell me anything." Leaning his elbows on the wall, he grinned. "It was Selwyn who eventually got it out of your brother."

I frowned, despite how my heart soared at seeing his face so unexpectedly. "Why did you come?" I asked him.

"I have a better one for you: why did you leave?"

Turning away from him, I threw the ball back over the wall to the young satyr, who snatched it up and ran away.

"I…loved you too much to cause you any more pain," I told him.

Aodh scowled. "You silly girl, who said I was in pain? Did I not prove to you that I wanted you?"

I nodded slightly, rubbing my finger where his ring used to be. "Then why, when I went to find you that night, were you crying as if I'd ripped your soul from your body?"

His face paled, and I clenched my hand into a fist.

He blew out a heavy breath. "I was…saying goodbye to someone."

"Who? There was no one there."

He pursed his lips. "The girl I used to love." He fixed his eyes on me. "You want to know why I wasn't already married when you stole my ring? The goblins had long pressured me to do so. But I'd made a promise to a sidhe girl when I was young. The whole thing was very childish, and I was a fool. I promised to make her my goblin queen. And even though she disappeared, never to be heard from again, I wanted to keep that promise. I still loved her. So I searched for her for years and years. But there was no trace of her. And then you show up, and you were beautiful and strong and far more than I could handle. I didn't want to want you. I didn't want to fall in love with you. So I pushed you away. But then…when I thought you would die, I couldn't do it anymore. Why was I wasting my life waiting for a girl who could be married to another or dead already when a woman like you was right there in front of me? Why would I waste the rest of my life on a silly, childhood promise? So that night, yes, I cried. I cried for the love I had to let go of so I could give you what you deserve."

Tears spilled down my face, and I took in a shaking breath. "It's not a silly, childhood promise," I told him.

He frowned, looking very displeased I'd said so.

Closing my eyes, I prayed my words would not be silenced. "I once met a boy, a goblin boy, when I sneaked out of the house to buy potion ingredients. My brother was worried for my safety, so he helped me glamour myself to appear sidhe. I loved this boy with everything I had, and I made him a promise, too: That one day, I would be his goblin queen. But before I could tell him the truth—before I could tell him I was human—my parents found out and took me away to Olympus."

His eyes widened, and his face lost all its color. He grabbed my shoulders over the wall. "You? You're Mischief?"

I nodded, smiling as tears of joy filled my eyes. "I'm Mischief."

He sighed, his brow scrunching as if trying to make sense of what I'd said. "That…explains a lot actually," he said finally. "But why didn't you say anything? Why didn't you send me a letter or something back then?"

I sighed and shook my head. "I did. But my brother never delivered it. He didn't even tell me he kept it from you until soon before we came back to Tír."

"But you could've just shown up at the palace. Why did you steal my ring?"

"I could have shown up and asked for your hand, but I couldn't tell you I was Mischief. My father had bound us all in magic secrecy. Until you loved me as Melody, I couldn't speak the truth."

Releasing my shoulders, he fumbled around on his side and placed his ring on the wall between us. "Will you keep your promise to me? Will you be my wife?"

I stared at the chunk of metal, the symbol of everything we'd suffered for. "Are you certain I'm worthy? I didn't pass all your challenges."

"What's this nonsense? You stole my ring, proving you are clever. You faced down a dragon, proving you have courage. You refused to renounce me or the goblins even when asked by the sidhe king, proving you're the most steadfast among us."

"But I wasn't persistent. I didn't stay until my goal was accomplished."

He leaned forward. "I thought your goal was to win my heart and the hearts of the goblins. You did that long ago."

My chest warmed, and I looked up at him. "How much do you love me?"

He grinned and finally repeated the words I'd longed to hear. "I never loved anyone but you. I would give up everything I have if I could only have you. I would do anything for you."

"Would you climb a wall for me?" I asked.

He hefted himself over the garden wall and landed gracefully on the other side.

I offered him my hand. Snatching his ring from the wall, he slipped it onto my finger.

"There's one more thing I need before agreeing to be your countess," I informed him.

"Name it, and it's yours."

Lacing my fingers with his, I tugged on his arm so he would follow me away from the revelers into the recently reaped field.

I smiled as we ducked behind a round bale of wheat. "Show me how much you want me," I told him. "Make it so I never doubt again."

Wrapping his arms around me, he buried his face in my hair as the sounds of the solstice celebration continued not far away. "You really are full of surprises," he whispered before pressing a fervent kiss to my neck.

"They don't call me Mischief for nothing." I grinned.

EPILOGUE

I smiled down at the baby, her pointed elf's ears peeking out from her ruddy golden curls as the setting sun fell on her sleeping face.

"She's tired," Aodh said, looking over my shoulder at her as he wrapped his arms around me from behind.

"It's exhausting having everyone adore you all day," I replied, reaching out to tuck her little hand under her blanket. "Is everyone gone?"

Aodh pressed a kiss to my neck. "Everyone but those staying." He trailed one hand up my torso, cupping my breast.

I leaned back into him, his cock stiffening against my backside. But I only enjoyed his touch for a moment before sighing. "I suppose we should go entertain our guests."

My husband nibbled my neck, and a jolt of desire ran through me. Squirming, I stepped out of his embrace and headed for the door before I lost the wherewithal to resist his touch. "Save it for later," I said with a smirk.

He followed me as if to catch me and drag me off to bed,

but instead, he simply snatched my hand and pressed it with a kiss. "Oh, I shall."

The day had been long, and I wanted nothing more than his embrace. But I couldn't indulge either of us right now. At least since most everyone who'd come to the palace—now called Goblinhouse—to give blessings to Ainslee on her blessings day had left, I didn't have to put on my countess-face.

After heading downstairs, we found the others still in the drawing room.

Selwyn smirked over the cards in his hand, and Gwendolen frowned from across the table.

Graeme hovered over his wife's shoulder, reaching out toward her cards as she swatted his hand away.

Ealar grinned from the seat between them. "I told you. No one in all Kelpania can beat my Selwyn when he's a mind to win."

Gwendolen pursed her lips. "We aren't in Kelpania," she muttered. Sighing, she laid her cards down face up.

Selwyn blinked in surprise, then scowled. With a click of his tongue, he threw down his cards to reveal he'd been beaten.

My sister-in-law cheered, and Graeme rested his hands on her shoulders in praise.

"Oh, don't be a sore loser, Selwyn. You can't win all the time," Graeme said.

Selwyn squinted at my brother, clearly not willing to let go of his loss so quickly.

Reaching out, Ealar rested his hand on Selwyn's. His touch elicited an immediate reaction. Selwyn's tension eased, and he smiled over at the other kelpie.

Ealar leaned closer. "I'll give you a reward later for being graceful in your defeat."

Selwyn's seawater eyes sparkled at his lover's words, and he lifted Ealar's fingers to his lips.

"How about you, Melody?" Gwendolen queried, collecting the cards in a stack. "Do you want to try your hand at beating me?"

I shook my head. "I wouldn't dare. I'm not nearly as graceful as Selwyn."

Selwyn's smile faltered.

Still, after all that time and everything that had happened, the kelpie didn't like me. I tried, I really did, especially after I found out Graeme and I had completely misunderstood him.

Perhaps some of his distaste for me had been from simple jealousy. But it turned out, Selwyn was far more honorable than we'd given him credit for. He'd loved Aodh truly, and he'd wanted him to be happy. For years, Selwyn had helped Aodh search for Mischief. And when I'd arrived, he saw me as an obstacle to the man he loved finding his heart's happiness.

Even when all was explained and Selwyn discovered I was Mischief all along, he couldn't seem to completely let go of his first impression of me. But we were getting better. I hoped with time we would figure out how to be friends.

"Speaking of Kelpania, how are the kelpies faring these days?" Graeme asked.

After Brochfael and his father had been implicated in the plot against the former sidhe king, there had been great unrest in their fiefdom. A shuffling of power had occurred, and the sidhe queen had chosen a distant cousin of Brochfael's to take over.

"The kelpies are still having a hard time accepting the new earl," Ealar answered. "Many can't understand why a goblin was appointed earl over Goblintown, but a sidhe must still oversee Kelpania. Some are calling for a kelpie to be lord."

My brother nodded seriously. "We've been getting similar petitions at court from all over Tír."

Gwendolen grabbed one of Graeme's hands, still on her shoulders—her sidhe eyes finding his without err.

"Let's not talk about politics now," Aodh insisted. "We're here as friends and family after all."

"I want to hear about Melody's project," Gwendolen said. "How is your refuge program coming along? Is there any way I can help?"

Since becoming countess of Goblintown, I'd thought long and hard about ways to help the goblins. I'd heard many stories of how the fae ended up here—the struggles they'd endured upon arriving as well as the trauma of what had made them come in the first place. With the assistance of Gaye and Odilie, I'd started a refuge program—a way to help newcomers get any help they needed as they settled into their new lives and came to terms with what it meant to be goblins.

I smiled at her. "It's going quite well, actually. I'd love some help if you'd like to come with me to make home visits next dorchae."

She nodded. "I'd like that."

"Well, as nice as this day has been, I think we ought to turn in," Graeme suggested. "We have to make the trip to Manderfeld tomorrow to visit Gwen's parents."

I blinked. That was the first I was hearing about Graeme leaving so soon after he'd arrived. "Is everything all right?" *As bad as kelpie unrest might be, it will be so much worse if the salamanders are unhappy.*

Gwendolen smiled. "Nothing to worry about. We just

haven't seen them since our wedding, so I thought it was about time we visit."

I looked to my brother to see how he was taking the impending visit to his in-laws, but he appeared to have made peace with it.

Rising from her chair, Gwendolen came to embrace us. Graeme followed, kissing me on the cheek and shaking Aodh's hand while congratulating us again on Ainslee's blessings day.

Selwyn and Ealar, too, decided to head up to bed, and they also congratulated us and wished us a goodnight.

As they closed the drawing room door behind them, Aodh's eyes slid to mine.

"They're gone," he said.

I raised my eyebrows. "I see that."

He closed the distance between us and slid his hands onto my hips. "The baby is sleeping."

I nodded with a smile, wrapping my arms around the back of his neck. "She's quite tired. I think she might even sleep through the night."

Leaning down, he brushed a kiss to my lips. "Shall we go up to bed, then?"

I smirked at him, pressing my body against his. "That seems very far away."

I heard the click of the lock as Aodh reached behind me to the drawing room door.

He took a step forward, and I retreated a step—my back pressing against the door.

"Aodh," I whispered, his dark gaze leveled on me.

"Yes, my love?" He leaned down toward me, hovering his lips over mine as his hands made quick work of the fastenings on his trousers.

My body flushed when he moved his hands down my sides. "I've been meaning to ask you for a long time."

"What's that?" He slowly started gathering my skirts in his hands.

"That…first Bealtaine night…" I trembled against him, trying to hold onto my thoughts as his touch pulled me deeper into oblivion. "Did you…?"

My skirts gathered at my hips, he lifted me up, and I wrapped my legs around him.

"Did I what?"

My mind was foggy as I throbbed with need. He was so close, only his will separated him and me from becoming one. "Did you, perhaps, visit me that night?"

He stilled, his blunt tip pressing against the very brink of my core.

I clenched my teeth in frustration.

"You mean, did I find myself at your door—turmoil churning inside me as to whether I should give in to my desire for you—only to hear you pleasuring yourself as you cried out my name?"

My face flushed. "A simple 'yes' would have sufficed."

"Yes." He grinned at me. As he slid deep inside me, I bit my lip to stifle my moan. "I'm due a little mischief of my own."

APPENDIX A: PRONUNCIATIONS

Ainslee (AYNZ-lee)
Aodh (Ay)
Aoife (EE-fuh)
Bealtaine (BALL-tuhn-eh)
Boingidré (BOHN-gihd-ray)
Brochfael (BROHK-file)
Capallré (KAWP-awl-ray)
Certaigidré (KARE-tay-gid-ray)
Cétalré (KAY-tawl-ray)
Chrysanthe (kris-AHN-thee)
Cináed (KEEN-eyed)
Conláed (KON-lied)
Conrí (KON-rree)
Dáire (DAW-ruh)
Domré (DUM-ray)
Dorchae (DOOR-uh-khay)
Dorcheré (DOOR-uh-kheh-ray)
Ealar (ee-lar)
Eirian (ey-RREE-an)

Eithne (EN-yuh)
Eulalia (yoo-LAY-lee-uh)
Gáethré (GAR-ray)
Gaimcenn (GAWM-ken)
Gemred (GEHM-red)
Glykeria (Glee-kair-EE-uh)
Graeme (GRAY-um)
Gráinne (GRAWN-yuh)
Gwilym (GWIL-lim)
Lorccán (LOR-kawn)
Lughnasadh (LOO-nah-sah)
Mairead (mah-rrad)
Odilie (oh-DEEL-ee-ah)
Oimelc (EH-melk)
Píobaire (PEE-buh-ruh)
Reannon (REE-ah-non)
Reódré (Ree-OHD-ray)
Samcenn (SAHM-ken)
Samhain (SOW-in)
Samrad (SAHM-rad)
Selwyn (SELL-win)
Sidhe (shee)
Siwan (she-wan)
Solus (SAW-luhs)
Solusré (SAW-luhs-ray)
Tadhg (TIE-guh)
Teré (Teh-ray)
Tír (teer)
Úardaré (OO-are-dah-ray)
Vissarion (vees-air-EE-awn)

APPENDIX B: FAE GLOSSARY

Asrai—A water-dwelling fae with green hair and webbed feet that can only surface at night. Sunlight kills them by turning them into a pool of water. The secretions from their skin can paralyze if touched and freeze from the inside out if ingested.

Banshee—Literally "woman of the fairies." A human who has gained fae magic by coupling with a sidhe.

Clurichaun—Similar to a leprechaun with a greater love of alcohol. *See leprechaun.*

Drake—Partial to humans, they are a type of house fae who form strong bonds with the masters of the house. They fly in the form of a streak of fire.

Dragon—Large, four-legged lizard with leathery wings, black eyes, sharp talons, and a barbed tongue and tail. From two distinct enemy groups—red and white.

Elf—Human sized with pointed ears, their flawless projectile aim is called elf shot. Hail from Elfton in Tír and Elfheim in Asgard.

Gnome—Earth elementals and talented miners. Hail from Gnomeburgh in Tír.

Gorgon—Winged beings with snakes for hair. Hail from Olympus.

Gremlin—Mechanically gifted, these fae have green skin, large ears, bulging eyes, and spindly fingers.

Imp—Native to Asgard, these fae are shorter than humans with lavender skin and amethyst eyes. They have bat-like wings, skinny barbed tails, horns, and long pointed ears. Mischievous in nature, they have a fondness for humans.

Kappa—Literally "river child." A water sprite the size of a small child. With green scaly skin, webbed fingers and toes, and a depression on the top of the head, which holds his or her life force in liquid form.

Kelpie—A shapeshifting water horse, identified in human form by seaweed in their hair. Enchantingly beautiful, they have great seduction powers over humans. Very dangerous to humans, with the habit of drowning them. Once touched, a human can't let go unless the kelpie allows it. Hailing from Kelpania in Tír.

Leprechaun—Short in stature with grey skin, red noses, and black eyes.

Lightning bird—Observed as a bird by women and a lightning strike by men, this bird lays its egg where lightning strikes the ground.

Luan—A bird born of the essence of the Divine Incarnadine Spirit. Its plumage is bright with five variegated colors though primarily incarnadine. It sings in a five-note range and appears when songs praising great rulers of the past are being composed.

Mermaid—A water-dwelling fae whose top half is human in appearance while her bottom half is a fishtail.

Oread—Mountain nymph. Long lived, they maintain the blush of youth for their entire adult lives. Hail from Olympus.

Penghou—A tree spirit, which can take the form of a black dog with no tail.

Piskie—Shorter than the average human with red hair, turned up noses, pointed ears, and upturned eyes. Hail from Piskieshire in Tír.

Portune—Very small fae (thumb-sized).

Puck—A fae with curly brown hair, hazel eyes, horns, and the lower half of a goat. Their ears and teeth are pointed. Hail from Puckford in Tír.

Salamander—Fire elementals. They have dry but vibrant red skin and glowing yellow eyes. Hail from Manderfeld in Tír.

Satyr—Native to Olympus. Similar to pucks, with the bottom half of a goat, their tops halves are hairier than their puck counterparts. They have the same pointed ears and horns as pucks, but they do not have pointed teeth.

Selkie—A seal fae who has a human form when it takes off its seal pelt. In human form, they generally have large, expressive eyes and hair the same color as their seal pelts. Hail from Selkby in Tír.

Sidhe—The aristocracy of Tír. Considered the most beautiful and most talented with magic. They appear almost human but for their beauty. On the tall side of human height, all have sea-glass green eyes and golden-hued hair.

Spunkie—A shapeshifting fae whose true form is a luminescent blue orb. They have a penchant for mischief and have been known to lure travelers off safe paths.

Sylph—Air elementals.

Trow—The descendants of the illegitimate children of the sidhe and the trolls of Asgard. Handsome with brown skin, large eyes, and either blond or red hair. They are slightly shorter than the average human. Hail from Trowstead in Tír.

Undine—Water elementals. They have green hair, ocean-hued eyes, and sand-colored skin. With the dangerous habit of falling in love with humans, they die if betrayed by their human lovers.

APPENDIX C:
CALENDAR OF TÍR

The fae of Tír use a lunar calendar with the start of the day commencing at sunset. Their year is separated into two seasons: summer (samrad) and winter (gemred). They group years in five-year cycles and thirty-year ages.

Each year begins on the first day of Samcenn. The month is bisected into two parts. The first half of the month is known as the solus half and begins on the night of the first quarter moon. The second half of the month (the dorchae half) begins on the last quarter moon.

The names of the months are as follows, beginning with year one of a cycle:

- Samcenn
- Dorcheré
- Reódré
- Domré
- Úardaré
- Gáethré
- Gaimcenn

- Solusré
- Capallré
- Boingidré
- Teré
- Cétalré

To keep the seasons in the right place in relation to the sun, a thirteenth month is added twice every cycle. Unless it is the first year of an age, the month Certaigidré is added before Samcenn on year one of a cycle. And then Certaigidré is added again in year three of a cycle before Giamcenn.

There are eight holidays celebrated throughout the year. They are as follows:

- Bealtaine (celebrated during the full moon of Samcenn)
- The Summer Solstice (falls in Dorcheré or Reódré, depending on which year of the cycle)
- Lughnasadh (celebrated during the full moon of Domré)
- The Summer Equinox (falls in Úardaré or Gáethré)
- Samhain (celebrated on the full moon of Gaimcenn)
- The Winter Solstice (falls in Solusré or Capallré)
- Oimelc (celebrated on the full moon in Boingidré)
- The Winter Equinox (falls in Teré or Cétalré)

Afterword

Thank you for reading! I do so hope you enjoyed it. If you have a moment, I would very much appreciate a review on the store where you bought it. Tell other readers what you thought, and help them make a decision on this book.

If you'd like to stay updated on news about my books and events, you can subscribe to my newsletter on my website: www.dlieber.com

On my site, you will also find my blog, where I post all my fun little tidbits.

Thanks again! I hope you will travel through my worlds with me again in the future.

D. Lieber

ABOUT THE AUTHOR

D. Lieber has a wanderlust that would make a butterfly envious. When she isn't planning her next physical adventure, she's recklessly jumping from one fictional world to another. Her love of reading led her to earn a Bachelor's in English from Wright State University.

Beyond her skeptic and slightly pessimistic mind, Lieber wants to believe. She has been many places—from Canada to England, France to Italy, Germany to Russia—believing that a better world comes from putting a face on "other." She is a romantic idealist at heart, always fighting to keep her feet on the ground and her head in the clouds.

Lieber lives in Wisconsin with her husband (John) and cats (Yin and Nox).

LINKS

Website: www.dlieber.com
Goodreads: www.goodreads.com/dlieberwriting
Bookbub: www.bookbub.com/profile/d-lieber

Milton Keynes UK
Ingram Content Group UK Ltd.
UKHW040909191024
449793UK00013B/110/J

9 781951 239312